all
made
up

Center Point
Large Print

Also by Kara Isaac and available from
Center Point Large Print:

Can't Help Falling
Then There Was You

**This Large Print Book carries the
Seal of Approval of N.A.V.H.**

KARA
ISAAC

all
made
up

CENTER POINT LARGE PRINT
THORNDIKE, MAINE

This Center Point Large Print edition is published in the year 2019 by arrangement with the author.
Published in association with MacGregor Literary, Inc.

The text of this Large Print edition is unabridged.
In other aspects, this book may vary
from the original edition.
Printed in the United States of America
on permanent paper.
Set in 16-point Times New Roman type.

ISBN: 978-1-64358-224-5

Library of Congress Cataloging-in-Publication Data

Names: Isaac, Kara, author.
Title: All made up / Kara Isaac.
Description: Center Point Large Print edition. | Thorndike, Maine :
    Center Point Large Print, 2018.
Identifiers: LCCN 2019011383 | ISBN 9781643582245 (hardcover :
    alk. paper)
Subjects: LCSH: Large type books.
Classification: LCC PR9639.4.I83 A55 2018 | DDC 823/.92—dc23
LC record available at https://lccn.loc.gov/2019011383

For my parents, Kim and Sue.
The most adventuring, selfless, generous,
faith-filled people that I know.

And for my grandmother, Erika.
After World War II, she got on a boat in
England and sailed to the other side of
the world to marry a man she barely knew.
You personify what it means to love bravely.

CHAPTER ONE

Reality TV. A misnomer if there ever was one. Katriona McLeod studied the sheet of paper the production assistant had just delivered to her dressing room. On it were the names and pictures of five women who were to be given extra attention in her makeup chair.

Mandy. Olivia. Lindsey. Jennifer. Adeline. They all smiled at her with big eyes, perfect teeth, and blow-waved hair. The same promo pictures would be going up on the TV studio's website just before the show aired, along with the pictures of nineteen other women who had no idea they'd been cut before they'd stepped a stiletto-clad foot out of the limo.

Kat folded the paper and shoved it into the front pocket of her black apron. The first set of women would be arriving any minute to be primped into camera-worthy perfection. No doubt frothing with excitement at being liberated from whatever Sydney hotel they'd been secluded in for the last couple of days. Might as well enjoy the last few moments of p—

BANG. The dressing room door flew open with

such force it smashed into the wall. Kat stumbled back, her hand landing in the palette tray she'd just laid out with different shades of liquid foundation. Cold cream spread across her palm and oozed through her fingers. Great.

"Good, you're here. I need a favor." Vince Oliver, executive producer and the only reason she was working on this ridiculous show, slammed the door behind him like he was being chased by a mob of angry kangaroos.

"The answer is no." She grabbed a wet wipe and cleaned four hues of foundation off her hand and wrist.

"I haven't even told you what it is." Vince grabbed a bottle of water out of the small fridge in the corner of the room and twisted off the cap. He took a few gulps before collapsing into one of the black directors' chairs lined up in front of the row of mirrors.

"I don't need to hear it to know my answer." Working on this crazy show for a third of what she usually made settled her debt to him. Not that he'd ever so much as hinted he saw things that way, but Kat knew this world. One where every favor was tallied and would be called in. Always.

The long hand of the cheap plastic clock on the wall clicked onto the eleven. Five minutes until she and her two assistants were scheduled to start the long process of turning twenty-four wannabe reality TV stars into the best-looking versions of themselves. She didn't have time for whatever Vince wanted.

He scrunched the now-empty bottle in his hand and threw it into the trash can. "I need you to stand in as one of the bachelorettes. Just for tonight."

"Are you drunk?" Kat studied him for the familiar signs but came up empty. His eyes were clear, his hands steady. Not drunk. Just crazy.

Vince ran a hand through his receding hairline. "I wish I were. Six of them have gone down with some kind of gastro bug. They're not in any state to be scraped off their bathroom floors, let alone squeezed into a gown and paraded in front of a bunch of bright lights and cameras."

They'd probably finally realized what they'd gotten themselves into and dined on raw chicken. That's what she would have done.

"We can make it work with twenty-two contestants, but no fewer. I've already got three of the staff subbing. I need one more. All you have to do is walk out of the limo and say hi. Then, at the end of the night, he'll eliminate the four of you and it'll be like you were never there."

Only a guy could say that. How many of his friends watched *Falling for the Farmer*? Vince could probably count them on one hand.

Kat finished cleaning her hand and dropped the wipe into her trash pile. "I work behind the

9

cameras, Vince. Not in front of them. Not even as a space filler or blonde number six. Not even for you. Surely you could call someone from your final round of audition cuts who lives in Sydney."

Vince stood and paced across the small space, his beer belly leading the way. "There's no time. We start filming in eight hours. I'm beginning to think this show is jinxed."

She couldn't blame him. The show was forced to replace the leading man after the first one realized he was in love with some girl he'd known since he was three. Which was very sweet and all but not exactly great timing when a studio has spent thousands plastering your looking-for-love face on billboards and bus shelters all over the country. As a result, the replacement had been kept so tightly under wraps only a few select senior staff knew who he was.

Kat picked up the palette tray and started cleaning off the smeared foundation with a cloth. "I'm sure someone else on the crew will do it. There are enough interns and assistants running around. Any of them would love to do you a favor."

Vince's gaze shifted, bouncing around the room, looking anywhere but at her. "None of them have the right . . . ah . . . look."

Kat stared at him. "What does it matter if they're just needed for a few seconds of camera fodder?"

"Look, we both know social media can be unkind. I don't want to take any chances."

It didn't take a rocket scientist to work out what he meant. With her blonde all-American/Australian appearance, she looked like the kind of girl who might aspire to find her husband on a TV show. She'd heard similar before. Her looks had both hindered and helped her entire life.

But she'd thought that after their years of friendship, Vince of all people, was beyond that.

Vince pinched the bridge of his nose. "Kat, I have never asked you for anything until this show. It has to be a success. My career depends on it." He didn't say the words, but he didn't need to. She owed him her success—up to and including the gold statue that lived in her closet. Until farmer guy and one of the chosen five rode into the sunset, she was indebted to him. Had been for the last ten years. And he was officially calling it in.

She sagged against the counter. "I don't have a dress." Forget the dress. Her mother watched the show. She'd have to avoid her for months if she did this.

Vince grinned. He had her. "We have plenty in costuming."

McLeods paid their debts. Always. Her father had drilled that into her since before she could talk. "One night, Vince. Thirty seconds of camera time. That's it."

His hand was already on the doorknob. "You have my word. We'll even put you in the last limo, so you can doll yourself up and change after you've finished with the others."

Kat looked down at her crew T-shirt emblazoned with *Falling for the Farmer*. Her stomach twisted. She'd already made that exact mistake once in her life. Almost a decade later she still hadn't recovered.

Caleb Murphy didn't belong here. Not in the big city. Not in a mansion. Not in a tux. And certainly not sitting under lights hot enough to scorch corn, two cameras positioned so close to his face that he could see his eyeballs reflecting back at him.

"Why did you decide to come on this show?" The hipster producer sitting opposite watched him with intense interest, as if he hadn't already asked Caleb the question multiple times.

Adam. That was the guy's name. Caleb preferred to think of him as his handler since the man—boy, really—never seemed to be more than a few feet away. Hovering. Asking questions. Offering him water and snacks.

Caleb blew out a breath. He knew what the TV-appropriate answer was. True love. Business success, but he just needed that special someone to share it with. Slim pickings of eligible women in rural Queensland, let alone any wanting to live on a farm an hour from the nearest city.

"I guess I'm just like everyone else. I want to meet someone to share my life with." That was the best they were going to get out of him. Not for anyone was he going to spout some guff about love and finding his soul mate. He'd had love twice in his life. He didn't believe in third time lucky.

Sweat trickled down his back. His shirt clung to him, and filming hadn't even started. How would he survive months of this scrutiny? His chest tightened despite his attempt at deep breathing. "Can I have a few minutes?"

"Of course. Water?" Adam held up the chilled bottle he always carried. Droplets of condensation coated the outside of the plastic.

"Thanks." Caleb grabbed it and ducked between the cameras and light stands, stepping over the cables crossing the floor.

Striding through the imposing front door, he stepped into the evening air and sucked in a couple of breaths. Beyond the manicured grounds, Sydney Harbour glistened under the warm light of the setting sun, the lights of its iconic bridge sparkling in the distance.

To his right lay a long driveway complete with turning circle. A flower-covered pergola covered most of the path that led from the driveway to the marked spot he'd be waiting on in a mere few hours.

The whole setup looked too good to be true.

And it was. The multihued flowers were as fake as some of the women he would soon meet. Staff had pulled the garlands out of boxes and draped them over the pergola the day before while he'd taken his introductory tour of the set.

He huffed out a breath, and stripped off his jacket.

"Let me take that for you." A production assistant appeared at his side, one hand extended toward him while the other held a clipboard of notes. A headset was perched on her brown hair. Where had she come from?

He handed it over. "Thank you."

"No worries." She tilted her head to one side, listening to something in her ear. "They need you back inside in a few minutes to finish up the interview."

"Sure. Thanks." Shoving his hands into his pockets, he strode across the grass, sucking in ocean-scented air as foreign to him as people watching his every move. The air he belonged in was earthy, scented with dust, fresh-cut grass, and manure. The predominant sound back home was the bellow of cows and hum of the milking shed, not traffic.

If anyone had told him a month ago he'd be standing here, the soon-to-be lynchpin of some looking-for-love TV show he'd never heard of, he would have laughed them off the front porch. Which was exactly what he'd done the day

Adam and his entourage had shown up. Then they'd shown him his audition tape. The one he hadn't known even existed, let alone had been submitted.

He pulled his phone out of his pocket, unlocked the screen, and brought up the video. Mum's kind face stared back at him, with wavy gray hair, skin wrinkled and tanned from years in the sun, and eyes the startling hue of spring grass.

There was no one else in all eternity he would have done this for. And he'd come so close to never knowing what she wanted more than anything else.

By the time she'd sent the video, the deadline had long since closed and the farmer been chosen. Her elegant words and heartfelt request had almost been lost to the archives of the TV studio, along with all the other failed audition videos.

Until that guy had experienced some kind of epiphany about his best friend and—according to the posse of TV executives who'd showed up on Caleb's porch—they'd jumped straight on a plane to Toowoomba because they'd wanted him as soon as they saw the video. How much of that was true, and how much was the flattery of desperate people who needed a new leading man? He didn't know. All he knew was he would do anything to make his mother's wish come true. And if he couldn't do that, what mattered was that she believed it had.

Facebook Messenger

Kat: Um, so, funny story. Sort of. A gastro bug hit some of the show's contestants, and the executive producer asked me to sub in as an extra for the night.

Paige: Good luck with that, buddy. I hope you told him he could put that request the same place as all the money he's NOT paying you.

Allie: You're doing this job for free. Why???? Isn't it for, like, three months?

Kat: Not for free. Just for less than usual. Long story. I owe Vince a favor from way back. He's the reason I first got my foot in the door working on films.

Allie: He's calling in a favor from ten years ago??? No way, José.

Kat: It's fine. I had a break in my schedule. Plus it might be nice to do something different.

Paige: If by "something different" you mean "something way beneath me and an insult to my intelligence," then sure. Anyway, I'm waiting for the funny part of this story. I'm really hoping it's your brilliant comeback line to his ridiculous and deluded request.

Kat: Not exactly.

Paige: You. Did. Not.

Allie: Didn't what? I'm so lost.

Paige: She didn't turn him down.

Allie: Wait. What? You're going to be on Falling for the Farmer? As one of the women?

Kat: For, like, two minutes. I'll get out of the limo, smile, say something inane, and get eliminated. No one will even know I was there.

Paige: Ha! Dream on. There's no chance that farmer is going to eliminate you. Not unless he's blind. Which I would be all for, by the way. Equal opportunities and all that. Plus, it would be the best TV watching—a bevy of women realizing their months in the gym and eating no carbs were for nothing.

Allie: I'm going to have to get all illegal now to find out a way to watch this show since it's not screening in the UK. And the academic in me has a real issue with breaching copyright. I hope you feel bad about making me violate my conscience like this.

Kat: Don't violate your conscience. Seriously. Paige can sit in front of the TV with her phone and just film all thirty seconds of it.

Paige: It's going to be way more than thirty seconds. Guaranteed.

CHAPTER TWO

At least Kat didn't have to sit in a limo filled with a bunch of half tipsy hyperventilating women, each doused in enough perfume to send them all up in flames if someone struck a match.

The last six hours had been long enough as the eighteen contestants rotated through her makeup chairs, toasting themselves with champagne, sharing dress choices for their big reveal, and speculating as to what the already decided man of their dreams might be like.

Leaning back, she took a sip of water and eased her feet out of the eight-inch heels she was sure had been retired from a previous life on the set of *The Real Housewives of Sydney*. Her options had been these or a pair of orthopedic-looking bowling shoes. She might be doing this under duress, but she had some standards.

Across from her, a sub who'd introduced herself as Leona had her head bent over her phone.

"How much longer do you think this will take?" Mary, one of the production assistants, nibbled on her thumbnail as she shifted on her seat. Beside her the final sub—Sarah—looked out the window with a bored expression on her face.

Kat leaned back in the plush seat, her full skirt rustling around her. "It could be hours. Depends on how many retakes the crew need to do of the women in the other limos."

"What do you mean?" Mary's eyes widened.

Oh, the poor dear. She must think reality TV was, well, *real.* "I'd guess at least half will need to have multiple takes. People get nervous. They fluff their words. Or a camera angle isn't quite right. A boom could fall into the shot. A light may flicker. Anything could happen. Even if everything goes right, the executive producers still like to have options when they put the episode together."

"So what viewers see on TV sometimes isn't the very first time the farmer and the contestants have met?" Mary said the words slowly, as if unable to believe they could be true.

Best to be kind. It was only a matter of hours before Mary was indoctrinated into how the world she had entered really operated. "Well, it's still the first time they've met. There may be just a few versions of it."

"What do we say if one of the other contestants recognizes us?"

None of them would recognize Kat. That fact was well established after ten years working in the media industry. Men noticed her. Women rarely. To the women, she was just a hand holding a brush and a voice telling them when to blink or pout their lips or lift their chin.

"We tell the truth—that some of the other contestants fell ill, so there are a few staff making up the numbers."

Sarah turned from the window, the pink streak in her dark bob shimmering under the passing streetlights, and slid further down in her seat. Her slumped posture and crossed arms folded her into herself. "They'll be okay with that?"

Kat smoothed her hands over her gray skirt. "They'll be thrilled. Less competition for the roses. In fact, none of them need to worry about going home on the first night."

"Horseshoes." Leona looked up from her phone.

"What?"

"The guy is handing out horseshoes. I had to buy a hundred of the things, and those suckers are heavy. Apparently, there's some kind of IP dispute with another studio about handing out roses."

Seriously? "Well, the producers can't have tested that with the focus groups. What kind of journey to love starts with 'Jemima, will you please accept this horseshoe'?"

Sarah snorted. "At least none of us are going to have our names associated with that."

"Maybe not." Mary adjusted the top of her

green strapless cocktail dress. "But won't people find it weird that all the girls from the last limo get eliminated?"

The poor girl really had no clue. "The viewers won't see that. The producers will cut the footage so it looks like we arrived in different limos."

Mary's eyebrows pinched. "But they fall in love, right? People really fall in love." Desperation rang through her words.

Kat looked at Sarah, who raised her eyebrows. They both shrugged as the limo took a right and drove over a bump. Hedges lined the narrow driveway passing outside Kat's window. "I think this is us." Finally. Time to get on with the show.

The limo slowed, gravel crunching under its tires.

"What if I like him!" Mary blurted out the words. "What if I get out of the limo and he's really great and I like him and want to stay?"

Sarah looked at her with pity. "I guess that depends. Do you have bills to pay? Do you want to keep your job? Because the only people who get paid to be on this show are the staff and him. If you can survive up to three months without any income plus however long you're unemployed once it's over, all power to you."

The limo stopped, and the door opened before Mary could respond. One of the producers stood outside consulting a clipboard, a halo of light behind her. She bent down and peered into the limo. "Okay, your order is Kat, Mary, Sarah, Leona. Walk through the pergola to the producer waiting at the end. He'll tell you when to go. You have thirty seconds." The door closed, and Kat jammed her feet back into her shoes.

"Good luck!" Leona wedged her phone into her bodice and knocked back the last of her glass of champagne.

"Um, thanks." What luck? The four of them were just a few seconds of TV fodder. Apart from their families and friends, everyone else who saw the show would forget they'd ever existed.

The door opened again, and a disembodied suit-clad body stretched out his hand to Kat. She gripped it as she stretched one foot onto the ground and stood. Bright lights seared her retinas, and she blinked a couple of times, trying to get her bearings.

Cameramen with cameras, halogen lights on stands, a couple of producers wearing headsets. One tilted her head to the right, telling her where to go.

A few feet to her right stood the opening to a long rose-covered pergola. Smoothing her skirt and trying to ignore the two cameras following her, Kat entered the tunnel.

Her stomach turned itself pretzel shaped as her eyes adjusted to the dimness. Why was she nervous now? The gravel crunched beneath her heels as she walked. She hadn't thought about her line. No doubt most of the women had planned something flamboyant, desperate to be memorable in a sea of blurring faces.

The cameras had halted at the entry to the pergola, leaving her alone for about thirty seconds. Then a producer came into view, standing a few paces back from the other end.

"Kat?" The man's voice was questioning. Like she may have fallen victim to body snatchers between getting out of the car and arriving here.

"Yes."

"Great. We're just going to be another minute. They're adjusting a couple of lights."

"Okay." She shifted on her heels.

"When I say go, once you leave here just walk to the end of the path, and he'll be waiting for you at the bottom of the steps. Got it?"

Kat bit back the desire to tell him that if she could pass advanced calculus, she could manage walking in a straight line.

"Okay. You're on." He gave her a tap on the small of her back. Any lower and he would have lost the use of those fingers for a few weeks.

Time to get this over and done with. Striding out of the dim flower-covered tunnel, she was hit full force in the face by even more and brighter lights than had met her outside the car. Trying not to squint, she focused on keeping her steps smooth and even.

Footsteps tread beside her. More cameramen no

doubt. Lifting her gaze, she looked for the steps the producer had mentioned but couldn't see beyond the glare hitting her eyes.

After four more steps the outline of a man appeared from the haze. Tall, broad shoulders. *Hi, I'm Kat. I'm a makeup artist and I live in Sydney.* Two sentences. Then he'd say something equally inane and that would be it. She could escape into the house and waste about eight hours of her life on idle chitchat and watching women fight over a man they didn't even know.

At least she'd have some good stories for Paige and Allie. Her cousin and best friend would be thrilled she could keep them updated in real time on the shenanigans. One of the perks of not being a real contestant: instead of being confiscated, her phone was safely stashed away in the borrowed clutch that waited inside for her.

There had better be some good catering. She was starving. And not stupid little hors d'oeuvres. A decent buffet with carbs and—

One spindly heel caught on the sidewalk while the rest of her kept going. Arms flailing like a baby chick tossed from its nest, she nose-dived toward the cobblestones.

So much for confident.

Just before her nose went from pert to button-mushroom-shaped, a pair of black dress shoes appeared beneath her and her fall was arrested by the sensation of being scooped out of the air.

"I've got you." The reassuring words whispered in Kat's ear and set the hairs on the back of her neck at attention. She knew that voice. She knew the broad chest she was nestled against. Knew the neck her hands had instinctively flung themselves around. The full lips that lingered hauntingly close, five o'clock shadow dotting the familiar jawline that she hadn't seen in over nine years.

She lifted her gaze and locked eyes with the only man she had ever loved.

God, help me.

Caleb had taken to not looking at the women as they walked toward him. Having to watch them approach, their eyes wide with expectation, in ridiculously tight dresses that left them hobbling like penguins, had proven too torturous after the first few.

He suspected the show wanted to create some kind of bride-walking-up-the-aisle feel filled with lingering glances and smiles, but he wasn't playing.

It was bad enough that he'd been lassoed into this whole charade. He refused to give any of the women false hope before they'd even met if he could possibly help it. Not when he believed he had about as much chance of finding love on a TV show as he did of making ten bucks a kilo on milk solids.

A few times the producer had halted a woman to make Caleb turn and watch her entrance. Woman number five twirled some kind of fancy sticks. Woman twelve played bagpipes and introduced herself with a crass innuendo-laden opening line that would see her going home tonight. Number sixteen wore a leotard and did flips and fancy acrobatic moves the entire length of the path.

This time he'd turned just in time to see the nineteenth trip over her own feet and fall in a blur of long blonde hair and full skirt.

He'd reacted on autopilot, just managing to catch her before she hit the ground. His heart had almost exited his rib cage when she'd turned her face toward him.

Kat.

He stared down, trying to understand how his first girlfriend could possibly be curled in his arms, all wide eyes and open mouth.

If an angel had fallen from the sky and landed in his arms Caleb would have been less surprised.

He breathed her in. The hint of citrus that was once so familiar sent him back ten years, a startling contrast to the rolling perfume factory he'd been subjected to over the last few hours.

She was even more beautiful at thirty-three than she had been at twenty-three. The youthfulness in her face from ten years ago had been replaced with a kind of ageless grace.

She certainly wouldn't think the same looking

at him. With too many years of early mornings and broken nights, long hours in the sun, and a receding hairline he tried to camouflage with a number one cut, he was definitely not an improved version of the man she'd left behind.

Somewhere, someone coughed. Then coughed again. He looked up to see two cameramen circling the two of them like buzzards around prey.

"Hi." He blinked, half expecting he would open his eyes and find a stranger in his arms.

"Hi." Her expression was wary. It reminded him of the way his cows watched him when they were getting close to calving.

"Are you okay?" He forced the words out while his mind spun questions faster than a combine harvester. Was this a setup? Did Kat know he was the farmer? How could the producers have found out about her? Their relationship had been mostly long distance. He could probably count on one hand the number of people who'd still remember they'd ever been together.

"Yes. Thank you."

When Kat removed her hands from around his neck, he took the hint and lowered her legs to the ground. He was supposed to take both her hands, look attentive, and hug her once the introductions were over. Those were his instructions. They'd already made him repeat the rigmarole with two women when he forgot one of the steps.

But as soon as Kat had her footing she stepped back and clasped her hands in front of her. If she'd received the same instructions she was ignoring them too.

You're a great girl, but I've realized I can't see us with a future together. The biggest lie he'd ever spoken rang in his ears.

He'd had to say something definitive. Something that would ensure she left and never looked back. But the betrayal on her face that day had haunted him for years.

"I'm Kat. I'm a makeup artist, and I live in Sydney." Her words were stilted. Unnatural. Like her subconscious was kicking in and parroting something she'd memorized.

This was how it was? They were meant to pretend they were total strangers? He'd play along. For now. "Hi, I'm Caleb. I'm a farmer, and I live in rural Queensland."

"I guess I'll see you inside."

"I look forward to talking to you."

For the first time all night, he actually meant it.

Facebook Messenger

Kat: I need to tell you both something, and I need you not to freak out.

Paige: Hey, she has her phone! I thought they stripped you of all contact with the outside world when you went on one of these shows.

Kat: I got to keep mine since I'm just a walk on.

Paige: Given you opened this conversation by telling us not to freak out, I'm sure you're the only one here who still believes you're just a "walk on".

Allie: I'm not allowed to freak out anymore. Jackson says it's not good for the baby. So consider me the voice of reason and sanity.

Kat: The farmer is Caleb.

Paige: It. Is. Not.

Allie: I feel like I'm missing something. Story of my life at the moment. Stupid pregnancy brain. Caleb???

Kat: We kind of dated awhile back.

Paige: He broke her heart.

Allie. Do you want me to fly over and break his legs? Because I totally will. And I'm sleep deprived and already carrying an extra twenty pounds, so I've got some serious anger ready and available for channeling.

Kat: Let me get back to you on that.

Paige: Did you slap him? Please tell me you slapped him.

Kat: Not exactly. I kind of tripped and he caught me.

Paige: There is no emoji for that.

Kat: You there, Al?

Allie: Sorry, I'm here. Needed to find some tissues because my eyes started leaking. Stupid hormones. Are you okay?

Kat: I have no idea.

CHAPTER THREE

K at stared at the screen of her phone from her perch on the closed toilet seat. As soon as she'd located her clutch, she'd hunted around the huge house until she'd found the bathroom farthest away from the festivities downstairs, then locked herself in.

An hour ago.

Her stomach rumbled. She'd never been one of those girls who lost their appetite when stressed. She got hangry.

Caleb. She hadn't been able to catch her breath since the moment she looked up and saw him. Older, more weather-beaten, with the slightly crooked nose he'd broken in a game of Aussie rules when they were dating, and eyes the color of the earth he loved so much.

He was meant to be safe in Toowoomba, living on his farm, happily married to some woman who canned preserves and looked cute in flannel. What had happened to her? Was he divorced? Widowed?

A knock sounded at the door, and Kat dropped her phone, the device skittering across the tiles before coming to a stop against the wall.

"Kat? Are you in there? Vince needs you to come down for some of the crowd shots."

"Just a minute." Her voice wobbled on the last word. She coughed and tried again. "I'll be right down."

She forced herself to her feet, picked up her phone, and dropped it into the sparkling monstrosity she'd borrowed from costuming.

Peering into the small mirror hanging above the vanity, she checked her makeup was still intact. No one could know she and Caleb had a past. That she'd once thought he was the man she was going to spend the rest of her life with.

Game face, Katriona. She had lots of practice at least. Years of tests and surgeries had given her a well-honed ability to compartmentalize her emotions. To make it through weeks, months, years, like her dreams for her life weren't being slowly stripped away. It would have made her father proud. If he knew.

She could do this. She could go downstairs and watch a bunch of women throw themselves at Caleb. Pretend he was a stranger instead of the man who had shredded her heart.

Sliding open the door, she stepped into the hallway, her full skirt rustling around her. Thank goodness the production assistant had taken her at her word and was nowhere to be seen.

Her traitorous heels sounded like gunshots

echoing down the wooden floor. Reaching the top of the stairs, too-loud laughter and a mish-mash of female voices floated toward her.

She reached the bottom in a few short steps and stashed her clutch behind a rose-filled vase. To her left lay a large seating area where women reclined on couches, their eyes scanning the room. To the right, a short corridor led to a large open kitchen with a countertop laden with food, and servers pouring drinks.

Kat made a beeline for the kitchen. She should be safe there. Producers preferred to pretend people on reality TV never ate. She grabbed a paper plate, and loaded it with corn chips, guacamole, and something that looked choco-latey but would probably be paleo and taste like dirt.

"Thank goodness you're here." Sarah sidled up beside her and dipped a cracker into a bowl of hummus. "I was beginning to think you'd snuck out the back."

"Almost. Upstairs bathroom." Kat downed a handful of chips in a couple of bites. "What's it been like down here?"

"About what you'd expect. At least six girls have screamed past tipsy and are well on their way to being completely sozzled. Two have already cried. I have no idea why. A few have declared themselves in love. The usual crazy."

In love? How could you be in love with someone when you didn't know he liked his poached eggs so well done you could play tennis with them? Or that he always put his left boot on first? Or that he made the best pancakes she'd ever eaten?

"Kat? Can I steal you for a minute?" And there he was. Standing beside her, hand out, a slightly hesitant look on his face as if unsure whether she might slap it away.

His hair was shorter than it used to be, and in the blur of their meeting she hadn't noticed his expertly tailored suit and dark blue tie.

Before she could respond a producer was at his side. "You don't need to waste time on her. Or her." He pointed at Sarah. "They're just stand-ins. You'll be eliminating them tonight."

"What?" Caleb looked down at the much shorter, much younger man beside him. Anyone who knew Caleb would recognize the edge to his single word signaled a man keeping his temper in check.

The man shifted on his feet. "I'll brief you shortly."

"I'd like to be briefed now."

The producer nodded to the cameraman, who lowered the camera and took a few steps back. "We had a few contestants go down with a bug at the last minute." He gestured toward Kat and Sarah. "These two and two others are part of the crew. They're just standing in for tonight."

A muscle on Caleb's jaw twitched. "Nice of you to let me know."

Sarah's gaze bounced between them, taking everything in. She tucked a streak of pink hair behind her ear. "If you want my advice, stay away from the girl with the bagpipes and the one with the boa. They're both nuts."

One side of Caleb's mouth ticked up. "Thank you. I appreciate it."

He turned to her. "What about you. Any advice?"

Choose me. Kat shoved the unexpected and wildly unwelcome thought aside. "No . . ." She cast her mind back to the women who had rotated through her makeup chair only a few hours earlier. Tried to conjure names of the few who had seemed normal. Nothing more than a haze of faces. "Good luck."

It sounded as flat as she felt.

It had been bad enough believing he had moved on and was happily married. This was so much worse. She'd be on the sidelines after tonight, forced to watch while the only man who had ever broken her heart fell for someone else.

If finding Kat in his arms had felt like a kick to the gut, discovering she was some kind of temp on *Falling for the Farmer* was like getting taken out at the knees.

Caleb tugged his collar, sweat trickling down

his back as he sat in front of the roaring fireplace. He'd been cooking in his suit even before a producer positioned him here for the latest speed date.

The earnest-looking redhead sitting next to him said something about an ex-fiancé and commitment issues. He wiped his palms against his pant legs in what he hoped was a subtle gesture, envying the redhead's bare arms and knee-length skirt.

"Want to take a walk?" Her face—what was her name? Ginny? Gemma?—lit up with a grin, and she shot to her feet like she'd been ejected off the stone ledge.

"Absolutely." She tilted her head toward a nearby set of couches where a few more women were chatting and tucked her hand under his elbow with a gloating grin. "Let's get away from prying eyes and find somewhere more secluded."

Dang it. She'd read his desire to escape the furnace as an invitation to a romantic rendezvous. Like that was even possible with a couple of cameras and a producer stalking their every move.

He'd been to calvings more romantic than this setup.

Was there somewhere they could go that would still be in sight of everyone?

"Excuse me." An olive-skinned woman in a

fitted black dress approached from the couches. "Do you mind if I cut in?"

As she spoke, Kat and Sarah came out of the doors leading to the patio and walked toward the couches. His hands clenched as he forced himself not to stride over and extract Kat for a conversation, whether the producers liked it or not.

Easy. Drawing attention to her in front of the other women wouldn't help.

"We were going for a walk." Ginny/Gemma's tone was already tinged with possessiveness and she gripped his arm even tighter. She'd need to go soon. A farmer's life did not allow for a clingy wife.

"Excuse me, ladies. I need to talk to Adam for a second. I'll be right back." Caleb extracted his arm and walked between the cameras circling him to his handler.

"Is everything okay?"

Caleb walked a few more steps away and placed his hand over the microphone attached to his lapel. "The blonde in the gray dress. I know she's a stand-in, but I want to talk to her. Can you set that up?"

Adam looked over to the couches, to where Kat was leaning into a conversation, hands gesturing. "Why?"

"Are you blind? Why do you think?" He had to force the words out. He'd wanted to at least navigate this process with integrity, yet here he was just a few hours in sounding like the average bloke who allowed something south of his brain to do the talking.

Adam frowned. "Honestly, the addition of the four crew was last minute. I don't even know if she's signed all the waivers we'd need to film her. The deal Vince made with her was walk in, a few crowd shots, walk away. I don't think she's even wearing a mic."

Perfect.

"What if I can convince her to stay? Off camera? Or is she completely off-limits?"

Adam sighed. If the guy thought him asking to talk to Kat was making his life hard, he had no idea what the next couple of months would be like. "Look. I can't make any promises. Vince would kill me if he knew I'd agreed to let you have an off-camera conversation. But . . . if you happen to ask her to talk to you and she agrees, I may remember she hasn't officially signed onto the show and tell the cameraman to err on the side of caution."

Tension eased from Caleb's shoulders. "Thank you."

Adam looked around to ensure no one was close enough to overhear them. "One word of advice. Don't be obvious about who your favorites are. It puts bull's-eyes on their backs with the other women."

"Got it." He strode across the patio to where the two women he'd left stood in stony silence awaiting his return.

He offered the redhead a loose hug. "I need to talk to the others, so thank you for your time." He turned to the woman who had interrupted them. He was ninety-nine percent sure of her name. "Shall we, Olivia?" He gestured to a nearby love seat, far enough away to talk in private, close enough to keep an eye on Kat in case she moved.

"Love to." After they'd settled in on the couch, Olivia leaned forward. The neckline on her dress was high, which made her a rarity. "I need to confess something."

She had his attention. "Okay."

"I'm only here because I drew the short straw."

Over her shoulder he watched Adam gesture to a guy holding a boom mic to get closer.

"I'm sorry?"

She sighed. "A group of friends and I made a promise when we were in university that those of us who were still single when we were thirty would audition for one of these cheesy reality shows." She clapped her hand against her mouth. "Sorry! I mean I'm sure it's all very genuine but . . ."

Caleb held his hand up. "No need to apologize."

"Well, there were four of us who met the criteria. None of us wanted to do it, so we drew straws. Whoever got the shortest one had to send in an audition video. I made the worst one I could, yet somehow here I am."

He'd have to ask to see that video. "Why didn't you withdraw?"

Her crossed leg bounced on her knee. "I kept assuming with every round that I would get cut. Lord knows I certainly did my best to convince them. Then I got laid off from my job and literally the same day I got the call saying I'd made the final cut. This is going to sound stupid, but I guess I thought maybe this was where God wanted me to be."

Modesty and an open admission of faith. That put Olivia two steps ahead of all the other women he'd spoken to.

Caleb leaned back in the seat. "I'm going to be honest. I'm not sure whether you want me to send you home or ask you to stay."

Olivia shrugged. "I have no idea either. It helps that you don't look like a Ken doll. That's what I was expecting. Some guy with product-coated hair, slightly orange-colored skin, terrifyingly white teeth."

Caleb bared his teeth. "I didn't get the memo about the hair and the tan but would like to say my family have always been complimented on our great teeth."

Olivia laughed. The cameraman filming them moved in a little closer and jolted Caleb out of a conversation that, for a few seconds, had felt almost natural.

"Do you think we'll ever get used to this?" As if reading his thoughts, Olivia gestured at the boom mic that hovered just a few feet above their heads.

"I have no idea." Off to the side a producer furrowed his brow. Apparently referencing that their every blink was subject to scrutiny by a hoard of onlookers wasn't the done thing. Well, Caleb didn't care about the done thing. Just because he was here didn't mean he was going to let them call all the shots.

Over on the couches, Sarah said something to Kat then stood. Now was the time to make his move, while Sarah was diverted.

"I should let you move on." He didn't know whether Olivia had picked up on his change of focus or whether she simply wasn't desperate to squeeze every second out of their conversation like all the other women. Either way, it gave her bonus points.

"Do you want to go home tonight?" He didn't want to keep her around if she didn't want to be here, even if she was one of the saner women.

She smiled as they stood. "Not tonight. Bad for the ego to be evicted in the first round."

He offered her his arm as they walked back to the couches. "Gotcha. Well, just so you know, whenever you want to go, just leave. I won't be offended."

He directed her to a spare spot on the couches. Six women suddenly sat straighter, flashed gleaming smiles. A couple tossed their hair like they were mares. Oh, Lord.

As expected, the one he wanted didn't so much as raise her eyes from where they contemplated a glass of lime and soda. Her favorite.

He cleared his throat. "Kat, would you like to talk?"

Her gaze jerked upward and locked with his. She looked at the two cameras circling the group and the other women, who had visibly deflated. "Um, sure." She placed her glass on the table, stood, and walked over to him like she was headed for the gallows.

"Let's take a walk. We'll see you ladies soon."

He held out his elbow and she regarded it for a second before placing her hand in the crook while still holding her body as far away as was possible.

Caleb kept an eye on Adam as they walked away from the group. He was having a word with the cameraman. Sure enough, as they walked across the patio and down some steps to the pool area, their entourage dropped back.

If he was lucky, his producer had bought him five minutes without scrutiny to bridge nine years of silence. Looking down at the beautiful woman beside him, he had no idea what to do with that time.

Even across the distance she was trying to maintain, Kat could feel the power rippling through Caleb as his legs strode across the pool area. They didn't build farmers weak or weedy in Australia.

What did he want? Worse, what could they say knowing their conversation would be beamed across the country for people's entertainment?

As if reading her thoughts, Caleb curled his other hand over the small mic attached to his shirt. She looked back, expecting to see a producer charging forward to make him uncover it. But the young man following them remained behind, and the cameraman was holding his camera at a slight downward angle that would only be good for shots of their feet.

"They're not filming, but we probably only have a few minutes before I'll be pulled away." Caleb's low voice tickled her ear.

"How did you manage that?" The idea of talking to Caleb without being filmed filled her with emotion.

"It wasn't me. It was you. Adam didn't think you'd signed the papers needed for them to film us having a private conversation."

She let out the breath that had been weighing her down all night. He was right. Some production assistant had delivered a wad of paperwork to the dressing room for her to sign, but she hadn't found time before she and the other stand-ins had to leave. Vince was probably firing the poor guy right now.

She pulled away from Caleb and turned. They'd walked beyond the main set lighting, but it glowed behind him, softening the rugged contours of his face.

"Why are you even talking to me?" She tried to keep her posture neutral. The cameras might not be filming, but that didn't mean she and Caleb weren't being watched.

Caleb scrubbed his face. "Who do you think I am, Kat? Did you think I would just eliminate you like I was told and pretend you were never here? Is that what you'd prefer?"

What she wanted was to go back to the day Vince had asked her to work on this stupid show and ignore her unspoken debt.

"No." She allowed the word to escape. That would be worse. To line up with all the other women and stand there, staring at the only man she'd ever given her heart to, knowing he wasn't going to choose her.

Again.

"How are you? You look well." Caleb shifted on his feet. Unclipped the microphone from his lapel and folded it into his hand.

Someone shoot her now. This painful, awkward

small talk was not them. She had to get off this show. As soon as she was eliminated tonight she would quit. Swap in one of her subcontractors and pay their salary herself for the next three months. Even though she couldn't afford it. Vince couldn't possibly say no to that. And if he did, well, he could just go ahead and fire her.

"What do you want, Caleb?" She tried to keep her voice steady. Forced herself to look right at him. Clenched her hands at the memories of the many times she'd run them along the stubble covering his jaw and looped them around his neck.

"I want you to stay."

Kat stared at him. For nine years she'd wondered what her life would have been like if he'd said those words. Her breath came in shallow bursts. Was he hoping for a second chance?

Her stomach clenched, reminding her of all the reasons she had to say no. Why the thirty-three-year-old version of Kat would never be able to give him what he wanted. What he needed.

He ran a hand through his short hair. "I trust you. Please stay for a couple of weeks and help me weed out the worst of them." He gestured back toward the house.

The insane piece of hope that had existed for a nanosecond unraveled. He didn't want her. He wanted a wingwoman. A mole. Someone to help steer him in the direction of his future wife.

"And why on earth would I want to do that?" She ground out the words through clenched teeth.

"Because . . ." His shoulders sagged as his words disappeared. "You're right. I have no right to ask you to help me. I'm sorry."

"You think? What are you even doing here, Caleb?" He was the last man in the world she expected to be on a show like this.

"Mum sent in an audition video."

She studied him. Caleb loved his mother. He would do anything for her, but something wasn't adding up.

He sighed. "She is apparently convinced drastic measures are required for me to meet someone."

"You've never married?" She needed to know what had happened to the fiancée Paige had Google-stalked for her once. Was he widowed? Divorced? Had someone broken his heart the way he'd broken hers?

He stilled. "No." The shadows cast by the trees overhead obscured his expression. "I was engaged a few years ago, but it didn't work out."

Why not? Kat caught the question before it could leave her lips. His breakup was none of her business. She didn't owe him anything, but he didn't owe her any explanation for the time since they'd split either.

"What about you?"

"No." The unvarnished pathetic truth. She'd broken up with every boyfriend she'd ever had—

bar one—because none of them had ever come close to making her feel the way she'd felt about him.

And now here she was, standing in front of the one man she'd even been prepared to give up everything for, and he wanted her to be his side-kick. "Annabella, Kristy, Brittany, and Lindsey."

"Sorry, who?"

"They're the craziest ones. You don't need to keep me around to find that out. You just needed to ask." With one last look into the eyes she knew so well yet not at all, she forced herself to turn around and walk away.

Facebook Messenger

Kat: I'm back. We talked. Off camera. For like three minutes.

Paige: And . . .

Kat: He wants me to stay. And help him find his wife.

Paige: HE DOES NOT!!!!

Allie: I've never even met this guy, and I want to pulp him.

Paige: Did you find out what happened to his fiancée?

Kat: He said it didn't work out.

Allie: Poor diddums. Cry me a river.

Allie: Sorry. Protective mama bear. I know you loved him once.

Paige: How do you feel?

Kat: Like I need to find somewhere to sit down and put my head between my knees. I told him who the biggest crazies are, so at least I can leave with a clear conscience.

Allie: You're a better woman than I am. If he were Jackson I'd have left him the crazies and taken the good ones with me.

Kat: I have to go. It's time for the awarding of the horseshoes.

Paige: ????????

Kat: Don't ask.

CHAPTER FOUR

How has the evening been?" Mark Caine, the host of the show, ushered Caleb into a small room filled with framed photographs of the women.

"Long." The hours had ticked by as the producers choreographed him conversing with all the women. He checked his watch. Almost one. A time he only saw when there was some kind of animal emergency.

"The good news is you don't have to make any difficult decisions tonight. You just have to eliminate the four crew members. But we'll need you to stay in here for at least half an hour so the women think you did some serious deliberation. Can I get you anything? A scotch? Whiskey?"

"I'm fine, thanks."

"Okay. Well, there's water on the table over there. Just knock on the door if you need anything. I'll be back to get you in a while."

Mark opened the door and disappeared, but not before Caleb glimpsed one of the security guards stationed outside. Did they think he was going to make a run for it?

Caleb glanced across the framed photos spread across the room. Kat's wasn't there, nor the other three crew. A piece of card rested on the table listing the eighteen names to go to the next round. He could connect maybe ten names with faces. For all the wrong reasons, apart from Olivia.

He picked a pen off the table, and put a line through Kristy, the crass bagpipe player who'd been so busy trying to thrust her chest out during their "talk" that he was surprised she didn't topple over. Keeping her was not an option, no matter what the producers wanted.

His phone vibrated in his pocket. He pulled it out to see *Mum home* on the screen. "Hello?"

"Hi, honey. Are you coming for dinner?"

One of the many curses of dementia: time no longer had any fixed meaning. "Mum, I'm not at home. I'm in Sydney doing that show you auditioned me for." Caleb paced the room, his phone clenched in his hand.

"Oh. Of course." She said the words slowly. The phrase she used now when something sounded familiar, but she was struggling to recall the details.

"It's called *Falling for the Farmer*. You signed me up to find me a wife."

"Have you found one?" The hope in her voice reminded him why he was doing this. He cleared his throat to try to get past the emotion welling in this throat.

"It's just the first night. They all seem very . . . genuine. You'll have to tell me what you think when you watch the episode."

That was the only reason he'd agreed to do this. The television network was turning around episodes in a matter of days to try and avoid another finale ruined. Which had happened last season when the "winners" were snapped on an overseas holiday a month before the final episode aired. For him, it meant his mother would get to see her wish come true.

Or at least some of it. Who knew how much time they had? Time he'd rather be spending with her, but she'd been in a lucid phase when the scouting team had showed up on his doorstep and had taken great offense at the suggestion she wasn't well enough for him to go.

"I will. I think I'll have the girls over."

He didn't even want to think what the pensioners from Toowoomba First Baptist would think of the show, even if his mother was in any state to host them. Which was highly unlikely.

"Oh, here's your uncle." There was a clunk and a, "It's Caleb" at the other end.

"Hi, son." Uncle Jared let out a yawn.

"Why are you up? Where's the carer?" His uncle had come out of retirement to help on the farm in Caleb's absence. He'd also insisted on moving in with Caleb's mum, but the last thing he needed at his age were broken nights.

"She's here. She's taking Marion back to bed now." His uncle's voice was heavy, the combination of running the farm and the 24/7 worry that came with a sister suffering from the same illness that had taken his wife. "How are things there?"

Jared hadn't wanted him to do the show. Still didn't. But once he'd seen the video he'd understood why Caleb didn't feel there was any other choice.

"Kat is here."

"Katriona?" Jared's voice lifted an octave. It took a lot to surprise his uncle, but he'd managed it.

"She wasn't supposed to be. She's the makeup artist on staff, and they had to sub a few extras in for the first episode because some women got sick. I'm supposed to eliminate her tonight."

"Huh." His uncle was silent for a few seconds. He was a man of few words, but when he spoke, Caleb listened. "How was it? Do you still have feelings for her?"

If he'd been asked that question yesterday he'd have scoffed. It had been nine years. He'd fallen in love with—almost married—someone else since. And as he'd watched Kat's glittering success from afar, he hadn't doubted for one second that he'd done the right thing in breaking up with her.

But the way his heart had leapt when he'd seen her in his arms. The way he'd had to clasp his hands together to stop himself from running a wayward lock of her hair through his fingers to see if it still felt like liquid sunshine. The way he'd been looking only for her the whole night. That felt like a whole lot of unresolved.

Asking her to be his insider hadn't been a genius move, but it was the best he could come up with in the moment. Served him right to have it thrown back in his face.

"You still there?"

Caleb blew out a breath. "I'm here. I don't know if I still have feelings for her. But she won't stay. She's made it clear she's leaving at the end of the night." *What was the point of that, God?* Had they really crossed paths tonight for nothing more than three minutes of broken conversation?

"What would you gain if she stayed? Has something changed?"

Jared was the only person in the world who knew why he'd broken up with Kat. "No."

"Be careful, okay? She really loved you."

Just like he'd really loved her.

The women had all been painstakingly positioned on a couple of steps, and now waited in strained silence for Caleb to appear.

Kat stood on the second tier at the end closest to the door, poised to make a fast and graceful exit at the end. Sarah, Mary, and Leona were all in the front row.

It was almost two a.m. At least half the women had kicked their shoes off, including her. A couple were swaying, as if falling asleep on their feet. Someone she couldn't see was letting out an occasional hiccup.

Romance at its finest.

One of the producers appeared in the arched doorway that led to a hallway. "Okay, ladies. He's ready. We'll start filming in a couple of minutes."

The room filled with sound as women shoved their feet back into shoes and adjusted necklines and hemlines. The swaying ones attempted to straighten up and look sober.

Kat slipped back into her heels and tugged in a breath, her stomach swirling up a storm. It would soon be over. She'd murmur something about it being "lovely to meet him" on her way out the door and disappear from public consciousness and his "journey" to find whatever he was looking for.

An assistant appeared with a tray of glittering horseshoes, and placed them on a small stand at the front of the room. Someone took a light reading, a board snapped, and the host appeared through the doorway.

Kat tuned out his droning words. She'd seen enough of these kinds of shows to know what they would be. Thank you for being here. Difficult decisions. Only going to get harder. Path to love. Blah blah blah.

Caleb walked out and stood beside the host, who gestured to the tacky horseshoes then took a few steps back. Sweat beaded his brow.

Kat stared at a generic painting of a countryside over Caleb's shoulder as he scanned the room. Kept her gaze on the gilded frame when he called out the first six names and the women gasped and teetered forward.

He disappeared.

"Where's he gone?" The dark-haired woman next to her sounded on the verge of panic. As if he might have decided to cut the show short about eight episodes and choose only half the women to consider for his future.

"He's gone to memorize the next set of names. He's met twenty-two women tonight. There's no chance he could remember them all."

The woman looked sideways at Kat. "How do you know that? Are you some kind of reality TV show obsessive?"

She said it with a sneer. As if she weren't currently standing on the set of such a show, with sweat patches under her armpits and the air of someone willing to trade all her worldly belongings for a U-shaped piece of metal.

"No," Kat said calmly. "I'm a makeup artist, and I've done some TV work." She was almost sorry she'd done such a great job with the woman's face, which still looked good after nine hours under hot lights. Kat had given her cheekbones that didn't exist in real life and helped defray attention from her larger-than-average nose.

The woman straightened and thrust her chest out as Caleb reappeared. Oh, brother.

He reeled off six more names, including Mirabelle, who turned out to be the woman next to her. She elbowed the contestant in front of them out of her way in her haste to take the horseshoe from Caleb.

The six remaining horseshoes glittered on the tray. The remaining horseshoe-less women stood ramrod straight like soldiers on a parade ground. Kat felt a little mean that they were all stressed out for no reason. The outcome of this ceremony had been predetermined before the women had even walked into the mansion.

He called out three more names, and three women said I do.

"Adeline." A statuesque blonde in a classy blue cocktail dress walked forward. The name rang a bell. She was destined to be one of the final five.

"Adeline, will you accept this horseshoe?"

"I will." Kat liked her. Adeline's words rang with confidence. Unlike the breathy little-girl sound of some of the other women.

He handed her the horseshoe, and Adeline took it with a flick of her wrist.

The whole room gasped as the thing slipped out of her hand and went flying. Over and over, the horseshoe whizzed through the air with a metallic gleam, gathering speed as gravity took hold.

It was headed right toward her section. Kat tried to bat it away, but it flew right past her sweeping hand, striking Mirabelle on the forehead.

The woman went down like Goliath.

Kat managed to catch Mirabelle under her armpits, but the best she could do was change her trajectory so the woman toppled sideways instead of straight back.

"Argh!" Mirabelle's dead weight hit Kat straight in her torso, and her heels slid forward across the tiled floor.

She was the last in her line. There was no one to catch her fall. So she slid straight down, her back hitting the hard floor, then her head. And Mirabelle landing on top of her.

"Oomph." All the air left in her lungs sprayed into a mouthful of Mirabelle's product-coated hair. Kat turned her head to the side to try and breathe. The entire crew stood frozen, bug-eyed.

The room soaked in stunned silence for a second. Useless, the lot of them.

"I think we may need a medic." She offered the advice from under sixty-odd kilos of dead weight.

That seemed to snap the crew into action, yelling and carrying on as if the woman had been hit with an asteroid instead of a wayward piece of equine footwear.

On top of her, Mirabelle groaned and started to move.

"It's okay. You're okay. Take it easy." This was easily the most ridiculous position Kat had ever been put in in her entire life. Flattened by a wannabe debutante on TV. So much for twenty seconds of walking out of a limo then disappearing.

There was no chance they wouldn't screen this, whether she'd signed the right paperwork or not. It was reality TV gold.

A medic finally appeared. Then another.

Mirabelle struggled to sit up, shoving an elbow in Kat's stomach to do so. Something hard pressed into her thigh as Mirabelle fought for her balance. Good grief. The woman was still holding her horseshoe. It was gripped in her right hand like it was the elixir of life.

"Easy." Both medics eased Mirabelle to a sitting position, holding one arm each.

Kat could breathe again.

The back of her head throbbed. She must have struck the ground harder than she'd realized.

She pushed up on her arm. "Careful." Caleb's voice came from beside her. "You took a pretty good hit too." From the breath on her cheek, he was close. Close enough that if she turned her head they'd probably touch noses.

"I'm fine." She shoved herself up to sitting, maneuvering her skirt and legs to try to keep a hold on whatever decency she had remaining.

He laughed low. "Still as independent as ever."

She swayed a little.

"Whoa. Easy." His hand gripped her upper arm.

"The back of my head hurts." She let the admission loose as the room swirled around her.

His fingers ran through her hair, and she tried to pretend they belonged to anyone but him. He'd always run his hands through her hair when he kissed her, his fingers looping around the strands as if claiming possession.

She winced as he hit a tender spot.

"Some help over here." He barked the words at one of the medics who said a couple of words to her partner before shifting over. "She hit her head."

"What's your name?" The older woman crouched in front of her.

"Kat."

"Kat, how many fingers am I holding up?" The woman flashed three blurry fingers and moved them from side to side.

"Three."

"Did you lose consciousness at all when you hit your head?"

"No."

"Not even for a second?"

Kat shook her head.

"Do you know where you are?"

"In Sydney on the set of *Falling for the Farmer*."

The woman's fingers probed along the back of her head. "You've got a nasty egg there. It's going to be tender for a few days."

"Is Mirabelle okay?"

The woman looked back as a stretcher was wheeled in. The other medic and a producer helped Mirabelle to her feet, horseshoe still clenched in her hand. A large piece of gauze was taped to her forehead. "We think so, but we're going to take her to hospital to run some tests."

Cameras circled them. Vince would be loving this. He couldn't have come up with a better way to start the season if he'd tried.

The medic flashed a torch into her eyes. "We should probably take you too. Just in case."

"No!" This nightmare dragging out for even longer was the last thing she needed. She lifted her full skirt off the ground then forced herself to her feet. Focused everything on remaining steady. "I'm fine. See."

The room blurred at the edges and her body swayed. Her hand grabbed for the closest secure thing. Caleb's arm. A camera hovered less than three feet away, trained right on them. "Sorry."

"Fine, huh?" His voice rumbled out of his chest and she didn't dare look him in the eyes. Forcing her fingers to uncurl from his forearm, Kat stepped back.

Her head tilted toward the camera. "Yes. You should check on Mirabelle."

"Mirabelle is being well taken care of."

This time she forced herself to look up. Concern crinkled at the corners of Caleb's eyes. "I'm fine. Please."

"Okay." After a long glance, he turned and strode toward the stretcher being readied for departure.

A producer appeared in front of her. "So you're okay to continue? We're going to film the final two once we can get everyone back in place."

"Yes." Regret settled through her at once. Why hadn't she claimed injury to escape this fiasco? The host could have done a sober announcement about how she'd hit her head and taken medical advice that it was best for her not to continue. "Actually . . ."

Too late.

Fifteen minutes later everyone stood in their spots, an obvious gap between Kat and the woman who had been on Mirabelle's other side. As expected, the host made some painful monologue about Mirabelle being in the hands of the best medical experts and everyone's hopes and prayers being with her and her recovery. Then Caleb was up.

Caleb lifted the second-to-last horseshoe and weighed it in his hands.

"K—"

Her heart leapt.

"Yes!" The busty brunette in some kind of tartan-striped dress shrieked and ran forward, hand out, before he'd even finished her name.

Kat let out a shuddery breath. It was okay. She could wish him well, walk off the set with her head held high, and move on with her life. This time when he rejected her, she'd leave with dignity.

Caleb looked down at the woman standing in front of him but made no move to give her the horseshoe. For the love, could he just do it already and put everyone out of their misery?

The woman stood there.

Caleb turned and looked at the host standing behind him.

The room was as silent as her gynecologist's waiting room as everyone held their breath, uncertain what was unfolding.

"I'm sorry. There's been some kind of mis-understanding." Caleb said the words quietly, but they filtered across the room. "I said Kat."

Chaos hit. The host and a producer leapt forward, dragging Caleb off to a corner where they huddled in a circle. The producer said something, hands flapping, and Caleb shook his head.

The rejected woman picked up her skirt and stormed from the room, another producer and cameraperson chasing her.

"Isn't that you? Aren't you Kat?" The woman standing next to Mirabelle's gap clutched her horseshoe as if afraid Kat might try to swipe it out of her hand.

"Yes."

He'd asked her to stay.

As his wingwoman. His sidekick. Her Robin to his Batman. That was all.

Vince appeared beside her, expression taut, a medic next to him. "Kat, the medic just wants to give you another check." He announced the words loudly as he tugged her off to one side.

The medic held up a light and shone it into her eyes.

"So, um, change of plan. I'm going to need you to stay." Vince uttered the words in a hushed and desperate plea.

"Absolutely not." She hissed the words.

"Caleb's right. He can't eliminate you. Not after you turned all Superwoman like that. You have to stay at least one more episode."

"Not a chance." She had done him his favor. He didn't get to change the rules on her now. One episode made her a walk-on, though with a slightly more prominent role than any of them anticipated. More than that made her a wannabe. Worse, she'd be forced to go on some contrived group date with Caleb. She'd fall down these stairs and put herself out of the game before that happened.

"Please don't make me beg for the second time in one day. I'll double your daily rate. Just tell me what you need for the week. We'll have someone at your apartment to pick it all up first thing in the morning. Or I can just send someone to David Jones to buy you whatever you want."

She needed the money. She couldn't pretend she didn't. But not even double the paltry amount she'd agreed to do this for would balance the torture of having to stay.

"Pupils look good." The medic stepped back and clicked her light off.

Kat looked around. Everyone was in their spot and ready to film except her. She picked up her skirt and stepped back into place.

"Please." Vince muttered one final plea then stepped away, disappearing into the crew.

Looking straight ahead she focused all her energies on Caleb. *Please don't say my name. Please don't ask me to stay.* Having him call her name and turning him down would just attract more attention. But having to stay and pretend to be one of his groupies? Watching him go out on dates with other women. That would be unbearable.

She'd done unbearable things twice in her life. Walking away from him being the first. The reason they could never have a second chance being the second. She didn't have any desire to add to her list.

Caleb returned to his position. Moving the horseshoe from one hand to the other, he seemed to be weighing his next words with it. Finally, he looked up and stared right at her. "Kat?"

Time stood still as she made her way down the two steps and the one, two, three, four, five paces it took to arrive in front of him.

"Kat, will you accept this horseshoe?"

She looked down at the tacky silver crescent in his palm. "I . . ." She cleared her throat. "I don't . . ." Well, that was a terrible start to the sentence. *I don't think so? I don't want to? I don't know? I don't think my heart could bear it?*

A finger underneath her chin tipped it up and forced her to look into his eyes.

"Please." It was the same worried, pleading gaze as the day he'd found her passed out on her bathroom floor, gathered her into his arms, and held her and told her to hang on.

Kat let out a slow breath. She had never been able to say no to Caleb Murphy. Apparently, she wasn't about to start now.

Facebook Messenger

Kat: So, slight change of plan. I didn't get eliminated.

Allie: Wait, what? He asked you to stay? But you said no, right?

Kat: Yes to the middle question.

Paige: You said yes?

Kat: It's hard to explain. A horseshoe knocked

one of the women unconscious, she collapsed into me, we both fell. There were medics and insanity and apparently he couldn't eliminate me after all that. So I have to stay for one more episode. You'll see what I mean in a couple of days.

Paige: Have to or want to?

Kat: Have to. It wouldn't have looked good if he'd eliminated me.

Allie: Um, yeah, I don't really care how he looks one way or the other. I care about you now spending, what? A week in his harem?

Kat: I'm sure it'll be fine. I'll hardly even see him.

Paige: I'm sure you have some kind of brain injury from your fall. Because of all the words that could be used to describe being hijacked into going on a matchmaking show where your ex-boyfriend is the match, "fine" isn't one of them.

Allie: Are you still in love with him?

Kat: NO!!! I just want this to go well for him. You guys have never met him. He's a genuinely good guy. I can at least help him weed out the worst crazies.

Allie: He has, like, a gazillion crew to help him do that. They want this to succeed just as much as you do. Probably more.

Kat: This will all be over in a week. You're always telling me I should relax and take some time off! P, I'm messaging you with some clothes I need you to pack for the week.

Paige: Not funny. If he breaks your heart again . . .

Kat: He's not going to break my heart. I promise.

CHAPTER FIVE

If Caleb believed in purgatory, this would be it. Being forced to make inane small talk with a bunch of strangers, all of whom seemed to want him to be someone he wasn't.

The crack of Kat's head hitting the floor still rang in his ears twelve hours later. All he wanted was to find her and check she was okay. Instead, he'd been situated in a cabana by the pool while producers fed a steady stream of women wearing not a whole lot his way.

"Hi." The next woman in the curated queue plopped onto the couch beside him. She had blonde hair and wore a bikini that barely covered the pertinent areas.

"Hi." Caleb had no idea what her name was. About ten blondes who looked terrifyingly alike counted among the women who'd made it through the previous round of eliminations.

She leaned in and placed a hand on his knee. "I'm Brittany, in case you don't remember."

"Thanks. I'm not great with names. But I promise I'll remember yours now." Caleb sat half-on, half-off the seat. How could he get her hand off his leg without being rude?

"It's totally fine." She curled her legs underneath her. "I know our spirit animals have connected at a deeper level."

Um? "That's, um, nice." If by nice he meant crazy weird. He shifted his position, but the talons remained wrapped around his knee.

Brittany leaned forward, and her hand traveled a bit farther up his thigh. Blimey. He gave her hand a pointed look, but she was oblivious. "Look, I know we're in a time-pressured situation here, so I think we should get right to things that are important to us. I believe that we, as human beings, possess at least one spirit animal that serves as our personal protector and guide."

"And how does one, um, find their spirit animal?" Caleb looked at her, hoping she would burst out laughing any second and tell him she was joking. But he suspected he had about as much chance of that happening as her keeping her hands to herself.

"Dreams. Usually. Like mine's a leopard." Brittany stared at him. "But it can also be a particular type of animal constantly crossing your path."

"In that case, mine would be a cow."

Her brow crinkled as she missed the joke and pondered his statement. "Well, I guess cows are calm and, um, productive. Those are good things."

Even though he'd been roped onto the show at

the last minute he'd told the producers a woman with a faith was important to him. They'd assured him there were some in the group. No one had mentioned their definition included spirit animal believers.

". . . it's common for us to have many spirit animal helpers throughout different periods of our lives. And, obviously, the more times we're reincarnated the more guides we have."

"Okay. That's, um, an interesting thought." Caleb looked up at the producer standing a couple of feet away. Like they could help him.

"Caleb, there you are." Gemma came swaggering up to them as if she hadn't been eyeing him like a piece of steak for the last fifteen minutes. "Can I steal him, Britt?" She reached over and grabbed his hand. "It's time to get that shirt off. Come have some fun in the pool with us."

The last sentence rolled off her tongue in a way he was sure was supposed to be alluring but sent chills up his spine. What had his mother signed him up for?

Caleb removed Brittany's hand off his knee then stood. "I'm sorry, ladies. I think I need to check in with Adam for a few minutes." He didn't think he was wrong. Adam had appeared behind the supervising producer with a pinched brow and crossed arms.

Gemma pouted as she turned toward the producer. "C'mon, Adam. Just let me have a few minutes with him. I've been waiting aaages."

"Sorry, ladies. It'll only take a few minutes."

Brittany finally got the hint and stood. "So I'll catch up with you again later?" It was a question Caleb let go unanswered. He'd find the nearest bathroom and lock himself in it before that happened.

With backward glances over their shoulders the women headed back to the pool, hips swaying in an exaggerated way he suspected he was meant to find sexy but looked more like they needed to find a good chiropractor.

He sat back down as Adam handed him a bottle of water. "Don't take this the wrong way but how long do I have to do this for?" Day two. He was only on day two, and he was supposed to be doing this for *months*.

"We have a problem." Adam twisted the top off his own bottle and took a gulp.

"Just the one?" Caleb tried to inject some humor into his voice but failed. He wasn't good with women at the best of times, let alone when trying to build rapport with strangers while a camera and a bunch of people stared at them like lab rats.

"Well, one big one." His producer sat down and leaned against the bench seat. "We've been filming for three hours now, and we have maybe, *maybe,* fifteen minutes of footage worth airing."

"Why's that?"

"You're terrible on camera." The man said the words bluntly. Caleb had to respect him for not even trying to soften the bald facts. But they weren't exactly a surprise.

"I told you I would be." The day they'd showed up on his front porch, armed with his mother's audition monologue, and asked him to be their farmer he'd said exactly that. That they couldn't pick a worse person for a reality TV show.

"I know. But, and I'm going to be brutally honest, there's average. Which is what we were expecting and is easily fixed with good editing. And then there's horrible. Which we can't fix no matter how good post-production is."

"What's the worst of it?"

Adam sighed. "You. Bluntly. You're stilted and awkward and reserved, and since you haven't even taken your T-shirt off, we can't even take the edge off that with some good ab shots. Not to mention that you recoil whenever a woman so much as leans toward you."

"Okay." Well, clearly it wasn't, but what exactly did they want him to do?

"I need you to be honest about something."

"Sure." He was good at being honest, which seemed to be a drawback when it came to TV.

Adam draped his arm over the back of the seat, trying to appear casual. His tense shoulders told another story. "Are you gay?"

A laugh hacked out of Caleb's throat.

"Because if you are, that's totally fine. I mean, it's problematic, clearly, since we have eighteen women here and if you prefer men—"

"Adam." Caleb interrupted him before this could go somewhere he didn't even want to imagine. "I'm not gay. I'm awkward and stilted and reserved because I'm an introverted farmer who spends most of his day with animals. But I am one hundred percent attracted to women. I promise."

Adam's brows pinched. "What's the problem? We have a group of attractive, smart, articulate women here who are literally throwing themselves at you, and you're responding to them like they have leprosy."

"No. I'm just not kissing them. Which is apparently the metric for success here. And I told you from the beginning I wouldn't be that guy who makes out with a different woman every ten minutes."

Adam was silent.

"What? I did."

"Look, you did, it's true. I guess we'd just assumed that would change once you got here and met them."

Now things made more sense. "You thought I'd trade in my old-school morals when women in string bikinis made it more than obvious they wouldn't turn me down?"

"Every other man in Australia would."

"We obviously know different types of men."

"We don't need you to kiss scores of women. Just a few." Adam leaned forward as if petitioning him. For a second Caleb felt sorry for the guy, banking the success of their show on not believing a world existed outside of their live-for-the-moment, do-whatever-you-feel-like ethos.

"Well, that's not going to happen. Last I checked, of all the things I signed away in that contract, a kissing quota wasn't one of them. The only way I'm kissing any woman is if I genuinely see a potential future with her. Whatever you guys need to do, you're going to have to come up with a new narrative."

Adam sighed. "Caleb, I like you, which is why I'm telling you that kissing a few women is a better option than Vince will come up with if he feels he needs to do something drastic to pull in viewers."

Caleb shrugged. As far as he was concerned, the worse the ratings, the better. "Look, I'll do my best to be less stilted and awkward and give you more to work with, but if the viewers of this show are after a bunch of steamy hot tub scenes then we should all go home now. That's not who I am."

Adam sighed. "Okay. Let's hope for your sake that's enough."

CHAPTER SIX

Kat found the first date card. Of course she did. The cream envelope embossed with the tacky horseshoe was leaning against the toaster when she crept downstairs to find a snack and avoid the pool party. The kitchen was empty. Apparently, she was the only person in the house who liked to eat.

She should just ignore it. Let someone else find it when they came foraging for a piece of lettuce.

"You need to pick it up and tell the others there's a date card. Gather them all in the lounge." The instruction came from Karissa, one of the five producers assigned to the women.

Kat pulled a face at the young woman with long mousy-brown hair. "Do I have to? We both know I'm out of here at the end of the week. I'll just go back upstairs and leave it for someone who'll be hanging around." God bless Paige. Along with sending her some clothes, her cousin had thrown in a couple of novels from Kat's nightstand. More contraband to go along with her phone.

Karissa shook her head. "Nope. You found it, you read it. Do yourself a favor and try to summon some enthusiasm. Otherwise we'll just have to refilm it."

Oh, brother. Well, here went nothing. Kat picked up the envelope and turned it over in her hands. Now she'd have to see Caleb. And she'd been doing so well for the last three hours, fighting the overwhelming temptation to check out how he was coping with his first official full day as a reality TV star.

Adeline walked into the kitchen. "What's that?"

Kat sucked in a breath. Held up the envelope. "Take a guess."

Adeline let out a squeal. "Date card!" She turned and ran out the door leading to the outdoor area. "Date card, everyone! Kat has the first date card! To the lounge!"

Stampeding elephants would have been quieter than the women as the announcement travelled around the house and across the pool.

Holding the card, Kat trudged into the lounge.

"Stand in the middle, in front of the coffee table." Karissa pointed to the spot and Kat assumed her position as women tumbled onto the couches and sat on the floor.

Kat caught a glimpse of Caleb and his producer Adam exchanging a few words outside the door. Then Caleb came in, pulling his T-shirt over his head. He must have been in the pool because it clung to his still-damp torso.

"Adeline and Lindsey, can you scoot over so

75

Caleb can sit between you?" One of the other producers spoke and the two women moved so fast they almost ended up in the laps of the people next to them.

Caleb squished himself between them, his broad farmer's body much too large for the small space.

"Everyone ready?" Kat inserted as much perkiness into the question as she could manage. There was no way she would reshoot this.

Claps and squeals filled the room.

She slid her finger under the seal, opened the envelope, and pulled out the card. Prepared to read the list of names for the first group dates. Hopefully they'd bundled all the crazies into one group so the rest of them could enjoy an evening of semi-serenity.

"Gemma. Tammy. Lindsey. Kat. *Kat?*" Her? What was her name doing there? That wasn't part of the deal. Sucking in a breath, she forced herself to continue. "Meghan."

Brittany. The last name hit her retinas. Uh-uh. No way. So far the group was a list of the possessive, the desperate, the ditsy, and her. She wouldn't make it through the night with her sanity if vegan-rawist-spirit-guide girl was the final addition.

"Olivia." Her roommate's name blurted out of her mouth before she could change her mind. The woman was actually sane, which counted for a lot in this house. And she was refreshingly cynical about the whole thing. "Let's dance the night away. Caleb." She slid the card into the envelope as a ripple of claps and sighs went through the room.

She paused, waiting for one of the producers to realize she'd switched names and rush in. None of them moved.

Caleb stood. "Thanks for a lovely afternoon, ladies. I guess I'll see the six of you in a couple of hours." He said his words with all the enthusiasm of a man headed for some serious dental work.

Probably because Caleb Murphy couldn't dance to save himself.

It had been line dancing. Not exactly his sweet spot but certainly better than the dark nightclub with strobe lights and pulsating music Caleb had braced himself for.

Best of all, it had provided limited opportunities for conversation or bumbling awkwardness on his part. That was coming up now. The three hours that had been set aside for one-on-one conversations loomed in front of him longer than a scorching Queensland summer.

He looked at the women arranged around the couches. Which one should he ask first? The entire evening he'd been focused on Kat. Every step, every turn, he'd known exactly where she was. But he couldn't ask her first. Like Adam had said, that would draw unnecessary attention.

"I'm going to propose a toast." Gemma leaned forward, picked up her glass, and waited for everyone else to do the same. "To Caleb, first dates, destiny, and happily ever after."

Caleb smothered a smile as he caught Olivia's eye roll even as she clinked her glass with the others. Eventually the clinking died away and an awkward silence descended. Gemma looked at him, as if her toast earned her pole position or something.

"Caleb, can I steal you for a few minutes?"

His head jerked up, convinced wishful thinking had him imagining the voice.

It was Kat. She'd been seated on the same couch as him, Adeline in between them. She'd already stood, drink in hand.

"Yes! Absolutely!" His words were out of his mouth before he could temper their enthusiasm.

Gemma shot Kat a look filled with pure venom. Either Kat didn't see it, or she ignored it. The other women registered various expressions of disappointment and resignation.

Caleb stood and grabbed Kat's hand, trying to remember the places Adam set up for one-on-one time, trying to remember which was the least conspicuous.

There was a balcony around the back of the building, tucked out of the way. Caleb led Kat outside the circle of couches, and headed toward the door in the opposite direction.

They could double back in the hallway, which he hoped would buy them some time if anyone came looking to interrupt them. Although if the producers wanted him to move on to the next woman they'd tell her exactly where to find him.

"Hey." He smiled at Kat. Ignored the cameras and crew following them.

"Hey." Her smile didn't quite reach her eyes, but he'd take it.

Caleb cut down a set of stairs then across the next hallway.

"Where are we going?"

"There's a balcony out the back with a nice view of the harbor."

He opened the door to the outside and ushered her through in front of him. The wind caught the back of her green wrap-thing as she walked outside, and he put a hand on the small of her back to push it back down.

She gave him a sidelong glance, and he snatched his hand back. Tried to pretend it hadn't fitted perfectly. Like always.

Kat leaned against the balcony railing, taking in the view while Caleb took in her. Her hair was caught up in a thick braid and the chunky necklace she wore rested against her fitted white T-shirt.

She'd always had a kind of effortless beauty,

but it showed up even more among a cadre of gorgeous women who seemed to think less was more and tighter was better.

Kat turned to him, her body less than a foot away. The balcony was smaller than he remembered. The cameraman and producer perched awkwardly in the doorway. But he wasn't complaining.

"I have a confession to make." A mischievous smile played on her lips.

"Oh?"

"I changed one of the names on the date card."

"What? Why?" A thought struck him. "Did you add yourself?" Why would Kat put herself on a date? Especially when—from what he'd seen of her conversation with Vince and her reluctance to accept his stupid horseshoe—she'd only remained on the show under duress. An unsettling spark of hope lit within him.

"No."

And died.

"Brittany was meant to be here. But I subbed in Olivia."

"Wow. Okay. Why?"

Kat turned and leaned against the balustrade. "Because you're a farmer, and Brittany is a rawist vegan who consults her crystals on major life decisions."

Most of that sentence made no sense. "She's a what?"

80

The sides of Kat's mouth rose. "A rawist vegan. She only eats unprocessed and uncooked plants."

Caleb stared at Kat. Was she joking? How could that even be a thing?

"It's a thing." He didn't know if he'd spoken aloud or if she'd read his mind.

"So you subbed in Olivia. Why?"

Kat just looked at him with the same *duh* expression she'd always given him when he asked the obvious.

Because he'd asked her to. The answer flooded his brain. He'd asked her to. He'd asked her to stay and help him weed out the crazies, and that was exactly what she was doing.

That was the kind of women Katriona McLeod was. He'd broken her heart, yet she still looked out for him.

Kat shrugged. "Olivia is great. She's genuine and, unlike at least half of them, she's not here to be an Instagram star."

"I have no idea what that means."

"It's a . . ." Kat waved her hand in the air. "Don't worry. It's not important."

"What about you? Why are you here?" The words were out of his mouth before he'd thought them through.

Kat's eyes widened, and her gaze bounced over his shoulder to where the camera had to be staring right at her.

He hadn't meant to put her on the spot. "You

seemed a little unsure last night." Now he sounded insecure.

Her gaze cleared. "I'm a makeup artist and work a lot in film and television, so I'm used to being on the other side of the camera. Being in front of it is . . . disconcerting. I guess I question how anyone can build a real relationship in this kind of environment."

"Well, that makes two of us." He probably wasn't supposed to say that being the star of the show and all, but fair dinkum. He was already a disaster on camera, so maybe they'd get better footage if he just said what he thought.

"So why are you here?"

Caleb looked out over the harbor view. The Sydney Harbour Bridge glittered in the background. Kat had stayed. He owed her the truth. As much of it as he could give her. "My mother sent in the audition video." He took a breath as the words choked him. Cleared his throat. "Her greatest wish is to see me with someone, and happy."

That was as much as he would say with a camera behind them. Mum was a proud woman, and he'd promised himself he wouldn't use her illness for TV fodder. "I had no idea she'd sent in the audition tape until the producers showed up on my front porch. But the truth is, I'm hardly meeting many eligible women working on the farm all day with a bunch of men."

"When was your last relationship?"

"A few years ago."

"What happened?"

"She left." Might as well put it all out there. "A couple of months before we were meant to get married."

"I'm sorry." Kat placed a hand on his arm, and he couldn't stop his body leaning toward her. Like she had her own gravitational pull.

Caleb looked down at her. All he wanted to do was cup the back of her head and discover if her lips still felt the same. See if she still tasted like peppermints and hope.

He'd loved Emma with his whole heart. Or so he'd thought. The day he'd walked into his house and found her note he'd thought he'd never draw a proper breath again.

But standing there he knew the truth. The woman standing in front of him was the great love of his life.

And he was going to have to let her go twice.

His fiancée had left him and, going by the haunted look in Caleb's eyes, he still wasn't over her. Kat's stomach twisted at the realization.

Caleb leaned over the balcony balustrade, fixing his eyes on the cars zooming around the city streets far below.

"Anyway, enough about me." The briskness of his words told her the conversation about his fiancée was closed. At least for tonight. "Tell me about your life, Katriona McLeod." He was the only person, other than her mother, who had ever called her by her full name. Most people didn't know what Kat was short for.

She leaned forward too as she curated her answer for the man who used to know her better than anyone else on the planet. "I work in makeup. Mostly for films and television. I've been doing it for nine years now."

She chanced a sideways look. Did he know anything about her life? Had he—like her—succumbed to the pull of Google to see what had happened since they split?

Or had he gone on with his life and left her in the past? She felt the sudden urge to prove herself. Prove she hadn't spent nine years heartbroken in the fetal position. That she'd made something of herself. Succeeded. "I'm quite good."

I have an Oscar. I've worked on some of the biggest movies in the world with the A-list of producers and actors. I can name my price and they will pay it. I don't want anything from you.

She swallowed the words back. Because the truth was that she wanted a lot of things from him. She wanted him to say he was sorry. She wanted him to say she was good enough. She wanted him to say he was a fool and he shouldn't have let her go.

A completely idiotic fantasy, given he'd never

been engaged to her. Never asked her to marry him. She was the kind of pathetic woman she yelled and threw popcorn at when watching a movie.

"Are you happy?"

His question robbed her of breath. No one had asked her that in years. Everyone assumed she was. Why wouldn't she be? She had her dream job. She had people who loved her. She had travelled to thirty countries. She owned her own company. She was beholden to no one.

Kat looked up to see Caleb staring down at her. "I love my job. But it's not everything."

But she would never have everything. She'd been robbed of that possibility, as the bills that kept arriving reminded her.

She blinked back unexpected tears. No one knew. Not her family. Not Paige. Not Allie. She'd told herself it was best. Better to wake up alone in a hospital room than deal with their sympathy. Or worse, their pity.

Fingers wrapped around hers where they clung to the balustrade. She looked at them then up at Caleb.

He was playing a role, she reminded herself. He was making sure the audience were fed.

If she stayed, she would have to do this. Hold his hand. Maybe kiss him. Her breath stuttered. How could she kiss Caleb Murphy knowing his heart wasn't in it?

"What do you want?" The question slipped out before she had time to think about it.

He thought for a second. "I want to be someone's home. I want to spend my whole life making one woman happy. I want to be worth staying for."

All she'd ever wanted was to be asked to stay.

And now he was. But for all the wrong reasons.

So why did everything in her want to remain with him on this show? To enjoy it while it lasted? Even if it was just a mirage, an illusion that would fade as soon as the cameras stopped rolling?

Text Message

Janine: So, color me dumbfounded when I turned on the TV on Thursday night and found one of my favorite parishioners on my big screen! A little bird told me you've somehow retained your phone, so your pastor is here and ready to listen. Anytime.

Janine: Anytime. Like literally anytime.

Janine: ANYTIME

Janine: Please. Don't make me beg.

Janine: I'm now at a conference in Texas. I was checking my phone so much that Beth thought someone was dying or something, so I've had to loop her in. She's desperate for an update too and feeling a bit Twitter trigger happy. And her Twitterati army is way bigger than mine, so you really don't want to keep her waiting!

Kat: Sorry! Yes, do have my phone but only get a chance to check messages when I can smuggle it into the loo without anyone seeing. I assume Paige has filled you in on everything?

Janine: A pastor can never divulge her sources ;-)

Janine: P.S. Thanks for legitimizing my FFTF obsession.

Janine: P.P.S. I don't suppose they need a chaplain? Because I can totally clear my schedule. Just waiting for the call . . . ready, willing, and eager to do the Lord's service.

Kat: I doubt the show can afford your fee for doing the Lord's service

Janine: *Ouch* Seriously though, how are you doing?

Kat: It was the second horseshoe ceremony last night. Another four women gone. Only fourteen left now.

Janine: And you're still there . . .

Kat: So it would seem.

Janine: I'm quite good at advice you know. Been giving it for a looooong time. Also, my son is going to marry your cousin, so that practically makes me your mother-in-law once removed. Or something.

Kat: JOSH PROPOSED?!

Janine: Um, no. Ahem. Anyhoooo. Moving on. Back to you.

Kat: Tell Josh he's not allowed to propose until I get back!

Janine: From what I saw on Thursday night that could be awhile . . .

Kat: I don't know. I don't know why I'm still here. I don't know how long I can bear to stay or if I can bear to leave.

Janine: Am I right in my presumption that Caleb is the guy from long ago you once mentioned? The one who broke up with you?

Kat: When did I tell you that?

Janine: Meh. Years ago. But he didn't have a name then.

Kat: Do you keep track of all the ex-boyfriends of North Point's zillions of single women?

Janine: Nope. Just the ones I can tell were life altering.

Kat: I have to go. If I stay in here any longer someone's going to think I have an eating disorder or something.

Janine: I'll be praying.

Janine: But no falling in love and moving to Toowoomba allowed. We only import. No exports.

Kat: Don't worry. I'm not moving to Toowoomba.

Janine: I once said I'd never pastor a megachurch. Look how that turned out.

CHAPTER SEVEN

If Caleb had sisters, even one, he might have had a clue what to do with a bunch of women who were so emotional, so anxious, and so wound up they made Ozzy Osbourne look like the epitome of emotional stability.

But he hadn't, so he was a man drowning without so much as a rubber ducky to stop him from going under.

They'd spent the day quad biking in the Glenworth Valley. An excellent choice since it involved limited time to talk and the chance for everyone to burn off some restless energy. But now it was evening. The part he dreaded as he was spun through musical chairs with all the women. Most of them wanted to dive into deep and meaningful topics while he still wanted to ask things like "Do you like Mexican food?" and "Will you mind if I disappear every Friday and Saturday night during the footy season?"

At least he'd been able to automatically add two women to his elimination list thanks to whining about chipped manicures and being terrified of getting muddy.

Huh. They would have no idea what mud was until they'd spent a few hours in the pouring rain, on their knees in a muddy puddle, with their arm buried up to their armpit in a cow's birth canal.

"Care to share?" Mirabelle fluttered her lashes at him as she sat squished against him on the couch. Mark had told them at the second horseshoe ceremony that another four women would be going home at the end of this week, so everyone was on edge.

For some insane reason, many of the women had responded to the announcement with higher hemlines, lower necklines, and eyelashes that reminded Caleb of massive spiders. Gemma had told him that the fact he hadn't kissed any of them was causing extra stress because it meant no one knew the pecking order.

"Caleb?"

"Sorry! What?"

"That looked like a deep thought. I wondered if you wanted to share it."

"It wasn't that interesting." He picked up his glass of juice and took a gulp just to have something to do.

She pouted, bottom lip sticking out in an overexaggerated fashion. Was he supposed to find that attractive?

"Caleb." Mirabelle ran a finger up his arm. She was wearing a coat while he was in a T-shirt and jeans. Must be one of those women who felt the cold easily. "I know farmers are meant to be the strong, silent type, but if we're going to grow our connection we need to be vulnerable with each other and share our thoughts."

Oh, sod it. He put his juice down on the table with a thud. "I was thinking about calving. Sometimes when a calf gets stuck it needs some human assistance, so a farmer puts his arm up the mother's birth canal to help wrangle it out."

Mirabelle's jaw dropped. "Well, that sounds very, um, manly."

It was disgusting, but whatever.

Mirabelle leaned in. Behind her, a camera moved a little closer. Caleb had almost stopped noticing them now. They were just part of the scenery in this game of survival.

"I'm sure you've been wondering why I brought you here."

He hadn't at all. He'd assumed it was just one of the many "private" spots the producers set up for every group date.

He looked around. They were on a couch in some kind of alcove. Candles flickered on the table in front of them while music crooned through hidden speakers.

If it was just the two of them it might have been considered intimate. It would probably even look that way to viewers who couldn't see the producer, sound guy, and camera guy all huddled in the corner.

Mirabelle dropped her voice. "I know you have to make some tough decisions this week, so I thought I'd take the opportunity to make our time together extra memorable." Her voice had gotten huskier as she spoke. Was she starting to lose it? She was definitely one of the biggest talkers in the group.

She leaned forward, placing a hand on his knee.

Oh, Lord. She wasn't going to kiss him, was she? What was he going to do if she did?

Instead she used his knee to push herself off the couch.

Phew.

She had on ridiculously high shoes. And she wobbled on them like a newborn foal taking its first steps.

She belonged on his farm about as much as one of those Kardashian people. He should send her home tonight. It wasn't fair to keep her around any longer.

The music had changed, gotten louder, and Mirabelle was swaying her hips like she was auditioning for a music video. She'd undone the belt on her coat and was doing some weird maneuver with it. Did she need to scratch her back?

What was she doing?

"Mirabelle." *I appreciate the time we've had together but I don't think I'm the right man for you.* He practiced the line in his head. Yes, that would do. Made it more about him than her.

"Shhhhh. Just enjoy." She'd dropped her belt and undone the top two buttons of her trench coat. Something red and lacy peeked over her lapels.

Enjoy? Enjoy what? Some woman dancing in front of him like he was in a str—Oh. No. His hands thrust out as if they contained the magical power to keep her clothes on.

Too late. The trench coat came off, thrown onto the coffee table, and she stood in attire that would have the senior citizens of Toowoomba First Baptist swallowing their dentures.

"Stop!" The word busted out of him in a strangled yell. "Please."

Where were her clothes? She'd been wearing a dress earlier in the evening.

Her coat. He went to grab it but just as he did there was a *whoosh* and the coat went up in flames.

Of course it did. She'd thrown it over a table laden with candles.

Mirabelle screamed and threw herself at him. Her arms wrapped around his waist, and her body pressed against his.

Stupid woman. He was in the wrong place. The couch blocked him from getting to the exit.

"That way!" He pointed toward the exit. They weren't in any danger. At least not yet. The table top was glass and there wasn't anything else flammable adjacent to where the coat spewed smoke and flames.

She didn't take so much as a step. Just clung to him like spring mud to his boots.

He was going to have to pick her up and carry her. Leaning over, he scooped her up under her knees and lifted her off the ground.

"Everyone stand back!" A producer holding a bucket of water barreled into the room and unleashed it toward the flames. And anything else within a three-foot radius.

Cold water sloshed across Caleb's chest leaving him spluttering. When he opened his eyes, all that was left of the coat was smoke and a few scorched pieces of material.

The fire was out. The fire was out, and he was holding a woman clad in wet lingerie.

Kat stood in the doorway, observing the scene like she'd taken a wrong turn and found herself in Oz.

He looked to where the crew stood completely bewildered. "Can someone please find Mirabelle a blanket?" He took a deep breath. "And once she's dry and dressed I think it's best if she goes home."

Mirabelle looked up at him, jaw hanging open. Then she hauled back and slapped him.

Kat was sure Caleb had never been slapped by a woman in his life. But if he had to be, it might as well be spectacular. And this? She absorbed the view of the smoking coat, the water splashed across the floor, Mirabelle wearing a whole lot of very little, and Caleb looking anywhere except at the mostly-naked body of the woman he'd almost dropped in the wake of her stinging palm. Well, this was definitely spectacular.

It was also one of the funniest things she'd ever seen.

She bit the inside of her cheek to try to stop herself from laughing.

A crew member brushed past her and handed Mirabelle a robe.

"You can't send me home!" Mirabelle's shrill words were edged with hysteria as she slid her arms through the sleeves and yanked the belt around her waist. "I put myself out there for you and this, *this* is how you repay me."

Caleb shifted on his feet. "I'm sorry. I wish you every happiness, but I don't think I'm the man you're looking for."

"I'm more woman than you can handle. Why don't you just admit it?" Half her updo slid down her face. Mirabelle swiped it away.

Caleb nodded. "I can't argue with that."

"Most men would fall over themselves for what I offered."

"I have no doubt." A twitch in Caleb's jaw said exactly what he thought about those men. He placed a hand on her elbow. "Mirabelle, you are a beautiful woman. Don't sell yourself short. The right guy won't need a strip show on the second date to recognize your value."

He said the words softly and Kat felt bad for being a spectator.

Mirabelle's lip wobbled.

Kat closed her eyes for a second. Here she was finding it hilarious that Mirabelle had made an absolute fool of herself, yet Caleb was taking the opportunity to speak deeper into whatever pain made the woman think she had to take her clothes off to get to a guy's heart.

She slipped out of the doorway and leaned against the wall outside. Caleb Murphy was a good man. If anything, he was an even better man than the one she'd left.

God, what was she doing here?

She tilted her head and directed her question to the ceiling. She was used to knowing what her next step was, used to feeling in control of her life. She was the smart one. The practical one. The one who had learned long ago to choose head over heart.

Yet when it came to Caleb she was no better than the woman who went to her ten-year high-school reunion hoping the guy who'd dumped her at prom would see the error of his ways and beg for a second chance.

Mirabelle brushed past. She didn't even notice Kat in her haste to leave. A cameraman followed hot on her heels, determined to wring every nanosecond of drama out of Mirabelle's departure.

"Want to take a walk?"

Caleb's words tickled her ear, and she steeled herself before looking up at him. "Are you sure you don't need a few minutes? That was quite something."

She could hear movement behind her. No doubt another camera crew.

Caleb ushered her toward a door that led to an outside patio. "I handled it badly." He opened the door and guided her through.

She shook her head as the cool evening air nipped at her bare arms. "Not at all. You were very kind." The lights of Sydney Harbour shone before them, highlighting a jagged skyline encompassing skyscrapers alongside historic buildings. Was *Destination NSW* sponsoring the show? This was an almost identical view to their first date. And the unfinished conversation that had been gnawing at her since. The desire for more information about his ex-fiancée was the driving reason behind why she'd said yes to another horseshoe. The insatiable need to find out what had happened to the woman he'd chosen.

"So . . ." Caleb's words trailed off as they looked at each other.

"What was her name?" The question tumbled out of her mouth. Kat didn't know why she wanted to know the name of the woman who had clearly inflicted as much heartbreak on him as he had on her, but she did.

Caleb blinked. "Emma."

"Are you still in touch?"

He stiffened. "No. We haven't had any contact since the day she left. Not for lack of trying." He gave her a wry smile. "Well, on my side anyway."

"Are you still in love with her?" Might as well go for broke getting the answers to the questions she couldn't let go of. As much as one could with a camera crew filming her every word to be screened across the country.

"No." He shoved his hands into his pockets. "But I'm not going to pretend I don't have questions. I wish I could give the next woman I'm with a series of past relationships that all ended neatly and got consigned to history, but that's not my story."

All Kat wanted to do was kiss him. Kiss him and remind him of their story. The story he had ended for reasons that still made no sense to her. But then, wasn't that love? Why some couples made it while others didn't was an eternal question.

Her hands gripped the balcony balustrade. "If you could only have one question answered, what would it be?"

Caleb scrubbed his hand through his short hair. "I don't know. What happened? How could it go from being so great to being nothing at all?"

Him and her both. Kat turned her head before he could see the same question in her eyes. To be fair, he hadn't left her without anything.

But the paltry explanations she'd extracted from him that night had never been enough. *We're not right for each other. We want different lives.*

Except those answers had to be enough. What was she hoping for? That nine years later he'd miraculously be able to give her some closure?

This was probably as good as it was going to get. He'd go on dates with other women for the rest of the week, then she'd be gone at the next elimination ceremony. Or maybe she'd salvage some dignity and make her own exit.

If she had something she needed to say, she had to say it now.

She shifted, turning so she faced him. "I was in love with someone once. I didn't see it coming when he broke up with me. I've always wanted to know when everything changed. What did I miss? How many dates did we go on when I thought we were having a great time and he was questioning us? How many times did he kiss me knowing he was going to end it? How long was he paving the path to his exit while I was seeing forever? What did I do or say that made him stop loving me?"

Good grief. So much for retaining some dignity.

Caleb knew she was talking about him, even if no one else did. She hadn't known all the questions she'd been nesting on, let alone intended to say. To him. *Him* of all people.

Why was she even doing this to herself? She hadn't been enough then, and she wouldn't be enough now. Not with the decisions she'd had to make.

A tear splashed down her cheek, and she swiped it away.

Caleb looked stricken. He swallowed. Once. Twice. "Kat, I . . ."

"Knock. Knock. Mind if I interrupt?" It was Gemma. Of course. She shoved herself past the cameraman and onto the patio. Her smug face indicated she knew she was interrupting something and was thrilled about it.

"Sure." Kat stepped away from Caleb, ducking past him before this could get any worse, maneuvering around Gemma to get to the door.

"Kat."

She turned.

Caleb's gaze caught hers. "I may not be the smartest man in the world, but I can guarantee no guy has ever kissed you while planning his exit. It's not possible."

What was she supposed to do with that?

CHAPTER EIGHT

What was it I did or said that made him stop loving me? Kat's question still haunted Caleb two days and two group dates later. Her aching question spun around his head as the chauffeured town car sped through unfamiliar Sydney city streets.

He should have sent Gemma away. Should have somehow found a way to tell Kat she had never, not once, done anything that made him stop loving her.

Should have found a way to tell her it was the opposite. He'd loved her too much.

But he hadn't. And they hadn't spoken since. The last two days had passed in a blur of bad dates, stilted conversations, no kisses, and increasingly tense conversations with Adam.

"Caleb, you have a meeting with Vince this morning."

Caleb turned his head from the window. "What? Why?" Caleb had seen the executive producer bustling around the set, a perpetually stressed expression across his face, but they hadn't had a formal conversation since before the show started.

Adam shifted in his seat. "He needs to discuss some changes with you."

Caleb stared at him. "What kind of changes?" He did his best to keep his tone low and controlled. He was a man of routine who liked knowing what every day held. This show was already pushing him to his limits. What else could they possibly intend?

"You'll find out soon enough. We're here."

"What—"

Their sedan pulled up to a stop outside the SBC headquarters, and the door opened before he could finish his question. Caleb got out of the car and walked to the front doors. At least there weren't cameras stalking his every move, although a few women did double takes when they saw him crossing the lot.

The second episode had aired last night.

His mother hadn't seen it. The entire reason he was doing the show, and she hadn't seen it. A bad day, according to his uncle.

"This way." Adam gestured toward the elevators, swiped a key card at the bank of floor buttons, and within a few minutes Caleb found himself ushered into a boardroom with spectacular views of the harbor.

They were so impressive that, for a couple of seconds, he didn't notice it wasn't just Vince in the room. He was flanked by two other men Caleb had never laid eyes on. Further along the table sat two female producers he'd seen on set but had little to do with.

"Caleb, thanks for coming. Take a seat." Vince gestured to a seat next to one of the unknown men.

Thanks for coming. Like he had a choice in the matter. Like he wasn't their captive 24/7.

"What's this about?" No point beating around the bush. They clearly hadn't assembled this entourage for coffee and a couple of sausage rolls. He mentally scrolled through his commitments. As far as he knew he'd kept every single one of them. "Is there a problem with the show?"

"A problem?" Vince flattened his palms on the table. "You could say that."

"Is this about me not kissing anyone yet?" Caleb tacked on the "yet" to try and appease them. As far as he was concerned, the only woman he wanted to kiss was Kat.

"It's not even the kissing. The only reason we had a second episode is because of your conversation with Kat on the balcony. And she isn't even supposed to be in the show! So we've been testing our footage for the next episode with some focus groups."

"And?"

"And the consensus is the same across the board. You have all the onscreen romantic appeal of a wooden spoon. We'd have nothing for the third episode if it wasn't for Mirabelle and the fire."

Again, something he'd told them from the beginning. Caleb leaned back in his chair as Vince looked down at some notes on the table in front of him. Might as well sit back and let the man get everything off his chest.

"In fact, it's getting worse as the dates go on. Yesterday's farm challenge date? I have some of the best editors in the business, and they can't get me more than seven minutes of usable footage of you with any of the women. No matter how they cut it."

One of the female producers joined in. "We thought maybe the big group thing wasn't working, which is why we switched it up and added more dates for this week but with fewer people. But those were even worse."

He couldn't deny that. Not when he'd hated almost every second of them. "What do you want me to do? I can't be someone I'm not. I've told you from the beginning I was never going to be a schmoozing womanizer." Caleb pushed his chair back slightly, his body coiled for departure if this was going where he suspected it was.

Vince ran a hand through his sparse hair and sighed. "We know. So we've decided to change the format."

"How?"

"We put the next episode to air as planned

next Thursday, and you're going to cut the group down to eight. Before ratings slide into a black hole, we want to take advantage of your profile to get viewers even more invested. You'll narrow the field down to eight, but the viewers will take it from there and vote for the final six, then four."

Caleb's gut twisted tighter than a pulled lasso. "What?"

"Then you choose one. The rest of the show is the two of you going back to Toowoomba, living together as a couple and seeing if you can make it work in the real world."

Many, many words exploded in his brain. None of which would have made his mother happy.

"Not on your nelly." He was not taking some woman he'd only known a few weeks back to the farm. Not ever. He shoved his chair back from the table. "Was that all?"

"No." The anonymous man next to him spoke mildly but with an underlying thread of steel. "Look. We see this as a win-win. You are obviously not comfortable dating a myriad of women, and the viewers have already latched onto a small number of favorites. You know that if we asked, you could send six of them home right now. So why waste their time and yours?"

Caleb remained silent. He couldn't deny that.

Vince flattened his palms on the table top. "You're an honorable guy, Caleb. We appreciate that. This way there's no dating multiple women for months. You and whoever you choose can go home, spend precious time with your mother, and pursue a more, um, intimate relationship. And if it doesn't work out . . ." Vince leaned back in his chair. "Well, you know you've given it your best shot."

He might not be a cowboy, but this also wasn't his first rodeo. "You want me to go home and have this woman move into my house like she's my wife?"

"Whatever happens between you is a matter for two consenting adults. But this is a show about finding love, and we would certainly hope you and your chosen lady find love in all its fullness."

Caleb's skin crawled like he'd just fallen into a nest of huntsmen. No, that was unfair to the poor venomous spider. "And what if I say no?"

"We hope it wouldn't come to that, but Hamish can take it from here." Vince motioned to the man sitting next to Caleb. "This is Hamish McAnulty, SBC's General Counsel."

Hamish opened a folder in front of him and removed a document with multiple tabs sticking out of it. He flipped through a few pages then stopped at a section highlighted in yellow.

"The highlighted section is the relevant part in your contract that covers changes to show format. As you can see, you've initialed the bottom right hand corner of this page." His tone oozed with condescension.

Caleb's fists itched to punch the smug lawyer in the mouth. "What if I say no? What if I say we continue with the current format or I walk?"

"Well, then." Hamish the weasel looked extraordinarily pleased Caleb had asked. "Unfortunately, since SBC can't see the show having any chance of meeting its rating and advertising revenue targets if we continue with the originally planned format, we would deem you to be in breach of contract. This page sets out those penalties."

He placed another piece of paper in front of Caleb. A line of figures ran down the page but all he could see was the seven-figure total at the bottom.

"I understand that may seem high, but obviously SBC has a range of commitments to both staff and advertisers for the period of the show. There would also be additional costs associated with replacing the show with something else at such short notice. The figure here is strictly an estimate. It could be higher. Oliver"—the weasel gestured toward the other anonymous man at the table—"can vouch for that as our head of programming."

The number was so ridiculous that Caleb almost laughed. "You can make up whatever figure you want. I don't have that kind of money."

"Maybe not." The weasel's voice became even more calculated. "But you do co-own a farm, don't you?" The insinuation hung over the room like Damocles's sword.

"It's in a trust. You can't touch it." Caleb sounded a lot more certain out loud than he did to himself. His grandfather had set up the trust, which Caleb had mostly ignored since he turned twenty-one and signed some papers to be added as a trustee.

Hamish shrugged. "Maybe. Maybe not. Either way, I hope you have deep pockets for all the lawyers you'll need to fight us."

Caleb's body went rigid. One of the farmers down the road had gone bust fighting a liability case after an accident on his farm. He'd won the case but lost his land and his livelihood to the lawyers.

He'd signed a deal with the devil. They knew he would never do anything to risk the farm that had been in his family for six generations. The ground his mother, grandfather, and generations of Murphys before them had poured their entire lives into since the days of the early settlers. The land he'd changed his name to match when he was sixteen. Abandoning his father's name the same way his father had abandoned his mum and him.

They had survived droughts, floods, stock disease, and blight, and they hadn't done it for Caleb to lose it all to some faceless corporation out for revenge.

There was only one possible option and for it to even have a chance he was going to have to play his cards right in the next thirty seconds. "We won't live together. I'm not that kind of guy. There's a house on the farm next to the main homestead. She can live there."

"Agreed."

"I'll tell the women about the changes myself."

"It may be better coming from Mark."

"I will tell them myself." He ground the words out.

"Of course."

He tried to keep his tone unchanged for the most important one. "I want some off-camera time with all of the women to help me make my decision."

"Not possible."

He eased a breath out. "If you would like me to go from fourteen women to eight to four to one in a few weeks, I'm going to need time with them. Not group date time, or one-on-one dates surrounded by cameras and producers. Real time. Just the two of us. The other option is I can leave here, walk down the street, find myself some fancy law firm, and we can see each other in court. There's no guarantee your contract will hold up, and I bet I could negotiate a no-win no-fee deal on a high-profile case like this."

Vince looked at Slimy McSlimy, and he gave a

small nod. "Okay. You can have some time with them. Very limited time."

He didn't need time with them. He needed time with one woman. She was the only one he could trust with this. If she didn't agree, he'd have to find himself a good lawyer. And if she did?

He would take Kat home. He would fall in love with her all over again.

Then, one day, she would leave. And he would never recover.

Text Message

Kat: Are you awake?

Allie: Yup. Pregnancy reflux. It's all sorts of awesome. On the upside, my sleepless nights mean bonus prayers for you.

Kat: Thanks. I think. How is the bean?

Allie: The bean is more like a watermelon. I'm tracking three weeks ahead on size. Thank you, Gregory genes.

Kat: Sorry???

Allie: Jackson certainly is sorry, since I currently have all the wifely charm of a sloth. But I'm assuming you're not messaging me at 2 a.m. to chat about my un-Pinteresty pregnancy. What's up?

Kat: They're changing the format of the show.

Allie: How?

Kat: At the next elimination it's going to go from fourteen to eight. Then the public is going to vote over two weeks to eliminate the next four. Then Caleb is going to choose the last one.

Allie: That's a big change from the original plan, right?

Kat: Huge. There was no public voting in the original plan.

Allie: What does this mean?

Kat: There's some kind of trouble. Maybe ratings? Whatever it is, it must be something big to have them completely change course only a few weeks in.

Allie: What are you going to do?

Kat: I don't know. Caleb's currently talking to all the women individually.

Allie: From what I've seen, there's no chance you're going to get voted out. You need to know that. If you're thinking the public may save you from having to make a decision, you should eliminate that option now.

Kat: It could happen.

Allie: No, it couldn't. That man has the charisma of a box of Wheaties with the other women. He's really not made for TV. And by really, I mean not at all.

Kat: I don't know what to do.

Allie: It all comes down to a very simple question. Can you walk away and move on with your life with no regrets?

CHAPTER NINE

Caleb deliberately scheduled his time with Kat after three others so as not to draw any unnecessary attention. He'd even asked a producer to find her rather than approach her himself.

Now a cameraman and a couple of others trailed behind them as they walked. He led them past the pool and into the garden. He'd seen a bench positioned against a wall where they could see anyone coming, but no one would overhear them.

The announcement about the change in format had sent a wave of panic through the women. The first three he'd spoken to had all been interrupted within a few minutes by others desperate to have their time with him. He wouldn't risk that happening with Kat.

He gestured toward the bench. "Why don't we sit here?"

"Sure." Kat looked at the camera then sat down and crossed one leg over the other. Her hair was loose, and it glinted the color of autumn straw.

She positioned herself so her legs tilted sideways, preventing him from getting too close. He sat, careful to give her personal space. But the floral scent of her still wafted across the distance, messing with his senses.

Her gaze flickered to the camera again. "So how are you feeling about the new format?"

He ran a hand through his hair. "To be honest, I don't think it's really sunk in. I only found out about it myself a few hours ago."

"Eliminating six women is huge."

He could eliminate them in a few minutes if he had to, but there was no way he'd say that. "It will be tough. That's why I've asked for more time with everyone this week. I just hope you won't be distracted by the prospect of the eliminations and can focus instead on our individual connection."

He was his own worst nightmare. Parroting off trite cliched words with little meaning. His uncle would be ashamed. That wasn't who Murphy men were.

The side of Kat's mouth ticked up slightly as if she could read his mind. "Rumor in the house is you haven't kissed anyone."

He started at the left-field question. "Um, no . . . Don't get me wrong. Kissing is fine. I mean, kissing is great. With the right person it can be . . ." He forgot his words as memories of the many times he'd kissed the woman sitting next to him flooded through his mind.

"Like coming home." Kat said the words softly.

"I belong. When I'm with you I feel like I belong. And I think you feel the same way about me." The memory of her long-ago words had him curling his fingers into his palms.

He'd never wanted to belong to anyone the way he wanted to belong to Katriona McLeod. The realization smacked him straight in the chest.

"Caleb?"

Caleb pulled himself back from the past. "Yes. Exactly like coming home."

She studied him. The hurt and disappointment he'd inflicted upon her years ago splashed across her expression.

"I'm not going to make my decision based on who I haven't kissed. I'm going to make my decision based on who I want to spend more time with." *And I want to spend more time with you.* Words he wanted to say but knew he couldn't. Instead he turned to the cameraman and producer.

"Do you have enough footage of us yet? Because if you have, I'd like to speak to Kat alone." He tried to sound blasé about it, but he was sure everyone could hear his heart thudding in his chest.

The woman looked disconcerted. "I'm sorry, but you don't get to speak to any of the women off camera. It's the rules."

"Well, the rules have changed. This whole thing has changed. And I negotiated some privacy. Feel free to check in with Vince or Adam if you need to."

The woman pulled her phone out of her pocket and swiped the screen. She walked a few feet away and had a short conversation with her back turned.

"What are you doing?" Kat looked at him with wide eyes.

Caleb dropped his voice. "I'll explain once they can't hear us."

Her mouth opened slightly, and she nodded.

The producer came back and nodded to the cameraman, who lowered his equipment. "Ten minutes. That's all you get."

"Thank you. Can you take my pack, please?" He stood and pulled it from where it was attached to his belt.

The producer opened her mouth as if to object then closed it. Caleb watched as she unplugged the pack.

"Hers too." He nodded at Kat, who stood and pulled her pack from behind her and pulled the plug out herself.

"Relax. I promise we're not going to run away. You guys are welcome to wait over there and keep an eye on us if you like." He gestured to where the path entered the garden about ten feet away. He hoped they waited so they could serve as an early warning sign of any of the other women approaching the area.

Not that it really mattered. He would orchestrate the same privacy with Olivia and Adeline so the crew didn't single out Kat as being special.

The cameraman and guy with the boom mic disappeared, but the producer stayed as a chaperone.

Now all he had to do was convince Kat to sign up to his plan. Then convince the viewers to keep her in the final four.

They were alone. Well, excluding the dragon glowering at them from the other side of the garden like they lived in Victorian England instead of twenty-first century Australia.

Kat sat back down on the bench, the wooden slats pressing into her legs. She didn't know what was going on, but she suspected she'd want to be sitting for whatever it was.

It had been three days since she'd opened her mouth and blurted out her ridiculous feelings about what happened almost a decade ago.

Why didn't she just tattoo *No, I'm not over you* on her forehead and be done with it?

She was better than this. Stronger than this.

"I may not be the smartest man in the world, but I can guarantee no guy has ever kissed you while planning his exit. It's not possible." She hadn't even been able to tell Allie about the words that had driven her almost crazy for the last two days as Caleb had gone on the other

group dates. Knowing he was never going to be able to give her a proper explanation for his cryptic proclamation as long as cameras filmed their every interaction. But now—for a mere few minutes—the cameras were gone.

But if she asked him to explain himself, she'd have to explain her moment of complete insanity.

Caleb settled down beside her, leaving an appropriate amount of space between them. A smart move on his part, but her heart faltered at yet another reminder of his rejection.

"We should talk about what you said on the balcony." He rubbed his hands together. The show must have hours of footage of him doing that exact move. He always did it during awkward conversations. The night they'd broken up he must have destroyed at least three layers of his epidermis.

"No, we shouldn't." Sitting here and having Caleb feel he needed to explain why he'd stopped loving her was not on her bucket list. "I'm deeply embarrassed, and I'm sorry I put you in such a difficult position. Especially on camera. You don't owe me an explanation."

Something flickered across his face. Relief? Uncertainty? She couldn't be sure.

"Are you sure? I know it was a long time ago, but I don't want to leave things unresolved between us. I don't want to do to you what Emma did to me."

Would it change anything? What could he possibly say that would make his rejection hurt less? If anything, his explanation would reopen old wounds. She should leave. He was eliminating six women next week. It was the best time to go. Just one of the crowd. Kat nodded. "I'm sure."

She was at the end of her emotional reserves. It was time to put herself out of her misery. She could tell him to choose Olivia or Adeline and leave with some of her dignity and sanity intact. "Caleb, it's time for me to go."

"You're the only one I can choose."

They spoke at the same time, their words clashing into each other.

"What?" *You're the only one I can choose.* She played the words over in her mind. That was what he had said, right?

"I trust you, Kat. I don't want to hurt anyone. I can't choose any of the other women because they will have, um . . . expectations. I can't do that to them or to my family."

She was so deflated she could've collapsed into the hedge behind them. "Right." He didn't love her. Didn't want her. He had made that clear years ago. Having expectations would be lunacy.

He was still rubbing his hands. She squashed the impulse to reach over and make them stop. "I'll pay you for your time, obviously. Whatever you would ordinarily make in a couple of months."

It took a couple of seconds for her to process what he was saying. But once she did her shock was overwhelmed by a roar of fury. "Are you kidding me? You broke up with me nine years ago, and now you're asking your ex-girlfriend to come back home with you and play happy couples for the cameras? And you'll pay me like I'm some kind of platonic call girl? How dare you! You . . . You . . ." Words flashed through her mind, but she couldn't say any of them aloud. "I have a life. I have a great, fulfilling, wonderful life. So no. No, thank you. I do not want your money and I certainly do not want to be your fake girlfriend."

She shot to her feet, ready to storm away. Except he moved as fast as her and looped an arm around her waist before she could leave. She thudded against his chest before shoving against it with both hands.

"Let. Go. Of. Me."

He might be the size of an outhouse, but she was sure she had enough adrenaline in her system to take him down.

Caleb dropped his hand like her back was molten lava. "I'm sorry. I shouldn't have done that. Please, please, just give me two minutes to explain."

Kat stepped back. "Why are you even here,

Caleb? If you don't want to fall in love and take someone home to Toowoomba and live happily ever after, then why did you agree to be on this show? I mean, I know you said it was for your mum, but you're the one here, doing this. And clearly hating every moment of it."

Nothing made sense anymore. Not him. Not her. Not this whole twisted, whacked-out situation.

"I didn't. I don't." Caleb glanced toward the dragon—who now watched them with keen interest—as he said the words quietly.

Kat looked at him, waiting for more. What could justify his obnoxious request? She couldn't imagine.

"I didn't tell you everything. I have to do this for Mum. I don't have any other choice."

She sagged onto the bench. "What do you mean?"

He sat down, one leg brushing against hers. "She has dementia. It's progressing rapidly. We don't know how much time we have before she's not . . ." He choked up, rubbed a hand over his eyes, and regained his composure. ". . . not her anymore."

"I'm so sorry." Kat's hand reached out of its own volition and covered his enormous one.

Oh, Marion. The woman Kat had known had been full of joy and hospitality. No one was a stranger as far as Caleb's mother was concerned.

She was warm and funny and had the air of someone who always believed the best in people but was never shocked by their deepest secrets. Leaving Marion had been almost as wrenching as leaving Caleb.

Caleb looked at her hand resting on his. "In the audition video she said her only desire, before she lost her memories, was to see me happy with someone."

Everything now made sense. Caleb was an only child. He adored his mother and would do anything for her. Including, apparently, pretending to find love on a trashy TV show.

"You want your mother to think we're together again? How would that even work? What would we tell her?"

Caleb leaned forward, clasped his hands over his knees. "Kat, she . . ."

And she suddenly got it. "She may not even remember who I am. Or who I was." That hurt for reasons Kat couldn't even pinpoint. They'd only dated for six months. Mostly long distance. Why wouldn't she have slipped through the cracks in Marion's memory?

He swallowed. Nodded. "I want my mother's last memories to include me being happy. And if she thinks that can only happen if I have a woman in my life, then I want to give her that."

"What happened with Emma?" The words fell out of her mouth and, for a second, she almost took them back. But the compulsion to know what had happened to the woman he'd intended to marry was too strong.

He sighed and stretched out his legs in front of him. "There was a fire in Emma's house a few months before we were meant to get married. She needed a place to stay while repairs were made, so she moved into my place and I moved in with Mum. Within a week she realized life as a farmer's wife was much more attractive in theory than in reality. She left me a note saying she was sorry. That she loved me but not enough to stay."

An irrational loathing for this woman she didn't know coursed through Kat. This woman had been offered the only thing Kat had ever wanted—to be asked to stay—and had thrown it away. "Would you have left the farm for her?"

He rubbed his hands across his face. "I'm not sure. She didn't ask me to make that choice. I'm a farmer, Kat. It's all I know. And I don't do it because it's been in the family for a hundred years or because Mum needs me—though those things matter. I do it because I love it."

"I know." Maybe Emma had known that too. Maybe that was why she hadn't asked. Hadn't forced him to make the impossible choice between the woman he wanted and the land he loved. Maybe Kat could hate her a little less for that.

"I am sorry. So sorry. I know I'm putting you in

a lose-lose position. And I completely understand why you've said no. I'll just have to walk away from the show and take my chances."

"What do you mean, take your chances?"

"I thought I could do this. For Mum. I thought that even if it didn't work out I could at least make it work for as long as I needed to. Until"—he swallowed—"until she wouldn't notice or remember. But I can't. I can't put someone through that, knowing that I don't see a future with any of the women here. I'll leave the show and find a good lawyer."

"Why?"

"SBC said they'll sue me."

Kat sucked in a breath. Of course they had. TV networks would not let one of their prime-time shows go mid-season without putting up a fight. Better a reluctant, resentful hero to fill in those hours of advertising dollars already sold than none at all.

"The contract I signed gave them the right to make changes to the format, and they said if I walk then they'll sue me for millions to cover lost advertising, paying out the crew, everything. They'll come after the farm. It's been in our family for 150 years. I can't be responsible for losing it. It would kill my uncle."

Kat didn't, couldn't, say anything. She couldn't assure him SBC was all talk and no action. They may well sue him.

"I didn't mean that you don't have an amazing life or that you don't have better things to do than to help me out of a situation that's entirely of my own making. I know you do. I'm sure you hadn't thought of me in years before you walked onto this set, and I know this whole thing will be consigned to a weird part of your history when you leave again."

Kat briefly closed her eyes. He had no idea how wrong he was. Though her little rant on the balcony should have given him a clue. But he'd always been the uncomplicated guy who'd said what he meant and assumed everyone else did too. He didn't waste his time trying to read between the lines. It was one of the things she'd loved about him.

"I can't ask any of these other women. I couldn't live with myself if I took one of them home knowing it wasn't going to work out. Not at my end. I just thought . . . well it's not like there's any chance of you falling in love with me . . ."

Again.

The word hung in the air.

Because they'd already done it once. Already had said *I love you* between kisses and with laughter and through tears. Made plans beyond next week, next month. Started to assume a future assured instead of unknown.

It had been almost ten years since he'd

dumped her. His assumption was reasonable. Rational. Except she'd never been either reasonable nor rational when it came to Caleb Murphy.

CHAPTER TEN

K at looked at the line of women set up along the bar stools in the biggest bedroom. She'd offered to do anyone's makeup as a way to keep her mind off her decision and almost everyone had said yes. They'd started five hours before the elimination ceremony and she was almost done.

Caleb's proposition had shadowed Kat's every thought for the last three days. To go back to the farm as his pretend girlfriend for the cameras, for the sake of memories his mother might no longer be capable of.

Meanwhile, he'd gone on more dates which only seemed to fuel the panic in the house about the looming elimination.

She had no idea what to do with the choice before her. She'd tried to pray but couldn't hear anything over the chaos churning within.

The dresser was clogged with everyone's makeup bags. Not the quality she was used to working with, but she'd done her best.

Multiple conversations buzzed around her. Women had packed themselves into the room to chat while they got ready for their last chance to charm Caleb. Their final few hours together before their numbers were cut almost in half.

Kat smoothed foundation across Adeline's face, then used a brush to start shading in the uneven spots in her complexion.

"Okay, we need to get this sorted once and for all." Brittany leaned against a chest of drawers clad only in a strapless bra and Spanx. "Has Caleb kissed anyone? A single person? We're doing the rounds. He hasn't kissed me. What about you, Adeline?"

The woman shook her head.

"Olivia?"

Kat cast a glance at her roommate. She had been trying to get a read on her all week but—unlike everyone else in the mansion—Olivia had remained discreet about how she felt about Caleb.

"Nope. And Lindsey, Marilyn, and Briana all say they haven't kissed him." Olivia didn't look in the least bit bothered as she studied two bottles of nail polish.

"Kat?"

Yup. Many times. And you girls are missing out. Kat tapped her brush back into the powder. "Pop your chin up, Addie. The last guy I kissed was my ex-boyfriend." That was true.

"Jen?"

The blonde standing in the doorway laughed. "You guys know I have no chill. You'd all know if Caleb had kissed me."

Brittany pursed her lips. "I'm pretty sure every-one else is a no as well. Sheesh. Talk about playing the long game."

"He's certainly no Ari." Olivia looked up from painting her nails.

"Ari would have kissed a potted plant if it got close enough. What were his *Bachelor* stats? Didn't he lock lips with, like, sixteen girls in the first three episodes and still managed to get it wrong in the end?"

"Pretty much. It was like, 'Oh, you like bacon? I like bacon. Let's make out!' " Jen wiggled her eyebrows as she wrestled full-body Spanx down her hips. The constricting material made Kat wince just looking at it.

Lindsey swallowed the piece of apple she was eating. "At least we're all in this together. I mean, kissing none of us is at least better than him having kissed most of us and being one of the few he hasn't."

"But how is he going to pick?" Brittany's voice lifted an octave. "How can he possibly narrow us down to eight tonight if he doesn't know who he's got chemistry with?"

"You don't have to kiss someone to know you've got chemistry. Chemistry is the thing that makes you want to kiss someone. For all we know, he wants to kiss plenty of us. Or maybe just one of us." Olivia lifted an eyebrow at Kat, which she ignored.

"Hmmm." Brittany looked doubtful. "Or you could just get in the game, kiss them, and discover you do have chemistry!"

"Why don't you try that tonight, Britt." Olivia said sweetly. "I mean, fourteen to eight. It's now or never."

"Maybe I will. I'm sure some of the other girls will do the same."

Poor Caleb. There were only so many ways a man could duck puckered lips before things went south.

She fished around in Adeline's makeup bag, and pulled out a couple of containers of eyeshadow. Neither were great colors for her. "Ad—"

The piercing shriek of a smoke alarm reached the room. Utter chaos reigned as the women screamed, hands over their ears, and streamed out of the room in various states of dress. Kat followed them down the stairs, monitoring the movements of the crew, whose lack of urgency denoted the alarm was either for something minor or a total setup.

"Help!" The voice came from the kitchen. "In here!"

Kat pivoted into the kitchen to find a flaming toaster, three women, and a camera crew. Marilyn and Brianna shrieked while Sienna flapped a tea towel uselessly at the flames. A plume of smoke spiraled to the ceiling.

They were an embarrassment to womankind. Kat grabbed the fire extinguisher from the pantry, elbowed Sienna out of the way, pulled the pin, aimed toward the toaster, and pulled the lever. Foam sprayed from the funnel, coating the flames, toaster, and half the counter with white fluff.

Once she was sure the fire was out, she ditched the canister on the counter for replacement.

At least she'd gotten it before the—

Water shot out from the ceiling, spray covering them all. The women screamed and tried to cover their coiffures and faces. Mascara slicked down cheeks and foundation ran down chins.

Sigh. There went two hours of her work.

The sprinklers stopped as quickly as they had started, leaving Sienna and Marilyn in sopping cocktail dresses. Brianna's beige Spanx gave an awfully accurate imitation of a drowned hairless dog.

At least she hadn't bothered to get dressed yet. She'd only brought one extra gown from the apartment.

Kat tipped her hair sideways and wrung it out on the floor. "You know," she said in a voice as non-accusing as she could manage, "you could have unplugged the toaster and taken it outside when it started smoking."

"But where would the fun have been in that?" Caleb's voice came from behind Kat. He had probably been cast to save the poor helpless females from the big scary fire. Whoops.

They'd changed the time on Caleb. Told him to be ready an hour earlier than originally scheduled. That he was going to surprise the women.

He'd suspected something was up, which meant he wasn't entirely surprised when his car arrived at the mansion and he'd found most of the women gathered on the driveway.

The colored hair rollers, weird clothing that looked like beige compression bandages, and two faces covered in green goop had been an interesting twist.

"Is everything alright?" At the sight of him, the women closest to the car scattered back toward the house like hand-sown seed.

Olivia looked up from where she was sitting on the low stone fence that surrounded the garden and painting her toenails. She shrugged. "One of the smoke alarms went off."

Olivia. His semi-secret weapon. Their off-camera time had been illuminating. She'd informed him she had no feelings for him but would be obliged if he could keep her around, so she could at least use the passport she'd had to procure to be on the show. Then she'd arched her eyebrows and enquired if he knew she was Kat's roommate.

"There was a fire in the kitchen. Sienna ran

131

toward it. She hasn't made it out!" Lindsey grabbed his arm. "You have to go in and rescue her. She may be trapped!"

Highly unlikely. The alarm might be shrieking, but there wasn't so much as a hint of smoke in the air. Besides, the extensive liability waiver everyone had signed wouldn't cover someone being trapped in a fire if the crew did nothing and kept filming.

"I'm sure she's fine, but I'll go in and see what's happening."

She looked at him like he was about to run into a burning building and put the fire out with his bare hands. He wished. At least that would make great TV and get the producers off his back about kissing someone.

Striding through the front door, it took him all of a second to work out the alarm was coming from the kitchen. He got there just in time to see the sprinklers open and water coat everything in the room. And everyone in it.

Including Kat, who didn't look one bit surprised to find herself getting drenched. The other three women clung together and screeched like a colony of bats.

Foam covered one of the counters behind Kat, and a fire extinguisher lay abandoned off to the side. He guessed what had once been a toaster lived under the pile of fluff.

The alarm cut out, followed by the sprinklers.

Water sloshed off counters and puddled across the floor.

Kat leaned over and twisted her hair like it was a damp towel, driblets of water adding to the puddle at her feet. The other women stood in soaked, stunned silence.

A camera crew filmed everything from the other side of the room. The producer finally looking like he was having a good day.

Kat straightened up. "You could've just taken the toaster outside when it started smoking." At least that's what he thought she said but the T-shirt clinging to her in so many right places had him somewhat distracted.

"Now where would the fun have been in that?" His voice sounded remarkably smooth and calm. He wasn't sure where the line came from, but it was probably the third best he'd ever managed.

Kat looked at him, a half-smile framing her lips. Gosh, he loved that smile. "Safety first, Mr. Murphy." She sounded like some kind of prim fire educator.

The other women looked like a silent parody of Cinderella's stepsisters, with wet hair, makeup running down their faces, and dresses squelching. Well, two dresses. He had no idea what Brianna was wearing.

He made a show of looking at all the foam. On the floor, over the counter, up the wall. "It seems Kat had that well covered."

Their gazes caught and something between them sparked.

Kat hadn't said yes, but she had stayed. All his foolish hope rested on her.

"We should get cleaned up." He didn't know which of the three said it and he didn't care. His attention remained firmly fixed on Kat.

She looked down at her clingy T-shirt, the water gathering at the rim of her cut-off shorts then dripping down her legs. Wet hair slapped against her shoulders. "I should probably go sort myself out too."

"Wait!"

She looked at him, her gaze wary.

"Why are a bunch of the women wearing compression bandages?"

She leaned back against the counter, her shoulders curving in around her. Her mouth opened and laughter filled the room.

"What?" He felt his own lips tip up at her amusement, but he had absolutely no idea what was so funny.

Eventually she stood up and ran her fingers under her eyes. "They're not compression bandages, Caleb. They're Spanx."

Learning another language would've been easier than trying to understand some of the terms tossed around on this show. "What on earth is that?"

"Shapewear. It goes under dresses. Or any

clothes. You know, to help smooth and, um, lift things."

Considering she was standing in front of him in clingy wet clothing, he could make some accurate observations about how she had nothing that needed smoothing or lifting, but it was probably best if he kept those thoughts to himself. "But why?"

She shrugged. "I guess it's like makeup. Gives women confidence."

He didn't get it. As far as he could tell, the only thing that contraption could give anyone was a restricted airway. "I can't be with a woman who needs to squeeze herself into a sausage-like casing to feel beautiful, Kat. That's not going to work on a farm."

She shifted on her feet. "It's not an everyday thing. Take it as a compliment. It's all for you. They want to look like the best version of themselves."

"I don't want them to always look like the best version of themselves. Not when most of my life involves looking like the dirtiest, smelliest, muckiest version of myself. I want them to be their actual selves."

"Maybe they're worried that being themselves won't be enough." Kat reached out and righted the fire extinguisher, avoiding his gaze.

Her biggest fear. One confessed in the stillness of night as they lay stargazing on the back of his truck. Born out of a lifetime of her parents making her feel like she didn't count. And he'd promised she would always be enough for him.

Kat brushed past him as she left the kitchen, and Caleb released a jagged breath.

He'd broken his word. He'd let her believe she wasn't enough for him. It was the only way he could make her go. The truth was she was more than enough.

He was the one who wasn't. Always had been. Always would be.

Text Message

Janine: I just watched the latest episode. How are you?

Kat: Tired. Confused.

Janine: How's your heart doing? Your conversation on the balcony was pretty raw.

Kat: I can't believe I said that to him. I'm mortified. It's been almost ten years. How can it still hurt so much?

Janine: You loved him, and you never got closure. It's not surprising that seeing him again has brought up a whole lot of stuff. Especially in this environment.

Kat: It was the latest elimination tonight.

Janine: And you're still there?

Kat: I am.

Janine: You sound like you're not sure if you should be.

Kat: I don't know what to do. I stayed because I can't imagine leaving. But I don't know what God wants me to do. Am I meant to trust Him and walk away? Or am I meant to trust Him and stay?

Janine: Is there a chance to talk off camera at all?

Kat: We talked a few days ago. For, like, ten minutes. He wants me to stay.

Janine: But what do you want?

Kat: I want to not be hurting anymore. And I'm so scared that I'm going to get to the end of this—whatever that is—and be even more broken.

Janine: It's okay to be scared. People were scared in the Bible all the time. It's possible to have both great courage and great fear. Being afraid doesn't mean you're making the wrong decision. Being afraid means you're invested in the outcome. Having faith is trusting God with whatever the outcome is. Even if it's not the outcome we hoped for.

Kat: I don't even know what to hope for anymore.

CHAPTER ELEVEN

You're the only one I can choose. Caleb's words hadn't stopped echoing in Kat's head since he'd said them. They churned round and round as she hammered on the door of the editing suite. It was only six in the morning and almost all the women were still asleep, but Vince would be here. He barely slept whenever he had a show rolling.

They were due to fly out to New Zealand this afternoon. Mark had made the announcement the night before over the sound of clinking champagne glasses and ear-to-ear smiles from the other women.

She had only a few hours to decide what she was going to do. She should have spoken to Vince before things had gotten out of hand.

"Come in!" Sure enough, his voice echoed from inside the trailer.

Kat opened the door, closing it firmly behind her. The last thing she needed was someone eavesdropping.

Vince turned from where he was reviewing footage. "Hey, Kat. Good timing. We need to talk."

He didn't sound the least bit surprised to see her.

Kat slid into the chair next to him, averting her eyes from the screens showing Caleb and Gemma.

"We do. What's up with switching the format like this?" Kat tried to sound neutral, like she was curious but not invested.

Vince reached for his glass that she hoped contained only Coke. The man looked like he'd aged ten years in the last few weeks. Not even the dimness of the room hid the bags under his eyes, and every pore exuded stress. "We're going down faster than the Titanic."

"What are you talking about?"

"We're losing viewers hand over fist. Ratings were good for the first episode, but dropped twenty percent for the second. When we tested early material from the third episode on a focus group, half said they wouldn't keep watching."

His tension jumped into the pit of her stomach. Vince needed this show to be successful. He'd signed on for three seasons. Moved his whole family over from the US.

"What? Why?"

Vince nodded at the screens showing Caleb. "Surely you've noticed. Our leading man has all the onscreen appeal of a brick. Along with a set of morals I'm sure are great in real life but are horrible for TV."

"What do you mean?" She had a good idea of what he meant but hearing it straight from Vince would tell her how real the threat of a lawsuit was.

Vince scrubbed his hand through his hair. "He hasn't kissed anyone. Heck, he barely touches them. It's like he's six and still thinks girls have cooties. Look at him." He hit a button and the footage rolled.

Kat forced herself to look at the screen. Caleb sat on a patch of lush grass, talking to Gemma. Unfortunately, even the gorgeous setting couldn't hide Caleb's awkwardness. His body language was stiff, eye contact was rare, and if Gemma so much as leaned a millimeter toward him he shifted away.

"You didn't screen test him before you cast him?"

"We did. A little. He wasn't great, but we were crunched for time and figured he'd be fine once he got used to the cameras. We never dreamed he'd get worse."

"What did you want to talk to me about?"

Vince averted his eyes. Took a gulp of coffee from the mug in his hand.

"Vince?"

"I need you to stay on the show."

She'd half expected it but somehow his words still shocked her like he'd doused her in iced water. "Why?"

"Because there are only two women that he isn't like a robot around. You're one of them."

"Um, thanks?" Olivia would be the second.

"Don't worry. You won't be the last one, but we do need you to stick around until the final round. We'll make sure of it."

"If it's such a disaster, why not cut your losses and run? Cancel the season. Let him go back to his farm."

Vince let out a croak of laughter. "Never going to happen. The studio won't allow it. They've got too much money tied up in this. Too many commitments."

Kat's breath hitched. "What if he chooses to go rather than picking someone?"

"Doubtful. He's got as much to lose as we have. More."

"You'd really sue him?"

"It's not my call. Heck, I like the guy even though he's making my life insanely difficult right now. But the studio is adamant the show must go on. That's been made clear to him."

Caleb was telling the truth. Not that she'd ever doubted it but hearing it straight from Vince solidified the stakes. If Kat walked away, Caleb would walk too. And it could cost him everything.

"Why is that?" Vince leaned back in his chair and studied her face.

"Why is what?"

"Why do you think he's different around you than around the other women?"

141

She could confess all to Vince. He was her friend and had always been good to her. But he was first an executive producer trying to save his show. And he would do anything if he thought it would bring in ratings, including exploiting her past with Caleb.

Kat shrugged. "Maybe because he knows that I was never meant to be on the show. I was just a last-minute stand-in. He may not feel the same kind of pressure with me he feels with the other women."

"Huh." Vince studied her. "What happened with what's-his-face? I mean, I'm assuming that you're not still together since you're here. Even if it's not real."

"Dan and I broke up over a year ago. It was mutual. Between our job schedules we hardly saw each other. It became obvious we weren't the right fit." All true. Though it wasn't their jobs that had been the death knell.

"What's the harm in staying? Just until the final four."

Kat studied the screen with frozen Caleb and Gemma. She couldn't make this kind of decision surrounded by cameras and crazed women.

"I need to go home." The certainty filled her to her core. She needed time away from this claustrophobic house. Time away from the cameras. Time to think.

Vince's jaw unhinged. "Kat—"

"Not for good. Well, maybe not. I've spent ten years building up my career, Vince. I didn't do that to become known as some sort of wannabe reality TV star."

She waited for him to say no. That it wasn't possible. If he didn't agree then she would have her answer. That it was time to go.

"You know how this works. The social media trolls. The tabloids. All of it. I've worked hard to build my brand as a makeup artist. You're asking me to throw all that work away for the type of celebrity I've avoided my whole career."

Vince picked up his glass and drained it, placing it down with a thump. "How long do you need? A few hours?"

"A day. At the most."

"You're supposed to be flying to New Zealand in less than twelve hours. What am I supposed to tell the women?"

"I'll leave you to figure that out. I'm sure you'll come up with something." She pressed her feet to the floor and rose from her chair, feeling the lightest she had in weeks.

She was going home. No matter what Vince said. She was going home.

Kat sagged against the elevator wall as it counted up to the twenty-second floor. Vince had insisted on filming her walking to the car in case she decided not to go to New Zealand. She'd never leave without saying goodbye to Caleb, but she wouldn't tell Vince that.

Caleb wasn't flying out until tonight, so if she decided she was done with the show there was at least time to tell him herself. Let him make whatever decision he needed to while still in Australia. No doubt with a coterie of hangers-on present, but she couldn't change that.

The plush carpet muffled her footsteps as she tapped in the key code into her front door and let herself in. Straight into Paige making out with her boyfriend.

The two of them leapt apart like scalded cats at the sound of the door slamming shut behind her.

"Hi, guys. Don't mind me." They were both wearing sweaty workout gear and smelled like endorphins, pheromones, and love. "Have a nice run?"

Paige smoothed an invisible kink in her pony tail. "Yes, very nice. Thanks."

"Well, don't let me interrupt your cool down." She raised her eyebrows. "Or warm up, as the case may be."

Josh quirked a half smile then looped an arm around Paige's waist and tugged her to him. "I do like a good warm up." He winked.

Paige flushed and gave him an elbow in the side. "Josh Tyler!" Her fake indignation did nothing to hide her smittenness with her boy-friend.

It was stomach-churningly adorable. Kat tried to stamp down the feeling of overwhelming jealousy that threatened. Her cousin had earned all the happiness that came her way. Kat just hadn't expected to be slapped in the face with it before she'd barely walked over the threshold.

Paige must have read something on her face because she reached behind Josh and opened the door. "Go. I'll see you later."

Kat headed for the kitchen and let the two murmur their sweet nothings to each other as she perused the fridge. She cracked four eggs into a bowl and started whisking. A generous pour of milk. Salt. Pepper. Back to whisking.

Behind her, a bar stool scraped across the floor as her cousin sat down. "Hope you're hungry." She banged two pans onto the stove top, turned on the gas, and threw some butter into one pan.

Paige cleared her throat. "Um, sorry about that."

Kat looked over her shoulder to see Paige clasping and unclasping her hands. Flushed cheeks and a furrowed brow had replaced the besotted smile.

"You don't ever need to apologize for being in love." She would not be one of those wowsers who rained on someone else's happiness. Especially not Paige's.

"I suspect the eggs may disagree."

Kat looked back down. Pale yellow liquid

145

spattered the counter where the mix had sloshed over the sides of bowl from the force of her whisking.

She wiped up the mess, poured the egg mix into the buttered pan with a hiss, and added bacon to the other pan. Paige brushed past and they stepped around each other with practiced ease as Paige popped bread into the toaster and got plates out.

Kat flipped bacon and scrambled eggs as she tried to find the words to unravel the knotted ball that had wrapped itself inside her over the last few weeks. "Have you been watching?"

"Of course." Paige dropped the toast onto their plates as Kat served the bacon and eggs. A sense of déjà vu hit her as she walked around the counter with the two plates and placed them down in front of the stools.

I miss Caleb.

How long ago had it been since she'd sat on this very seat and confessed her secret shame to her cousin. A year? More?

Paige settled in beside her and placed two glasses of water in front of their plates.

Kat focused on chopping up her toast. Shoveled in a mouthful. Eating meant she couldn't talk and talking was too hard right now. She didn't know what she might say if she started talking. And she didn't like not knowing. It scared her. Even with Paige.

She chewed and swallowed, not tasting a thing.

Paige took small, dainty bites. Mostly eggs. Probably thinking about fitting a wedding dress Kat would put money on being in her near future.

She shoved her plate away. There was no point trying to eat her feelings. There wouldn't be enough food at a Denny's buffet for that.

"So? What do you think?"

Paige put her fork down and took a sip of water. "I cried when I watched your conversation on the balcony. Until then I didn't realize how much you were still hurting. And I worry he could hurt you even more."

"I know." Kat knew how that felt. She'd watched Paige stay in a dead-end relationship for years, her hope only ever being traded for more hurt.

It was Wednesday. The next episode would be screening tomorrow. "They're altering the format."

Paige frowned, forehead crinkling. "How?"

"Tomorrow Caleb goes from fourteen women to eight. Then they're going to let viewers vote for the top six and four. Then Caleb will choose the final one. To go back to his farm to see how they work in 'real life'."

Paige blew out a breath. "Well, I can see why that made you leave. Are you okay?" She picked up her fork and scooped some more eggs.

"I haven't left." Kat shook her head. "I've been

allowed off the reservation for a few hours to decide what I'm going to do. The final eight fly to New Zealand later today."

"And you're considering going?" Paige's attempted politeness couldn't mask the incredulity in her question. Kat couldn't blame her. And her cousin didn't even know the half of it.

"I don't know." She took the leap. She had to tell someone. To get this thing out from inside her own head. "Caleb has asked me to stay. Until the end."

"I'm sorry. What?" Paige's fork clattered back to her plate, her open mouth displaying the remnants of her breakfast.

"His mother has dementia. She was the one who sent in his audition video. He's doing this for her, so the last memories she has are of him happy. He says he can't see a future with any of the other women."

"And he sees a future with you?" Paige picked up her glass and took a gulp.

Shaking her head took all her energy. "No."

"No?" Paige's voice shot up a notch.

"He trusts me. Plus, he can't quit the show because they'll sue him."

"Do you still love him?" It wasn't really a question. Paige had watched Kat lose her mind on the balcony in the last episode. Caleb might not read between the lines, but Paige sure could.

"What does it matter?"

Paige stabbed her fork into her toast. "What does it matter? Oh, I don't know. Maybe because there is a big difference between doing a favor—the world's hugest favor—for an ex-boyfriend you no longer have feelings for, and moving back to his hometown and pretending to be in love with the guy you're really in love with on a TV show." She stabbed her toast-clad fork in the air. "For his mother."

When put like that, the scheme sounded insane.

"I need ice cream." Her cousin pushed her half-eaten eggs away.

"It's too early for ice cream."

Paige slid off her seat and marched around to the fridge. "It's never too early for ice cream."

No point arguing with that.

Paige opened the freezer door and yanked out a tub of Häagen-Dazs. "So Caleb thinks he's asking you to be what? His wingwoman? His Girl Friday? And what happens when the show finishes and the cameras leave? You just put out a statement announcing it didn't work out and you both have great respect and mutual admiration for each other?"

"I don't know. We haven't talked about that yet."

Paige muttered something under her breath as she slammed the freezer door shut and grabbed a spoon off the drying rack.

"You think it's a bad idea."

"No." Paige sat down next to her and ripped the lid off the tub. "I think checks and stripes are a bad idea. I think pumpkin spice lattes are a bad idea. I think diets where you only eat foods hand-harvested in the Alps by Swiss virgins are a bad idea. This one left bad in the rearview mirror hundreds of miles ago." She waved her spoon around like she was trying to conduct her argument. "How can you even consider it?"

"Maybe it's what I need to do to get over him." The words burst out of her, her chaotic thoughts coalescing around them. Maybe this was what she needed. To go back to Toowoomba. To realize the life Caleb had ripped away from her wasn't the life she wanted.

Paige paused, her loaded spoon halfway to her mouth. "Explain that to me. Because I'm hoping it makes a lot more sense in your head than it does out loud."

This conversation had to be a nice change for Paige. Kat was usually the sane one handing out the good advice while Paige wallowed in drama.

Kat eyed up the ice cream and tried to unravel her thoughts. "It's been over nine years. Nine years, Paige. And I'm not over him. You're the only person who knows that. Almost a decade, and I can't find a way to love anyone like I loved Caleb. I have literally travelled to the four corners of the earth. I hadn't seen him or spoken to him since we broke up. I've dated. Not casually, but seriously. And he still has a hold on me. I don't know why. I don't know how. Maybe the only way I'm ever going to get over him is to go back. Get some closure."

Her cousin swallowed her mouthful. "Alright. I need you to hear this knowing how much I love you. Okay?"

"Okay." Kat steeled herself for whatever was coming.

Paige leaned forward and looked her straight in the eye. "You are one of the smartest people I know, but that is one of the stupidest things I've ever heard."

Kat opened her mouth, but nothing came out. Her eyes stung as she choked back the tears that had been building for weeks.

"Look." Paige softened her tone. "I know how it feels to be stuck. You know that more than anyone. But do you honestly think going back is the path to going forward?"

"What if it is? What if I do go back and realize we aren't right for each other. That I would have been miserable trying to make a life with him on a farm in the middle of nowhere. Then I'd be able to move on."

Paige reached across the counter and grasped Kat's hand. "What if you go there and fall more in love with a guy who doesn't love you? In a couple of months you could be right back where you were a decade ago."

"Maybe that would be better than trying to live with not knowing what went wrong."

Paige pulled in a breath. "What does Allie think?"

"I haven't told her. Well, she knows about the change of format but not about Caleb's request."

"Why not?"

"I don't want to stress her out with the baby. She's got enough on her hands as it is."

"You have to tell her. She'll be so hurt if you don't."

"I know." She didn't want to hurt her best friend for anything, but the more people she let in the worse off she was going to be.

"Just be careful. Be careful with your heart."

That was part of the problem. She'd been careful with her heart ever since Caleb had broken it. And it had mended jagged and raw, like a bone needing to be rebroken before it could ever be whole again.

CHAPTER TWELVE

When Caleb had been told he needed a passport for the show he'd imagined all sorts of far-flung and exotic destinations. Not a short jump across the ditch to New Zealand.

Which was a perfectly nice country. He'd seen *The Lord of the Rings* and *The Hobbit* movies like the rest of the civilized world. But it wasn't Barcelona. Or Venice. Or the Rockies.

Peering into the bathroom mirror, he rubbed some product through his hair. Four one-on-one dates down, four to go.

So far he'd been bungee jumping in Queenstown, skydiving in Christchurch, jet boating in Taupo, and luging in Rotorua. He couldn't blame the producers for spending each day trying to scare his heart out of his chest. When he had all the onscreen personality of a slab of cheese, it was probably the only trick they had left to try and make some decent reality TV. Whatever the standard for that was.

He'd also suffered through four "romantic" dinners and couldn't understand why any of the women were still around. Surely it was as plain to them as it was to him that they had about as much chemistry as two bricks.

That certainly hadn't stopped a few of them from finally flinging caution to the wind and going in for kisses. A couple he hadn't been able to dodge.

"We're just asking you to kiss her, not sleep with her." That had been the gritted-teeth instructions from one of the producers the night before while he was on his way to dinner with Gemma. So he hadn't fended her off when she'd leaned in and planted one on him. But good luck to the editors making it appear like he was an enthusiastic participant.

Kat was still here. And she was the only reason he was still participating in this ridiculous show.

A knock sounded at his door. He checked his watch. He had thirty minutes until his next date.

Kat stood there, looking over her shoulder. As soon as she saw the door had opened she ducked though it. "We probably only have a few minutes."

"How did you know where I was?"

She gave a small smile. "Great connections."

"Why don't we go talk over there?" Caleb gestured to the sitting area in the suite. He hadn't seen her since the last elimination night. His eyes drank her in and he had to restrain himself from reaching out to touch her as she brushed past him.

"Sure." Kat plopped herself down on one of the couches. "I'm supposed to be today's date."

He let a sigh of relief escape. "Thank God."

Her gaze bounced around the room, and a slight downturn to her lips conflicted with his response. *Supposed to be.* Supposed to be meant there was a chance she wouldn't be. Supposed to be left space for doubt. Space for changes.

"I think we might be going caving. Allie and I did it once when we were on a filming break from *The Hobbit*."

"How'd you even end up working on those movies?"

Kat crossed one leg over the other. "Vince helped. He set me up with some contacts of his who were working on pre-production."

"Vince, as in executive producer Vince?" Caleb dropped into the chair opposite Kat.

"Yeah. I owe him a lot. He's the reason I have the career that I do instead of selling makeup at a David Jones counter."

Something froze in his stomach. "Is that the reason you're still here? Because you owe Vince?" That made sense. Stupid. He'd let himself hope that maybe her staying around had something to do with him. But that would have been too good to be true.

Kat ran a hand through her hair, avoided the question. "We had a good thing."

"We did." Good. Good was a nice steak. Good

was a cold beer on a hot day. Good didn't even come close to what he'd had with Kat.

"But not good enough." For a moment her gaze flickered and hurt traveled across her face.

Caleb swallowed back his vehement denial. Kat'd had great things written all over her from the second they'd met. He was a farm boy from the middle of nowhere. He'd considered himself the luckiest man on earth every second they were together. But when the offer came in for her to work on a big-budget movie, he'd known that trying to hold on to her would have been as cruel as trying to keep an eagle in a cage. "I never wanted to hurt you."

"I know." She whispered the words, not meeting his eyes. "Are you sure there isn't another woman you can consider taking home? Olivia is really nice."

Olivia was nice. But he didn't lose his breath when he looked at Olivia. Olivia didn't have him tossing and turning at night, wishing he were worthy of her. Olivia didn't have him wondering if he had officially lost his mind because he wanted to take the woman he loved back home while knowing she would never stay.

Caleb shook his head. "No."

"Okay. So how are we going to win over the viewers?"

Win over the viewers? Was she saying what he thought she was? "You mean you're going to stay? To the end?" His voice cracked a little on the last question and he coughed to try and cover it.

A pause as her gaze bounced everywhere except at him. "Yes."

"Is this because you owe Vince?"

She looked at him then to the window then back again. "My debt to Vince is more than settled by now. Besides, you know no one can make me do something I don't choose to."

"Then why?" Kat was saying yes. She was going to come back to the farm. Caleb's body jolted up in the chair as the enormity of what she was saying hit him.

She shrugged. "Your mum was always good to me. If this is what she wants, I want to help."

"You would do this for her?"

Kat dragged a finger along the back of the couch. "I've seen a few legal battles in my time. The studios always win. Even if they lose in court, they will make your life miserable for as long as it takes to play out. Your family doesn't have much time left. It's too precious to be wasted on lawyers and court proceedings."

She was right. "Thank you."

"Don't thank me yet. We have to win over the viewers first."

Caleb sagged back into his chair. For a second, he'd forgotten this all rested on a bunch of strangers' votes.

Kat bit her bottom lip, a rare sign that she had something more to say but wasn't sure whether to say it or not. "Do we maybe tell them we have a history?"

"Why would we do that?"

"I've watched these types of shows for years. Viewers hate it if they feel things are unfinished between the lead and a contestant. The way that Rachel and Peter ended on last year's season of *The Bachelorette* almost set Twitter on fire. I'd get votes if they knew we have a past."

Caleb's heart thundered in his chest. For years he had considered them to be as finished as two people could be. More finished than Rachel and Peter, whoever they were. "How would we do it?"

Kat gazed at a spot over his shoulder, thinking for a few seconds. "We tell them the truth. At least some of it. That you broke up with me. That I left to work on films and never came back. That we haven't seen or spoken to each other until I walked out of the limo. That it feels like some of the old spark is still there."

She gave a brief smile. "They'll want a few more details than that, so you'd have to come up with a few more words to make it believable."

Caleb tried to conjure up what he would say. There was no way he was telling the bunch of watching piranhas the truth. Not when the woman sitting in front of him didn't even know it.

His skin crawled at the idea of sitting in front of a camera and talking about his relationship with Kat—their break up, the aftermath. Especially when it probably wasn't even required. Like Vince had said, the audience could already see she was the only one he had a real connection with.

"I don't think we need to be that drastic."

"What do you suggest?"

Caleb shifted on his chair. "Look, part of the reason this has all fallen apart is because I don't fancy locking lips with enough women to form a hockey team. So all we really need to do is . . ." He couldn't even finish the sentence. Kissing Kat. Again. He hadn't let himself go there.

Kat leaned back and crossed her legs. "Appear like we have chemistry?"

"Yes." He wasn't stupid. Persuading reality TV viewers that he'd found love without kissing the object of his affection wouldn't work.

"It'll be fine. It's not like we've never kissed before." She waved her hand like it was no big deal. And it probably wasn't for her. She hobnobbed with A-list celebrities and no doubt had actors falling over themselves to offer their lips in service.

Meanwhile, excluding the excruciatingly awkward clash of teeth with Holly Smith at his Year 12 ball, two women comprised his entire kissing repertoire.

"What about at the end? If this works, we'll have half of Australia expecting a wedding and for us to get cracking on our five adorable children."

He froze when he realized what he'd said. They'd always joked about having five children—a compromise between his six and her four.

Kat didn't even give it a flicker of acknowledgement. "The paparazzi gets bored fast. I'm booked with a job in the US for eight weeks once filming finishes here. After that I have four weeks in New Zealand. After six months or so, if anyone still cares, we can just say long distance proved too difficult."

Her words brought reality piercing him like a missile. The only reason Kat was here was because she had been contracted to work on the show. She was in front of the cameras under duress. And because Kat had a huge heart she would do this for his mum and to help rescue him from his own stupidity. She was no more looking to fall in love then he had been.

"We haven't talked about your lost income. If you're square with Vince, won't you be off the payroll if you've chosen to stay?"

Kat visibly bristled, her posture going from slouched to rigid. "I don't need your money, Caleb."

"I'm not saying you do. But I'm insisting. This is a business transaction. I pay my debts." Maybe watching cold hard cash leave his bank account would help him keep his heart in line.

She sighed. "Fine. Two grand a week."

Caleb was sure that wasn't even close to what she really earned, but he wasn't about to haggle. He had savings but the farm might also need them after a winter of low rainfall.

Kat leaned back against the couch. "So we're going to do this? Go out there today and try to convince Australia they should vote for us?"

He nodded. "Are we good? Is there anything we need to talk about? I mean . . ." He blew out a breath. They had a past. A past they'd skated over and dodged around. "When we broke up . . ."

Kat stood. "We're good. You were right. I'm not the woman for you. You just realized it before I did." She gave him a smile. "Don't worry, Caleb. I'm not going to fall in love with you. I promise."

It wasn't her he was worried about.

Six hours in wetsuits in the dark and the wet. Not exactly a setup for romance. Kat couldn't decide whether that was good or bad.

A freezing wind whipped across the grass they were standing on. Kat clamped her teeth together to try and stop them from chattering as one of their guides flattened the fluttering pages against his clipboard. "Just a reminder there won't be any bathroom stops on this trip and while peeing in your wetsuit may be nice and warm it's horribly bad for them. If you didn't go to the bathroom before we left base, these bushes are your last chance until we return."

Oh wow. Those were fun options. Strip off the piece of rubber that was the only thing between her and hypothermia or hold it for six hours. "What do they think people have? Bladders the size of watermelons?"

The guide stopped talking and stared at her. "Did you have a question?"

"Um, no. No question." Wow. It was like being back in school.

Next to her Caleb's shoulders shook with silent laughter.

The guide droned on and Kat tuned out to try and distract herself from both the cold and the massive hole they were about to rappel down.

She'd rafted the Waitomo Caves with Allie a few years ago on a girls' weekend. They'd almost done the Black Abyss tour then, but she had chickened out when she saw it included rappelling and a massive cliff jump. Heights she could deal with. But dangling over a hole into the earth and jumping off a cliff in the pitch black into a river you couldn't even see was a definite deal breaker. If she knew then she'd be here today about to do the hardcore tour with Caleb, she would've choked on her complimentary bagel.

Caleb reached out and took hold of her hand,

as if he knew that her bravado was unraveling. Kat looked down at their fingers wrapped around each other's palms.

Being with Caleb had always made her braver than she actually was. His steady, calm, unwavering nature was a safe place for her to land if she failed. Until it wasn't.

Should she have told him about her conversation with Vince? She was reasonably sure she'd made the right call, but the decision didn't sit well. Caleb was a terrible actor, as the entire country already knew. She couldn't risk that he might do or say something and give away his belief that the ending was predetermined.

Putting their efforts into wooing the viewers into legitimately voting for them made far more sense. She didn't want Vince to have to choose between her and someone who got more votes unless there was no other way.

The guides came around doing one last check of their harnesses.

"You okay?" Caleb's voice came low into her ear. The camera on his helmet clunked into hers. Kat tried to ignore the large cameras circling around them. At least they'd get to leave those behind soon.

"A bit nervous. You?"

Caleb glanced down the hole they were about to throw themselves into. "A little. There's nothing like this in Toowoomba."

They watched as the first two crew members clipped themselves onto the line then disappeared into the darkness. No screaming or sounds of bodies falling echoed up from the hole. That was something.

They were next. "Do you want to go first, or do you want me to go first?" Caleb ran his hand down her arm. Even with a thick layer of rubber between them, her skin still prickled like he'd touched her bare skin.

"I'll go first." Having Caleb standing below and staring at her rubber-clad and tightly harnessed rear would be worse. A girl had to retain some dignity.

She stepped forward onto the rickety-looking wooden platform and watched as the safety guy clipped her harness on.

"Just lean back. Feel the harness and the rope take your weight. Then push off and let the rope flow."

Kat forced herself to tilt back. She had done this during their rappelling practice only thirty minutes before. But walking down a barely-there slope in a field was completely different to dangling on a rope over a sheer drop.

She forced herself to breathe. She'd climbed the Sydney Harbour Bridge with Paige for her birthday last year. If she could scale that massive structure surely, she could do this.

But she'd been attached to steel. Something

solid and unwavering beneath her feet. Not so much here. She tilted herself too far out to be able to get back onto the platform so now she was suspended in midair, but she couldn't force her feet to slide off the platform. To relinquish her last hold on stability.

"Bring me back. Bring me back, please." The last word came out as a half-hysterical scream.

The guide opened his mouth as if to say something then clamped it shut and hauled on the rope to lift her up until she got enough leverage with her legs to get herself back onto the platform.

"It's okay. Take a moment." He put his hand on the small of her back and guided her away from the drop.

Caleb stood on the edge of the platform. Why wasn't he coming for her? Oh, right. Only one person allowed on the platform at a time. She forced her legs to wobble toward him.

"I'm okay. I'm sorry. I just need a moment."

"You don't have to do this." He tucked a piece of hair behind her ear. "We can go and do something else."

She looked at the drop she would have to confront to go on this adventure. Her fear of the unknown. Of dangling over a black hole and trusting one slim rope to keep her safe.

"Will you be disappointed in me?"

"No. Never." She could see in his eyes that he was telling the truth.

"I think we would have fun doing this, but I know we would have fun doing something else too."

"I'm scared."

"Me too." He looked into her eyes as he said the words and suddenly they didn't seem to be talking about rappelling anymore.

His arm wrapped about her waist, and he tugged her closer. "You can do this, Kat. I know you can." He leaned in toward her and she stopped breathing. Their helmets cracked against each other.

Sometime today Caleb was going to kiss her. For the cameras. For the viewers. For the votes.

And she would have to kiss him back without her heart getting involved.

CHAPTER THIRTEEN

Traversing the dark depths of the earth with Kat was the most fun Caleb'd had in years. The sound of rushing water and the echoing vastness of the caves and tunnels they travelled gave the two of them an almost-private experience.

"I can't believe we're doing this." Kat murmured the words from where she sat next to him on an overhanging ledge.

"I know. It's incredible." He wrapped his hands around a warm metal cup filled with hot chocolate that the guide had distributed to their group.

After rappelling they'd hiked, climbed, swum, and floated in tubes along the surface of the water, Kat growing more relaxed as time had progressed.

He'd long since lost track of the number of times he'd wanted to kiss her. The helmets made it impossible. He wasn't sure whether to be thankful or frustrated.

Below them, in the gloom, he could just make out the meandering river.

"What are you thinking about?"

Kat looked up at him, the light on his helmet casting a glow over her face. "I was wondering if they're going to make us jump off here."

"Probably."

She turned her head, her gaze covering the distance between them and the water, then scanning the opposite walls. No doubt assessing her own capability versus the perceived risk.

Kat was all about control. The remnant of a childhood in which she had none.

Caleb tugged on the end of the braid lying over her shoulder. "Don't overthink it just because it's dark. This isn't nearly as high as the old swimming hole. Thousands of people do this every year. They wouldn't be operating if people got hurt."

She tugged at the strap on her helmet. "I know." She undid the clasp, lifted the helmet off, and rubbed her head. "That's better. Man, that is heavy with all the camera gear on it."

He looked around. The guides were talking farther up the ledge, and the crew was occupied with their own drinks and snacks. "I'm pretty sure we're not supposed to do that. Health and safety and all that."

Kat shrugged. "I don't know about you, but I suspect I signed my life away on those three pages of liability waivers."

She had a good point. Caleb took his helmet off and placed it on the ground behind him, facing the camera toward the back wall. There would no doubt be words when it was discovered, but it would be worth it.

"How's your mum doing?" Kat sipped her hot chocolate.

"Good days, bad days. I've talked to her once since we arrived in New Zealand. She seemed okay, but my uncle told me the night before she'd misplaced the fish for dinner and they couldn't find it anywhere. Guess where it showed up."

Kat crinkled her nose as she thought. She was ridiculously cute. "The mailbox?"

He shook his head. "Nope."

"The car?"

"What's the worst place you could think of?"

"Her bed? Oh, his bed!"

Caleb laughed. Climbing into bed and discovering fish would definitely be up there. "Close."

"Okay, I give up."

"The washing machine."

"That's not too bad unless . . ." Her eyes widened. "Oh no. She didn't."

Caleb nodded. "She did a hot wash."

"Were there . . ." Kat covered her eyes. "Oh, there were, weren't there?"

"A whole load of clothes covered in boiled salmon. Then she got angry at Uncle Jared and insisted that he did it. The clothes are gone, and he thinks the washing machine might be too."

169

Kat's shoulders started shaking. "I'm sorry. I know it's not funny, but imagine the smell." She wiped her eyes. "Imagine your uncle's face when he opened the machine and realized what had happened to dinner."

Caleb couldn't help but laugh. Had to, or he'd cry. "I wish I'd been there."

Two weeks. He'd be there in two weeks if all went to plan. And Kat would be with him.

"What would I do if I came home with you?"

"Whatever you want, I guess. You could help on the farm if you wanted. Or I'm sure you'd have plenty of women desperate for your makeup skills."

He groaned. The woman sitting beside him had an Oscar and he was suggesting she should content herself doing makeovers on farmers' wives. "I'm sorry. I know that's probably beneath you."

Kat leaned in, her arm brushing against his. "Not at all. I like helping women feel good about themselves. I'm on a team at my church that works with women trying to reenter the workforce. I teach them how to do their makeup."

"Toowoomba isn't nearly as glamorous as Sydney." The city had barely 100,000 residents to Sydney's millions. She was used to the bright lights and the glamor brigade, and he was offering her what? Two months on a farm in the middle of nowhere while he worked long hours.

170

What was she going to do all day? Kat needed to be challenged. She would be bored out of her mind in about three days.

Even Emma—who was rural born and bred and said she loved him and was going to marry him—couldn't manage a week on the farm.

"Hey." Kat tilted her head to look up at him. "Now who's the one overthinking things?"

He ran a hand through his hair. "I don't want you to regret coming."

She turned her whole body so that she faced him. "Your life is not beneath me, Caleb."

"But . . ."

Kat moved in and placed a finger on his lips. "No buts." She took her finger away. "I'm all in. I promise."

The cave took on an ethereal quality as they watched each other, like a spell had been cast over the gloom and removed all but the two of them. Caleb raised his hand and ran it over Kat's cheek.

"I don't deserve you." He whispered the words across the space between them as his fingers trailed down her braid.

"You're right. You deserve much better."

Even in the dim light he could see pain and hurt radiating in her eyes. Had he caused that? Or had someone else?

His hand roamed down her damp wetsuit-covered back. He leaned in and caught a whiff of chocolate on her breath. There were no helmets in their way this time. He didn't know if there were other cameras catching this or not. Didn't care. His palm caught the curve of her waist.

Kat's hand landed on his shoulder and then her fingers traced a path up behind his neck.

"I missed you." Caleb didn't know which of them said the words. And it didn't even matter because all he cared about was kissing the woman in front of him.

So he did. And suddenly they were twenty-three again and loitering on her porch at one in the morning like they were sixteen and out past curfew.

As past and present collided he knew only one thing.

He had never stopped loving her.

CHAPTER FOURTEEN

Almost a million votes cast. How many more would have voted if he'd been halfway decent at this reality TV thing? At least Vince looked happy as he'd clapped Caleb on the back and asked him if he wanted a drink before the six "winners" were announced.

Kat had to be one of them. She was the only one he'd kissed. Women were a mystery to him in most regards, but he couldn't believe the kiss they'd shared wouldn't give her a leg up on the voting front.

Caleb paced the small room where he was being held as the crew set up and finished positioning the eight women.

It had been three days since they'd filmed the last date. The least amount of time possible to allow them to get the episode aired and allow a twenty-four-hour voting window. Three days of being stuck in a hotel and driving himself completely crazy.

Pulling his phone out he checked the time. Nine in the evening in New Zealand was six in Queensland. Opening his messages, he tapped out one to his uncle. The last he'd heard, the new meds hadn't done anything for his mum, and her lucid times had become further and further apart.

Every day he questioned his decision to be on the show. Yes, his mother had auditioned him and practically frog marched him out the door when she heard he'd been chosen but if he'd refused it would've been a few days—at most a week—before she'd have forgotten it ever happened.

But if he hadn't come—Caleb's chest tightened just at the thought of a parallel life where he stayed on the farm and Kat never walked up that path and stumbled into his arms.

His phone buzzed in his hands. Still no change. At this rate, by the time he returned home his own mother might not know him anymore.

A knock at the door and Vince walked in. "Okay, we're all set. Ready?"

Caleb shrugged. "As I'll ever be." As long as he walked out that door and saw Kat all would be okay. If she had come to her senses in the last few days and gone home . . . Well, at least that was definitive.

Though he assumed that hadn't happened since he'd bet the show would drag a heap of drama out of a woman deciding to leave voluntarily at this stage in the game.

He followed Vince down an echoing corridor, and found Mark waiting for him at the end. He wondered what the part-time host had been up to while Caleb had been on eight back-to-back dates, because he hadn't seen the man since they arrived in New Zealand.

Mark held out his hand, two cameras filming over his shoulder. "Caleb, big night. How are you feeling?"

"To be honest, a little relieved to have the decision taken out of my hands. It's been a weight off my shoulders not having to decide which two to send home tonight." He couldn't believe they were going to have to do this all again next week.

"I'm sure, I'm sure." Mark's head jerked up and down as if he were a puppet on a string. "Okay. Let's go see the ladies, and you can say a few words." He gestured through another set of doors to a room that was lit brighter than a U2 concert.

Caleb followed Mark into the room, searching for one person. Kat. He found her in the front row, wearing some kind of blue one-shouldered number. His thudding heart slowed incrementally. She was here. There was a chance everything would be okay.

"Caleb, ladies." Mark nodded to the room at large. "A momentous evening tonight. Over a million votes cast in a life-changing poll never before done on *Falling for the Farmer*. And I can tell you there were a mere handful of votes between the women staying and leaving."

Caleb blanked Mark out as he droned on for a

few seconds and tried to catch Kat's eye, but she studiously focused on the host beside him.

"I'm going to pass it over to Caleb to say a few words before we announce the results. Caleb." Mark stepped back then made a theatrical show of drawing a white envelope out of his jacket's inside pocket.

"Ladies." Caleb cleared his throat, and six out of eight looked at him like deer caught in a spotlight. Olivia gave him an encouraging smile, and Kat stared at a spot somewhere over his shoulder. "Thank you for your time this week. This show has been an adventure. Each of our dates were different and I will remember them for the rest of my life."

He stepped back. Mark didn't say anything for a second, as if he expected Caleb to say more. Except Caleb didn't have anything else for the women. He just wanted to be done with this.

"Caleb, can I speak to you for a second?" Olivia was already walking forward as she asked the question.

"Sure." He knew what she was going to say. She was leaving this contrived mess. Good for her.

Olivia smiled up at him. "I really enjoyed our date. It was lots of fun, but I've been considering things for the last few days, and I think we both know that what we have is a friends thing. Not a forever thing. So it's time for me to go home. I wish you all the best in finding the woman you're looking for."

There was resounding silence in the room except for the footsteps of a cameraman.

He should say something. Everyone was waiting for him to say something. "Thank you. I wish you all the best as well."

Olivia lifted her arms, and he leaned down to give her a hug.

"You already know who you love. You haven't been able to take your eyes off her since the first night. Good luck." The words whispered into his ear. He hadn't even processed them before Olivia stepped back and gave him a wink.

Then she was out the door with a smile and a wave.

"Caleb, ladies, if you're ready." Mark stepped forward again brandishing the envelope like it was a weapon.

You already know who you love. Olivia's astute observation lingered with her citrus-scented perfume.

She was right. What was he doing? Was he really going to allow these women to go through another two weeks of this insanity when he knew the only woman he would take home was Kat?

He should have taken the chance and pulled the plug on the whole thing a week ago.

Mark pulled a large cream card out of the envelope and looked at it like he had no idea what it would say. Ha! "Remember, I am announcing these in no particular order. The first woman voted in by viewers is . . . Gemma!"

Gemma let out a little squeal and started moving forward.

"No." Caleb shook his head. Determination filled him. "No." The second one was louder. All eyes were on him, including Kat's, her brow puckered and her head tilted.

Gemma froze, halfway across the floor to him.

"I'm sorry." He looked at them all. "I'm sorry, everyone. This has gone far enough. It's not fair to keep putting you all through this."

"Caleb . . ." Mark stepped toward him, but Caleb held up his hand to stop him from coming any closer and attempting a bro hug or who knew what.

"I don't care how the viewers voted. I don't care who the top six are. I already know who I want to take home." He looked straight at her. "It's Kat or it's no one."

"Cut." That was Mark, waving the card in front of his face like it was a fan.

"No." Vince's voice barked from behind the cameras. "Keep rolling."

He looked at Gemma and then the six women behind her. "I'm sorry, ladies. You are all exceptional women. But it's not fair of me to do this to any of you when I know Kat is the only one I can see myself taking home."

The silence was weighted with shock for a few seconds until Gemma tossed her head.

"It's fine." Gemma's tone could have frozen fire. "You're boring. A boring farmer from a no-name town. I was planning to leave tonight anyway." She picked up her skirt and swept from the room, a cameraman and producer in pursuit.

Kat still hadn't moved. He wasn't even sure she had blinked. "Kat? Can I talk to you?"

Shaking her head as if awaking from a dream, she lifted her skirt with one hand and stepped forward.

There was nowhere they could go where they wouldn't be filmed, so he placed his hand on the small of her back and guided her into the passageway he'd entered from.

"Are you okay?" She tilted her head at him with concern in her eyes as if wondering whether he'd had a psychotic break.

Caleb reached and took both of her hands in his, wrapping his fingers around her freezing ones. "It wouldn't have been fair, Kat. It would have been cruel for me to let three other women invest another week on this when I already know you're the one I want to take back to the farm. Only you."

She shook her head. "I can't believe you just did that."

He didn't regret it. Not for a single second. Even if she said no. Even if it all ended here.

Even if his unexpected changing of the agreed plan drove her away. There was no way he could date other women after that kiss. His days of playing pretend were over.

"I don't know what to say." She whispered the words with her head bowed, and his heart flung itself into his feet.

Caleb tugged in a breath. "You don't have to say yes now. I know this is unexpected, so take as long as you need. I'll head back to the farm. Hopefully, I'll see you there."

Facebook Messenger

Kat: Caleb flipped the show.

Paige: He did what now?

Allie: I have no idea what that means but it doesn't sound good.

Kat: They went to announce the six who made it through the first round of voting and right when they announced the first one he said no. That it was me or it was no one.

Paige: Well, you've got to give the man points for being definitive. I guess.

Allie: The studio definitely can't complain about him not giving them any good TV now.

Allie: Where are you? Are you okay?

Kat: I'm in an apartment in Brisbane. I flew in this morning.

Paige: What did you say? When he said it was you or no one?

Kat: I didn't know what to say.

Paige: So what now?

Kat: He's gone back to the farm.

Allie: And if you don't go too?

Kat: Show's over. And he might get sued for ruining the season.

Paige: I vote let the stupid show be over. Then you can wait a week and go there by yourself. Work out whatever this thing is going on between you guys without it being TV fodder for half the country.

Kat: Can't. There's a ninety day no-contact clause in the contract.

Allie: You can't contact him for three months?

Kat: Not without giving them an opportunity to film any in-person meeting.

Paige: I can go. I'll be your middleman. Josh and I can go on a road trip to Toowoomba. Pay him a little visit and let him know you'll see him in ninety-one days. I wouldn't mind having a few words with him.

Allie: Yes! Can I come? I have some words too!

Kat: You guys are enjoying this way too much.

Allie: Sorry. But you have no idea how nice it is that you're the one having the drama for once and we get to be the fierce friends.

Paige: Amen to that. When do you leave for the farm?

Kat: I haven't decided to go yet.

Paige: You're totally going to the farm. His farm is like my Christchurch.

Allie: Or my Iowa.

Paige: It's the crazy scary thing that you really don't want to do but you're going to do it anyway.

Allie: Because you love him.

CHAPTER FIFTEEN

It's Kat or it's no one.

Two days later, and Caleb's words still tumbled through Kat's mind as she watched the brown hues of rural Queensland pass by.

They were the words she'd held onto as Vince had pleaded with her to go to the farm, promising to triple her daily rate if she did. As she paced a Brisbane apartment while the crew waited for her to tell them what she was going to do.

But Paige was right. Kat had known she was going to go to the farm from the moment Caleb had found the courage to throw the show into turmoil. She'd just needed a couple of days to breathe first.

But Paige was wrong about Kat loving him. She was doing this for closure. Because she knew herself well enough to know she had to see this through to the end. No matter what.

The SUV sped up, overtaking a meandering people mover. She knew these roads. Even after nine years absence they still resided in her bones. She'd driven them many times when they'd been dating. They were only a few minutes away from the farm.

She pressed her head back into the leather seat and scrubbed her face with her hand. Had it only been four weeks since she'd stepped out of the limo?

The kiss lingered. Every time she closed her eyes she could feel Caleb's hand in her hair and his lips firmly on hers.

Their plan had worked. Even if it was a reconfigured plan where Caleb had thrown the original out the window and Vince had hustled her into a side room and informed her through clenched teeth that if she didn't say yes to Caleb the show would be over and court papers filed.

The tight control she'd held on her life was unraveling like a spool of thread slipping through her fingers.

The gravel crunched beneath the tires as the car turned into the long driveway leading to the homestead. Signs dotted the fence line. *Private property. No trespassing.* Those were new.

She smoothed her palms against the skirt of her patterned sundress and leaned forward. The air-conditioning in the car couldn't totally cover the heat emanating from outside. Once the door opened she'd be stepping into an oven.

As if to torture her even more, the car slowed.

"Sorry." Karissa gave her an apologetic look

between the seats. "They've asked us to hold back a few minutes."

She sucked in a breath. Tried to ignore the camera facing her, catching her every facial tic.

"Are you nervous?"

"Terrified." At least that much was true.

"What are you scared of?"

"Everything."

"What are you looking forward to most?"

"Just living a normal life again." Yes, there would still be cameras. But at least she would have some freedom to do things like watch TV and check her phone without hiding in the bathroom for fear someone would see her and take it away.

The car gathered speed again, dust flying up under the wheels and gravel pinging off the underside.

Kat looked out the tinted windows. A rectangular metallic shed stood where a paddock had been. Cows ambled in the fields. Nothing out of the ordinary for them.

The homestead had been repainted. Cheerful red trim accented the doors, windows, and porch where green used to be. The porch swing rocked back and forth in the light breeze, the same swing she and Caleb had spent many an hour snuggled in—his mother usually close at hand and popping out at unexpected moments to ensure no one got too cozy.

Her fingers gripped the armrest, nails digging into the firm surface.

Production trailers filled one corner just off the driveway. Cameras and boom mics gathered in a posse around the spot where the car would be disgorging her. No lights thanks to the blazing sun overhead.

The front door opened. Caleb stepped out onto the porch, strode down the four steps to the ground, and stood where a taped X marked the brick path. His broad-brimmed hat shaded his face so she couldn't see his eyes.

The car rolled to a stop. Crew and cameras swarmed into position a few feet away from her door, blocking her view of the one person she would do this for.

Kat put her hand on the handle and pulled it only to discover herself locked in.

"Wait for the driver," Karissa reminded her.

Kat tapped her fingers against the doorframe as people outside shuffled around doing who knew what. Finally, the driver opened his door and stepped out.

The next moment her door snapped open, shining light bursting in. At least one person believed in efficiency. Kat blinked in the glare like a baby possum. Sunglasses—one of the many things not allowed on reality TV.

A breeze whipped into the car, and the bottom of her dress fluttered. She grabbed the edge of the hem. Giving all of Australia a full-frontal view of her purely functional underwear wasn't the impression she was going for.

Walk slowly. Karissa's instructions echoed in Kat's mind as she navigated the hive of people and equipment surrounding her. Her hair whipped around her as the breeze picked up, and she grabbed it, holding it away from her face as she stepped over cords and around lights.

Why hadn't she tied it back? Because Caleb had always loved it loose. That was why. She was making decisions based on the preferences of the other person in a fake relationship. It was a new low.

Her sandal-clad feet slapped against the bricks. One step, two, three. Still she couldn't see him. She tried to see over the shoulders and heads and cameras for a glimpse, but it was like trying to find Where's Waldo in one of those books she'd had as a child.

The crowd opened up and he was here. They locked gazes and a grin spread over his face.

They'd made it.

Caleb strode toward her.

"H—" The greeting stalled in her throat as he placed his palms on her waist and lifted her off the ground. Her hands flung themselves around his neck.

"Hi." His breath fluttered against her cheek as he shifted to support her back.

"Hi." It was almost a whimper as his strong arms squeezed the air out of her lungs.

"You came."

For a moment she pretended it wasn't a charade. That cameras weren't filming their every expression, their every word. That it was only them and this was real. Her arms tightened around his neck as Caleb leaned in, the brim of his hat grazing the top of her head.

Kat closed her eyes as his breath feathered her lips. Her heart thundered in her chest as if attempting a jailbreak from her ribs.

"Who's this?"

The shrill voice cut through the moment. Kat looked over Caleb's shoulder to see his mum barreling down the porch stairs, brows pinched, salt and pepper hair awry, Caleb's uncle in hot pursuit.

Kat stumbled as Caleb released her from his arms, bouncing against his chest before she regained her footing.

His mother arrived in front of them. Grabbing Kat by the arm, she glared up at her. "You're not Emma. Where's Emma? What have you done with her?"

Caleb closed his eyes for a second, foolishly hoping that when he opened them his mother wouldn't be manhandling his ex-now-fake girl-friend.

Mum wasn't even meant to be here. Uncle Jared had planned to take her into town so they would miss the insanity of the big reveal, but Mum was like a heifer sensing a change in the wind. On their way to the car, she'd planted her feet on the porch and refused to move.

"Hello, Mrs. Murphy. I'm Kat."

His eyes jerked open to see his mother's response to Kat's calm words. Would she recognize her name? Her voice?

"Marion, why don't you let the girl go." Jared hovered beside his sister and patted the hand wrapped around Kat's forearm.

Jared had promised not to let Mum out of sight, or near the front door, until Caleb could bring Kat in and privately introduce her. But his mother was wily and seemed to have a sense of when something was going on that they were trying to keep from her. She looked at Kat with confusion and distaste but not recognition.

"Mum." Caleb stepped in and loosened her fingers from Kat's arm. "This is Kat. Remember? I'm on a TV show. Kat's the woman I chose to bring home to stay here for awhile."

His mother's eyes flashed. "Well, I certainly hope she doesn't think she's staying in our house. I'm not having any loose woman under my roof."

Caleb shifted closer to Kat and placed his palm on the small of her back. "No. She's going to stay in the cottage."

"She can't do that. Emma's in the cottage."

The sainted Emma. Mum had adored her, and he'd occasionally wondered if she'd been more hurt than she'd ever let on by Emma's unexpected departure from their lives. "Emma left me. A long time ago. Remember?"

A sheen glazed his mother's eyes. "She did? Are you okay?"

"I'm fine. It was years ago."

"And who are all these people?" His mum jabbed a finger at the cameras and crew all entranced by the made-for-TV spectacle.

"They're all with the TV show."

"Are they staying for lunch? If they are, you're going to have to get more bread. I don't have enough for all of them. And make sure they take their shoes off before they come inside. I've just swept the floors. Don't want their dirty feet all over them."

"Marion, why don't we go inside. Let Caleb show this young lady around." Jared took his sister's arm and turned her toward the house. She went without complaint, her housecoat flapping behind her in the breeze.

"Sorry about that."

"No, it's fine." Kat attempted a smile, but the tightness around the edges said otherwise. He couldn't blame her. Being forgotten and falling short because she wasn't the favored ex-fiancée was hardly an auspicious start to her time here.

190

"Why don't I show you the cottage?" Caleb gestured toward the fork in the path that led away from the homestead and toward a smaller house that stood about fifty meters away.

Aware of the cameras and crew following their every move, he wrapped an arm around her shoulder and she slotted against his side, her feet matching his rhythm as always.

His house hadn't existed in Kat's time. He'd built it the year after their breakup when he needed something—anything—that would distract him from her absence. Waking at four in the morning for milking, working twelve hours, and spending the last remaining hours of daylight building a house had been his escape. He'd exchanged the pain of heartbreak for mind-numbing exhaustion.

She slanted a look up at him as they approached. "It's cute."

"Thank—" His step faltered as he took in the cottage with fresh eyes. Oh, no. He hadn't even thought.

She'd described this very house one night as they'd snuggled on the porch swing up at the homestead.

He knew she realized too because she came to a complete stop, taking it all in. The swing, the bright tulips, the yellow door. When they walked inside, she would see the window seat and the wooden floors. The large master suite with a

191

walk-in closet he only used a quarter of. The bathroom with eons of storage.

He had broken up with her and built her dream house. How on earth was he going to explain that?

Facebook Messenger

Kat: He built my dream house.

Paige: What do you mean he built your dream house?

Kat: When we were dating I said that one day I wanted a house with a porch swing, tulips, and a yellow door. Since we broke up they've added a cottage to the property. Caleb lives in it. Guess what it has?

Paige: No way. It DOES not.

Kat: You'll get to see it on the next episode.

Allie: Your ex-boyfriend dumped you then built your dream house? And moved in?

Kat: I know.

Allie: That's either the most romantic thing I've ever heard or the creepiest.

Paige: Have you asked him about it?

Kat: How could I? We were surrounded by cameras and crew. What was I going to say? Hey, guy I've supposedly only known for four weeks, what's with building the house I told you about ten years ago?

Allie: It's like his own little Taj Mahal.

Kat: Except I'm not dead.

Allie: Maybe it was his way of grieving your break up.

Paige: Want to know what a good way is of avoiding grieving a break up? Don't break up.

CHAPTER SIXTEEN

She'd wanted to kiss him. That had been Kat's impulsive and oh-so-foolish reaction when she realized that the house standing in front of her was the very one she'd told him she dreamed of.

But that would have been ludicrous because, as Paige had pointed out, what kind of guy breaks up with a girl then builds the cottage of her dreams?

Kat rolled the question over in her mind as she tossed and turned in bed. Caleb's bed. Though he had relocated to the homestead while she was here, he was still everywhere. From the masculine furnishings to the color palette of creams and browns—which made no sense with the yellow door—to the clothes still neatly folded in his drawers and hanging in his closet.

Thank goodness the bedding didn't smell like him or she would have had to relocate into the spare room with its single bed, random junk, and tiny windows.

Did he regret it?

The question kept floating back. Every woman who'd ever been dumped held onto the hope that the guy would one day wake up and realize he'd made the biggest, stupidest mistake of his life when he let her go. Even if he was a sprat in the ocean of mandom and she'd subsequently landed herself a 200-pound marlin.

But Kat wasn't hard to find. Unlike Caleb, with his distaste of social media. Kat was on Facebook, Twitter, and Instagram, and even had her own website. It would have taken him two clicks to contact her if he'd ever been of a mind to.

Instead he'd built her dream house, gotten engaged to another woman, been dumped by the other woman, and gone on a reality TV show.

Or maybe he'd gotten engaged to another woman, been dumped by the other woman, built his ex-ex-girlfriend's dream house, and then gone on a reality TV show.

Whatever way she diced it, the numbers didn't add up. And she was good at math.

Something knocked on her window, sending her scrambling for her sweatshirt and yanking it over her head. She padded over the wooden floor, slid the curtains to the side and wrenched open the window.

Sure enough, Caleb stood outside.

"Hey."

"Hey." Kat leaned a hip against the window ledge. "How can I help?"

The last time she'd seen him had been when

the camera crew had trailed them through the house and she'd had to both attempt to conceal her shock and play up her Caleb-smittenness for the cameras. His hand had stayed firmly on the small of her back the entire time he showed her around the house, as if he knew she might need some extra assistance to stay upright.

"Do you have a few minutes to talk?"

"Considering I'm on a farm in the middle of nowhere, it's after midnight, you don't have a TV, and I can only get cell reception if I stand on the kitchen counter with my arm outstretched like Lady Liberty, yes, I think I can spare you a few minutes."

"Sorry about that. I'll give you the wi-fi password."

"Great. See you at the front door." She inched the window back down.

"Oh, okay."

"What were you planning to do? Climb through my window like Romeo? I doubt you'd even fit." From the sheepish look that flitted across his face, that was exactly what he'd been planning on doing.

Boys.

He shifted on his feet. "I didn't want to risk waking the crew."

"They don't have anyone covering the ten to six shift unless there's a specific need. The network deployed some of the cameramen to other projects." Yes, she'd shamelessly eavesdropped on every call Karissa had made during the drive from Brisbane to Toowoomba.

A smile stole across his face. "Well, I guess that's when we should have all our fun."

Something tempting and dangerous traveled through her at his words. Kat slammed the window shut and jammed her feet into her Ugg boots before she could dwell on the feeling.

She pulled her hair into a ponytail, and closed the bedroom door behind her before heading for the front door. She opened it to find him already leaning against the door frame. "Should I come in or do you want to talk outside?"

He'd changed his shirt since she'd last seen him. Now a T-shirt covered his broad torso and did nothing to hide what many, many years of farm work had sculpted.

Kat swallowed. Neither was neutral territory. Beside Caleb, the porch swing swayed invitingly in the breeze. Tempting but no. There were way too many memories and way, way too many kisses associated with porch swings.

"Come on in." She stepped back, found the light switch, and flicked on all the lights in the living area as he closed the door behind him. Maybe bright lights would help her keep her wits about her. "Do you want a drink?"

He sat down on the only couch, legs stretched out comfortably in front of him. "No, thanks."

"Okay. I'm going to make myself a cup of tea." She busied herself boiling the jug, opening and closing cupboards trying to find cups, then digging in her purse for a tea bag.

"You brought your own tea bags?"

She fished one out from the bottom of her bag. "Oh, sorry. Do you happen to have a strawberry and raspberry herbal blend in the house?"

He smiled. "I do now."

Kat plunked the tea bag in the cup, poured boiling water over the top, and carried her steaming mug over. She could sit on the couch or one of two armchairs. But they were on the other side of the coffee table. It would look weird if she went all the way over there. Make it obvious she didn't want to sit next to him.

"Do you want me to use a coaster?"

"A what?"

"A coaster." She gestured at his gleaming coffee table. "To protect the table."

"Kat, do you seriously think that in the last nine years I have turned into the kind of man who even owns a coaster, let alone cares about someone using one?"

"Good point." She placed her cup down on the table, then squeezed herself into the corner of the couch and tented her knees up in front of her as an additional barrier.

Caleb smiled at her from the other end of the couch. Not even a smile. More like a smirk.

"What?"

"You still do exactly the same things when you're uncomfortable."

"I'm not uncomfortable!"

"Remember after our second date when you told me we'd be better as friends? You were in exactly the same position. Wedged into the corner of the couch behind a barricade of knees. It was as if you were hoping an escape hatch would open up behind you."

It was true. She'd fumbled over excuses that ranged from not really looking for a relationship to not thinking they had the right kind of chemistry. Not wanting to crush the earnestly chivalrous but kind-of boring farmer boy who she'd been told never asked anyone on a date. Ever.

And he'd taken it all very stoically, not uttering a word of self-defense or rebuttal. Instead he'd thanked her for her honesty as he'd gotten to his feet. Then he'd held out his hand to help her up and . . .

"Just for the record, you're wrong."

"About?" Kat didn't make a habit of being wrong. About anything.

"All of it."

"I'm sorry?"

"You are looking for a relationship. You just don't think I'm your type. Because you usually go for the life-of-the-party guys, the

always-on-the-move guys; the full-of-opinions-and-keep-you-guessing-where-you-stand guys. And I'm none of those things. I'm the show up when I say I will guy. I'm the do what I say I will guy. I'm the know where you stand guy."

Then he'd run his hand down her arm and unfurled a smile that caught her at the back of the knees. "I'm the guy who didn't kiss you on the first date or the second because I happen to think first kisses are for anticipating, not squandering."

As Kat looked into his eyes she'd seen herself mirrored there. Felt as though she'd been truly seen for the first time in her entire life. And as he lifted a piece of her hair and twirled it around his finger, his breath wafting around her face had sparked a longing that came from the depths of her soul. She'd closed her eyes and leaned in.

And, unlike every other guy ever given the same opportunity, he hadn't kissed her.

"Hey, Kat." His words whispered across her lips. The ones he was supposed to be kissing.

"Mmm."

"If you happen to change your mind, you know where to find me." Then he'd winked and seen himself out, leaving her a molten heap of equal longing and frustration and the realization that every arrogant assumption she'd made about Caleb Murphy was wrong.

· · ·

Why, for the love of God's green earth, had he brought that up? The next two months were going to be hard enough without confusing things even more by referencing their history.

Kat bit her bottom lip. Her knees scrunched even closer into her chest, arms now wrapped around them.

Something that glimmered in her expression, in the way she looked at him, had Caleb flirting with the idea that maybe she still had feelings for him. But even if she did, so what? Feelings were like the weather. They couldn't be relied on. Feelings could change in less time than it took to harvest a field. He'd learned that lesson the hard way, first with his father and then with Emma.

"I'm sorry. I shouldn't have said that."

"It's okay. We have a past. We can't ignore it. That's the whole reason I'm here, after all." Kat leaned over, picked up her mug and took a sip. She placed it back on the table with a thunk, a ripple of tea splashing over the side. "What's with the house?"

The weight of her question, though he had expected it, hit him square in the chest. There was no good or rational reason why a guy would build a house to his ex-girlfriend's specifications. "I missed you."

Her gaze hardened. "You broke up with me."

"Just because I realized we weren't right for

each other doesn't mean I didn't miss you." *Or stop loving you.*

"Do you have any idea how weird it is to be staying in the house I used to dream of living in?"

"No." The worse thing was that she looked exactly like he'd always thought she would. Like it was made for her. Like she fit. But she didn't. And wishing otherwise didn't change a thing. "I can repaint the door, pull the tulips out, remove the swing if it helps."

Kat shook her head fiercely, her hair swishing across her shoulders. "Don't you dare. I do love it. I just . . ."

"Just?"

She sniffed. "I just . . . wish . . . you'd made it for me."

Oh, God.

It took everything in him not to reach across the leather that separated them, pull her into him, and tell her the truth. That there hadn't been a day as he was building the house that he didn't think of her. That as he'd painted the door and hung the swing and planted the tulip bulbs, a crazy piece of him had selfishly hoped that one day he would turn around and find her standing behind him.

Even though he'd known the right thing for her was to stay away, to live the big, amazing life she was destined for.

And she had. She had left and lived exactly the

life he'd wanted for her. The life that deserved her more than he did.

He fought for control of his heart. If this was what it was like on night one, what would the next six weeks be like? Six weeks of seeing her every day. Of pretending to build a life with her. He couldn't bear to think about it.

He needed to get out of her space. Fast. Before he said anything that would cause her even more hurt. He forced himself to his feet, he strode to the kitchen, and poured himself a glass of cold water from the jug in the fridge. Contemplated emptying the entire container over himself.

When he turned around Kat was still in the same position, her tea cup bouncing between her hands. It must be empty.

Caleb returned, sat down in one of the arm-chairs, and leaned forward with his hands steepled. "I'm sorry. I never thought of the house when I asked you to come. Never really thought about how hard coming back would be on you."

Kat looked up from her mug. "I'm a big girl, Caleb. I chose to come. You didn't make me do anything I didn't want to." She stretched her legs out then retracted them underneath her.

"I'm sorry about what happened with Mum."

"There's no need to apologize. How is she doing? How's her memory?"

"Spotty." Caleb leaned back in his chair. "Some things are hazy, some things are gone, and some things that happened years ago are like they happened yesterday."

"Like Emma." Kat took a careful sip of her tea.

"Like Emma." Caleb had talked, thought, more about Emma in the past few weeks than in the last few years.

"I guess it's a good thing she didn't remember me. It would have been awkward trying to explain things if she had." Kat tried to make light of the interaction, but Caleb could tell it had hurt by the way her shoulders slouched forward.

He couldn't imagine how it would feel the first time his mother didn't recognize him. The day was coming, possibly sooner than any of them were anticipating.

"What are we going to do tomorrow?" Kat tried to smother a yawn as she asked the question. "Or should that be today."

"I'll get up early and do the milking with Uncle Jared. Then I thought I could show you around the farm."

Kat gave a wry smile. "That should give them at least some good footage. Cliché. But good— city girl meets big farm."

"That's what I was thinking. The more footage we give them of that kind of thing, the less footage they'll need of us being, well, you know . . ."

Kat nodded. "Good point. Fill up their seventy minutes or whatever they need with me looking

204

like a complete fish out of water. Chuck in a few lingering glances over some cows, and that should buy us a couple of episodes at least."

That wouldn't be hard. At least not from his end. The greater difficulty would be taking his eyes off her so he could get his work done.

He cleared his throat. "We should probably drive into town. Get you fitted with some farm-appropriate clothing. As cute as your sundress and sandals are, you're going to need some jeans, boots, and at least a couple of big hats. That kind of thing."

Kat pulled a face. "Just as long as I don't have to wear any flannel."

"It's your lucky spring. Way too hot for flannel now."

"Good. Oh, yeah, before you head back, can I have the wi-fi password?"

"Sure. It's—" The digits rolled through his mind like numbers lining up in a slot machine. *080808.* "Um, I'll have to double check it and get it to you in the morning. Is that okay?"

The house was bad enough. There would be no explaining why his wi-fi password was the numbers of their first date. She'd think him an utter lunatic. What other aspects of his life had he permeated with Katriona McLeod's existence without realizing?

CHAPTER SEVENTEEN

Kat didn't have to open her eyes to know a bright light was shining in her face. The question was whether it came from the sun, her ceiling light, or a hideous stage light accompanied by a camera in her face, all before she'd had coffee let alone a chance to put on any makeup.

She rolled over and shoved her head under her pillow, then used the few seconds it bought her to work out if there was anyone else in her room. Yup. Breathing. Shifting of feet. It all indicated the presence of a producer and at least one cameraman.

She sucked in a muffled breath against the cotton of her pillow cover. This was what she'd signed up for. For the next two months. Producers and cameras on her heels for most of the day. She should be grateful the house wasn't fitted with hidden cameras to observe her every move when the crew wasn't here.

"Karissa." She eked up her pillow enough to talk and chanced a guess.

"Morning, Kat!" The producer's voice was hyper-cheerful.

"Is this really necessary?"

"Vince wants shots of your opening moments on the first day of your new life."

Hurray for Vince. "What time is it?"

"Just after seven. Caleb will be here at seven thirty for breakfast."

Twenty minutes to shower and make herself camera ready. Tight but doable. Kat flipped the pillow off her head and sat up. Eyed her producer in her cute T-shirt and cut-off shorts. "You can get some shots of my new life once I've had a shower and gotten dressed."

"Um." Karissa's brow pinched as she studied Kat's old T-shirt and shorts.

"What?"

"Do you have anything cuter than that? Vince was thinking a kitchen scene in a cute bathrobe, messy bedhead look, bare feet. That kind of thing." The woman at least had the grace to look embarrassed as she conveyed her boss's 1950s setup.

Kat stared at her. "Does this little scenario also include cooking Caleb some eggs and hand-squeezing oranges for his morning juice?"

Karissa coughed and mumbled something.

"What was that?"

"Bacon. He's a farmer. There also needs to be bacon."

She knew exactly what they could do with their bacon. Kat flipped her cover off her legs and slammed her feet onto the cool wooden floor. "I'm going to shower."

The red light above the camera blinked, signaling it was filming. Good. Hopefully Vince was watching this live back in the production trailer. She stared down the lens with the glare she gave men with large egos and wandering hands.

"I will cook him bacon because I like bacon. But if Vince wants someone wearing a barely thigh-grazing robe and batting come-hither eyelashes then he is welcome to come down here and do it himself!"

Karissa eyed Kat. She'd probably never imagined this when she signed up for the show. Probably thought she'd get some malleable wannabe-celebrity happy to do whatever she was told. Say whatever lines she was fed.

Kat sighed. It wasn't Karissa's fault. The woman had a job to do too. But there was no way she was facing Caleb without the chance to put on some cosmetic armor and give herself a pep talk in the mirror while she did it. "Look. Give me fifteen minutes then I'll give you your on-camera and start cooking Caleb's eggs."

Twenty minutes later, she was dressed and made up. Her hair was pulled back in a severe French braid, the pinching around her temples strategically designed to remind her to keep her wits about her when Caleb walked into the room with his slow smile and knowing eyes.

A camera hovered over her shoulder as she cracked five eggs into a pan.

"Why fried eggs?" Karissa's question came from where she was perched against the counter, just out of view of the camera.

"Caleb's favorite is fried. Well done. Preferably with the consistency of a hockey puck."

"How do you know that?"

Kat froze, the eggs hissing in the pan. She didn't. At least, Kat who had only known Caleb four weeks didn't. "Um, I guess he must have mentioned it." She tried to force some nonchalance into her voice as she dropped bacon into a second pan. Let the spatter of fat hitting heat cut off further questions.

"He's heading up the path now." Karissa pushed herself off the counter, and the camera moved away from Kat. Just a few paces.

That was the upside to two people being followed around by a crowd of others. No such thing as surprises or spontaneity.

Another camera crew entered and positioned themselves a few feet into the open space to capture Caleb's arrival.

Some people had genuinely fallen in love in this kind of arrangement? It boggled the mind. This setup had all the romance of canoodling with a porcupine.

Kat scooped her two eggs out of the pan. "Am

I supposed to open the door?" Might as well play the game when it didn't matter and save her resistance for when it did.

"No. You just stay there. Act oblivious." Viewers who believed that would believe anything, but whatever. So she put four pieces of bread into the large red toaster. Rummaged in the fridge for some butter. Flipped the bacon and tried to pretend she wasn't waiting for the click of the door handle turning. Tried to pretend it had been almost twelve hours since she had last seen him. Not six.

The toast popped, and she turned off the elements for the pans. Starting a grease fire had some appeal for its ability to provide great TV footage without requiring any emotional investment from her. She helped herself to a piece of bacon and popped it in her mouth, allowing the crunchy saltiness to distract her from her knotted emotions.

There was a knock, then the door handle turned at the same time she did. Caleb strode through the door all scrubbed up and carrying a large bouquet of bright flowers.

This was not a man who had come straight from the milking.

"Morning!"

"Good morning." She couldn't stop grinning in response. The opposite of the reserved smile she'd lectured herself on in the bathroom mirror.

He stalked through the room, ignoring the cameras and crew. An art she had yet to master.

He rounded the island style counter, pervading her space. Kat waited for him to stop, to offer her the flowers, but instead his free hand captured her waist and tugged her to him.

"Hi." The word fumbled on her lips as she stared up at his rugged face. *It's just for the cameras, Kat. Remember, it's all for the cameras.*

"Hi." The word rumbled out of his chest as he looked down at her, a mischievous smile on his lips. And then they were on hers. Firm yet gentle. She leaned into the kiss, one hand reaching up and capturing his cheek, the other settling on his waist.

Step back, step away. That's more than enough for the cameras. Her brain issued the warning, but her body betrayed her, her toes inching up, her hand pressing into his hip, her eyes closing.

She was in so much trouble.

Caleb had once thought that there was nothing better on this earth than kissing Kat McLeod. Turned out there was. Kissing Kat McLeod when she'd been sneaking bacon.

He hadn't intended to kiss her. Had thought they'd get at least a couple of days grace on that front before he started getting grief from the production staff.

After all, she was, supposedly, pretty much a stranger living in his house.

But the sight of Kat standing in his kitchen, cooking him breakfast, smiling at him . . . It did something to his heart. He'd thought a quick peck for the cameras wouldn't hurt.

How that had turned into the kind of scorching kiss that left them both breathless he wasn't entirely sure.

He didn't know which one of them had finally broken it off, but he would put money on it not being him. "These are for you." He finally remembered the flowers in his hand and thrust them toward her. Anything to put a barrier between them.

They looked a lot less fresh than they had a minute ago. One poor flower hung at ninety degrees to the stem like a soldier wounded in battle.

"Thanks." Kat took them, looking a little dazed. She gave her head a little shake. "Do you own a vase?"

"Um, no." Great planning, Romeo. "But my mum has some."

Some wisps of hair had come loose from her tight braid. He forced himself not to tuck them behind her ear. Not to touch her. His senses hummed. The problem with kissing Kat had always been that once was never enough.

For some reason, he'd thought that would

have changed over the years. Like he could kiss her for the cameras without his brain and body making the connection to the girl of so long ago. He couldn't have been more wrong. If anything, the feeling had intensified as if he were trying to play catch-up for nine years. Or seven, if he excluded the time he'd been kissing someone else.

She's leaving. At the end of this she's leaving. She's already told you that. This is all made up.

He forced the words into his brain. Tried to make them override the desire to scoop her back up in his arms, evict the camera crew, close the door, and try to convince her to stay.

He cleared his throat and took a step back. "Breakfast smells good."

Kat placed the flowers on the counter. "Thanks. Why don't you get some cutlery and glasses? I'll serve."

Caleb made quick work of setting the table and returned to the kitchen to find Kat holding two plates loaded with toast, bacon, and eggs. His eggs sat solid, cooked almost to shriveled, and coated with a generous amount of pepper. She'd remembered just how he liked them.

"Let me take those." He grabbed the plates from her hands, trying not to read too much into something as basic as the cooking of eggs.

Kat grabbed a jug of orange juice off the

counter, followed him, and slid into her chair before he could pull it out.

"Grace?"

Kat nodded and bowed her head.

"Lord, thank you for this food. Thank you for this day and thank you for Kat being here. Help us to trust you on this crazy adventure." Over Kat's shoulder he caught a crew member rolling his eyes. Whatever. Production could edit it out for all he cared, but he wasn't going to quit saying it. "Amen."

Kat poured them both a glass of juice then picked up her cutlery. "How was milking this morning?"

"It was fine. It's good to be back." His workload would be limited until after the show was over, but it was good to be back. He needed a sense of normality in this situation. Also, cameras were banned inside the milking shed for health and safety reasons, which limited the crew to a few scene-setting and general activity shots from the doorway.

He'd make a list of the other places on the farm where he could get away with doing the same. The liability insurance with the exorbitant premium he resented paying every year would finally come in handy.

"Oh, by the way, the wi-fi password is murphyfarm. One word, all lower case." He'd changed it as soon as he'd gotten home after talking to her last night. Along with his internet banking password. It had been a sobering lesson of his unrealized patheticness.

His knife cut through his toast and eggs with a screech across the plate. He stabbed at a pile and thrust them into his mouth.

Kat's mouth twitched, and her fork paused halfway to her mouth. "You realize murphyfarm is barely one step up from 12345."

"Considering it's almost a mile to the next property, I'm pretty sure I'd notice someone hanging around trying to bludge off our internet."

"Good point. So what's the plan for today?"

Hadn't he already told her that? Caleb opened his mouth as Kat's eyes widened, and she tilted her head toward the cameras. Ah, right. Keeping track of what was said on camera and off was going to be tricky. "I need to feed my mum's menagerie of animals after breakfast. Then I thought we could go into town. Get you some boots and hats and whatever else you need."

"Not possible," Karissa spoke from off to the side. "The public won't know what's happened until the episode airs tomorrow night. You guys can't be seen in public for at least the next two days. But don't worry. We've ordered some farm-appropriate attire for Kat. It should be here later today."

Something like panic flickered across Kat's face. She was a city girl. Being stuck in the middle of nowhere for days was probably akin to being trapped in an elevator.

A sense of foreboding simmered through his body. The last time a woman had been on the farm for two days, she'd left. For good.

CHAPTER EIGHTEEN

Kat sat on the porch and jammed her feet into Marion's spare pair of gumboots, which Caleb had delivered to the front door of the homestead. She'd been looking forward to leaving the farm even if it was only to go to Toowoomba with a posse of hangers-on. No doubt they would have gotten plenty of odd looks. Maybe even interceptions.

Shopping she could do. Being around anyone, even strangers, to help distract her from this thing with Caleb she could do. Being stuck on a farm with only Caleb and the crew whose job it was to watch them like two bugs in a jar? Not a fan.

Not even his family were around to provide some relief. His uncle was determined to stay as far away from the cameras as he possibly could. His mother was spending the day at a care facility since she was considered a potential danger to herself and life and property if left unsupervised.

Kat looked down at her cute T-shirt and shorts, the best she could do until the mysterious delivery arrived this afternoon. She hadn't even owned any farm-appropriate attire when they'd dated. She'd had a real job, which meant their dates were in evenings and weekends. Apart from porch swinging and general canoodling, her farm presence had involved the occasional dinner with his mum and sometimes his uncle, not helping out with the chores.

Something buzzed around her head and she flapped it away. At least she'd only applied light makeup this morning. Didn't have to worry too much about it melting under the heat of the sun, which was getting fiercer with every minute.

Caleb had gone to collect slops for the animals. He hadn't invited her to come, and she hadn't asked. She'd never had much to do with animals, apart from the occasional friend's cat or dog. The life of a jet-setting diplomat's daughter didn't allow for the luxury of pets. Or any other emotional attachments.

She'd left her phone back in the cottage. Paige and Allie would want to know what was going on, but she didn't know how to describe the morning's kiss. And they were the types to ask. *Yes, we're kissing. For the cameras. And I can feel them down to the tips of my toes. I'm sure that will wear off.* They'd be about as convinced by that answer as she was.

Caleb appeared from the side of the house carrying two medium buckets sealed with lids. He swung them up and over the trailer of his truck with ease before dusting off his hands.

"Ready, milady?"

She walked down the porch steps, the gumboots about a size too big and thumping against the ground. "Where's the crew?"

"They've gone ahead to set up at the petting zoo." Caleb opened the passenger door and stepped back to allow her to hop in. No hand to help. She wasn't sure whether to be glad or disappointed.

He walked around the front of the cab, he got in the driver's side. "It's not far. Just a couple of minutes."

"What's the petting zoo?"

"Just a few animals Mum keeps. Chickens, pigs, a couple of lambs." He reversed a few feet then switched into drive.

"Oh, that's sweet."

Caleb slid a glance at her as the gravel crunched under the wheels.

"What?"

"Don't get attached."

"What do you mean?" Kat pushed a piece of hair behind her ear and turned toward him.

"Well the chickens are kept for their eggs and are pretty ornery, so you probably won't like them. But the piglets and the lambs are cute. They're for Christmas."

"You mean I'm going to be feeding animals today that will be your Christmas lunch." She'd be gone by then. They finished filming the first week of December.

He nodded and quirked a smile. "And a very delicious one at that." He reached across a hand, tapped her knee. "It's okay. I know it may seem cold to non-farm people. We don't have to do this if you don't want to."

Kat let some cool slide into her voice. "Don't worry, Caleb. I'm good at not getting attached."

Silence. Caleb's fingers were clenched over the wheel, the muscles in his jaw ticking. What was his problem? He was the one who dumped her. He was the one who asked her to come here and do this whole fake relationship thing. He had no reason to get annoyed.

Caleb pulled off the road. They bounced over some potholed grass and dirt for a few seconds before he slowed in front of a small collection of structures set among the trees.

The crew waited alongside the vehicle with a couple of cameras and boom mics. Kat flung open her door and got out before Caleb could move, shutting it with enough force to be definitive but not enough to make people think they were in the middle of an argument when the last they'd seen was she and Caleb making out in her kitchen.

A chicken coop stood to the right of the space, and a fenced pen with a corrugated iron-roofed shelter sat in the middle. Four snorting and snuffling pigs roamed the yard. They were bigger than she'd expected. When Caleb had said piglets, she'd envisioned little pink pigs she could cradle in her arms. Not that she'd want to. But these ones had long since left the cute piglet stage. Their large hairy bodies were covered with black and pinky-white fur, and they had to weigh close to fifty pounds each.

The pigs stampeded to the fence as she approached. Their snouts jammed though the gaps between the slats, and the snuffling turned into squealing. Their hooves pawed at the ground, and their mouths frothed.

Suddenly her breakfast bacon didn't taste so good.

Caleb arrived beside her and placed one of the buckets down between them.

"Do they always act like this when you feed them?" Kat nodded to the jostling porcine, trying not to let their robust movements intimidate her.

"Pretty much. We're later than their usual breakfast time, so they're extra hungry." Caleb bent and pulled the white plastic top off the bucket. A large metal scoop sat over mix of grains and vegetable scraps.

"Want to feed them?"

Not really. No. "Sure." She forced the word out with a smile, not wanting to look like some high-maintenance blonde bimbo. She could do this. They were just some pigs, not a group of rampaging T-Rexes.

Caleb scooped a serving of the food and handed it to her. "Give them about five scoops. We put them down in different parts of the yard so they don't maul each other trying to get to just one."

"Okay." Kat took the scoop off him. "Do I need to go in the pen?" Please say no.

Caleb shook his head. "Nah. Just work your way around the fence line." He moved in behind her, his chest resting against her back. "Like this."

Focus on the pigs, Kat. Focus on feeding the pigs.

A camera moved around them as one of his hands rested on her waist and the other steadied hers. For a few short seconds she'd managed to forget they were there.

"Just lean over the fence." Caleb's breath tickled her neck. "Then reach down and tip it out."

Kat leaned over the waist-high fence, scoop held high. The second the pigs saw it they started snorting and fighting underneath. How on earth was she supposed to get it onto the ground?

Oh well. At least if she got bitten they'd have to let her off the farm for a tetanus shot or whatever. She flipped the scoop and dumped the feed. Only half of it made it to the ground. The other half coated the heads and backs of the herd.

The pigs all dived at the slop as if they hadn't eaten for days.

"I'm just going to grab a couple of things from the ute. There's a couple of slats that need renailing. You okay?"

"Sure. Fine." Kat forced certainty into her voice. Four more scoops. How hard could it be?

She scooped another serving out of the bucket, walked a few feet up the fence line, leaned over, and tipped the slop onto a spot of bare earth. A couple of pigs immediately diverted from the first pile to the second.

So far so good. She headed back to the bucket. Three more scoops, then chickens. Fresh eggs from happy chooks. This wasn't so bad. Maybe she could make a passable country girl after all.

She'd show Caleb. *Show him what, exactly?* Her foot slid in her too-big boot, and she tripped, ploughing right into the bucket of feed. It tipped, and feed poured over the ground.

Kat pulled herself onto her knees, and righted the bucket. Far more than three scoops was piled on the ground. Did she try and scoop the top back into the bucket, or was it contaminated?

Ear-piercing squeals drew her attention. She looked up to see the five pigs throwing themselves at the fence, trying to get to the feed that was just a few inches on the other side.

"Hold on, piggies. Give me a sec." She picked up a scoop of the food and tried to throw it between the slats at them but some of it caught on the breeze and sprayed back over her. Brilliant.

One of the boards creaked and started loosening itself from the post at one end. Oh no.

Two pigs threw themselves at the board, as if recognizing it was the weakest link. With a crack, the nails holding it in came free and the board swung out. The two pigs resumed their charging with gusto and it split. One pig forced himself into the gap. The remaining upper and lower boards strained against his back and large stomach. There was no way he would get through it.

Then suddenly he was. And the next pig was smaller and followed right after him.

Kat screamed and took off, two hairy, hungry pigs on her heels. She leapt at the closest tree, put some distance between herself and the ground, then kicked off her boots and scrambled through the branches until she was a good six feet up.

By the time she looked down again all the pigs were free. Two of them gathered at the bottom of her tree, two more happily gorged themselves on the original spill and the last one was sprinting past the chicken coop and heading for freedom.

Most of the crew had scattered, their screams and shouts and shrieks telling her they'd had the same reaction as her to the stampeding pigs. One of the cameramen—who had the look of a farm boy from way back—had his feet planted wide, his camera firmly pointed straight at her.

And she was perched in a tree covered in

pig food and not coming down any time soon.

She was so not cut out to be a country girl.

"What happened? Are you okay?" Caleb appeared under the tree. His hand shaded his eyes against the sun, and two planks of wood were tucked under one arm. A tool belt rested around his waist. Three minutes too late.

"They mutinied."

Caleb let out a low chuckle. "So it would seem." He leaned down and patted the back of one of the pigs that snuffled happily around his feet, snorting up the few remaining grains of food. "I'm sorry. That fence was fine when I left for the show. Uncle Jared can't have had a chance to check it while I was gone."

Spoken like a man who hadn't just had a few years carved off his life by stampeding ham hocks.

Caleb leaned the wood against a low-hanging branch then removed his tool belt, draping it over the same branch.

He placed his foot against the trunk of the tree and lifted his hand toward her. "Can I help you down?"

"It's okay. I'm fine. I can do it."

Caleb tilted his head at her. "I know you can. But since it was my pigs that chased you up there, the least you can do is let a penitent farmer help you down." At his slow smile she almost forgot his life was out of her depth.

Now their hunger had been satiated, the pigs milled around aimlessly, snuffling into the grass. The runaway had decided against escape and settled down on his stomach next to the chicken coop. They looked about as scary and vengeful as the average cocker spaniel.

She sighed. "Fine. But I warn you. I stink of pig food." She lowered one sock-clad foot to the next branch down then levered herself to the next lowest one and reached for his hand.

He grasped hers firmly, his other arm wrapping around her backside and lifting her off the branch. "Pig food never smelled so good." Caleb grinned up at her as she rested her hands on his shoulders. Slowly he lowered her until she dangled just off the ground, her torso pressed against his.

"Sorry I left you. I didn't anticipate Harry, Larry, Curly, and Mo would find you quite so irresistible that they had to stage a jailbreak." Caleb murmured the words against her mouth.

Kat opened her mouth to say something then her gaze caught the mic attached to the collar of Caleb's T-shirt. She closed her eyes for a second. She'd forgotten their every move was being filmed, their every word recorded.

If they were together the way everyone thought they were, this was a kissable moment. The way Caleb's gaze had jumped from her eyes to her lips said he knew it too.

It was so tempting. She hadn't been kissed the

226

way she'd been kissed that morning in a very very long time. The magnetic pull of another kiss was undeniable, but giving into the pull of kissing Caleb every time the cameras were rolling would only make things harder when it was time for her to return to her own world.

Her body betrayed her, leaning into his hold, her chin lifting. His lips landed on hers, soft but firm. Her arms wound around his neck as his tightened around her back.

Kat forced herself to pull away. Their breath mingled in the air between them.

"Kat." Caleb half said, half sighed her name, his gaze more than a little glazed.

Kat sucked in a breath, trying to force oxygen into her lungs and some sense of self-preservation into her brain.

"And cut!" Adam strode toward them. "That's perfect. Vince is going to love it."

Caleb lowered her the remaining inches to the ground but kept one hand firmly on her back as they turned toward the producer.

"We're going to pack up here, batch this for editing, and set up for the next shoot. We'll meet you at the house in about an hour." The crew were already half done with packing down and loading their gear back into the SUV.

Thank goodness. She needed the break to pull herself back together.

Adam clapped Caleb on the shoulder looking

the happiest Kat had ever seen him. "Turning up the heat level a notch or two isn't so bad, is it?" He grinned at Caleb. "Bet you're wondering why it took you so long. Feel free to keep turning that dial." With a wink he clapped Caleb's shoulder again and headed to the SUV.

Caleb and Kat watched in silence as the vehicle started, churning up a spray of dust as it chucked a U-turn in the paddock and disappeared.

"So." Caleb looked down at her, a question in his eyes.

Chemistry is not the same as compatibility. She tried to remind herself of reality while her traitorous body urged for her to curl her fingers into his T-shirt and go back to where they'd been a few minutes before. But with the cameras gone that created way more issues than a few moments of mind-blowing chemistry were worth. Kat stepped away. Just a couple of inches but enough that Caleb got the message.

"I should see to that fence." He tucked a piece of hair behind her ear.

Her lips tingled, indignant at being robbed of another spectacular kiss. "Can I help?"

"It's okay. I'll do it." The weathered voice came from behind them and they both leapt like they'd been caught doing something wildly inappropriate.

"Kat. Nice to see you again." Caleb's uncle gave her a nod from underneath his wide-brimmed weather-beaten hat as he approached. He'd aged since she'd last seen him. New crevices lining his tanned face and his snow-white eyebrows were fuller than some men's mustaches.

"Hi, Jared. You too." They both shifted on their feet. Should she hug him? Miss Manners hadn't exactly covered etiquette for situations like this. She looked at Caleb, but he was no help whatsoever. "So I'll . . . I'll let you guys finish the fence and meet you back at the cottage."

"Take the ute." Caleb held out the keys, but she brushed them away.

"No, thanks. The walk will do me good." She turned and looked down at her feet. Socks. No gumboots. Sigh. She trudged over to the tree and shoved her feet into the too-big boots.

One of the pigs looked up at her and she swore she could see laughter in its eyes. Brilliant. Even the Christmas ham knew she could be bested.

CHAPTER NINETEEN

Kat paced the floor of the cottage, phone pressed against her ear as she wrenched her mic pack off the back of her shorts. Stupid, uncomfortable piece of equipment.

The phone rang and rang as she fished the cord snaking up her torso out of her top.

C'mon, Paige, pick up. If she didn't, Kat would have to call England and wake up Allie in middle of the night. And angry pregnant women needed their sleep.

"Hey." Paige didn't bother to hide the surprise in her voice. "Is everything okay?"

"Do you have a few minutes?" Her cousin's work day was always frantic but she'd answered. Maybe she'd managed to catch Paige in a break.

"Give me two secs." Muffled murmurs followed, her cousin apparently unable to operate her mute function. The line cleared, and the sound of a door closing came through the phone. "Okay, I'm here. What's up?"

"You were right."

"I'm always glad to hear it but what exactly about?"

"I . . ." Kat tried to breathe. "This . . ." She couldn't even get a sentence out, struggling against the boulder of emotion sitting squarely on her chest.

"Take your time."

Kat dropped onto the couch, dropping her head into her hand.

"It's okay. Just breathe. In. Out. Just focus on that. In. Out."

Kat focused on her cousin's voice. On following her instructions. Her world narrowing down to that one task. Getting air in and out of her lungs.

What had this show done to her? She didn't panic. She didn't need to be coached to perform the most basic bodily function. Even on her worst days she'd never experienced the churning anxiety that raced through her veins as she walked back to the cottage.

She sucked in a breath, then let it out. Another. Another. Finally, her chest started to loosen.

"Better?"

Kat nodded, then remembered her cousin couldn't see her. "Yes. Thanks."

"Can you tell me what happened?"

"You're right. I'm never going to get over him here." What had ever made her think this could be a good idea? Six weeks. Six weeks of kissing Caleb. Of pretending to be his girlfriend. She'd been on another planet to hope this could ever end up in anything other than heartbreak.

Paige was silent for a few seconds. "Do you think there's a chance he might feel the same way?"

"Please don't try and feed me hope, Paige. I don't think I can bear it. He hasn't said anything to indicate he regrets breaking up with me."

"Don't get me wrong. I don't know why Caleb broke your heart, and I'm still pretty peeved about it, but whatever it is between you isn't finished. It's plastered across his face every time he looks at you on the show."

"Maybe not, but it will be finished in two months. It has to be." Even if the man could kiss in a way that made her forget all the reasons why she wasn't meant for his life.

"Why? I don't understand why."

"Physical attraction isn't the same as compatibility. We're not compatible. I've been here less than twenty-four hours and that much is already clear."

"What do you mean?"

"I was meant to feed the pigs, but I couldn't even do that. I spilled the feed, the pigs busted out of the pen, and I freaked out and climbed a tree." She was so unequipped for this life. She hadn't even made it through the first day without a disaster.

Paige tried to muffle her laugh but was

woefully unsuccessful. "Please tell me they got that on camera."

"Of course." Production was probably rushing through a highlights reel to feature at the end of tomorrow night's episode as they spoke. Kat sighed. "This is his life. I'm not cut out for this. I'm a city girl. I love crowds of people and busy streets and travel and new experiences." Her fingers gripped her phone as she held back the other reason. The one no one knew about. The one she could never ask Caleb to accept. Even if everything else could be worked through.

"You do remember we had this conversation months ago except it was about Josh and me, and you were the one being the voice of reason and sanity. Where has that Kat gone?"

Kat pulled open the pantry cupboards in search of comfort. The man had to have some chocolate in the house. Candy. Biscuits. Anything. "That was completely different. You and Josh have so many things in common. You were just too pigheaded to see it."

"You're afraid."

"Afraid? Of course I'm afraid. I'm in a fake relationship on a reality TV show with the only guy I've ever loved, the guy who broke my heart. And before this is all over he'll probably do it again. What's not to be afraid of?" The intensity of her words shocked Kat to her core. She wasn't usually this honest with her feelings, not even with Paige. Feelings, her father had long ago taught her, were fickle. Only the weak were controlled by their feelings.

"You're forgetting something."

"What?"

"God is bigger than your fear." Paige let her words fall into the space between them.

"Easy for you to say." Kat was trying to get the words back before she even heard them. "I'm sorry. That was unfair." And the last thing that her cousin deserved. Yes, her cousin was living the dream romance, but she deserved every piece of it. Had earned every moment of happiness.

"You think I'm not afraid? I'm afraid more than I want to admit. I'm afraid Josh is going to wake up and realize he could do so much better than a neurotic post-traumatic wreck. But I'm doing my best to trust in him, in us, and in God. I'm trying to ignore all the voices telling me this is too good to be true. Too good to last."

"But Josh has never broken your heart. Never said you aren't enough." Even now, so many years later, she could still close her eyes and see Caleb's blank distant expression. Hear his cold clipped words telling her he'd realized he didn't see a future together.

She hadn't been enough then and she was even less of a person now.

"Have you asked him about that?"

Kat let out a bitter laugh. "Why would I do

that? 'Hey, Caleb, what was it about me that wasn't good enough for you?' No, thank you."

"It's just . . . I know it's reality TV and edited and all that, but I can't reconcile the guy I see on my screen with what happened nine years ago. I can't believe there's not more to what happened than him suddenly deciding that you weren't right for him."

Kat bit her lip. Paige meant well but indulging in the dream that maybe there was more to the story of their breakup felt foolish. "He's had years to contact me if he had any regrets. I'm not exactly hard to find. Instead, he chose to go on a TV show to try to find someone new. Even if it was mostly for his mum. If he thought there was a chance he'd made a mistake, why wouldn't he have done something—anything—to reach me?"

"Have you ever Googled yourself? You're a big deal. Oscar winner. Friend to the stars. Romantically linked to a bunch of them."

"I've never dated an actor. Not once." Kat forced the words out through gritted teeth.

"I know that. Google? Not so much. If I wasn't your cousin I'd be intimidated by you. I mean, the guy broke up with you, and you went and conquered the world. You can't blame him for assuming you probably didn't even remember his name."

"He knows me better than that, Paige." She'd caused a scene when he'd broken up with her.

A sobbing, begging, shame-inducing scene. No woman ever forgot that.

I'm also just a girl standing in front of a boy asking him to love her. The memory of standing on her porch, hysterical and snot-faced, using Julia Roberts's famous line from *Notting Hill* was one she had tried to bury deep in her psyche. It was humiliating but true. That was how she'd felt with Caleb. And the answer had been a big fat resounding *No.*

And she'd vowed never to degrade herself like that in front of a man ever again. Never risk being the one in a relationship who loved him more than he loved her. Never allow someone to inflict that kind of pain on her.

She hadn't come all this way to let the same man do it to her twice.

CHAPTER TWENTY

"You own horses now?" Kat whispered the words to Caleb the next morning while assessing the two enormous mares tied to the fence railing. Behind them came the now-familiar sound of the crew setting up for filming.

"Nope." Caleb muttered the word out of the corner of his mouth as he leaned against the railing beside her. "But I guess my quad bike doesn't have the aura they're going for." His gaze lingered on her for a second. "You okay?"

"Yup. Fine. Why?" She'd had a terrible sleep but with the extra time she'd spent on her makeup this morning there was no way he'd be able to tell. "Paige says hi."

"Paige?" His brow rumpled.

"My cousin." Then she remembered he'd have no reason to remember that. He'd never even met any of her family. "I talked to her yesterday when you were fixing that fence."

"Where does Paige live?"

"In Sydney. We're roommates. For now."

"For now?"

"Well, she's from Chicago. Came over on a

237

work visa but fell in love with an Aussie. Sooner or later I'm going to lose her to immigration or marital bliss. Hopefully the second one."

"And what does Paige think of all of this?" Caleb shifted his body so that it turned toward her. She felt herself leaning closer to him, like he had his own gravitational pull, despite all the pep talks she'd given herself the previous afternoon while he worked with his uncle.

"Kat?"

Oh, she hadn't answered his question. "She says we're convincing."

"Must be the only thing I do on the show that is." Their eyes caught, and one side of his mouth tilted upward. She couldn't help but smile back.

Kat was saved from herself by Karissa.

"Here's the plan. You two are going to go for a romantic horse ride ending with an even more romantic picnic down by the river. Caleb, make sure you show Kat across your land. Woo her. Impress her." The producer looked down at the clipboard with the run sheet listing their rendezvous down to ten-minute blocks.

"I'm pretty sure she's already impressed." Caleb turned to Kat and raised an eyebrow. "Aren't you, baby?"

She bit back a snort of laughter. "So impressed." Kat pulled her hair up and tied it into a loose knot on the top of her head. If this was spring heat, summer was going to be brutal.

"Romance. Just remember there is no such thing as too much romance." Karissa scribbled across her clipboard.

Easy for her to say when she'd be traveling in an air-conditioned SUV while they rode under the blistering sun without so much as a breath of wind to take the edge off.

Even Caleb, presumably used to this heat, was pulling his T-shirt from his torso, the back already damp with sweat.

"Do you guys want to wear helmets?" Karissa checked off something else on her clipboard as Kat raised her arms so a sound tech could attach her mic pack to her waistband.

He shook his head. "Nah. We'll go slow so Kat has plenty of time to be impressed by the grandeur of my empire."

"Okay, we're good. Let's start filming." Just like that, the crew around them vanished and it was just the two of them.

"So? What are we doing?" Kat inserted a little verve into her line as she'd been given in the pre-brief.

She'd also been told to grip his strong manly farmer arm and act as if he'd just conjured up a trip to the moon, but that wasn't going to happen.

"I thought it would be fun to show you around the old-fashioned way. Have you ridden before?" Caleb said his lines with all the enthusiasm as if he'd told her they were taking a romantic trip to the dentist. Hopefully the crew would figure out scripts were never going to work if they wanted anything screenable. The man had horrible delivery.

"A few times." She was a good rider but might as well keep something in reserve for the cameras. And for him. The Kat he knew from ten years ago had never ridden a horse. He was probably expecting her to be reluctant and nervous.

They approached the two mares, who snorted as they got closer. "Let me give you a leg up." Kat put her booted foot into Caleb's threaded hands and boosted herself onto the horse.

Caleb landed on the top of his horse with a thump a few seconds later, and grabbed the horn of the saddle to stop himself tipping over the other side.

"Very graceful, farmer boy."

"That's farmer man to you." Caleb gathered his reins into one hand, and tipped his hat slightly forward. With a click of his tongue he turned the horse's head away from the fence then looked back to her. "You good?"

"Yup." Kat clicked her tongue and gave her horse a little kick. "Where are we heading?"

Caleb pointed to a stand of trees on the horizon. "Over there. But we'll take it as slow as you need. We're in no hurry."

How sweet. He thought they were going to take

a painfully slow walk there. Yeah, nah. "I think I'm good."

Kicking her horse again brought it into a trot, and she moved ahead of Caleb. She looked over at him and grinned. "Race you!"

"Wh—" His words were lost as she kicked the horse into a canter and pulled away. Her hair whipped around her face and her speed created a breeze where none had previously existed.

The SUV bumped over the uneven ground of the paddock to her right, a camera peering out the window. Good luck getting useable footage that way.

No doubt Karissa was also freaking out about the liability issues of not making them wear helmets.

A thumping sound came from beside her. Caleb was coming up on her right, leaning forward, one hand holding the reins, the other holding his hat onto his head.

She grinned at him and gave her mare, Starlight, another kick and leaned into the powerful rhythm of the horse.

Turning her attention forward, she left all the craziness in the dust and focused on the stand of trees that were maybe a kilometer away.

"C'mon, Starlight. Let's show them what we're made of." She glanced to her left but there was no sign of the camera crew. Unsurprising. Anything faster than twenty kilometers an hour over this terrain would have them bouncing into the ceiling.

The trees loomed closer. They were maybe another minute away. She glanced over her shoulder. Caleb was right behind her, leaning over the neck of his horse, hat gone and face set in concentration.

He'd never been the type to let her win because she was a woman. Or because he wanted to make her feel good. If she won, it would be because she'd earned it.

She smiled to herself. But he'd gripe for days about how it wasn't a fair race because she'd had the advantage of surprise and gained a head start.

The trees came ever closer. She was going to have to slow down in a few seconds. She wasn't an idiot. Trees meant roots and a change in terrain from the hard, dry ground she was galloping across. If she came off with no helmet on she'd likely break her neck. Tightening the reins, she slowed Starlight into a canter then into a trot.

Her eyes were gritty and dust and sweat clung to her like cling film, but she felt freer than since she first walked onto the set.

Caleb pulled his horse into a trot a few meters behind Kat, unable to believe what he'd seen.

Kat had just taken off. One second she was there, and the next she was racing across the field like she'd been born in the saddle.

She leaned forward, stroked the neck of her mare, spoke a few words to it, and sat up. For the first time in Caleb's life, he was jealous of a horse.

"Just a couple of times, huh?" Caleb steered his horse to pull up beside hers.

Kat grinned across at him. Her shirt stuck to her back and her face was flushed with heat and victory. She'd always had a competitive streak.

He reached into his saddle bag, pulled out a bottle of water and handed it to her, then pulled one out for himself. He knocked back most of the bottle and splashed the rest over his face.

"That's all you have to say? No complaining about my head start or taking you by surprise?"

Caleb glanced back. The SUV with the crew bumped over the uneven ground, still a few hundred meters back. It would probably take them another couple of minutes to catch up.

He glanced down at the camera on his saddle. It was only good for footage if he was on the horse. He dismounted then lifted his hand to Kat. She stood tall in her stirrups, brought her leg over, and he grasped her waist and lowered her to the ground.

"Where on earth did you learn to ride like that?" Caleb's breath stirred the hair on the back of her neck.

Kat shrugged as she turned, an impish smile on her face. "Oh, you know. Places."

"That's all you're going to give me? Places?"

Kat took another swig of her water. "Fine. I learned on the set of *The Hobbit*. One of the stuntmen taught me."

Her casual words cut through him. While he'd been here, filling all the hours that God gave to keep his mind off Kat, she'd been on the set of *The Hobbit* learning how to ride like a rodeo girl. That stuntman would've pulled out all the stops to impress her. His gut twisted. How could he even begin to compete?

The crew had arrived. One of the cameramen practically tumbled out the car door in his haste to get them back on camera.

"Boyfriend?" He tried to keep his voice neutral.

Kat raised her eyebrows. "I don't date colleagues."

"Their loss." He tried to inject some levity into his tone, aware of the camera now capturing everything.

Kat didn't say anything, but her empty water bottle crumbled between her fingers with a crunching sound. "Maybe." Her words gave him the benefit of the doubt, but her eyes called him a liar.

This was the part where, if this was real, he'd utter some charming words and seal it with a kiss. But this wasn't real, and he—or the him of ten years ago—was the reason she was currently throttling a piece of plastic. A kiss wasn't happening. No matter what Karissa had scheduled on her piece of paper.

"Where to now?" Kat stepped back, tucking a piece of wayward hair behind her ear.

Caleb stepped back, giving her some space. He shoved his empty water bottle into his back pocket and gestured toward the trees. "We'll cut through here. Head down to the river." River might be a generous term. It depended on how much rain there'd been in his absence.

"Okay." Kat tucked her mangled bottle back into her saddlebag and turned back to him, conjuring a smile that didn't make it from her cheeks to her eyes. "Lead on."

He grabbed her hand, ignoring the two cameras circling them, and tugged her toward the shade. As soon as they reached it, the temperature dropped a couple of degrees, his eyesight taking a couple of seconds to adjust to the changing light.

Kat skipped over a fallen log. "Is this all yours?"

"Yes. Down to the river. That's the border between our farm and the McCafferty's. At least on this side." He tightened his grip on her hand as she clambered over another fallen tree trunk.

"Have you ever thought about doing something else? Other than being a farmer, I mean?"

"Not really. This is in my blood. And not just because it's the family business. The hours are antisocial and the work is hard and having your livelihood at the mercy of the elements isn't an easy ride but . . ." He didn't know how to describe his connection to the land they'd just ridden over, the land they were walking on.

"But?" Kat turned and looked at him.

"I can't imagine any other job giving me this level of satisfaction. I can't imagine any other job I'd want to commit my life to the way I commit to what's here. It might sound crazy but there's something about knowing this is mine. That everything I'm putting into this isn't for some faceless corporation but for my family. For my future children." He grabbed a tree branch to pull it out of Kat's way. "I want them to have the childhood I had. Roaming the farm. Learning to swim in our river. Appreciating where their food comes from and how hard people work to produce it." Except his children would have a father. His children's memories would include him in all those things.

"They'll have a wonderful life." The wistful way Kat said it had him reaching down and taking her hand. She was an only child as well. She got it. The dream of a big family and lots of voices. They'd talked about it a lot. He looked down at her just as she brushed her hand across one eye.

"You okay?"

"Just a piece of dirt." But her voice caught as

she said it. Could she see his dream as vividly as he could? Their children racing down to splash in the water. Blond hair glinting in the sun. Laughter trailing behind them. He would give anything to secure that future.

A couple of meters away from her one of the cameramen stumbled and muttered a curse, ruining the moment.

A checked blanket and a picnic hamper awaited them down by the water. A bottle of bubbles and two champagne glasses stood beside the basket.

"Just a little something you prepared earlier?" Kat grinned up at him.

"Something like that."

He led her down to the blanket, and they both settled on the ground. Jeepers. Caleb shifted on the blanket, trying to find a comfortable spot, but rocks jutted through the thin covering. Kat wiggled next to him.

"Should we move it?"

"No!" Adam barked the order from behind them. "No moving allowed. It's been set up there because it gives us the best framing for the shot."

"Well, that's fine." Caleb stood, grabbed the bottle and glasses, and held out his hand to Kat. "We'll move. We wouldn't want to ruin your perfect shot."

He found a less rocky spot on the bank, settled onto the grass, and Kat sat beside him. Popping the cork off the bottle, he poured the bubbly into the two glasses, handed one to her, and tipped his glass in her direction. "To the winner of the race. Even if you did cheat. A little."

Kat grinned as she tapped her glass to his. "I was wondering how long it would take you to bring that up again. If it's bugging you, we can have a rematch on the way home."

Something in his heart shifted at her use of the way home. He gulped. "Honestly, I'm not sure if my farmerly pride could take being beaten by a city girl in a horse race again."

He took a sip of the bubbly and winced. Definitely not his thing. Placing it on the grass beside him, he propped his heels into the bank and loosely draped his arms over his knees.

Kat took a sip of her drink, her legs crossed in front of her. "So . . ." She looked sideways at him.

Uh-oh. That kind of opening always meant something awkward was coming. "So."

"Tell me about Emma."

"Um . . ." Caleb twisted toward Kat, ignoring the cameraman inching his way in front of them. "What would you like to know?"

Kat shrugged. "How did you meet? How long did you date? What happened?"

"We met through her brother. Conrad was my best friend."

"Was?"

Caleb shifted, looked down at her. "Things tend to get a bit complicated when your ex-fiancée is also your best friend's sister. It's not his fault. Blood over water and all that."

Complicated didn't even begin to cover it. Toowoomba wasn't a big city to begin with. It was even smaller when you moved in church circles. Emma came from a big family, which meant half of his old social circle were related to her by blood or marriage. Even the ones who did their best to keep a foot on either side of the divide didn't know how to navigate the rocky terrain.

"I'm sorry. That can't have been easy."

"No, it wasn't." Caleb stared across the water to the neighbor's farm. A fence post needed mending. He should let Stuart know.

The cameraman crossed his field of vision. For a second, he'd forgotten they were even there. The sun beat down on his uncovered head. Man, he hoped he found his hat on the way back. It was one of his favorites.

"What about you? What happened with the last guy you dated?" He felt an irrational streak of jealousy as he asked the question.

Kat picked up her drink and took another sip. "Dan. We were together for four years, but he worked on an oil rig six weeks on, six weeks off. With the travel required for my job, we spent maybe a quarter of those four years actually in the same city. Maybe less. It was good but it wasn't enough."

"Was that why you broke up?"

"Sort of. It became obvious we didn't miss each other enough. I just . . ." She gazed into the distance. "Whoever I end up with for the rest of my life, I want distance to be unbearable. I want to feel like part of me is missing when one of us is away. That's how I'll know it's real."

"And it didn't feel like that with Dan?"

"With Dan, it was always nice when he was back but once he was gone . . ." She shrugged. "I carried on with my life. It was mutual. We both realized the other person wasn't the one we felt compelled to make big sacrifices for to be together. Three months after we broke up he got engaged to some Norwegian fitness blogger, so there's that."

Kat couldn't hide the flicker of hurt that traveled across her face. Or the way she drained half her glass of bubbly in one long draw.

If he knew Kat, and maybe he didn't anymore, there was more to the neatly packaged mutual break-up than she was telling. But he was a patient man. He could wait. And he certainly wasn't going to probe into whatever created that tender spot while cameras circled like vultures.

"How long ago did you break up?"

She put her glass down. "Just over a year ago." She glanced at him. "I'm completely over him, for the record. Don't get me wrong. The whole getting-engaged-three-months-later thing was a bit of a kick to the ego, but I don't wish it was me. In fact, I'm thrilled it's not."

"Me too." He nudged her knee with his leg and managed to get a smile out of her.

Leaning back, he propped his elbows on the ground and stretched out his legs. A fly buzzed by and as he swatted it he caught sight of a couple of assistant producers hovering nearby. One of them caught his eye and mouthed *kiss her.*

Kat leaned back, then rolled over so she was lying on her stomach, propped on her elbows and facing him. She shielded her face from the sun with one hand. He hated the rule about no sunglasses when it was him being blinded, but it was a definite benefit when it came reading her moods and thoughts.

"How's your mum doing?"

"She's . . ." There were no words to describe witnessing someone he loved mentally unravel in front of him. "We're doing the best we can, I guess. Some days are better than others. Her lucid times are rapidly diminishing." He plucked some grass, rolled the strands between his fingers. "There's been a big difference even in the last month."

"Do you regret leaving? Doing the show?" Kat leaned forward, her shoulder nudging his ribs, her long hair grazing along his arm.

251

"I guess it weighs on me. Not knowing the conversations we would have had. The things she would have told me if I'd been here. The missed moments I'll never have a chance to get back."

Kat smoothed the front of his T-shirt with the palm of her hand and his stomach clenched. "But she wanted you to go." Her pointer finger started tracing idle patterns along the cotton. He didn't know if she realized she was doing it, but every cell in his body did.

"She did. Practically kicked me out of my own house."

She smiled but her eyes were still troubled.

"And no." Caleb lifted his head up and let his gaze roam her dusty face. "To answer your question, I'm not sorry I did the show."

Feet shuffled behind Kat, but he ignored them. Tried to pretend it was just the two of them.

He captured her wandering hand, winding his fingers through hers before he lost the ability to think.

"Do I miss the time I could have had with Mum? Of course. But it also means I'm here with you now, and I would do it all over again for that. I promise."

He could tell by the guarded look in her eyes that she thought he was bringing it for the cameras, fulfilling the requirement for romance, but he wasn't. He wasn't that good an actor. And he felt things for this woman he couldn't even begin to hide.

He lifted her hand and kissed her knuckles, allowing his breath to whisper across his skin. "I'm glad you're here, Kat. I wouldn't have wanted it to be anyone but you."

It was the perfect moment to kiss her, but he held back. She'd probably let him steal as many kisses as he wanted when the cameras were around. But he wanted more than that. Even if this wasn't real. Even if it would all disappear like dandelion fluff in a few short weeks. He wanted some of the moments to be instigated by her.

Which was probably about as likely to happen as his mother's disintegrating neurons knitting themselves back together.

So he was wretched but not surprised when she squeezed his hand and pulled away.

CHAPTER TWENTY-ONE

A photoshoot. Followed by a cozy couple interview with the women's magazine of choice. That was how they were going to spend their third day.

Of course.

Kat smoothed her palms down the cream dress she'd been provided. A cream slip with a lace overlay and a pink ribbon around the middle. It was completely adorable.

For a four-year-old.

In what world had a stylist thought it was a good look for someone who was thirty-four? She didn't want to know. *Pick your battles, Kat. Pick your battles.*

At least they'd let her do her own hair and makeup.

Her hands shook as she pinned back the end of the half-braid that she'd woven along her hairline and down one side. Then unpinned it again and letting it hang loose. Second-guessing her every decision.

Reality had slammed into her right about the moment Caleb had picked her wandering hand from his torso and she'd realized she'd been absentmindedly manhandling him like they were a real couple.

A fact she'd had more than ample hours to reflect on during her second afternoon and evening spent solo, while he finished some farm work and helped his uncle with his mum.

She pulled in a breath, her fingers gripping the door handle of the car.

The latest episode of the show would air tonight. Then they would be plastered from one end of Australia to the other as a couple on the cover of one of the most widely read women's magazines. Nowhere to hide. No other women in play. Just the two of them and thousands of eyes watching their every edited move. The SUV pulled into one of the fields, wheels bumping along the uneven ground until it pulled to a stop in front of a familiar dark-haired woman with a canvas camera bag slung over one shoulder and a Nikon hanging around her neck. Bee.

Kat had done makeup on a couple of her shoots before. Bee was one of the best when it came to the kind of natural feel-good shots brands paid big money for.

Kat slipped out of the car, the impractical wedge heels she'd been given sinking into the grass. A woman she didn't recognize waited just outside the SUV.

"Hi." She shut the car door behind her. Caleb was nowhere to be seen.

"Hi, Kat. I'm Camille, VP of publicity at SBC. I'm going to be overseeing the shoot and interview today." Camille, one hundred percent Sydney—or maybe Melbourne—from the tips of her caramel-colored hair extensions to her Kate Spade boots, flashed a smile that didn't quite reach her eyes.

Wow. They'd pulled out the big guns for today. Whether that was good or bad remained to be seen.

"This is Belinda, your photographer." Camille gestured to Bee as she approached.

"We've met." Bee smiled as she passed her camera bag over to the assistant trailing behind her. "Good to see you, Kat. Though I have to say I never would've picked the occasion."

"That makes two of us."

"And this is Lauren with *Aus Weekly*." Camille gestured to a blonde curvy woman who Kat hadn't noticed.

Lauren nodded with a friendly smile. "I'm so glad it's you. Even if Caleb hadn't cut the whole process short, Australia would have voted the same way."

"Thank you. It's a bit overwhelming." At least that much was true.

"That must be Caleb." Camille nodded to where his truck was turning off the road. "Great."

The white farm vehicle pulled in behind the SUV and Caleb cut the engine, opening the door almost simultaneously. He jumped out of the cab, swung the door shut, and strode toward them.

Kat couldn't stop the grin that climbed up her face. Looked like she wasn't the only one who hadn't gotten to choose her outfit.

Brown corduroy trousers, oatmeal-colored shirt, beige suspenders. All he needed was a corn stalk between his teeth and he'd be a cliché straight out of Hollywood central casting. His scowl said he knew it.

She walked to meet him, her wedges wobbling on the uneven ground. He covered the last few feet to her in long strides, catching her under her elbows before she could stumble.

"Nice dress." His words brushed her ear.

Reaching out she plucked on one of the elastic bands traveling from the waist of his pants over his shoulders. "I could say the same about the suspenders."

They weren't miked up, thank goodness, but no doubt there were still cameras catching their every move for some "behind the scenes" footage.

His hand closed over hers. "After this is done we are never ever going to talk about me and this *Beverly Hillbillies* getup ever again."

"Deal. As long as it includes the *Mary Poppins* dress."

"I happen to be a fan of the dress." He tugged

her a little closer and she stumbled onto his toes. "Though I hope they're not expecting you to cover much ground in those shoes."

Kat looked down to where his hand covered hers, and her breath caught at the brown woven bracelet encircling his wrist.

He looked down. "Recognize it? It's my contribution of style to this terrible outfit. Well, yours I guess. As always."

Her thumb ran over the woven cotton, her mind spooling as many threads as the bracelet. "But . . ." She struggled for words. None came. Why did he still have it?

"I'm sorry," Caleb murmured into her ear. "I shouldn't have worn it. I didn't think it through."

Kat forced herself to breathe, to look up to where he was studying her with concern. It was a bracelet. It wasn't like the guy had shown up blaring the mix CD she'd made when they were dating, complete with a mortifying number of songs from the *Dawson's Creek* soundtrack.

A wrist band. It was just a wrist band. One with no particular meaning or linked to any particular occasion. Just one item in a huge number of items that could be tagged to their time together. The guy hated shopping so much he probably still wore the clothes she'd bought him—if they hadn't fallen apart.

She had to stop reading meaning into things when there clearly was no meaning. Otherwise she'd be mainlining Prozac before the week was through. "No, it's fine. I'm sorry. It just took me by surprise."

His hand reached out and brushed a lock of hair back from her cheek. "You sure?"

She forced a carefree smile. "I'm sure."

"That's perfect! Just hold that for a few more seconds." Bee's words were accompanied by a whirr of clicks.

Kat glanced over to find Bee crouched on her haunches, camera lens pointed up at them. "Eyes on Caleb, Kat."

"Yeah, eyes on Caleb, Kat." He threw her a mischievous grin while twirling a strand of her hair around his finger. His other hand splayed across the small of her back, her traitorous spine wilting in the warmth.

"You think you're so funny." She murmured the words while switching her gaze to a spot in the middle of his nose.

"A man has to find humor in something when he's about to be on the cover of some women's tabloid trussed up like an Austrian yodeler."

"Great. Now Caleb, I want you to pick her up and spin her around like when she first arrived at the farm."

Kat wound her hands around his neck, and his arms went around her lower back. He lifted her, and she dangled in midair.

There was no magic. Awkward silence ensued

as they stared at each other. The only sound was Bee's camera clicking away. Even the birds had quit chirping, as if they'd voted to boycott the whole charade.

"How was last night?" Kat was all too aware of the way his body was taking the full weight of hers. Better to make fake conversation than dwell on that.

"Not so good." Caleb's brow wrinkled and jaw tensed.

Kat averted her eyes over his shoulder, focusing on the waving grass, the trees in the distance, anything other than Caleb's arms around her. "Is there anything I can do to help?"

"Can you turn back time?" Caleb murmured the words as Bee stopped taking photos and walked toward them. The pain in his voice pinned her heart against his ribs.

"Okay, let's try something else."

Caleb had Kat back on the ground before Bee had even finished her sentence.

Bee exchanged one camera for another. "Okay, Kat. I want you to hold Caleb's hand then walk away, glancing back over your shoulder. Caleb, you follow her."

Just do it, Kat. The sooner they get their photos, the sooner this will be over. Caleb's fingers wound loosely around her left hand and Kat started walking, allowing their arms to stretch out between them.

"Good. Now look back," Bee shouted.

Kat twisted her head to look back, her gaze catching Caleb's.

The whole thing felt wrong. She moved with all the grace of a marionette, her uncooperative limbs heavy and sluggish. Where should she look? How should she look? What expression should she portray?

What was the appropriate look for pretending to be in love with the guy she'd never gotten over?

"You know," he raised an eyebrow. "You could look a little more thrilled at field walking with a hot Austrian yodeler."

Focus. Just keep it superficial. "I'm sorry. I think I'm overwhelmed in the presence of such great suspenders." She forced some levity into her tone and tried not to notice how the early morning sun emphasized the natural highlights in his hair, the curve of his jaw, the flecks in his eyes.

Caleb lifted his eyebrows at her. "Oh, don't go mocking the suspenders, Julie Andrews." He gave her arm a strong tug and she was flying back toward him, stumbling over the uneven ground before landing against his torso.

Kat looked up from where she was now anchored against his chest. "Who knew yodelers had such smooth moves."

"Better than farmers, that's for sure." Caleb's

261

arm draped around her back, keeping her close.

"Oh, I don't know about that. I once knew a farmer with some pretty good moves." The words were meant to be teasing but they turned into something more when their faces were all of inches apart.

Then his hands were cradling her face and his lips were on hers. All the awkwardness disappeared as she leaned into his kiss, her hands gripping the front of his shirt like it could somehow magically block out everyone and everything else around them.

It's just pretend. This isn't real. Kat tried to remind herself as her body melted against Caleb's, his rough thumbs feathering along her jawline, his fingers weaving into her hair.

Except there was nothing that felt pretend about this.

Caleb broke off the kiss, pulling back. "Well, hopefully that gave them what they needed."

Kat reeled back, forcing her fingers to let go of the front of his shirt. Her diaphragm expanded and contracted more fully as she forced her lungs to take in air.

"Sorry about the lack of warning." Caleb ran his hand over his head. "Figured they would require a kissing shot and it was better to just get it over and done with before we could overthink it."

Better to get it over and done with. If there had

been any air left in her lungs that would have stolen it.

"Good thinking." She couldn't be mad at him. It was typical pragmatic Caleb thinking. They'd want a kiss. Might as well just take her by surprise before they had to stage one and it got awkward.

"Did you get some good shots?" Caleb directed the question to where Bee had her head tilted downward, staring at the screen of her camera.

She popped her face back up with a grin. "So many. You two are naturals." She walked toward them, her boots making much better work of the terrain than Kat's sandals. "Have a look." She offered Caleb her camera. "Just hit the right arrow to scroll through."

Caleb took the camera and Kat leaned in to see the screen. The first set were of him lifting her up and looked as awkward as they'd felt, all tight faces and rigid bodies. Caleb scrolled through at them with only enough time for a glance at each one.

Then of them walking, frame by frame of her turning, turning, turning. Just photos of two people walking and turning. Some blurry. Nothing even halfway magazine worthy.

Caleb paused on the next one.

Oh, Lord.

She'd completed the turn and their gazes had connected.

Caleb staring at her, expression indecipherable.

But every woman in the country would be able to see the longing in her eyes.

She couldn't save herself if she tried.

CHAPTER TWENTY-TWO

D o you think that went okay?" Two hours later, Caleb leaned back on his couch, propped his arm up along the back.

"Seemed to. Bee looked happy enough." Kat had taken off her tottering heels and rested her bare feet on his coffee table. She was scribbling something on a piece of paper.

"Here." She ripped the page out of her notebook and held the paper toward him. He reached for it. A line of numbers was written across the page in black in her precise handwriting.

"What's this?"

She closed her notebook with a thud. "My bank account number. If you don't mind making the first payment by the end of the week that would be great. Sydney rent and all that."

He stared at the stark reminder of their agreement. Tried to smother the despondent thud of his heart against his rib cage. This was a business arrangement. Nothing more. No matter what story the photos told.

"Thanks. I'll sort it out tonight." He pulled his wallet out of his pocket, and tucked the paper inside as someone knocked on the door.

Kat rose from her chair and padded to the door, opening it and stepping back to usher in the next reporter in the long line they'd welcomed today.

"Hi, Lauren. Would you like a drink of anything? Coffee, juice, tea? I have to warn you there's no herbal in the house."

"A water would be great. Thanks. Camille said to tell you we can start without her. She has to make a few calls." The reporter crossed the room and settled herself into the chair where Kat had been sitting, placing her iPhone on the coffee table and tapped the screen a couple of times. "I'm recording the whole thing anyway, so she'll receive a transcript of what we cover before she gets here."

"All good." Kat poured two glasses of water in the kitchen then returned to the living room, placing one in front of Lauren and the second in front of Caleb.

Sitting down on the couch beside him, Kat curled her legs underneath her and tucked herself into his side as if that was exactly where she'd been before answering the door.

If it wasn't for the bank account number burning a hole in his wallet he'd almost believe it.

Lauren surveyed them with a benevolent smile. "This shouldn't take too long. I've jotted down a few observations and notes from the shoot, so now I just need some quotes to fill in the article."

"Sounds good," Kat said.

"Kat, let's start with you. Did you know going into the vote that you were the only woman Caleb had kissed?"

"No. It was an open secret in the house he hadn't kissed anyone before we went to New Zealand, but I didn't know what had happened with any of the other women that week. Obviously, you always hope you're the only one but . . ." Kat trailed off and bit her bottom lip. "I've seen enough of these shows to know everyone thinks their connection is special."

The woman had spent her life on the wrong side of the camera.

"Caleb, talk to me about that kiss in the cave. It looked magical, especially knowing you hadn't kissed anyone else. Was it your plan when you kissed her for that to be a signal to viewers she was the one you wanted them to vote for?"

"No. There was no secret strategy at play. The truth is that in that moment all I was thinking about was kissing Kat. Not about the cameras. Not about the show. Not about the other women. None of it."

Lauren gave a small sigh. "Great answer. Tell me about the moment when Gemma was announced as the first one through the voting round. When you decided to throw the show into turmoil and choose Kat then and there. What were you thinking?"

"Mostly that it wasn't fair to the other women to keep going. Not when I knew Kat was the only woman that I wanted at the end."

"That sounds like a very clear-cut decision."

Caleb looked down at the top of Kat's head. "It was the easiest decision I've made during the whole show."

"And what about you, Kat? What were you thinking when Caleb said it was you or no one?"

Kat shifted beside him on the couch. "Shock. Surprise. Disbelief. It was so surreal."

"Is that why it took you a couple of days to decide to come here?"

"Yes." Kat's eyes turned to him. "I wanted to be sure."

"And you, Caleb? What were those two days like? Returning home from New Zealand yet not knowing if she would come?"

"Pretty stressful." Especially when SBC had provided him with a revised figure of what his little stunt was going to cost him if Kat said no. "I knew there was a chance she may not come, not with the way I'd cut the process short by a couple of weeks."

"And when you saw Kat get out of the car? I've seen the footage. Your face when she got out of the car will have most of the country naming your children when it airs tonight."

Kat tensed, and he moved his arm off the back of the couch to tuck it around her shoulder. "I couldn't have been happier."

"There are some who are saying the other girls never got a look-in. That it was clear you and Kat had chemistry no one else had from that first night. What do you say to that?"

"Kat stood out from the beginning. It would be dishonest of me to pretend otherwise."

"And what about you, Kat? Was there magic there from that first night?"

There was a pause. "I wouldn't have stayed if there hadn't been something."

"Are you in love?" Lauren leaned forward as she looked between the two of them.

Unfortunately. Irrecoverably.

Caleb huffed. He didn't like lying. There were enough lies by omission in this setup without adding more.

Kat let out a laugh. "I think it's important to remember the show was truncated to get Caleb back home sooner. It's only been a few weeks since that first night. I guess that's what the next couple of months is about. To see what happens."

"You're a city girl, Kat. Can you see yourself living here long term? In the middle of nowhere? A forty-minute drive to the nearest beautician and hairdresser?"

Caleb bristled at the implication. Kat reached up and squeezed his hand. "I guess it's lucky for me that I'm my own beautician, and I'm pretty sure Caleb hasn't paid for a haircut in years."

"Forty minutes isn't exactly far," Caleb said. "Most people in Sydney spend longer commuting every day. I'll take my open road and beautiful countryside any day."

Kat grinned up at him. "Defensive much?"

He dropped a quick kiss on her smiling lips before he'd even realized what he was doing. Kat's fingers twisted around his, her thumb running across his wrist band.

"Well, you clearly have chemistry. There's no doubt about that." Lauren's observation broke the moment and Caleb reluctantly returned his gaze to the reporter.

Kat shifted again, this time moving away from him. The movement was so slight that Lauren wouldn't notice, but it felt like a chasm had just opened up between them even though their hands were still entwined. "Well, a relationship takes a whole lot more than great chemistry."

The front door opened. Camille stepped into the cottage, heels clicking on the wooden floor, phone to her ear. "Okay, anything else? Great. I'll call you around two."

She lowered her phone, and glanced at the three of them. "Sorry for being late. Crazy day. I may need to duck out again. How's everything going?"

Lauren looked down at her notebook. "Good.

I think we're almost done. I just have a couple more questions."

"Great. I'll just clear some emails while you finish up." Camille pulled out a chair from the dining table and sat, turning her gaze back to her phone.

"Kat, you're an internationally renowned makeup artist. You work on huge movies with some of the biggest stars in the world. Why did you audition for the show?"

"I didn't."

Camille's head jerked up from her phone, her eyes narrow.

"You didn't what?"

"Audition."

Caleb tightened his grip on Kat's hand. Whatever she was about to say, he would have her back. No matter what.

Lauren raised her eyebrows.

"Okay, Bee has just sent through some sample photos from the shoot." Camille stood. "We should review them now, given your designers are holding the cover for them."

Lauren looked between Camille and Kat, clearly torn between not wanting to anger the hand feeding her and knowing there was more to the story than she'd been told.

Kat made the decision for her. "I didn't audition." She sat up straighter, pulling right away from Caleb. "I was meant to be the makeup artist for the show, but the night it was due to start shooting some of the women who had been cast got sick. I was asked to stand in for the first episode. I was supposed to be eliminated that first night."

Going by Camille's glare, she'd eliminate Kat from the planet given half the chance.

"So what happened?"

"Alright, I think we're done here. Lauren, a word?" Camille grasped her phone in a death grip.

"Relax, Camille. What are you worried about? It's a great story. Very Cinderella-esque. The woman who was supposed to spend the series on the sidelines is thrust into the spotlight and on a path to love. The readers will devour this. Why on earth did you want to cover it up?"

Camille considered the words for a few seconds. "Okay, fine. As long as that's how you spin it."

"I'm hardly going to risk losing our exclusive deal, am I?"

Camille sat in the chair next to Lauren, her fingers tapping on its arm. "Just a couple more questions."

Lauren nodded at her then focused once more on Kat. "So what happened? Why weren't you eliminated?"

Kat and Caleb exchanged a quick glance.

"The farmer was Caleb." Her simple words

only hinted at the complexity beneath the statement.

Lauren turned her probing gaze to him. "You knew she hadn't signed on for the show? That she wasn't one of the women competing for you?"

"Not at first. I was told during the course of the night that Kat was a stand-in, and I was supposed to eliminate her at the end of the night."

"And why didn't you?"

"I wanted her to stay." His heart swelled as he looked at Kat. What would he have done if she hadn't been there?

"So . . ." Lauren's gaze bounced between him and Kat. "In the first episode there's no footage of you and Caleb talking beyond your initial meeting until the elimination ceremony. Did you have a conversation, or did everything change from that first meeting?"

"We had a brief conversation. It wasn't filmed because my substitution was last minute and I hadn't signed the paperwork needed to allow the crew to film it." Kat sounded remarkably calm while Caleb's insides were twisting like an angry snake.

"Are you still on the staff? Of the show?"

Camille rose from her seat, her right eye twitching. "Okay, time's up. I said a couple more questions and we're past that."

"If you're trying to infer I'm in this for financial gain, you couldn't be more wrong." Kat shifted

273

and leaned forward in her seat. "I took this job as a favor for a friend. I would be financially better off if I were anywhere else right now, on any of the numerous other contracts that I could have accepted. I—"

"Okay, we're done." Camille had shifted closer to the couch while Kat answered Lauren's last question and now stood in between the three of them.

Something niggled at Caleb but he couldn't work out what.

Lauren stood. "It was lovely to meet you both. I'll see you in a few weeks for our next interview."

Camille showed Lauren to the door, casting an epic evil eye over her shoulder at Kat. "We need to choose the photos from the shoot, but I'll be back in a few hours to debrief."

As the door closed behind them he realized what was niggling him. Kat had never actually answered the last question.

There were only so many lies, half-truths, and omissions Kat could manage, and she'd reached her limit today. Relief at discarding one of them coursed through her, although the way Caleb sat at his end of the couch, almost unnaturally still, was dampening that relief.

He could have been a statue if not for the occasional blink and the rise and fall of his chest.

"What time are the cameras coming back for more filming?" He didn't answer, so she levered herself off the couch to review the run sheet on the table.

Midday. She checked the clock. Just past eleven. Time to get changed out of this Pollyanna dress and catch up on a few messages and emails.

"I'm going to get changed."

Caleb still didn't say anything. Was he mad she'd told the journalist she hadn't auditioned for the show? Had his male ego taken a blow knowing in a few days all of Australia would learn she hadn't been one of the women vying for his affections?

Well, he wasn't the only one in a difficult position. If that was the problem, he could just get over it.

She turned to head to her room. His room. The bedroom.

"So." The quiet calm in his voice raised the hairs on her neck. She turned around. "They're paying you *and* I'm paying you."

Oh. That was the problem.

"I never asked you to pay me, Caleb. If you recall, you insisted." Kat strode over to where he sat, her remaining patience for machismo evaporating. Soon the cameras would invade their space once more, and she and Caleb would have to play happy couples again. Might as well get this sorted out now.

His fingers folded over his palms and his shoulders bunched up. "Except you never mentioned you were on SBC's payroll as well. You didn't think that maybe you should disclose that?"

Something ugly surged within her. She had been financially independent for fifteen years. She didn't need Caleb Murphy and his macho provider instinct thinking he had any say. "And why do you think any of this is any of your business? I also earn some money from my YouTube channel. Should I have declared that as well?"

Caleb opened his mouth, but she wasn't done yet.

"This is a business arrangement. That is what you have asked of me, isn't it? That I put my entire life on hold to come here and parade myself in front of the whole country to head off the risk of SBC suing you. You don't own me. My other income streams are *my* private matter, so don't you sit there like some petulant child offended I'm not dependent on your money."

Caleb stood and scrubbed his hand across his head. "You're right. I'm sorry. I guess sometimes I forget. That it's just business, that is."

Kat stared at him. What did that mean?

Caleb puffed out a breath. "I'm not built for this. Spending half our time pretending we're something we're not. Trying to remind myself it's just make believe. That you'll be gone again in a couple of months."

Unless you ask me to stay. The thought ricocheted through Kat's mind, but she shoved it back. She liked her life. She liked traveling and working in a different location every month. Just the thought of staying here, in the middle of nowhere, made her hands itch to grab her battered passport and jump on the next plane.

Caleb'd had every opportunity to ask her to stay nine years ago. When life had swung out like an endless horizon in front of them and everything was a lot less broken. He hadn't. Instead, he'd forced her to go. Told her they had no future.

If he'd thought they didn't have a future then, they certainly didn't have one now.

She steeled herself. Whatever happened here, shattering her heart into pieces wasn't one of the options. "You don't get to talk to me about money ever again. I chose to be here, and I own that. It was my choice. But you don't get to pretend a few grand covers what this is costing me."

Caleb open his mouth, but she put her hand up. And he had the good sense to close it.

"I'm going to spend the next however many years of my life as the woman from that reality-show couple whose relationship didn't last. For the rest of my life, whenever people Google my name, the gossip from this show will come up first along with a bunch of slurs about me choosing my career over love. That's what people are going to think they know about me. Not my business. Not the ten years I've spent building my career. But some stupid C-grade reality show where I skipped through the fields in a flower girl's dress holding your hand. Don't you dare stand here thinking you have the monopoly on this being hard."

Her voice shook. She hated that. Hated anything that undid her in front of this man who managed to do it so utterly with as little as a glance.

"Kat, I didn't—" Caleb reached out his hand. If she let him touch her she would be undone.

She stepped back out of his range. "Let me know when the crew are here." And she forced herself to walk away without a backward glance.

CHAPTER TWENTY-THREE

"Want to have dinner at the big house tonight?" Late the next afternoon Caleb hooked his arm around Kat's waist and settled her in close as a camera stared at her over his shoulder.

The day had passed in a blur of publicity meetings taking them through the media and viewer responses to the reveal of Kat as the "winner" the night before.

"Hey, you." Caleb palmed the small of her back. "Did you hear me? Dinner? With Mum and my uncle?"

"Will that be okay? I don't want to upset her again." She had tried not to dwell on how much it had hurt that Marion remembered Emma but not her, but she wasn't keen on a repeat performance.

"Honestly, I don't know." Caleb ran his hand through his hair. "But if you're going to be here for weeks it doesn't seem right for you to be secluded out here in the cottage."

"You don't have to have dinner with me. I get that you want to spend as much time with your mum as possible. I'm happy pottering around here by myself." Dealing smack to some social media trolls would improve her mood. Maybe she could set up a fake account and have some real fun.

Besides, she wanted to give Caleb an out. There'd been a weird vibe between them since their fight about the money. She wanted to tell him exactly where he could put it, except she needed it. She had to clear the bills still hanging over her head.

"Why don't we see how tonight goes and take it from there?" He leaned forward. "Besides, my mother is off limits, so we get to be off camera. That is, if you don't mind being chaperoned by a grumpy retiree and a confused old lady."

Kat glanced at the two cameras filming their every word. They'd already started fading into the background. Which made things dangerous. Made her more likely to say things that wouldn't be wise. Think this was real rather than make believe.

"Hey." Caleb's voice rumbled up from his chest. "No pressure. I totally understand if you'd rather give it more time."

"No. Your family is important to you. I want to spend time with them." Which was true in a flagellating-sucker-for-punishment kind of way.

"Good. Because I want them to spend time with you as well. I want Mum to know what an incredible woman I've brought home." Caleb pulled her into him and dropped his lips to hers. She could already hear the swoons of thousands of Australian women watching this in the next episode.

She pressed her lips to his. Her body melted into Caleb of its own volition, her arms wrapping around his shoulders and her toes lifting her to the perfect kissing height.

Church kiss, she reminded herself. Just like Drew Barrymore and Adam Sandler in *The Wedding Singer*. No need to get carried away.

She pulled away before it could turn into the scorching kitchen kiss from their first morning. Those would need to be rationed, otherwise she had no chance of her heart not running away from reality.

"Shall we go?" She smiled up at him.

"Sure."

"Caleb, we'd like to get a few minutes of you guys walking into the house, that sort of thing." Adam spoke from behind one of the cameras.

"Not a chance." Caleb didn't so much as glance at the producer.

"But the viewers deserve—"

Caleb swung on him. "Adam, I couldn't care less about the viewers. The rules are clear. No filming my mother in her home. Not ever. If anyone does I will put them through a wall. Are. We. Clear?"

A few minutes later, and liberated from their

microphones, Kat and Caleb walked up the path, his hand clasped in hers. Cameras filmed them from the porch of his house.

As Caleb placed his hand on the doorknob, Kat's insides seized with dread. "Caleb, what if she's having a good day? What if she's lucid and remembers me?"

"It's unlikely. A good day for her means she remembers those closest to her, but a lot of this millennium is blurry. On the off chance it's a great day, it'll be fine. She always liked you."

"But she loved Emma. And she remembers her." Kat couldn't keep the petulance out of her tone and it infuriated her. She wasn't used to being jealous. And being soul-searingly envious of a woman she'd never met, who Caleb hadn't had anything to do with in years, was a sharp reminder of her feelings for him.

He gave her a long look. "If she's that lucid, she'll also remember Emma left."

"What about your uncle? What does he know about us? Does he know that, you know . . ."

"That this is an arrangement? He does. He thinks you're very kind." Caleb squeezed her hand. "He's on your team, Kat."

The problem was she didn't know what team she was on anymore.

"Don't stress. You've had dinner with my mum and Uncle Jared plenty of times."

Like that was comparable. Sitting around the

kitchen table, in love and believing his people would one day be her people wasn't the same as knowing her presence was a means to an end. No matter how noble and well-intentioned that end was.

Caleb opened the front door and ushered Kat through, his hand firm on the small of her back. She could do this if Caleb were here. He'd take the lead and she'd follow.

"Caleb, is that you? Come into the lounge. We have a spatula!"

Difficulty finding the right words. The phrase flashed through Kat's mind from the Googling she'd done on the early stages of dementia. One on a list of things she could expect.

They headed down the familiar photo-lined hallway, their feet echoing across the wooden floors. The first two-thirds of the photos were the same ones she'd walked past a hundred times while they were dating. The rest were more recent. Thankfully no sign of the woman who haunted her.

Kat reached for Caleb's hand and found comfort in the familiar hold. A spatula could be anything from a TV to a . . . Kat rounded the corner and walked into Caleb when he slammed to a halt.

"Conrad?" Caleb sounded like he'd seen a ghost, but Kat couldn't see who he was talking to because he'd stopped right in the doorway.

Why was that name familiar? Kat squeezed through the small gap between the door frame and Caleb and popped into the lounge room.

A man about their age sat on the couch—floral and new since Kat's time—holding a cup of tea and looking perfectly at home. He had brown hair, a chiseled jaw, and she had never met him before in her life. Marion sat next to him. Her gray hair was pulled up in a bun but her floral top had been buttoned haphazardly and she only wore one slipper.

Her eyes darted between the man and Kat as if knowing she knew them both but couldn't make the connections.

"Mum, you remember my girlfriend, Kat." Kat wasn't sure whether her grip had tightened on Caleb's or his on hers but whichever it was their hands were wound around each other tighter than a garter on a bride.

His mum's gaze brightened. "Oh yes, your girlfriend. How lovely." She smiled then, happiness rippling across her features.

Kat let her breath leak out. Caleb hadn't exaggerated when he said how much his finding love meant to his mother.

"Hi, we haven't met. I'm Kat." She stepped forward and held her hand out to the stranger.

"Conrad." He stood and shook her hand, glancing at Caleb as he did.

They had talked about a Conrad. When? Her

mind scrambled through all the conversations they'd had over the last few weeks.

"Where's Alice?" Caleb grabbed her hand as soon as she stepped back.

His mother's face darkened. "I told her to go home. I don't need a babysitter. And this nice young man said he would stay with me until you came home."

Conrad shrugged, sympathy in his eyes. "Alice and your mother were having, um, words when I arrived. Your mother had locked Alice out of the house. I thought maybe I could help."

Caleb's face sagged. "Thank you."

Marion pushed herself up. "Let me set two more places. This young man can stay for dinner too. He tells me he's an old friend of yours, Caleb."

"Kat, honey, can you help mum in the kitchen? I'll be there in just a few minutes." Honey? Caleb had never called her that. Not ever.

"Um, sure." Caleb relinquished his grasp on her hand and Kat followed Marion down the hall. Her walker squeaked across the floor as she shuffled past the photos documenting her life.

Who was Conrad? She was usually good with names. She had to be when she often worked on sets with hundreds of people. But she could not place him. It was like being on this show had blown a circuit.

Kat paused in the kitchen door and caught her

breath. It was like entering a time warp. Every-thing was the same, yet it wasn't. The freezer door hung open, a bag of peas defrosting on the floor. Despite dishes scattered across surfaces, no appearance or smell of dinner greeted them.

Scattered pieces of paper filled with unfin-ished lists covered the large dining table where she'd eaten many dinners. Cutlery lay splayed in the center as if someone had placed them on the table then become distracted with another chore.

It was a far cry from the spotless kitchen and perfectly set table of ten years ago.

"So," Kat forced some cheer into her voice, "can I help with anything for dinner?" She picked up a couple of nearby plates and stacked them beside the sink.

Marion looked at her, brow wrinkling. "It's not dinner time. I haven't even had lunch yet."

"Well, let me see if I can find you something to eat." Kat scanned the front of the fridge to see if there was any kind of menu plan but found nothing among the assorted photos, pamphlets, and coupons.

Maybe they cooked in bulk and ate the same thing for a couple of nights? She opened the fridge and peeked inside for leftovers. The usual contents stared back at her but nothing that looked like it could be dinner.

Kat opened the oven. Ah, there it was. A

chicken still in its packaging. She pulled it out of the oven, its temperature indicating it hadn't been liberated from the fridge too long ago. Well, it would be a late dinner. She switched the oven on, then turned to find Marion hovering next to the table.

"How about you take a seat and I'll make you a nice cup of tea?" Marion had always loved tea. Perhaps that much hadn't changed.

Once again Marion's brow crinkled, but at least she sat down at the table. "Who did Caleb say you were again?"

"I'm Kat. His girlfriend."

"Oh!" Another look of delight, accompanied by surprise. "Do you love my son?"

"I do. Very much." If she couldn't have an honest conversation with someone who probably wouldn't remember it tomorrow, who could she have one with? If Caleb happened to overhear the truth, he'd just assume she was doing exactly what he'd asked her to: help him convince his mother he was happily in love.

"Does he love you?"

"I don't know." Almost one hundred percent no. But he had once. *We even made out sitting at that table . . .* Whoa. Kat's body flushed from her forehead to her toes. Some memories should remain buried.

"Where do you . . ." Marion's face scrunched for a third time. Kat's heart went out to her. She

287

couldn't imagine losing words you'd known and used all your life. "Appear from?"

"All over. My father is American, and my mother is Australian. He was in the diplomatic corps when I was young, so I've lived all over the world." She'd lived everywhere but never belonged anywhere.

Until she'd landed here. The first time.

Checking the kettle for water, she flicked it on then opened the fridge again and assessed the contents for sides. Meanwhile, her pretend boyfriend and some guy of significance were still alone. Talking about who knew what.

The fridge beeped at her. *Focus, Kat.* She grabbed some vegetables to add to dinner, piled them up into her arms, and knocked her hip into the door to close it. As she turned toward the counter, her elbow skimmed a lone magnet holding down a stack of pamphlets. They all cascaded to the floor.

A postcard landed at her feet and her stomach contracted as if she'd been punched.

Caleb and Emma stared up at her. Well, actually they stared at each other. Two blissfully happy in love people, walking in one of the paddocks, holding hands, laughing.

And she remembered exactly who Conrad was.

"Thank you for helping Alice." Caleb floundered for neutral ground. Not that his mother was exactly neutral, but it was the closest he was going to get with the man who used to be his best friend.

Conrad placed his cup and saucer down on the coffee table. It was still full. He'd never liked tea. "Alice was upset. She blamed herself for leaving her house key inside while she got something from the car. Your mother was determined not to let her back in. Something about Alice stealing her glasses?"

That wasn't anything new. One of the curses of dementia was his mother constantly misplaced things, then blamed everyone around her for taking them.

"Anyway, I managed to talk her into unlocking the door. Alice said she finished at five, and I thought maybe it would be better to let her go a little early. I'm sorry if I did the wrong thing."

Caleb slumped into his uncle's recliner. "You didn't." But then, who knew what the right or wrong thing was anymore? What calmed Mum one day would enrage her the next.

"She didn't recognize me."

"No." Conrad looked like he expected more, so he tried to explain. "The last decade is the worst of her memory. Some things she remembers once in a while, but a lot of it is just gone."

"I just . . . thought she would. After the . . ."

"After what?"

"The preview at the end of the episode last

night. Kat arriving, and your mum being upset she wasn't Emma." Conrad shrugged. "I guess I'd thought if she remembered Emma she'd remember me."

Caleb stared at Conrad, fists clenched. "They showed that?" The words ground out of his mouth like gravel. Of course the producers had elected to keep that scene in the episode. It was too good to pass up. Even if anything they filmed of his mother on their property was supposed to only be included with his explicit permission. Which he'd never been asked for.

"Did you think they wouldn't?"

He hadn't given it any thought at all. The entire day had been overwhelming. First, the sheer relief that Kat had come, to the heart-thumping realization that it meant he would see her every day for the next six weeks.

"I didn't even think about it. Stupid." The studio would argue consent was implied by his mother involving herself in the scene. That Kat's arrival was one of the most significant moments of the series and it was impossible to edit his mother out of it. It would have made great TV.

"Can't say I picked you for a reality TV watcher." Caleb's joke fell flat.

"Can't say I picked you for a reality TV star."

"Yeah, well. I guess we all change." Caleb folded his arms across his chest. "So what's up?"

His stomach plummeted like he was on The

Giant Drop at Dreamworld. Emma had left, their friendship had hobbled along for a few months but eventually they'd both wordlessly accepted that it was better to let it go. There was one reason why Conrad would be here. "What's happened to her? Is she hurt? Sick? Is she. . ." *Dead. Is Emma dead?*

"What?" Conrad's jaw sagged. "No. No, she's fine. Emma's fine."

Caleb's breath came out in a whoosh. "Then what?"

"She's back."

"What are you talking about?"

Conrad shifted on his feet. "Emma's back. In Toowoomba. Has been for a couple of months. She got a teaching job here."

He was sitting down. At some point he'd gone from standing up to sitting down and he didn't know when.

Emma was back. After four years she'd chosen *now* to come back. He realized Conrad was still talking.

". . . she was going to come and see you but then we heard you'd left to be on this show. Why didn't you tell anyone you were on it?" Why did Conrad's question sound like an accusation?

Caleb rarely had anything to do with Emma's family beyond awkward nods when they crossed paths. When Emma had left he'd lost more than her. Her brother, his best friend. The siblings he'd wanted all his life. The nieces and nephews he'd already attended birthday parties for. The kids they'd started planning so they'd be close to their cousins.

And yet here he was. No wife. No kids. With his ex-fiancée's brother in the parlor wanting to know why he hadn't notified them he was planning to go on the show, and his ex-girlfriend in the kitchen pretending to be his new girlfriend. You couldn't make this stuff up.

Caleb stared at the floor for a few seconds, trying to harness his thoughts. "So why are you here, Conrad? Is she married? Engaged? What message have you been sent to deliver?"

Nothing in him reacted at the idea of Emma being with someone else. He'd assumed she'd move on. Having a name and a few details made no difference.

"No. She's not with anyone. And I'm here because she wants to see you." Conrad had sat down again. He leaned forward, his hands clasped between his knees.

"Has the show done this? Have they put her up to this?" If they had, he would wring Adam's scrawny little hipster neck.

"No. She has no interest in being on the show. She just wants to talk to you. No cameras."

"What does she want?" Caleb shifted in his chair. "Is she looking for absolution? Forgiveness? Because you can tell her I forgave her a long time ago." Caleb let out a wry laugh. "I thought I had, but it's obviously an ongoing process."

"Are you willing to talk to her?"

"I don't know." That was the honest truth. He didn't want to say yes, but he also couldn't say no.

"Do you really think you can build a life with Kat?"

He had to be careful what he said even without any cameras around. "I don't know, Con. But I'd like to try."

"You really think she could be happy here? In the middle of nowhere? When she's used to travel and cities and movie stars?"

No. She couldn't. Trying to fool himself otherwise would only make things worse for both of them. If his love hadn't been enough for Emma—country-girl Emma—it certainly wouldn't be enough for Kat. But there was no way he was telling Conrad that.

"I know I'm hardly a neutral party, but I don't want to see you getting blindsided at the end of all of this." Conrad pulled out his phone and tapped on the screen. "Have you seen this?" He handed his phone over, and Caleb started scanning an interview Kat did after she'd won the Oscar.

I love big cities. Love travel. Love always being on the move. Every job is different. Every month is different. I can't imagine being in the same place for life.

The words sliced through him and he let out a long breath, aware of Conrad watching his every twitch. The article was dated 2013. Years ago. She might not still mean what she'd said when surrounded by bright lights, fancy outfits, and golden statues. People changed their minds about the life they wanted all the time.

But could they change that much?

CHAPTER TWENTY-FOUR

*D*o you really think you can build a life with Kat? . . . I don't want to see you getting blindsided at the end of all this.

The words vibrated through Kat's mind as she stood just beyond their line of sight watching Conrad hand Caleb his phone. Conrad was right. More right than he knew.

Caleb wouldn't know it. Even Conrad might not know it. They were blokes. But she knew the only reason Emma would have requested a meeting was because she wanted to put her foot in the door of second chances.

She sucked in her breath. If she cared about Caleb, truly cared, she had to tell him to say yes. This was just an arrangement. But he was a man of his word. He wouldn't dream of pursuing something with Emma while he and Kat were "together." No matter that it wasn't real.

Not that he could. But she also couldn't let him jettison any chance of a future with his country-life-ready ex-fiancée. Because the show would soon be over and once the furor died down she wanted him to be free to move on with someone else. Even if it was someone she didn't think worthy of him. Single eligible women didn't exactly grow in the fields.

"Caleb, can I talk to you?" She popped her head around the door and put on her best breezy tone, the same tone she'd used in those long months when she was all but dead inside.

"Of course." He handed Conrad back his phone and was at her side in an instant.

Emma's brother stood and rubbed his hands on his jeans. The similarities were obvious now she'd seen Emma's photo. Same coloring, same noses, same freckles spattered across both faces.

"I should get home. But I'll watch Marion for a few minutes while you talk." He shuffled past the coffee table, turning to Caleb when he reached the door. "You know where to find me once you have an answer." Then he closed the door firmly behind him.

"Is everything okay?" Caleb stood and closed the space between them.

Emma was back. Kat let the knowledge seep into her bones. Was it a sign from God that she shouldn't have come? Or was it just the return of a woman who couldn't stand the thought of the man she'd abandoned moving on with someone else? "I think you should see her."

"Excuse me?"

She should get a medal for this. Trying to convince the love of her life to give his ex-fiancée another chance. Or at least be open to it. "I'm just saying. I'll be gone in a few months. This will all be over. And I don't want you to miss a second chance at happiness when it could be standing right in front of you."

His gaze hardened. "First of all, Conrad said nothing about her wanting a second chance. Second, even if she did, why would I want to be with someone who broke my heart?"

And there it was. The million-dollar question.

"People change. That's what we believe, right? That people can change. Be transformed. It can't have been easy for her to come back."

"I don't love her anymore, Kat."

"But maybe you could again. One day." *Or me. Maybe you could love me.* The words welled up inside her. But she wasn't stupid. There was a big difference between being the dumper and being the person left behind. One was definitive. The other was open ended with a tail that seemed to last as long as time itself.

Caleb rubbed his face. "Let me get this straight. You want me to be open to being with the woman who abandoned me without so much as a word of explanation or the decency of saying good-bye?"

"No!" The word came out with too much force, and she tried to modulate her tone. "I'm just saying don't close yourself off to the possibility of anything once I'm gone. I want you to be happy. I want you to have someone to love. I want you to have all those kids you've dreamed of. And I don't want you to go through everything coming with your mother alone."

His gaze softened as he looked at her. "You're a good person, Katriona McLeod."

Didn't she know it. "Also, this fell off the fridge." She pulled the card out of her back pocket and handed it to him.

He looked down, his expression changing into something she couldn't read. "This was on the fridge? How'd I miss it?"

"It was buried behind a stack of pamphlets."

"I'm sorry you had to see that." He shoved the card into his back pocket.

"It's okay that you loved her." Kat whispered the words even though everything inside her wanted to say otherwise. She'd known he'd loved Emma. Otherwise he wouldn't have asked her to marry him. But to see it written across their faces made their love so much truer.

Caleb shook his head. "I'm not sorry I loved her. But I'm pretty sure what Emma and I had can't be salvaged. The trust has been broken. I don't see how we could ever get that back."

"I'm not asking you to chase after her. Certainly not before we've seen this through. Just saying don't write anything off as impossible. You never know what God will do."

He refused to look at her, his eyes remaining

downcast on the chestnut floorboards. "We should get back to Mum." Caleb moved past her and opened the door. Kat followed him into the kitchen where Marion had been settled in an easy chair by the window. As soon as they walked in, Conrad moved toward the door.

"I'll leave you guys to it."

"Con." Caleb put his hand on his old friend's elbow and he paused.

"Yes."

"I'm sorry. I don't want to hurt her, but it's a no. It's too late. I've moved on."

Conrad nodded. "I'll let her know." His footsteps echoed up the hall followed by the thud of the front door closing.

"Are you okay?" Kat touched Caleb lightly by his elbow as he watched his mum in her chair. Her head lolled to one side and even though her eyes were open she didn't seem to be looking at anything.

"No." He shook his head. "Not really. I hate that I don't know how to navigate all of this. Mum. What you saw before was good. Mum actually made sense. Most of the time she's angry or confused or nonsensical. Even with Alice's help I don't know how we're going to be able to keep her at home for much longer, but Uncle Jared won't hear of her going into a care facility. What are we supposed to do, Kat?"

When Kat asked if he was okay, she'd meant

about Emma, but it was like the last fifteen minutes hadn't even happened.

"I want to go home. Please let me go home." The words came from his mother. She had her hands on the arms of her chair and was struggling to rise.

Caleb was beside her in a second, kneeling in front of her. "Mum, it's me, Caleb. You are home. Remember? This is your home."

His mother looked up at him with an accusing expression. "I don't believe you. You're just like the others who are coming to find me." Her hand lashed out, but Caleb caught it easily and returned it to her lap.

"No, we don't hit. You're safe here." He spoke to her like she was a toddler.

Kat picked up a pot of lavender hand cream off the table, needing to do something to help. Anything. She unscrewed the lid and breathed in the fragrant aroma. She'd read somewhere that favorite smells could sometimes calm people with neurological disorders.

Approaching Caleb, she held it out. "Does she like this? I could rub some into her hands."

He looked up at her, a defeated expression on his face. "I don't know. Anything is possible."

Kat pulled a chair out from the dining room table and sat in front of Marion. "I'm just going to rub some of this cream into your hands, Marion. Okay?"

Kat held Marion's right hand in a gentle clasp, and rubbed the cream into her papery skin in a gentle circular motion, running her fingers down Marion's then back up again.

Caleb's mother's hands, which had started off stiff and tense, gradually relaxed into the massage. Kat worked in silence for a few minutes then switched over to Marion's other hand.

Caleb appeared beside her with a blanket and a footstool. "Here you go, Mum." He draped the blanket across her lap, placed the footstool on the floor, and gently propped Marion's feet on it. A small snore rumbled from her mouth.

"You're a miracle worker." Caleb smiled down at Kat. "It usually takes much longer to calm her down once she's gotten herself worked up."

Kat stood. "Will she sleep for long?"

Caleb brushed a piece of his mother's hair out of her face. The small movement almost broke Kat's heart. "It's hard to know. Hopefully for a little while."

Kat leaned forward and tucked in the blanket around the older woman. Marion had always been larger framed but now her collar bones stuck out like sticks. "Should we get started on dinner while she rests?" Pushing her chair back, Kat stood up and screwed the lid back onto the hand cream, and placed it on the dining table.

"Sure." Caleb glanced at the clock that hung

on the wall. "We should have a little while before Uncle Jared gets in."

"I'll sort the chicken out if you can find some more veggies to go with it." Making her way around the table, she grabbed an oven tray from the same cupboard it had always lived in, and pulled a knife from the knife block. She cut into the packaging, and the chicken's slippery carcass tumbled out into the roasting dish.

They worked in silence for a few moments, busy with their respective tasks. Kat tried not to overanalyze everything that had just happened. Caleb was a man of his word. He wouldn't have said no if he wanted to see Emma. But was he letting his pride get in the way instead of listening to his heart?

Kat pulled a block of butter from the fridge then turned to see Caleb with his head buried in the bottom of the pantry. "Can you get me some bread or breadcrumbs while you're in there?"

Caleb reappeared with a handful of potatoes which he dumped in a clear space on the counter. "I feel like we need to clear up a few things." Something in the way that he looked at her while he said it had her stomach clenching.

"Okay, shoot."

"First, I'm sorry about the money thing. You're right. It's none of my business. Second, I'm not getting back together with Emma."

"Well, there's no need to make any hasty—"

"I'm not being hasty. Whatever used to be between us is gone. Gone. I'm not mad at her. I don't need an explanation from her. There's nothing in me that sees her reappearance as a possible second chance. So while I hope she has changed and I hope she has a great life with someone one day, that someone isn't me."

"Okay." Kat tried to squash the uninvited spark of hope that had lit itself inside her. Him saying no to seeing Emma had nothing to do with him having feelings for her. It had everything to do with his feelings about Emma.

Caleb arched an eyebrow at her. "Okay? That's all you have to say after your impassioned don't-write-her-off pitch?"

"You can't make someone feel something that's not there. I learned that a long time ago." Kat turned back to the fridge as it started beeping at her. "Any chance there's any bacon in here?"

A laugh rumbled out of Caleb's chest. "You're in a farmer's house. There's always bacon." With one stride he was beside her and reaching into the fridge to pull out a newsprint wrapped package. "That should be some. What are you making?"

"I thought I'd do some stuffing with bacon in it." Kat moved to close the fridge, but when she turned back Caleb still stood behind her, an intrigued smile on his face.

"You do stuffing now?"

"I do lots of things you don't know about." Her

303

words came out sounding a heck of a lot more flirtatious than she'd intended.

"Like what?" Caleb might not have physically moved toward her when he said the words, but that didn't stop her heart rate kicking up a notch.

Kat held up the package in her hands as a barrier. "Well, horseback riding and stuffing for two. Now, are you going to get out of my way and find me some bread so we can get this chicken in the oven, or what?"

"I guess that depends."

"On?"

Caleb gave her a mischievous smile. "On what the option is for the 'or what' part."

"You remember there's no cameras here, right? You don't need to flirt with me." Kat forced herself to try to bring some sanity back into the conversation.

"Maybe it's more fun because there are no cameras here." Caleb anchored his palm against the fridge and leaned toward her. Whether he remembered it or not, he had performed this exact maneuver against this very fridge before, and she knew exactly where it led.

Kat closed her eyes even as her body hummed with awareness of him. Of course it did. It didn't differentiate between the presence of cameras or not. Caleb Murphy had the same impact on her regardless of what was happening around them. It just wasn't like him to play recklessly.

"You sure you haven't had a swig of moonshine while you were in the milking shed, Farmer Murphy?"

"I don't know. Would it help or harm my case if I said yes?" Caleb leaned forward, his fingers brushing across her cheek, his touch melting her resolve to keep their physical chemistry purely on camera. They were kissing all the time anyway for the show. What would another one hurt?

But as Kat leaned in, Caleb shifted back, blinking as if awakening from a dream. "Breadcrumbs. Right. Let's find some breadcrumbs."

CHAPTER TWENTY-FIVE

Caleb sat watching Kat in his parents' kitchen, caring for his mother, prepping dinner. The sight did weird things to his heart. And his brain. Like making him forget she wasn't his. Instead, he'd gotten carried away in a few moments of insanity thinking this was his life. That Kat McLeod belonged in his kitchen and would welcome being thoroughly kissed against the fridge. Just like she had many years before.

"Can you see if you can find some dried oregano while you're in there? Or tarragon?" How could she sound so calm and collected? He was still struggling to recover his breath, to remind himself that, as she had told him just a couple of days ago, their arrangement was purely business. A proposition he had instigated.

He needed to pay her. He'd been avoiding it even after their little dustup. Seeing the money disappear from his account would be like a hard kick from one of his cows, but maybe it would stop him flirting with fantasy and bring him back to reality.

Loading his arms with a loaf of bread, the container of bread crumbs, and a couple of packets of dried herbs, he turned and dumped them onto the counter next to the bacon pieces.

"Thanks." She smiled at him from where she was melting some butter in a pot. "Is everything okay? You look like you've just seen a ghost."

"Yes, fine." He shook his head as if that would cure what ailed him. "Just a weird sense of déjà vu. From having you here."

Kat's glance flickered to the fridge, and he was ninety-nine percent sure she was remembering the same thing he had been.

"It's weird." She picked up the plate with the bacon and use her wooden spoon to add it into the melted butter. "Whenever you get close to me I half expect your mum to pipe up from the corner reminding us to remember to leave room for the Holy Spirit."

Caleb laughed at the memory. "Well, I have to admit I preferred that to her quoting First Timothy about how I should treat you like my sister."

Kat sautéed the bacon and butter, then added some diced onion she must have found in the fridge. "That was my introduction to First Timothy. At least it got me reading the whole book."

Caleb turned his attention to finding the potato peeler. "Where do you go to church in Sydney?"

"North Point."

"The megachurch?" Had to be. There wouldn't be another North Point in Sydney. The church of a gazillion people and a few rock stars. Kat would fit right in. He hoped they weren't one of those prosperity theology places.

"Yup. And don't look at me like that. It's a really good church."

"Sorry. I just find it hard to imagine going to a church where you can't know the pastors." Toowoomba Baptist had three hundred people on a good day. The entire congregation could probably fit into one of North Point's bathrooms.

"I know them."

"You know Greg and Janine Tyler?" Caleb couldn't stop the edge of incredulity that creeped into his voice as he started peeling his first potato. But then, it would make sense that she knew the lead pastors of North Point. She was, after all, an Oscar award-winning makeup artist. They probably made it their business to know about congregants like her who could enhance their church's brand.

"I do." Kat's tone brought a chill to the room. "Please tell me you haven't turned into one of those critics who hates big churches you know nothing about. Greg and Janine are two of the nicest and most down-to-earth people you could ever meet. And, unlike what the rest of the world seems to think, they aren't in it to build an empire." Kat banged her pot for extra emphasis.

Caleb bit down on the defensiveness that rose within him. Kat was a smart woman. She wouldn't be sucked into something that wasn't right at the core. "You're right. That wasn't fair of me."

"Are you still at Toowoomba Combined?"

"No. I . . . I moved after everything with Emma. Started going to Toowoomba Baptist with Mum and Uncle Jared. I thought it would be for six months or so, until I wasn't the scandal of the month anymore. Especially with her family there." Caleb finished his potato and rolled it into the sink. "But I never went back. I guess it felt like it would be easier for everyone if we went to different churches."

"I'm sorry. I know you liked it there." Kat tore some chunks of bread into smaller pieces and added them into the bacon pot.

"Well, there are upsides. The ratio of senior citizens to younger people at Toowoomba Baptist means the baking is always superior."

"But you still keep in touch with people at Combined?"

"Sort of." Until Kat had showed up he hadn't realized how few friends he had in Toowoomba. Between people moving away and the invisible line drawn between his social circle and Emma's after their breakup, he didn't have a lot of friends. If the crew announced it was time for some kind of Kat-meets-the-friends-episode, he'd only have a handful of people to invite.

"That must have been hard when everything happened. Losing Conrad as well as her."

"It wasn't great. Her family is big. Her nephews and nieces had already started calling me Uncle Caleb. To be fair, her family tried. Conrad invited me to his daughter's birthday a month after Emma left, but it was too hard. Too awkward." Caleb sliced his potato peeler across the spud with more force than necessary, and the next thing he knew it also had taken a strip off the side of his finger.

"Ow!" He held up his hand, a trickle of blood dripping down the side of his hand.

Kat took one look at it and flung herself over her bowl. "Don't you dare bleed on my bacon!"

Caleb shoved his hand under the tap, and turned the cold water on full, rinsing the blood away to inspect the damage. Just a surface cut, but he'd need to trim it away and get it covered. "Do you mind getting the first aid kit? It's at the bottom of the pantry. I need the scissors and the box of wide Band-Aids."

Kat picked up her bowl, still holding it close to her torso like he'd cut an artery. Only after she'd placed the bowl on the dining table did she get the first aid kit and fish out the scissors.

"Thanks." He took care of his injured finger while Kat washed her hands then cut a piece of plaster from the roll.

She peeled the plastic strips away from the

center and held it up so he could place his cut against the gauze. Then she wrapped the sticky sides firmly around his finger. "Done!" She surveyed her work with pride.

Caleb started to laugh, struggling to contain the volume so he didn't wake his mother.

"What?"

"Don't you dare bleed on my bacon? Thanks for the heads-up that I should only have a medical emergency when no pork products are nearby."

Kat crossed her arms over her chest. "First of all, slicing your finger open with a potato peeler is hardly a medical emergency. Second, that is some great stuffing. If you'd gotten blood on it, we would've had to throw the whole bowl out. I stand by my prioritization."

"What would I need to beat bacon? A broken bone? Heart attack?"

Kat turned and grabbed the bowl off the table. "I'm going to ignore you now and stuff this chicken. We've already taken too long getting it into the oven. At this rate it'll be tomorrow before we eat." Brushing past him, she grabbed the roasting tray and started shoving her magical stuffing into the cavity.

Caleb hovered behind her. "Stroke?"

"Stop it."

"Brain aneurysm?"

"You're not nearly as funny as you think you

are." She finished filling the chicken and opened the oven door to put it inside. A blast of warmth hit them both.

"Asthma attack."

She closed the oven door with her hip as she turned around. "Don't make me slap you with my chicken hands." But she was laughing, and a sense of victory filled him.

"Concussion?"

Kat washed her hands under the tap, pumping the soap dispenser more than needed. "I'll concuss you if you don't quit." She held up her wet hands toward him. "Where's a towel?"

Caleb held up the one streaked with his blood. "How about this?"

"You are so gross." She wiped her hands on the front of his shirt, his abs clenching as her hands traveled down his torso.

"I'm just saying that had better be the best stuffing I've had in my life."

She smirked at him as she leaned against the counter. "Well, you just feel free to apologize when it is."

"How do you like your apologies?"

"I'll take them however they come." The air between charged with attraction, something in their last exchange tipping things from fun to fiery.

His hands were on her hips and hers were . . . well, he wasn't sure where hers were because he was distracted by the way she was biting the very bottom lip he wanted to kiss.

This isn't real. The words knocked on a door somewhere in the back of his brain, but he ignored them. Because this felt real. Nothing over the last few years felt more real than Kat McLeod prepping dinner in his kitchen and giving him the kind of look that said he was all she wanted.

"Oh, sod it." At least those were the words he thought she muttered before she wrapped her fingers around his shirt and pulled his lips down to hers.

Text Message

Kat: So we kissed tonight. When there were no cameras.

Allie: Totally forgiving the jumbo bean for waking me up at two am for this! Details, please . . .

Kat: There's not much to tell. We went to his house for dinner with his mother and uncle. The cameras aren't allowed in there because he won't let them film his mum. We were making dinner together and it just kind of . . . happened.

Allie: To be honest I'm surprised it hasn't just "kind of" happened before now. The chemistry between the two of you could keep half of Toowoomba lit at night.

Allie: What are you thinking? Feeling? Do you think it happened just because you guys have great chemistry and you're kissing on camera, so the lines have blurred? Or do you feel it's more than that?

Kat: I don't know. I feel it could be more, but what if I'm delusional? What if it was just a moment but doesn't reflect anything more on his side?

Allie: I know I'm just watching it on TV and it's all edited footage but I'm with Paige. I don't understand how there can't be anything more on his side. I mean, the way he looks at you . . .

Kat: But if it is more then I need to tell him before it gets any further.

Allie: About the endo?

Kat: Yes.

Allie: How has it been since the last surgery?

Kat: Fine.

Allie: So that's positive.

Kat: Living without having to mainline Class A drugs just to function is positive.

Allie: If he's a man worthy of you, then it's not going to be a deal breaker. It's not.

Kat: There's something else. Emma is back in town. And she wants to see him.

Allie: His ex??? What did he say?

Kat: That he didn't want to see her.

Allie: Huh. Interesting.

Kat: I told him he should.

Allie: Of course you did.

Kat: ????

Allie: It's an out. If he was to see her, that would give you another reason to put your walls back up. Have you considered maybe he knows that?

CHAPTER TWENTY-SIX

No good things came tagged with the word "surprise" in reality TV. Kat knew that for a fact.

She'd also known something was coming. Had watched it on the crew's faces over the last week as Caleb and she had spent most of their on-camera time doing farm chores—the reality TV equivalent of watching grass grow. They'd also finally been allowed off the farm for a date. But the strawberry fields had been closed for their exclusive use, so she still hadn't seen anyone other than the crew.

By some kind of mutual unspoken understanding she hadn't visited for dinner since the unscripted kiss in Marion's kitchen. Another place to avoid, along with the porch swing. Which made tonight their first evening together since that night.

"How much am I going to hate this, Karissa?" Kat leaned over in the car and tightened the buckle on her strappy sandals.

"What's to hate? You get to wear a cute outfit and go out to dinner with a hot guy. I would've thought you'd be thrilled to get away from the farm." Karissa wrinkled her nose, clearly no more—possibly even less—of a farm girl than Kat.

"I would be. Except that you said there was a surprise." Kat checked her lipstick in the mirror. "C'mon. Is it karaoke? Because they know I can't sing. Am I going to have to croon some cheesy love song to Caleb in all of my off-key glory?"

She glanced out the window. Caleb was a few meters away doing an interview with Adam about who knew what. Maybe Adam would give them a clue about what lay in wait.

Outside the front of the restaurant a sign announced *Closed for a Private Function*. She wasn't sure whether she was relieved or not that they wouldn't be eating in a fishbowl, surrounded by diners ogling their every move and dissecting their every expression.

"While we're waiting, there's a tweet you need to send."

Kat pulled out her phone. The show's publicity people had wanted to take over her Twitter account for the rest of the season and send who knew what kind of moronic material. But since she didn't intend to spend her life purveying her reality TV experience into some kind of C-list celebrity career, she'd politely told them what they could do with that idea.

So now they fed her material and she tweeted

the less insipid stuff. "What does this one say?" She opened the Twitter app and ignored the circle telling her she had 1,739 new notifications.

"I've just messaged you the photo."

A photo of her trying to gather eggs from the chicken coop flashed up. Her mouth was contorted in a grimace, like some high maintenance city girl thinking the chore was beneath her. The truth was that the chicken cropped out of the photo has just pecked her ankles.

"The line is 'City girl meets her match. Tonight on SBC at 8:30'."

Well, it could be worse. At least it wasn't another photo of her cooking Caleb's eggs captioned by some 1950s housewife line. Kat tapped in the words, added the photo, sent it into the ether, and shoved her phone into her clutch.

The car door opened, and Caleb stood outside with his hand outstretched. Grabbing it, she exited the car and flattened her palm against her skirt in case a breeze caught it.

"Hungry?" Caleb's fingers closed securely around hers, staying there even as he closed the door with his other hand.

"Starved." They had better be planning on serving real food at this place. If she found the kitchen shut and a couple of ornamental bowls of lettuce on the table, she'd unleash some serious hanger. They walked up the stairs as the cameras circled around them. She'd got to the point where she barely noticed them half the time. They just blurred into the background. "What did they ask in your interview?"

"About our families mostly. Not that there was a heck of a lot to say."

Caleb paused and opened the large wooden door for her. As she stepped through the door, the dots connected and she knew exactly what the "surprise" was.

Her mother.

"I'm so sorry." The words came out of her mouth before she could filter them.

"What was that?" Caleb looked down at her, a quizzical smile on his mouth.

"Katriona!" The word trilled across the room, expanded from its usual four syllables to about six.

She was too late. She should have warned him. And now he would be going in unaware of what was coming his way. Like one of those little piggies being fattened for Christmas.

But it wasn't just her mother. There were two people at the table. Surely her mother hadn't brought a date.

The person in the second chair turned, and she almost fell off her shoes.

"Dad?" Kat clung to Caleb's arm as if it were a life preserver holding her above water. He shifted closer.

What was her father doing here? Her parents

hadn't coexisted in the same space in fifteen years. Not since her father took out a restraining order against her mother after an incident involving his Mercedes and the bottom of his swimming pool.

Caleb squeezed her hand then nudged her farther into the room. She moved forward on wobbly feet, the high strappy sandals providing no support to her shaking legs.

She summoned up her strongest voice. "Caleb, these are my parents, Robert and Darlene. Mum, Dad, this is Caleb."

Caleb held out his hand to her father and they shook. He then gave her mother a brief hug. Kat didn't miss the way her mother pressed herself into Caleb's chest, but she could only hope he had. She didn't want to imagine what the woman would get up to during her one-on-one time with him.

Caleb pulled a chair out and she sat, leaning against the back for support. He dropped into the one next to her, unperturbed, which made sense considering she had neglected to give him any forewarning about what he'd just walked into.

A waiter hovered around offering red and white wine. Kat declined. She didn't drink in the company of either of her parents. It would be way too easy for a glass to turn into a bottle.

Instead, while Caleb asked about their journey to Toowoomba, she grabbed a roll from the bread basket in the middle of the table and slapped some butter on the top. Maybe she was overthinking this. Maybe it wouldn't be as bad as her gut was insisting it would be. Cameras would soon beam their every word to hundreds of thousands of people. If there were ever a reason for her parents to be on their best behavior, surely now would be it?

"Caleb, are you a family man? Kat is getting on and a woman only has so many eggs, you know." Her mother took a delicate sip of her wine as if her question were nothing more than an observance about the interior decor.

Kat choked on her roll, sputtering around the mouthful of carbs, and Caleb slapped her on her back.

"I am. I'd like to have at least four kids, but there's plenty of time for that." Caleb gave her the kind of wink that would have ordinarily sent her pulse raising but instead knotted her stomach with dread.

"Darlene, we've just met Caleb, and Kat has only known him for a matter of weeks. Why don't we start with something a little more appropriate than their reproductive plans?" That from the man who had once offered to pay to put her eggs on ice—an offer she should have taken him up on.

Caleb slid a gaze toward her, a question in his eyes. Kat shook her head. She had never told her parents about Caleb. They had no idea they had a past.

Something shadowed Caleb's face, but he covered it quickly and plastered a smile over the top. "I'm happy to answer any questions you would like to ask me. This is an unusual situation, and I'm sure there's a lot you'd like to know." His statement was underscored by a boom mic swooping low above their heads.

"Indeed." Her father's ruddy face expressed exactly what he thought of the arrangement as he took a gulp of wine.

"What made you choose Katriona?" Her mother leaned forward, artificially perky cleavage on display.

Kat restrained her desire to run after the waiter with the wine.

Caleb smiled at her mother, doing an impressive job of focusing on her face. "Kat is everything I could ever ask for in a partner. She's funny, feisty, independent, and smart, and we share similar values. I consider myself blessed she agreed to come on the show."

He casually draped his arm across the back of her chair, his fingers circling around her shoulder blade. Even though she knew his words and actions were all for the cameras, her breath caught at the sensation of his finger skating across her skin.

"And what about you, Kat?" Her mother's wine

glass had barely skimmed the table before she raised it again.

"He's safe." The words were out of her mouth before she'd even thought them. Safe. Not exactly the most romantic of attributes. But the one she'd been missing for her first eighteen years. People didn't know how important a sense of security was until they had to live without it.

Her father barked a laugh. "If you want safe, darling, I'll buy you a dog."

"I don't want a dog." Kat managed the sentence through gritted teeth.

He leaned back, wine glass in hand. The liquid sloshed in the goblet as he gestured with his hands. "Fine. A gun. You still have your firearms license, right?"

"You have a gun, Katriona?" Her mother was all wide-eyed and high-pitched. "Caleb, has she told you about her gun?"

"No, Mother. I have a piece of paper that says I can own a gun. There's a big difference." Which was a good thing given she had a bit of a temper. Packing a pistol in her purse right now wouldn't be ideal.

"The point being that if you want safety, a dog or a gun would be better options than splashing your personal life all over television in the misplaced hope of finding love with a stranger."

"I'd like to think I'm a better option than a

dog." Caleb said the words mildly, but his hand tightened its grasp on his water glass.

Her father ran his hand through his cropped hair. "Maybe. Maybe not. I have an idea. Let's put bets on how long this is going to last. I give it three months."

How dare he. "Or how about we put bets on how long your latest marriage will last?"

Caleb's arm tightened around her shoulder. "Can you give us just a second." Not waiting for an answer, he pushed back his chair and stood. Pushing her own out, Kat took Caleb's hand and let him lead her across the restaurant and back outside.

A warm breeze blew but he wrapped his arms around her and tucked her against his chest under the glow of a streetlight. "What's going on?"

"What? You're okay with him sitting there attacking us like that?"

"No, but they're your parents. They deserve some credit. After all, they did manage to raise you." Caleb tucked a piece of hair behind her ear.

She'd always taken the view that she'd somehow turned out okay despite her parents, not because of them. But she certainly wasn't going to say that on camera.

A breeze circled them, and she stepped closer. "I'm sorry I said you were safe."

"Why?" He looped his arms around her and

the question rumbled from his chest through her body.

"It's not exactly sexy, is it?"

Caleb's arms tightened around her. "Ah, but that's where you're wrong. I happen to think safe can be incredibly sexy."

His hand trailed up her back, bumping over the mic pack tucked into the back of her dress, and weaved itself into her hair.

Kat raised her gaze from his chest and stared into Caleb's eyes. They studied her back. Safe had never looked better.

Her fingers reached up and brushed his stubbled jaw.

"You know what safe says to me? Safe means you trust me. Safe means you feel you belong. Safe means you know I will never betray you. Safe means something is secure. Not fleeting or passing or a whim."

All those words were Caleb Murphy. All those words were what she'd been looking for in a person her entire life. All those words were what she'd thought she'd found in him. And then he'd broken her heart.

Safe, this time, meant keeping her distance and maintaining her guard but knowing her head had nothing on her heart when she was within Caleb's orbit. The inevitable coming heartbreak that soon paled compared to the tug of living in this moment.

Kat raised herself onto her toes, tugged Caleb's head down, and pressed her lips to his. Caleb deepened the kiss, his hands cradling her face. Her hands wound around his neck, pressing him closer, her body molding against his.

He broke off the kiss only to feather more along her jaw. She sucked in her breath with desire.

Caleb wasn't safe. Caleb was fire and ice and a high-flying trapeze with no safety net. Caleb was the man who deserved to have every single one of his dreams come true.

Which was why she had to leave, no matter how hard it would be to walk away.

"Okay, I think I can face them now." Kat pulled away before she succumbed any more to his touch.

"Are you sure?" Caleb ran his thumb across her cheek. "Because I am more than happy to perform an encore just to make certain."

"Tempting, but who knows what will happen if we leave them by themselves for much longer."

Might as well get this over and done with. His fingers wound around hers, warm and comforting as they returned inside. No matter how badly dinner went, it would be better for him being there. As their table came into view, she came to an abrupt stop, and Caleb knocked into her side.

"Sorry."

But she didn't say anything, just stared at her parents who were looking . . . guilty?

"What was that?" Kat walked up to her seat but remained standing.

"Nothing." Kat's mother picked up a roll from the bread basket. "I had something in my eye. Robert was helping me extract it."

"And he needed his lips to do that?" Kat blinked. She hadn't been wrong, had she?

"Don't be silly, Katriona." Her mother laughed but her hand shook as she cut into the roll.

"Mother, he wasn't getting something out of your eye. He was nuzzling your neck!"

Her mother didn't say anything, but the flush creeping up her face sure did.

Oh, wow.

She looked between the two of them. "Would someone please tell me what is going on?"

Her father tugged at the cuffs on his short. "Look, Katriona, you're an adult. The truth is your mother and I sometimes still . . . see each other."

Kat pulled her seat out with a screech and thumped into it. A plate of pasta had appeared while they were away but she had lost her appetite. "What do you mean?"

"Just because we got divorced doesn't mean a level of attraction, a certain familiarity, didn't remain. Can you pass those rolls, Darlene?"

"Are you trying to tell me you're friends with benefits?" The question was out of her mouth before she'd even processed what she was asking. "Wait! Stop! Do not answer that!"

Her father was married. To a woman half his age who Kat had met all of twice, but still. Cavorting with his ex-wife on a TV show was a new low. Poor Mindy. Hopefully she'd had a decent lawyer on the prenup.

A smile tugged on her mother's mouth. "All I'll say is when you're in the dating game it's nice to sometimes be with a man who already knows how your engine works."

"Oh, my gosh!" Kat slammed her hands over her ears before her mother could scar them further.

Caleb had made the mistake of taking a drink right as her mother brought up her "engine." Water sprayed out of his mouth, spattering his food and the front of his shirt.

Kat grabbed her napkin and threw it at him. How could this be? It didn't make any sense. Her parents had been divorced for almost fifteen years. They hated each other.

She looked straight at her mother. "Please at least tell me you haven't been the other woman." Her father had been married twice since he and her mother had split up. Did she have no self-respect?

"That's none of your business."

Now, *now,* her mother decided to be discreet?

"Just so we're clear, we're not getting back together." Her father leaned into his chair and took a sip of his wine.

The thought hadn't even occurred to her. Their marriage had seemed ordinary at the time. The ending, however, was one of nuclear proportions. She would have thought that bridge had been well and truly napalmed. But then she'd thought they couldn't even stand to be in the same room together. Look how wrong she'd been about that.

"Whatever you do, I don't want to hear about it. And I don't want to know about it."

"An arrangement that has been working well for years until you surprised us. Also, Cindy and your father have separated." Her mother's tone implied Kat had burst without warning into her bedroom instead of catching her making out with her ex-husband in a public restaurant, in front of a film crew.

Cindy. Not Mindy.

Caleb cleared his throat. "So how about that weather we've been having . . ."

Silence. Then Adam appeared at the table. Kat had never been so glad to see the producer. "We have some areas set up for individual conversations. Why don't we move to that now?"

"Great idea." Her mother gave a perky smile. "Caleb, shall we chat?"

"I'd love to." Caleb pushed his chair back.

Kat shoveled a lukewarm piece of ravioli into her mouth. Her mother would probably hit on him. Or at least make a point of shoving her surgically enhanced assets front and center.

At least it could be worse. If this were real, the man would be running for the hills.

CHAPTER TWENTY-SEVEN

Well, one thing was for sure: Kat's family might be small in number, but they weren't small in impact.

Caleb shifted, trying to get comfortable on the bar stool he'd been shown to. Next to him Darlene teetered on her own perch, her fingers playing with the stem of her wine glass.

"So, ma'am, what would you like to know about me?"

A cameraman hovered on the other side of the bar.

Kat's mother lifted her glass and swirled her wine before taking a slow sip.

Caleb's stomach growled. Man, he should have brought his food with him. He could have eaten while she pondered. They'd edit it out anyway. Long stretches of silence did not make good TV.

"What five words would you use to describe yourself?"

Caleb took a sip of his juice. "Well, safe. Obviously." At least Kat had given him a starter. "Loyal, determined." *Desperate. In trouble. Crazy.* "Reserved."

"What do you mean by that?" Her mother placed her glass of wine back on the bar.

Caleb shrugged. "I don't feel the need to talk a lot. I spend a lot of my days working alone on the farm, so I'm content with my own company."

"What about with someone that you love? Do you tell them how you feel or hold your feelings back?"

Caleb rubbed his hand across his scalp. "I guess it kind of depends on the situation. But once I know I love her and that she loves me, I'm all in."

"Your fiancée left you, didn't she?"

Wow, Kat's mother really didn't pull any punches. "She did. Yes."

"And how many relationships have you been in since then?" This time she picked up her glass and gulped back the remains.

"None."

"None?" Her eyes widened, and her voice pitched an octave higher. "I'm not just talking serious relationships. I'm talking short-term ones, casual ones, dating ones."

"Still none. I'd been set up on maybe three dates since I was with Emma. None of them made it to a second. Until Kat."

The woman crossed her leg. "Are you in love with my daughter?"

"She's a wonderful woman. I care about her deeply."

He'd been badgered all week during his solo interviews as the producers tried to get him to say the word. He wasn't falling for it.

There was only one way he would say he loved Kat—to her, and only to her. And only if he reached the point where he was willing to put everything on the line in a foolish and undoubtedly useless attempt at asking her to stay.

Which would only happen if the thought of living the rest of his life without her became enough that he was willing to ask her to consider a life that was less than she deserved.

"But you don't love her?"

"Mrs. McLeod . . . " *Was that even her name?*

She waved him off. "It's Ms. but whatever."

Caleb rested his elbow on the bar and decided to be as honest as he could. "Your daughter lives an impressive life. It's literally the complete opposite to mine. She has planes, big cities, movie sets, famous people. I live on a farm that's forty minutes from the closest town, and five minutes from the nearest neighbor. My life is dictated by seasons and animals and milk prices and the weather. For me, leaving isn't an option. Not even for love. I'm not naive. Kat could easily decide after a couple of months here that no matter how she feels about me, this isn't the life for her."

Her mother put down her glass, studied him.

"You're right. This isn't the life for her. I'm glad you're smart enough to see that."

Caleb deflated. Part of him had been foolishly hoping she'd say he was wrong. Say she could easily see Kat embracing this life. Loving it. Thriving in it.

"But there's also a chance I could be wrong." She circled the rim of her glass with her fingers. "I love my daughter more than life, but it doesn't take a genius to work out we're not close. Between her uprooted childhood and the divorce, her father and I probably didn't provide her with the stability she needed. We also have some different values." She quirked a smile that seemed to aspire for deprecating but instead just seemed sad. "As is probably self-evident."

"Do you have any advice for me?"

She thought for a second. "She had her heart broken a long time ago. She thinks I don't know about it, and it's true I don't know who he was or what happened, but I do know a broken heart when I meet one. She's never trusted anyone with her whole self since. Living on a farm in the middle of nowhere isn't your biggest obstacle. That is."

Caleb's heart thudded against this rib cage. Knowing Darlene was talking about him. Knowing the chances of Kat trusting him with her heart when he was the guy who had wrecked it in the first place were infinitesimally small.

"You're going to have to go all in first." Darlene tapped a finger against her empty wine glass. "If you want a chance at a life with her, you're going to have to be the one to take the risk and ask for it. She isn't going to hand it to you on a platter. She isn't going to give you a wink and a nod, signs she feels the same way. In fact, she will probably make it really, really hard. She'll make you prove you mean it."

He deserved that. But the thought of going all in for it not to be reciprocated, or for them to try and Kat to eventually leave? The thought left him hollow.

"Other than that . . . do you believe in God, Caleb?"

"I do."

"Then the only other good advice I have for you is to pray. Because you're going to need all the help you can get."

Kat shoveled the last piece of rubbery ravioli into her mouth. The fuller her mouth, the less conversation she had to make with her father.

Her father seemed to be okay with that arrangement. Drinking his wine, eating his pasta, ignoring the camera hovering a few feet away.

Kat looked at her empty plate, and her gaze wandered to Caleb's. Would it be rude to eat his food too? Before she could debate the ethics, Karissa pulled out his empty chair and sat down.

"We need you guys to talk to each other. Our viewers will be expecting a father-daughter chat, which means we need you to, you know, chat."

Kat cast a glance across the table at her father. The first man she'd ever trusted with her heart. The first man to break it.

Memories of her childhood rushed to the forefront of her mind. She was eight, begging him not to accept another posting. Begging not to be uprooted once more. He'd knelt in front of her. For a second, she'd thought he'd heard her. That maybe, for once, she would be more important than his job.

Then he'd grasped her chin between his hands and hissed at her. "You are a McLeod. You do not beg. Not ever. Not for anything."

She never had again—until the night Caleb broke up with her.

"He's not enough for you." Her father's voice broke through, forcing her into the present. He jerked his head toward where Caleb and her mother sat talking at the bar, as if who he was talking about might need clarification.

"What are you talking about?"

"Don't be foolish. He's a small-time small-town farmer. Attractive if you like the type. Nice enough for something interim, but you're not a small-town girl. When the butterflies and heady feelings of being the 'chosen one' die down, you will be bored out of your mind. What would you do with your life?"

"Exactly what I do now. It's not far to Brisbane. Considering Sydney traffic, it's probably about the same commute to the airport. I could pick up more work in Australia so I don't have to be away for so long."

Her father leaned back, his dyed-black hair glinting under the light. "Let's chase that rabbit down its hole, shall we? Let's say we reach the end of this journey or process or whatever it's called, and in two months you two are madly in love and want to make it work. He's here on the farm and you're flying in and out for jobs. Maybe that's workable for a year or two. But what if it's not enough? All his friends have wives or partners who are here. He's always the one going to things by himself, coming home to an empty house while you're cavorting with the rich and famous. Do you truly believe he would be okay with that? Because I'm telling you as a man, he won't."

Maybe if she wanted to marry a man like her father she'd listen to him. "I dated Dan for years and it was never a problem."

Her father barked out a laugh. "Because he was off on an oil rig for six weeks at a time and up to who knows what."

"Just because you go through women like popcorn doesn't mean all men do." Kat forced

337

in a breath before she lost her temper in front of all of Australia. "I'm not saying this is the perfect situation. I'm not saying we won't have challenges. But has it occurred to you for one second that a man who knows how to stay in one place is exactly what I need? It would certainly be a nice change."

Her father reached for the bottle of wine in the center of the table and poured himself another glug. "I know I'm hardly ideal father material, but don't choose a guy just because he's the opposite of me. You have a lot of me in you. You could have chosen any job in the world, but you chose one that keeps you on the move. You did that. Not me. Why do you think that is?"

Her father's statement set Kat back in her chair. He was right. She had chosen a life that involved having one foot in and one foot out of any given situation. Not having to commit to anything or anyone for longer than the space of a contract.

It meant nothing could ever get too serious. No one could get too close. Because there was always an end point. Always a date where she would be on another plane heading somewhere else.

What if her father was right? What if she was just like him, destined to live life as a nomad? What if staying wasn't in her DNA?

"Look, Kat, nothing would make me happier than to see you blissfully in love. But people like us aren't cut out for this kind of small life. Trying to pretend that we are will only lead to heartbreak. Both yours and his."

Text Message

Kat: So . . . Caleb met my parents.

Paige: I'm assuming separately.

Kat: Nope.

Paige: Oh. Wow. So how was that? Everyone still alive to tell the tale?

Kat: Apparently, they have been seeing each other. In a "friends with benefits" kind of way.

Paige: There's a mental image I never saw coming. Thanks for that.

Kat: If I'm going to be scarred for the rest of my life, you get to be too.

Paige: What did they think of Caleb? And vice versa?

Kat: My father thinks this is a phase. That in a few weeks I'll be desperate to be on a plane and in a big city. That I'd never cut it here permanently.

Paige: No offense, but your father isn't exactly known for making good decisions when it comes to marriage or parenting or relationships in general. See Exhibit A: Lindy. Why would you listen to him now?

Kat: I don't know. He made a good point. That I've chosen this nomadic life. He thinks that I don't have it in me to stay in one place for longer than a few months. That it's inevitable I'll get restless.

Paige: You are not your father. Don't let him project his stuff onto you.

Kat: He's right though. I love my job. I don't want to give it up. And Caleb can hardly circumnavigate the globe with me. He belongs here.

Paige: You realize you're talking like this is an actual thing, right? Not just a made-for-TV thing.

Kat: There are moments when it feels real. That maybe something has shifted for him. But maybe that's my wishful thinking. Wanting to see things that aren't there.

Paige: What if things have shifted for him? Then what?

Kat: I don't know if I could do that to him. Tell him there are feelings when I don't know if I'll be able to stay here. What if I wake up in a couple of months with the unquenchable desire to go?

Paige: But what if you don't?

CHAPTER TWENTY-EIGHT

Five days since her parents had left, and Kat hadn't had a decent night's sleep since. Her father's words about how she'd never be happy in one place continued to ring in her ears.

They taunted her as she'd "helped" Caleb around the farm and as they'd been sent on dates to secluded parts of the region to remain out of sight of the public.

If sleep was going to be impossible to come by, she might as well do something with her time. She crawled out of bed, slipped on a hoodie, grabbed her phone and padded toward the living area. Anything would be better than staring at her ceiling, playing her two weeks on the farm over and over in her mind. Analyzing Caleb's every move. Over-analyzing her every response.

She turned on the TV, flicking through channels of infomercials, music videos, and late-night talk shows. Off.

She'd tried books and magazines already. She could reply to one of the many trolls on social media, maligning everything from her intellect to her nose (must have had work done. No one has a nose that perfect). Scratch that. Starting her morning with a lecture from some SBC millennial with a degree in Twitter didn't appeal.

She needed to stretch her legs. Get some fresh air. But the world outside was pitch black, the nearest street lamp kilometers away. She pulled open a curtain and squinted at the main house, which lay shrouded in darkness apart from a dim light shining through the bathroom window.

The walls pressed in around her. She needed a torch, something with more grunt than the flashlight app on her phone. Surely Caleb had a proper torch.

"C'mon." She muttered the word under her breath as she opened the cupboard that held random stuff. Board games. Heavy boxes that looked like they held documents. A couple of blankets, a first aid kit . . . "Ta-da." She grabbed the black industrial-sized torch and hefted it into her hands. It lit with a click of the button.

Not as handy as a head lamp would have been, but it would do. She slipped her phone into her hoodie pocket, shoved her feet into her sneakers, opened the front door, and peered into the night.

A quick stroll to the animal yard and back. Twenty minutes of fresh air was all she needed.

Caleb would hate her roaming the place alone at almost midnight, but what he didn't know wouldn't hurt him.

She closed the door behind her and switched on the torch. Its sharp beam pierced the darkness in front of her and bounced off the cobblestone path as she walked. Perfect.

She soon hit the dirt road that would lead her to the highway if she walked far enough. The surface masked her footsteps into dull, almost-indistinguishable sounds.

Her steps lengthened, shoulders loosening with every stride as she passed the homestead. The beam of her torch became the only light. A cow bellowed somewhere across a paddock. Kat sucked in the fresh unpolluted air.

The minutes rolled by as she followed the torch's narrow beam down the road, never able to see more than a couple of feet on front of her. The story of her life.

The stars blanketed the heavens, a view rarely seen among the bright lights of Sydney. Despite the vastness, which should have made her feel insignificant, she felt seen.

"God, what am I doing here?" She whispered even though no one would overhear her.

She hadn't really prayed since she'd gotten to the farm. Instead, she'd retreated. Found it impossible to form the words she wanted to say. Possibly because she didn't know if she wanted to hear His answer.

"I know . . . I know I'm supposed to trust you." She barely managed to get out the words. "But this man has already broken my heart once. I've had enough to deal with this year without adding a second round into the equation."

That was it for her. She watched the light from her torch bounce along the path for a second. *C'mon, Kat. There are other people you could spare a few seconds for.*

"Please look after Allie and the baby. And don't let Paige get engaged while I'm gone. I'd like to be around for that. Oh, and my crazy parents." Her voice rose. "I know You love them and I'd like them to know You too, but they are horrible together. So if You could keep me away from whatever their little arrangement is, that would be awesome. Also, if this stupid show means we have to see them again, if You could stop my mother from flirting with Caleb, that would be great."

"She was flirting with me?"

Kat screamed and swung toward the sound of Caleb's voice.

He approached, hands in front of him. One held a hammer, and a head torch shone from his forehead.

"Oh, my!" Kat plastered her hand against her chest in case she needed it to catch her heart, which was doing its best to escape. Her other hand shielded her eyes from his torch.

"Sorry!" Caleb tilted his lamp up so the light didn't blind her. "I wasn't sure what was

344

worse. Surprising you or hearing something I wasn't supposed to. And I only had a second to decide."

"What did you hear?" When had she talked about him? Had he heard it?

"Just your mum flirting with me. I'm still trying to work out whether to be flattered or weirded out."

"I can't believe you missed it. She was looking at you like you were dessert and she was the spoon."

Caleb winced. "That's terrifying. How about we make a deal to never talk about me and your mother like that ever again?"

Kat couldn't help but laugh at the look of horror on his dimly lit face. "Sorry. But at least now you know why I never wanted you to meet her when we were dating."

Caleb scrubbed his hand across his head, apparently at a loss at how to respond.

Kat swung her torch around. Behind Caleb stood a fence missing its railings. Some pieces of wood sat propped against a post.

"Why are you mending fences at midnight?"

Caleb shrugged. "Sleep is overrated." Something about the way he averted his gaze said there was more to it than that.

"What else?"

Caleb spun his hammer in his hand. "Mum's not sleeping well. Sometimes it takes Uncle Jared an hour or longer to get her back to bed. She gets agitated if I try to help, so it's better to be out of the house. Doing something useful for him since I'm no use with her."

"I'm sorry." Kat kept her feet planted despite her desire to grab his face and kiss away the shadow of defeat in his eyes. She settled with placing a light touch on his hand. "I can't imagine how hard this must be. The last thing you need is me and all the cameras and the drama with the show . . ."

"Kat." The word rumbled out of his chest, and she looked into his shadowed face, which had somehow gotten a lot closer. "You are the best thing about all of this."

Oh. What did that mean?

Caleb shifted on his feet. "How about you? What's your excuse for roaming around at such a late hour? Which, for the record, I'm not a fan of."

Kat shrugged her shoulders. "Same. Not sleeping. Wanted to get out and stretch my legs without some camera peering over my shoulder and a mic recording every word."

"If it's too much, I would understand if you left."

Kat gave a soft laugh. "I don't think my two hundred thousand new Twitter followers would be fans of that plan."

Caleb caught his hammer as it faltered in its

spin. "Man, I'm glad I'm not on whatever that thing is. It sounds like a nightmare."

"Oh, you're on it."

"What do you mean?"

Kat pulled her phone out of her pocket. "Look." She opened the app, typed in @CalebFFTF, and pulled up his profile, complete with a photo of him leaning over a fence similar to the one he was currently deconstructing. "See."

Caleb leaned in, his arm brushing against hers. "But that's me!"

"Yup. Somewhere in your contract you would have given SBS permission to set up a social media account for you. You'll be on Facebook as well. Instagram. Maybe Pinterest."

"And then what happens?"

"Someone in their social media team is sending out tweets as you. See." Kat scrolled down showing the long list of tweets and photos of him promoting the show, teasers about upcoming episodes, short reflections on what happened in the last one. "You have a couple of hundred thousand followers as well."

"And these tweeters think this is me." His breath brushed against her cheek.

"Some will. Others will assume it's a publicity person."

"And what's that?" He pointed at the bell icon. The number attached to it had long since passed four figures.

"That's the notifications. Any time anyone sends a public tweet or retweets a tweet I'm tagged in, I get notified."

"And why do you have so many of them?"

Kat shrugged. "I hardly ever look at them. It's easier to ignore the trolls if you don't see what they're saying."

"So trolls are bad."

"Trolls are generally cruel, vindictive, horrible people online who hide behind anonymity. To be fair, there will be some nice people, but most of the time it's not worth scrolling through the garbage to find them."

Kat could see from his expression that he had no idea the depths to which people could stoop when given the cloak of internet obscurity. But then, why would he? Caleb had about as much use for Twitter as he did for a non-fat soy caramel frappe with no whip. "You can take a look if you like."

"Are you sure?" He looked down at her. "It's your messages."

"They're not private. Just think of Twitter like a massive billboard. Anyone can see what is written on it." She handed him her phone. "Just tap on the bell and scroll."

He took the phone, his calloused thumb tapping the screen at a slow pace. Kat took a few steps away. Whatever he was reading, she didn't want know.

He scrolled for a couple of seconds, his jaw tensing. "I'm not reading this!" He thrust the phone away from him as if it harbored anthrax.

Kat grabbed her phone before he could throw it. "If it makes you feel any better, you probably have just as many that your social media person has to sift through every day."

"I just . . ." Caleb swallowed. "I'm so sorry. I had no idea you would be dealing with ugly stuff like this."

"Hey." Kat nudged him with her arm. "It's okay. I knew. And it's after midnight, so why don't you channel some of that anger into the fence."

He looked back at the work as if only now remembering why he was there. "Do you want to stay while I do? It shouldn't take me too long. I can get you a blanket out of the ute." He gestured off to the side, and Kat realized she'd somehow missed the hulking farm vehicle parked only about ten feet away.

"Sure. You fix the fence. I'll get the blanket."

Caleb swung the hammer with all his force. The satisfying crack of it against the wood didn't come close to dulling his anger.

Kat lay on the blanket a few feet away, hands propped under her neck, feet crossed at the ankles, studying the stars. She'd turned off her torch, so the light of the moon and the occasional flicker of his headlamp when it bounced in her direction outlined her in a soft glow.

How she could be so calm was beyond him. All he wanted to do was hunt down the people who spewed hate across the internet and deal out some good old-fashioned Queensland justice.

Hey @KatMcLeod. I hear the QLD average IQ has dipped since you moved in.

Hope my next girlfriend has a rack like @KatMcLeod.

Most women end up just like their mother. Suggest you run from @KatMcLeod as fast as you can @CalebFFTF.

He slapped the final piece of board onto the post and powered the first nail in with a resounding whack.

"Are you trying to fix that fence or tear it down? It's hard to tell from here." Kat's words held a hint of amusement.

"How can you find those troll people funny?" Caleb slammed the next nail in, the hammer just missing his thumb.

"I don't. At all." Her voice sobered. "Okay, sometimes I do. The ridiculous ones. But don't forget, I've watched people with a much higher profile than me deal with this for years. I knew it came with the territory, which is why I've hardly looked at them since I arrived."

Caleb pounded in the last nail then dropped his

hammer into his tool belt, and tested the board with his foot. It held strong.

He picked up the leftover wood, propped the boards over his shoulder, and headed back to the ute. He tossed them into the tray then chucked his tool belt into the backseat before slamming the door shut. "Let me drop you back to your place."

His words came out brisker than he'd intended. The combination of the anger still swirling around his gut and the sight of Kat lying on his picnic blanket stirred so many emotions he felt as out of control as a spinning top hurtling across a wooden floor.

Kat propped herself up on her elbows, studying him through the torchlight. "Why don't you take a few minutes to calm down?" She lay back down before she'd even finished the sentence.

Caleb walked to the blanket and stood over her, hands shoved in pockets, not sure what to do. He could hardly leave Kat here by herself, but she clearly wasn't in any hurry to leave.

"Sit down, Caleb. You're blocking my view. Relax."

Caleb lowered himself onto the blanket as far away from Kat as he could manage without making it obvious. Quite a feat considering his fingers itched to tangle themselves in her hair, which was spread beneath her like a halo.

He tried to rid his mind of stupid people roaming the internet and focused on the broad expanse of sky. Tried to enjoy a rare waking moment without having a camera and producer scrutinizing his every word.

"How was your time with your father the other night?" With all the cameras around, they hadn't had the opportunity to properly debrief.

"It was fine. Thanks for the money, by the way." Kat flipped so she faced the sky once more. Changing subject was the tactic she always used when she didn't want to discuss something anymore.

And maybe the darkness had his eyes playing tricks on him, but she seemed to have shifted further away from him.

"I'm sorry you had to ask for it. I'm sorry all this is costing you far more than I knew." The jibes on Twitter started unraveling through his brain again. His hands clenched.

"I'm sorry I got mad at you about it. I . . ." Her fingers curled around the blanket. "I've had some health problems, and I have some bills I'm still paying off. That's the only reason I'm taking your money."

"How much do you need?" Caleb wasn't a rich man, but he had some savings stashed away. Living at home and working the family business was good for that. Paying off a few medical bills was the least he could do.

Kat waved away his question. "It's fine."

"Kat."

"Caleb." Her voice matched his with a similar edge. "They are my bills, my problem. It's not your job to rescue me. It's not anyone's. I'm a big girl."

He didn't want to rescue her. He wanted to love her. The desire expanded every day she was here.

"Are you okay?" She had to be. If something was wrong with Kat . . . He sucked some air into his lungs, unable to continue the thought.

She tilted her head toward him. "Don't worry. I'd hardly be here if I were dying of cancer, would I?" She reached across and poked him in the ribs. "I hate to break it to you, but if I were dying, being on a reality TV show definitely wouldn't have been on my bucket list. Not even for you."

A breath he didn't even realize he'd been holding leaked out like a deflating balloon. She was okay. He could take however this ended as long as Kat was okay.

Caleb caught her hand, wrapping his fingers around her wrist. "Are you happy? Do you ever get lonely? All the travel. Always being in a different place." This was probably the best time he'd find for a real conversation about her life. To see if she'd changed her mind since that article Conrad had showed him.

She rolled onto her side. Her head propped in her hand. "Sure. But doesn't everyone? I don't think that's a travel thing or a job thing. I think it's a human thing. Some of the people I've worked with are the loneliest people I've ever met. Yet they're always surrounded by a crowd. Always at the next party or the next place to be seen. It's why they'd rather go home with a stranger than leave alone. Alone is terrifying for them. It's made me realize what a gift it is to be content with your own company. You taught me that."

"I did?" Caleb couldn't have been more surprised if she'd said that he'd taught her how to knit.

"You probably don't remember, but when we first started dating I asked you how you could stand it. Spending hours alone most days on the farm. Do you remember what you said?"

"There's a big difference between being alone and being lonely." He couldn't recall saying the words to Kat, but it was the same thing his uncle had always said to him.

"Yeah. I always remembered that. Especially on some of the early movie sets when I was still trying to prove myself. I soon realized it was better to be alone but safe in my hotel room than lonely in a crowd with people I wasn't sure I could trust."

Something in her tone told him her conclusion was more than theoretical.

"Were you ever . . ." Caleb swallowed. "In a dangerous situation?" He'd never, not for one second, thought about that. Never thought that letting her go to live her dream could be placing Kat in harm's way. Never thought about the possible underbelly.

The weight of her pause flattened the air. "I've been well protected."

"What do you mean?"

She was silent for a second. "At the wrap party for *Alice*. I put my drink down on the bar and I went to go to the bathroom. The line was crazy long, so I decided to try again later. I was walking back to the bar when I saw the crew member I had been talking to drop something into my glass. I wouldn't have seen him if I had waited in line or if the crowd had delayed me for a couple more seconds."

Caleb couldn't breathe. Even though he knew she was fine. Even though she was right in front of him. "What did you do?"

"I caused a massive scene. Grabbed my drink and told him I had seen him put something in it. Told him I was calling the police and giving it to them for testing. I figured if I had been mistaken in what I saw, then he would say I was crazy and let me. But he freaked out. Grabbed the glass out of my hand and smashed it on the ground. One of the executive producers saw the whole thing. The guy's never worked in the industry since. At least, not that I know of."

Caleb's stomach turned. "It's my fault. You were there because of me."

"Caleb, it's not your fault." Kat's hand reached out and found his. "I'm glad I was there. What if I hadn't been? What if he'd decided to target any other woman in that room? He probably would have gotten away with it. I love my job. I love traveling. I love meeting new people and discovering new places. The Oscar means I have credibility. A voice. Which means I can watch out for other women. Help make my small corner a little bit safer."

"If something had happened to you, I could never have forgiven myself." He'd thought he'd been doing the right thing. Had been sure of it.

Kat's hand brushed his arm. "It's not on you, Caleb. My safety. My happiness. My life. None of it is on you. It's on God."

God. Where was God in all this? Kat had been praying when she'd walked up the road, chatting away like it was the most natural thing in the world. Her faith had clearly strengthened over the last decade. His had floundered when Emma left, then taken another nosedive with his mother's diagnosis. Not that either of those things were bad compared to what many people were going through. But still. There was something in him that felt cheated by the way everything had unfolded. "Honestly, God doesn't feel like He's been around much lately."

Kat raised herself to a seated position and

pulled her knees to her chest. "I know how that feels. The thing I've realized is that God always shows up. But a lot of the time, it's not in the way I want him to."

CHAPTER TWENTY-NINE

The sun was barely a hint on the horizon when Caleb finally gave up on sleep at five and trudged into the kitchen to make himself a cup of coffee.

"Morning." His uncle grunted the word as he dropped a pod into his coffee maker. The machine whirred into action.

"Morning." Caleb pulled open the pod drawer and selected a Ristretto.

"You were out late last night."

"Fixing some fences. And Kat was out for a walk, so we talked a bit."

"No cameras?" Jared waited for the last drip of coffee to finish falling then pulled his cup away. Caleb would miss their familiar kitchen routine when filming finished and his uncle returned home.

"No cameras." Caleb poured some milk into his cup, put it in the microwave, and set the timer for ninety seconds. "What do I do? Being here is costing her more than I ever imagined. You should see the hammering she's getting on social media. And I only read a granule of it."

"Are you asking me because you feel bad about what she's going through, or are you asking me because you still love her?"

"I love her." It was as simple and as complicated as that.

"Does she know that?"

"No." Caleb took his cup out of the microwave and placed it under the coffee machine.

"You planning on changing that any time soon? Because, if I'm not mistaken, there's only a few weeks left of this setup." Caleb heard his uncle's unspoken *thank goodness.* He probably couldn't wait for filming to be finished so he could trade farm work in for pottering around his vegetable garden and flirting with all the widows at the community center.

"What would be the point?"

"Well, I'm no Romeo, but even I know the point of such things is to see if there's a chance she may love you back."

"She *loves* her life. She told me that literally a few hours ago. She loves the travel. Loves seeing new places. Loves her work. She doesn't want the life I can offer."

"Yet she is still here." Jared looked at him pointedly. "Getting hammered on social media, whatever that means. Here. Not on some movie set on another continent."

Caleb couldn't deny the frisson of hope that sparked through him at his uncle's words, but he knew what this setup was, no matter how much he wished it otherwise. "She's here because she has big heart and I put her in an impossible spot to say no."

"Are you sure?"

"What do you mean?"

"I'm just saying you've been given a second chance with the woman you love. Not many men get that. If you love her, now's the time to do something about it."

"I don't want her to have to choose."

"Maybe it's time to let her be the one who makes that decision."

"She doesn't love me. She's here because I pressured her into staying. Because she has medical bills to pay and I'm helping. Because she's contracted to the show. Because it's her job."

"You don't think it's possible that can all be true, but she may also be here because she's no more over you than you are over her?"

No. It couldn't be possible. There was no way that someone as incredible as Kat hadn't moved on from him. She'd dated some guy for four years, for crying out loud.

His uncle placed his mug on the bench and pulled a loaf of bread out of the pantry. "I'm just saying that a long time ago you made a choice. Whether that was the right decision or not, it is what it is. But not putting yourself on the line because you think you're somehow protecting her isn't love. That's fear."

"What if it's just business for her?"

Jared shrugged. "Then at least you'll know and be able to move forward. You won't be left wondering if you let the love of your life go for a second time. What are you really afraid of?"

"That I'll tell her I still love her and find out she does have feelings for me. But months or even years from now, she'll realize this isn't the life she wanted and leave. I don't know if I could recover from that." He stared at the milk still white in his coffee cup.

"Caleb." His uncle peered at him with discerning eyes. "We've talked about this. Kat is not your father."

"I know she's not." He did. But he couldn't silence the part of him that told him that if he and his mother weren't a big enough reason for his father to stay, then he also wouldn't be enough for Kat. She might not be his father, but they shared big-city roots and a love of travel. In the end, trying to force his father to adjust to life on a farm had been like trying to force a rooster to be a chicken. What if it were the same for Kat?

His uncle slapped a couple of pieces of bread into the toaster. "So what? You'd rather take the chance of building a life with someone you love less? So it hurts less if they leave? There are no guarantees in life, Caleb. You don't go all-in with the person you can live with. You go all-in with the person you don't want to live without."

Easy for him to say.

"If love's staring you in the face, grab it with both hands while you have the chance. I had a great love with Susan, and even though we had years to say goodbye, I still carry regrets about everything I never said, never did while I had the opportunity. And now it's too late. For the love of God, Caleb. Be brave. Tell the girl you love her."

CHAPTER THIRTY

W e need more romance." Caleb had barely had a chance to say good morning to Kat before Adam stalked through her front door and delivered the edict with his usual finesse. "More kissing. More making out. Some wandering hands would be great."

"You ever tried to have a moment while a bunch of cameras and people stare at you, Adam?" Kat poured some kind of nut milk over her muesli. "It's not exactly conducive to romance."

Her robe slid off her shoulder, revealing a white singlet and tanned arm underneath. Her hair was tied into a messy bun on the top of her head, a pen sticking out of it at an odd angle—her storage place for when she was taking a break from the crossword puzzle. Reading glasses perched on the end of her nose—glasses she'd only fessed up to owning after she'd spent minutes trying to read the crossword held as far away from her face as her arm could get it and admitted she'd run out of contact lens solution. A problem he wasn't in a particular hurry to solve.

If it weren't for Adam being in the room Caleb

might have done exactly what the man had asked.

At least Adam had brought coffee, although the drinks would undoubtedly be lukewarm since the nearest coffee shop was twenty minutes away.

"Almond milk latte for the lady." Adam placed the coffee in front of Kat. "Flat white for you." He pressed the cup into Caleb's hands.

"Thanks, mate." Caleb took a sip. Yup, tepid. Oh, well. He lifted the cup to his lips for a second go. Adam wasn't so bad. He was just doing his job.

"Look." The producer sat down at the dining room table across from where Kat ate her breakfast. Ditched his satchel on the floor. "Don't pretend we don't know that as soon as filming finishes for the night you're all over each other."

In his dreams.

"We just need you to bring some of that to the camera, because you've been too restrained since the night at the restaurant. I don't know if you're having some kind of lovers' tiff or what, but I do have something I think might help." He reached into his bag, pulled out a laptop, and opened it.

Tapping the keys, he turned the laptop to face Kat but spoke to Caleb. "Take a seat next to your woman."

Oh, he wished.

The screen flashed up with the *Falling for the Farmer* logo complete with a photo of him and Kat holding hands and walking through the fields. One of the many taken on the photo shoot the day after she'd arrived.

Caleb stood behind Kat. "Look, mate, we've already told you we have no interest in watching the show."

"I know, I know. It's not an episode. It's just some snippets. To help you get the juju back. I promise. It's only a couple of minutes. Literally."

"Okay." Kat threw her hands in the air. "We'll watch it." She jabbed the enter button, and the photo dissolved into a video montage.

Kat falling on the first night and Caleb catching her. On the balcony during the first date. In the kitchen after the "fire" she'd foamed to death. Kissing in the cave, the shot dark and blurry. Caleb spinning her around when she'd arrived at the farm. The sizzling kiss in the kitchen the next morning. A heated look she'd given him after the great pig escape. Entwined in each other's arms outside the restaurant the night he'd met her parents.

Watching it all created a rolling desire to kick Adam out of the house and hold Kat captive until she agreed to stay forever.

The montage ended and Adam closed the laptop.

"I'm not sure what you were trying to convince us of, but it's certainly not that you have a shortage of romance."

Adam leaned forward. "That's the problem. We didn't have anything at that level in the last episode. The Twitterverse thinks something is wrong."

Like he cared what the twitterers thought.

Caleb stayed silent. He didn't have an answer to Adam's statement. He'd tried to connect with Kat all week, but she'd put up a wall. The night on the picnic blanket was the only time he'd managed to glimpse through a crack. If he were a betting man, he'd put his money that something had been said during the conversation with her father. She was pulling back while he was falling forward. His heart battered against his rib cage at the thought.

For the love of God, Caleb. Be brave. His uncle's urging echoed in his head.

Adam tapped the table. "Look, I'm not saying that we need some big cliché romantic scene. We just need thirty seconds of something that looks like a real connection. Today."

"And if not?" Kat raised her eyebrows as she picked up her coffee, a spark of the real her blazing in her eyes.

Adam sighed. "Then Vince may feel compelled to liven things up some more, and I don't think any of us want that."

No, no. They did not. The man had done them all a favor by cutting the disastrous dating-many-women format short but messing with it more?

Caleb didn't want to think about what that could entail.

But the last month and a half had shown Vince would do whatever it took to keep the ratings up. "Okay, let's see where today goes. Adam, can you give us a few minutes?" He glanced at the clock. "We'll be good to go at nine."

Adam stood and shoved his computer into his satchel. "Sound will be here at quarter to. We're heading offsite, and we need to leave at nine." He left through the front door, closing it with a click.

"Is everything okay?" Caleb asked.

"Sure. Why?" Kat pulled her pen out of her hair, averting her gaze. "I'm stuck on another word for purse, seven letters."

"You haven't seemed yourself the past week." *What did your father say to you? How can I counter it?*

"Sorry. Just a few things on my mind."

"You can leave, Kat. Anytime. We're far enough through that you could walk and the studio wouldn't be able to do anything about it. We can stage a fight. You can say you realized I'm not for you. This life isn't for you."

She stood and wrapped her robe tightly around her. "No. Definitely not. I'm here to do a job. I always finish what I start."

Her words were like a punch to his chest. He was still just a job. A job to be finished. It was one thing to be brave when you had the hope of success. Another thing completely when you were practically guaranteed failure.

It had been half an hour since they'd left the farm with a convoy of crew following them. Both of them were lost in thought.

I'm not my father. Caleb's not my father.

The thought hit Kat as Caleb had offered her a way out. Again. She didn't want to be anywhere else. She wasn't missing the buzz of planes and travel and movie sets. The only place she wanted to be was eating her cereal and doing her crossword right where she was. Forever.

She'd been flustered, so she'd blurted out something about finishing the job. The opposite of how she felt.

Caleb wasn't selfish. He wouldn't make major life decisions without her and expect her to follow in his wake. He would include her, consult her. He didn't spend his life striving for things that never kept him satisfied.

He was everything her father wasn't. That was the reason she'd loved him first and the reason she loved him still.

She wanted to stay. Not for days or weeks. *Forever.*

Caleb pulled his truck over to the side of the road and waited for the next car to pull in behind them. A sign announced Toowoomba was only five kilometers away.

He looked over and cast her a quick smile that didn't travel beyond his lips. "You okay?"

"Fine. Just thinking. You?"

"Same."

Her fingers yearned to touch him, so she took a chance and reached for the hand lying on his lap, fingers sliding into his like they belonged there. Caleb wound his fingers around hers and gripped them firmly.

Adam tapped on Caleb's window and he lowered it. "C'mon you two. You look like we're taking you on a trip to the morgue. I promise it's going to be a good time."

"It would be more fun if you told us where we were going." Kat didn't feel up for surprises. If they were going to be together and thrown off a bridge, she'd like to know about it.

Adam sighed. "Fine. The Toowoomba Carnival of Flowers is on. You're going to the wine and food festival."

Her whole body slumped in relief. She could do that. Eat some food. Drink some wine. Except . . . "So you've got us exclusive entry? It'll be just us?"

Adam laughed. "Hardly. That's not in the budget. You and a few thousand other people. It'll be great. Get you out of the bubble. Meet some people. Charm the viewers."

Kat's stomach clenched. Now she wished she and Caleb had watched at least one episode of the show so they'd know what people had seen. What they'd heard. What they knew. Or thought they knew.

"You do have special reserved parking by the entrance. We're heading to Upper Queens Park, so just follow us."

"You excited about getting out and about?" Caleb asked as he flicked on his indicator and followed the crew's car onto the road.

Kat glanced at the camera on the dashboard capturing their every interaction. "Excited. A lot nervous. We haven't been watching the show, so not knowing what people have seen is a bit crazy." There, stick that on TV.

Caleb squeezed her hand. "I'm sure everyone loves you just as much as I do."

Kat felt her eyes widen as his words filled the cab. *It's not real, Kat. It's not real. It's just for show.* And a smart move too. In any other situation, viewers would expect her to launch herself at him and some serious kissing to occur, but she couldn't do that while he was booting it down a highway at a hundred kilometers per hour.

"You love me?" The words leaked out of her mouth. Stunned. No acting required.

"I've loved you since the first night you fell into my arms. Before that, even." He gave her a long look before returning his gaze to the road. What was real and what was for show blurred at the edges.

The city limits of Toowoomba flashed past and Caleb dropped his speed.

What on earth was the squeaking sound? Oh, that would be her lungs trying to suck in air.

She should say it back to him. All the viewers would be waiting for it. But she couldn't—not knowing if everything, their entire arrangement, had just been tipped on its head or if Caleb was just upping the romance factor as he'd been instructed.

Caleb followed the crew's car in the park where large signs and banners proclaimed the Carnival of Flowers Food and Wine Festival.

They came to a stop. Crew exited SUVs on either side of them. Kat tried to unlatch her seatbelt but her fingers fumbled, somehow failing to complete the most basic of maneuvers.

Caleb leaned over and pressed the button for her, his fingers grazing against hers.

"Is it true?" She kept her gaze focused on her lap knowing she wouldn't be able to keep her expression neutral if he found some way to signal to her that no, it was just TV-Caleb talking.

Caleb unclicked his belt and lifting his hand, twisted a lock of her hair around his fingers. "Kat, look at me." His words were barely above a whisper, and her head lifted without her permission to face him. "It's the truest thing I know." His gaze never left hers, and no hint of pretense or reservation laced his eyes. "I know I'm just a man living on the farm in the middle of nowhere. I know you have this big, exciting life. I'm not stupid enough to think I can compete with that. But I'm here. And I'm yours. If you want me."

Everything faded around her. All she could see was the man she had never managed to let go. Leaning in, her hands travelled up his shadowed jaw and around his head, her thumbs smoothing themselves across his cheeks. *I love you too. I've never stopped.* But she couldn't say the words. Not until he knew everything that lay between them. He might think he loved her, but he wasn't making an informed decision.

Instead she pulled his head down and channeled everything she had into a kiss. Caleb's hands funneled through her hair then danced down her back.

Her body moved farther into him, bones liquifying at his touch. She longed to be in his arms, but the gear stick and handbrake hadn't got the memo.

Cheering broke through their kiss and they wrenched apart. A crew in front of the windshield directed a camera their way. Worse, a crowd around them clapped and cheered and whooped.

Caleb took in everything and grinned. "Well, so much for making a low-key entrance." He gave everyone a wave then leaned forward and kissed her again.

• • •

It had been, literally, the last thing Caleb intended to say. And he could've pretended it was just for the camera, but the surprise in her eyes replaced the look of wariness and reservation. He couldn't take the words back. Even if he wanted to.

And he didn't want to. He was tired of playing games. It was time to step up and put everything on the line. At least then he'd know he'd tried. Even if he ended up alone.

He hit the ground to the sound of whoops and cheers. Waving, he headed around the ute and opened Kat's door. She stepped onto the running board. He placed his hands on her hips and lifted her to the ground to the accompaniment of a chorus of female ooohs from the crowd.

Kat grabbed his hand and looked at him from under lowered lashes. He couldn't stop himself and she let out a startled yelp as he dropped her into a dip then kissed her soundly. Her back stayed as straight as a plank of wood for a few seconds. Then she relaxed, her arms creeping up to his shoulders and her lips softening into his.

Looked like he'd spontaneously kicked off his campaign to convince her to stay. For real. He stood, lifting Kat back onto her feet, lips plump from all the kissing. "Should we go?"

"Sure."

Their group moved like a swarm. A camera crew in front, then Caleb and Kat, then a small area of clear space, then another crew and a crowd of people milling behind them. It was a shock to be in a crowd after weeks of living in relative isolation. He squeezed Kat's hand, not intending to let it go for the duration of the outing. "Where should we go first?"

She could say Mars and he would get her there. Somehow.

"What is there?" Kat tucked herself into his side as he opened the program. Her lemon-scented hair lured him in, and he had to hold himself back from burying his face in it.

"Excuse me?"

They looked up to find a gaggle of young women surrounding them. Late teens, maybe? Their nominated spokesperson, a brunette with braces and an adoring gaze, approached Kat.

"Hi." Kat smiled. Better she than he, who leaned toward introverted grumpy farmer at the best of times.

"We just wanted to say that we love the show. And you guys. We all wanted it to be you from the beginning. It was like love at first sight."

"Thank you. We appreciate it."

"Can we have a picture?"

Before he could blink, the girls surrounded him and Kat on all sides, squishing against them. The brunette held up her phone, the camera showing a haze of faces. "Chelsea, you need to squish in more. I've only got half your face." The girl next to him got so close he hoped her father wasn't anywhere nearby.

"Smile, baby." Kat whispered the words in his ear, and he looked at the camera to see his face contorted into a grimace.

He managed to pull his lips back into an approximation of a smile while around him Kat and the girls somehow worked angles to make themselves all look like supermodels.

"Three, two, one, cheese!" The screen flashed as the girl took multiple photos.

"Thank goodness that's over," he muttered after everyone double-checked they were captured in flattering poses and the girls moved on with giggles and waves.

"You're going to be disappointed if you think that's the only time that's going to happen today. And we need to work on your selfie smile." She jabbed him in the ribs.

"I have a better idea." He placed his hands on Kat's hips and tugged her close. "I will do as many selfies as the fans want if I get to kiss you in every one. I can guarantee my selfie kissing face is a whole lot better than my smiling one." He waggled his eyebrows at her and she laughed.

"Food first, Romeo. I'm starving." She pointed to a caravan advertising tacos. "Mexican, please."

They headed over to the van, bought a couple of tacos, took a selfie with the server, and headed on their way. Kat didn't even wait to find somewhere to sit before digging into her taco. "Oh my gosh, this is so good." She mumbled the words through the mouthful of Mexican, the tip of her nose dabbed with sour cream and salsa.

She looked up at him as she placed the remains of her taco back in the cardboard tray. "What?"

He leaned over and swiped his thumb over the tip of her nose. "Nothing now."

She captured his hand as it dropped and wove her fingers through his, settling herself into his side. He knew it could all be an act for the cameras. That they might get back to the house and she'd return to the same distracted distance. But his foolish heart held out hope by the way she'd asked him if his declaration was true.

"Churros!" Kat pointed to another caravan.

"You haven't finished your taco yet!"

Kat tilted her head up at him. "Your point is?"

"Just don't blame me when you crash off the sugar high."

They headed toward the churros van, Kat's hand settled in his. If he ignored the cameras constantly moving in and out of view, the mic pack digging into the small of his back, he could almost believe they were just another ordinary couple on a date.

"Chocolate or caramel sauce?"

"Whatever." He didn't care if his sauce was chocolate, caramel, or jalapeño. All that mattered was whether he might have a chance to win back

Kat's heart. After all this time. After the way he'd stuffed it up. They were going to have to talk about why he'd broken her heart ten years ago. And he had no idea how she would take what he had to say.

"Relax." Kat traced a finger down the front of his shirt. "You look stressed. It's just sauce."

Caleb heaved out a breath. If only it were just sauce.

Kat leaned into him for a second, her head tucking into the side of his neck, her breath tickling his chin. She tilted her chin to look him in the eyes.

"What are we doing?"

He almost missed her whispered words among the sound of the churros frying and coffee machines grinding beans.

He rubbed his thumb along her bottom lip and watched her summer sky-colored eyes widen. "I don't know. But I'm done pretending about how I feel about you." He leaned forward and captured her lips. Wrapped one arm around her waist. Lifted his other hand up to her cheek.

He waited for her to pull away but instead she deepened the kiss, painting his world in technicolor. Her hands gripped the front of his shorts and pulled him closer.

"Oh my gosh, Kat." He whispered the words against her lips when they finally broke apart, gasping for air.

A cough in front of them broke the headiness. "Sorry. That will be eight dollars please." The teenage server looked mortified as he held out a box of still-steaming churros. Caleb dug into his pocket for his wallet.

Over the top of the crowd he caught a glimpse of brown curly hair he'd know anywhere.

"I'll get it." Kat had already pulled out her purse and was extracting some cash.

When Caleb looked back Emma was gone.

CHAPTER THIRTY-ONE

"What's next?" Kat uttered the first words since they'd left the Toowoomba city limits as Caleb's truck rolled to a stop in front of the big house.

Caleb eyed the crew's SUV pulling up next to them. "I'm not sure."

They'd attempted some idle chitchat for a few minutes after leaving the festival but had fallen into electric silence, hyperaware of the dashboard camera watching, waiting, judging every word exchanged.

Kat ran her hands through her hair. What were they going to do? How was she supposed to get through the rest of the afternoon with cameras recording their every move?

Caleb jumped out of the cab, and Adam approached him as he walked around the front and offered a high five.

Kat unbuckled her seat belt and got out of the car. Caleb reached out his hand as she approached, giving her the kind of smile that rendered her knees unstable.

"Vince is thrilled with the footage from the

festival," Adam said. "I'm going to review the first cut of edits with him and we need to swap out some gear, so you've probably got half an hour before we start filming again. Use it wisely." He gave them an ostentatious wink before turning back to the SUV.

Kat watched in disbelief as the SUV peeled away. Waited for him to spin around and declare it was just a joke. But the car disappeared down the road, spewing dust behind it.

"So . . ."

"So . . ."

"Should we go inside?" Caleb gestured to the big house.

"Sure." Kat's voice trembled. The game had changed at the festival. At least, she thought it had. But was she about to find out it hadn't? That it had all been an act?

She held Caleb's hand as if it were a life preserver keeping her above water in a raging ocean. "The churros were good."

Caleb looked across at her, a smile on his lips. "The churros were good." He pushed open the front door. "Not my favorite, but good." The door closed behind them, and they pulled out their mic packs and disconnected them as if by unspoken agreement.

"What was your favorite?" Kat tried to keep her tone neutral but only made it about halfway.

Caleb swung around from where he'd placed

his pack on the dining table and covered the distance between them in two steps. He tossed her mic pack onto the couch, and tugged her toward him. His breath feathered her face as he lifted one hand and grazed her cheek. "You, Kat. You're my favorite." His gaze probed hers.

Her breath faltered, words buried deep in her chest.

"I don't want this—us—to be pretend anymore. I want it to be real. I'm in this. Not for the cameras. Not to save myself from being sued. Not for my mum. I'm in this for you."

Kat could barely process what he was saying. "So all the things you said in the truck . . ." Once more she couldn't finish her thoughts, the implication of his statement too much to take in.

"All true. Every single word. We've been given a second chance. A crazy, unexpected second chance. I wake up every single morning and the best thing about my day is that you're here. And I don't want it to end. Not when the cameras leave. Not ever." Caleb ran his fingers down the side of her face, across her lips, and she leaned into them. No cameras. No demanding producers or viewers wanting romance. Just them.

"Please, Kat." He dropped his words to a whisper. "I know I broke your heart. I can't change that. But I would give anything to have another chance to win it again." He kissed her then, a slow, lingering kiss that pushed her fears of inadequacy away and erased her sense of everything except him.

The kiss lengthened and she was pressed against the front door, her fingers curled around the lapels of his shirt, and his forearms braced on either side of her head.

They finally broke apart, breathless.

Caleb tipped her chin up with his fingers. "Should I take that as a yes?" His voice was gravelly, his eyes glazed. His other hand was buried in her hair, his fingers spinning it in loops.

"It . . ." A warning gong sounded in her mind.

I love you. I want to spend my life with you. She'd heard this all before. Ten years ago, they'd sat on the porch swing she could see out the window, and he had made all sorts of promises about a life together.

She'd been expecting a proposal. Instead she'd gotten her heart broken. And he had never so much as sent a text message until this insane show threw them back together.

She moved sideways, ducked under his arm. "I don't know."

Caleb stepped back and shoved his hands into his pockets, confusion swirling across his face.

"What happened to us, Caleb?" She sucked in a breath. "You can't make grand proclamations like that and think it wipes away the need to tell me what happened."

She walked into the kitchen and switched on

the kettle for a cup of tea. Not that she wanted one. But she needed something to do with her hands. Something to give her mind a few minutes to catch up. Because all her body wanted to do was be back in his arms.

He came up behind her as she ripped open the packet of her herbal teabag and dropped it into a cup. Her body tingled at his nearness. *Don't turn, Kat. Whatever you do, don't turn. Because if you do and he tugs you back into those arms, you won't get the answers that you need. The best chemistry on the planet doesn't fix a broken past.*

"We were so young, Kat."

Kat poured the boiling water into her cup. Watched it turn light pink. Stirred. Watched it darken. "We were twenty-four, Caleb, not seventeen."

She picked up her mug and walked toward the sitting area, forcing herself to put one leg in front of the other. Not to look at him. She sat down in the single chair, wrapped her hands around the cup, and allowed the heat to seep into her cold fingers.

After they'd broken up all she'd dreamed about was Caleb Murphy showing up and admitting that he'd made a mistake. That he couldn't live without her.

Now that day was here, but a few words and some heated kisses couldn't undo years of hurt. Not without any explanation as to what had caused the hurt in the first place. Not when his declaration that she wasn't enough rang in her ears as she'd worked every day to prove him wrong. When they'd overshadowed every significant achievement.

Caleb dropped into the couch opposite her. He leaned forward, forearms propped on quads. His gaze studied her face. "What do you want to know?"

"When did you stop loving me? Why?" The questions that haunted her spewed forth without hesitation. She hadn't seen their breakup coming. Years later she still didn't have a clue when everything changed.

"I never stopped loving you." He said the words without hesitation, as factually as if saying the sky was blue instead of tilting her world on its axis.

"I'm sorry. What?"

"I broke up with you because I loved you so much I knew I had to let you go."

Kat stared at him, unable to process what he was staying. He had to let her go? What did that even mean?

The silence stretched for a few seconds. Her hands shook, hot tea sloshing over her fingers. She leaned forward and placed the cup on the coffee table. Pink liquid spilled over the sides of the mug and dripped onto the wood.

"I'm not following." It was her voice yet not

her voice. "You're going to need to run that by me again."

"You were going to turn down that job on *Alice in Wonderland*. For me. It was your big break. I couldn't let you do that."

That job had been her first step onto the movie ladder. It set up a chain of events that led to *The Dark Knight* and *The Hobbit*. Her entire career.

"I hadn't decided whether I was going to take the job or not." She'd been vacillating, half of her wanting to embrace the adventure and the other half reluctant to leave the only place she'd ever felt like she belonged. The only person.

Caleb shifted in his seat. "You were leaning toward turning it down. Staying here. Because of me. I couldn't let you do that. I loved you too much. I had to let you go even though it broke my heart."

He had to be joking. "It broke your heart? It broke *your* heart? I was expecting a proposal and instead I got a 'You're a great girl, Kat but I've decided you aren't right for me' speech. And I never knew what had happened or what had gone wrong. Don't you dare talk to me about your broken heart!" Her voice rose in pitch, in volume. In anger and disbelief.

Caleb's jaw tensed. "Yes, I made the decision. But that doesn't mean it didn't cause me pain. You're living in the flipping monument to it!"

She couldn't believe this. She hugged her legs

into her body just to give herself something to hold onto. "But that's the point. You made the decision. Not me. Not us. You. You decided what was the right thing for me. For my life."

She'd thought he was different. Had been sure he was nothing like her father.

"And look at the life you've had. Your dream of working on major films has come true. You can name your price. Choose your work. You've won an Oscar."

How could he not get this? "Who cares? Want to know a secret, Caleb? Heaps of people have won Oscars and a lot of them are miserable. A golden statue doesn't keep you warm at night. A golden statue doesn't comfort you when you've had a bad day. It's not a husband. It's not a family."

If Caleb had given her the agency to make her own decision they'd be a family by now. The thought barreled from her with the force of a tsunami. She launched out of her seat, adrenaline hurtling through her body.

Caleb's hands clenched. "You needed more than this. You deserved more than this. I knew that if you decided to stay you would regret it. That eventually you would resent me. I couldn't live with myself knowing I had robbed you of that opportunity, robbed you of the life that was made for you. So yes, I made the decision I thought was best."

"It wasn't your decision to make!" She roared the words so loudly the crew in the editing suite probably heard them. She stopped pacing and zeroed in on him hunched over on the couch. "Would you do it again? If we could do it all over, would you do the same thing?" Only one answer could save them now.

He looked up at her, haunted determination in his gaze. "Without the benefit of hindsight? Yes. I would rather you hate me than resent me. Be trapped by me."

She brushed past him, grabbing her suitcase out of the closet on her way to the bedroom. Once there, she emptied all the drawers and grabbed clothes and hangers out of the wardrobe, shoving them in without rhyme or reason.

"What are you doing?" Caleb appeared in the doorway.

"What does it look like I'm doing? I'm leaving. It's time for this to be over."

"You can't mean that."

Kat stormed into the bathroom, sweeping products off the counter and into her makeup bag. Returned to find Caleb where she'd left him. She threw the bag onto her crumpled clothes.

"Please, Kat. Calm down. Take a minute. Let's talk about this."

"We have nothing to talk about, Caleb." Shoes. She needed her shoes. She dived back into the wardrobe, snatching up flats, sneakers, and sandals and tossing them into her suitcase. The boots the show had provided could stay. "You knew. You knew how much being in charge of my own life mattered to me after a lifetime of being dragged around by my father's postings. Of never having any say. Of never getting to decide. Of never even getting to have an opinion." She looked around the room. Grabbed her Bible and vitamin pills off the nightstand.

"Kat." His voice cracked with the three letters. Snapped her attention back to his face. "Please. Don't."

"You robbed me of the choice to decide who I loved, Caleb. To choose what I wanted for my own life. I never would have resented you or felt trapped. I would have loved our life. If you had let me choose." Her own voice broke and tears streamed down her face. "I would have loved you."

"You can't know that." Caleb scrubbed his face.

Kat jerked the lid down on her suitcase, leaning her body weight into it to zip it up. "I can. Because ever since, I've been trying to find a person who makes me feel like you did. Trying to find a place to belong like I felt I belonged here. All this time, I've thought the problem was with me. That I wasn't enough. That when you got to know the real me, the true me, I wasn't what you wanted. But the problem wasn't me. It was you. Your fear. Your insecurity."

Kat hauled her suitcase off the bed and pulled it toward the living area.

She turned and looked at him as she reached the front door. Had they really been making out right here only a few minutes ago? "We could have had a second chance." She shut her eyes, almost unable to bear how close they had been. "All it would've taken was for you to admit you were wrong. That the choice was mine to make. Not yours. Not ever yours."

Caleb watched Kat storm to the front door. If she opened it and walked out, that would be it. There would be no third chance.

"I'm sorry. I'm sorry, Kat. Please don't go. Just give us time to talk about this. We can quit the show. Whatever it takes. I don't care. Can't we at least take some time? Talk about this. Please."

Kat let go of her suitcase handle, rubbed one hand across her cheek. "You cost us everything, Caleb. You cost us everything and you don't even know it."

"Tell me, Kat. Tell me what I don't know." He took a step toward her, but she took a step back. He took a step back. And another. Whatever it took to keep her away from the door.

"Ten years, Caleb. We could have had ten years by now. We could have had a family. Kids."

"We're not sixty. We can still have them. I

know we've lost time. We're older than we would have liked, but that's the new normal."

"We can't. We can't." The anguish in her voice almost split him in two. Her fists clenched at her sides as she took a couple more steps away from the door. "Seven or eight years ago, maybe. Even five. But not now. Not now."

He heard the words but couldn't comprehend what she was trying to say to him. "What do you mean?"

"There will never be any children, Caleb. Not for us."

What was she talking about? They'd talked about having kids. Four of them. Six.

"I don't understand."

"You don't have to understand. I. Can't."

His eyes narrowed. "Can't? Or won't? Is this because of your messed-up parents? We're better than them, Kat." The words hit the room loud, accusing, and she flinched. He'd just uttered something unforgivably cruel without even really knowing what it was. "I'm—"

"Look!" Kat had yanked up the bottom of her T-shirt, revealing a horizontal scar across her lower torso. "Does this look *optional* to you?"

"What . . ." Caleb's jaw hung.

She tugged her T-shirt back down. "I can't have children because I had a hysterectomy. Nine months ago. The part of me that would have made me a mother was cut out of me and discarded with medical waste. After years of excruciating pain and every medical test under the sun and consults with the best doctors in the world, the answer was that some things just can't be fixed."

She wasn't angry. Angry he could have dealt with. Angry meant she had some fight left. It was the slump of her shoulders and the defeat in her eyes that undid him.

He scrambled for words, but none came. Instead, a memory resurfaced. They'd been dating a couple of months. He'd arrived to pick her up for a date to find her pale and lifeless, curled in the fetal position beside her bathtub.

He'd lifted her off the floor and she'd come around. Refused to go to the hospital. Told him it was female issues. And he'd been too awkward, too mortified, to inquire any further. "That day you passed out on the bathroom floor. When we were dating. It was because of this."

She sighed. "Yes. It was endometriosis, but it took the doctors years to work out. By then it was too late. The damage was done."

"What does that mean?" He'd never heard the word before in his life.

"Think of it like cancer. Except not. It doesn't kill you. Though it certainly makes you want to die."

Caleb tried to process the information. Kat couldn't have children. They wouldn't be able to have children. If she loved him. If she stayed.

And staying was hanging on a knife edge. His brain stuttered over that. Whenever he'd envisioned their future together, it had always included a cadre of kids.

"That doesn't need to change anything." The words were out before he'd thought them through, but since he'd said them he had might as well bulldoze on.

Her finger stabbed at him. "Don't be so naive, Caleb. Of course it does. It changes everything. This land is your legacy. And I can't give you an heir." Then she started to cry. Great big aching sobs.

He took a step toward her, but at her upheld palm he froze like a Roman statue. "It doesn't. There's adoption, fostering, surrogacy."

She sucked in a breath. "I'm not going to do that to you."

"Do what to me?"

"None of those things offer any guarantees. Not even close. I can't let you give up your dreams of a family. You deserve to be with someone who can give you that."

Caleb stilled. The hairs standing up on the back of his neck told him whatever he said next could be the difference between Kat staying or leaving.

"I don't care about anyone else. Not their uterus or their eggs or any of it. I want you. Even if we never have children, I still want you."

She looked at him with pity clouding her eyes. "You have no idea what you're saying."

He knew exactly what he was saying. He didn't need to think about it. Process it. To know he would rather have Kat with no kids than anyone else with a passel of them. "I know exactly what I'm saying."

Kat sighed. "You may think that now. But eventually you'd resent me. We'd grow old and you'd look out on this farm you'd have no one to pass it on to and you'd wish things had been different."

"I wouldn't. With God as my witness, I wouldn't."

"Well, now you know what it feels like."

"What?"

She gave him an exhausted smile. "To have the decision made for you."

Someone knocked. Kat grabbed the door handle and flung the door open. There, on the porch, stood Emma. A posse of cameras and crew surrounded her.

Caleb stumbled back, his body tensed like someone had thrown him against the wall. He swung around. If the cameras were outside, they were also inside.

There they were. In the corner of the lounge. Half hidden in the alcove. The crew must have come in while he and Kat were in the bedroom.

She hadn't seen them. Had no idea that all her

pain and heartache had just been filmed for the country to see.

God, what had he done?

Kat yanked her suitcase across the threshold. "He's all yours, Emma. I'm out."

CHAPTER THIRTY-TWO

This could not be happening.

Caleb scrubbed a hand across his eyes, certain that when he pulled it away his ex-fiancée wouldn't be standing there. Except she was. Looking like she hadn't aged a day since she'd left. Even wearing the boots he'd given her for her birthday.

Behind Emma, a door slammed, then an SUV peeled away with Kat in the backseat.

To be fair, Emma looked as stricken as he felt. One hand clutched the door frame and her face about two shades paler than usual.

"What are you doing here?" He tried to keep his voice neutral in a situation that was about as neutral as Chernobyl. Whatever it was, he guessed she wasn't here to pick up the sweater, two books, and scented candles she'd left behind.

It wasn't Emma's fault. Why ever Emma was here, she wasn't the reason Kat had just left. No, he'd managed that one single-handedly.

Emma looked over her shoulder at the SUV tearing down the drive kicking up dust. "She's gone?"

"Yup. I guess you got your wish." His words tainted with bitterness.

Emma took a step inside the house. "That was never my wish."

"Then why did you send Conrad here to speak with me right after she came to the farm?"

The camera crew in the house crept out of the alcove and closer to him. Vince would probably be having a heart attack over what great TV this was. Caleb couldn't even summon up the energy to attempt to have his first conversation in four years with his ex-fiancée in private. What did it matter when he'd just lost Kat?

"That wasn't why I wanted to talk to you."

Emotion churned within him, most of it ugly. The woman standing in front of him had left. Just disappeared, leaving him with no answers and an entire wedding to cancel.

Every second they stood here Kat was getting further away. "You know what, Em? I don't actually care. I said no. Yet here you are." He crossed his arms over his chest. If she thought he was going to invite her in and make her a cup of tea, she could keep dreaming.

"I knew you'd never gotten over Kat." She said it as a fact. No resentment or bitterness. Just flat out.

He was not taking this. Especially not right now. Caleb walked up to her until he was almost in her personal space. As he looked down at the woman he'd once planned to marry he felt nothing but tired. "I loved you. I asked *you* to marry me. Not Kat. I chose to build a life with you. And you left." And now Kat had left. He didn't even try to hide the anguish in his voice.

"I know." Emma didn't look away. Didn't make excuses.

"Four years, Emma. It's been four years. How many times did I call you and you never picked up? How many voicemails did I leave that you never replied to? How many texts did I send that you didn't answer? The only reason I knew you were okay was because your mother took pity on me." On what was supposed to be their wedding day. She'd showed up at the farm and sat on the porch and told him it was time to let Emma go. That she wasn't coming back. Handed him a check for the lost deposits and cancellation costs. Which he'd torn up and thrown into the wind.

Emma stared at the floor for a second before squaring her shoulders and looking back up. "I got scared. I didn't think I was ever going to live up to her."

"What are you talking about?" Emma and he had talked about Kat maybe twice. He'd shared the bare bones of their relationship, a relationship that had already been years in the past.

"Your front door. It was yellow."

That blasted front door. Again. "What about my front door?"

"She wanted a yellow front door. Your mum let it slip. This whole house is pretty much a tribute to Kat." Emma straightened her shoulders and crossed her arms like she had something legitimate to be offended about.

Caleb stared at her. "That had nothing to do with you. With us. I built the cottage long before I met you."

"But you kept the front door yellow. Like you needed it to be yellow in case she came back." She looked at the offending door swinging wide open behind her.

"Are you kidding me?" What was it with women and reading something into every little thing? "I kept the front door yellow because it was yellow and I had no reason to change it. If it bothered you, why didn't you just say so? I would have let you pick whatever color you wanted."

"I didn't want to have to ask!" The words burst out of Emma. Full of hurt and fury.

If he were a swearing man . . . "Are you telling me you left because I was supposed to somehow magically know the color of my front door bothered you because it reminded you of my ex-girlfriend. One who I broke up with years earlier and hadn't contacted since."

"I know it sounds ridiculous."

"It sounds worse than ridiculous. It sounds like an excuse. You can't seriously expect me to believe that's the reason you left. That after eighteen months you chose to abandon us and everything we had planned rather than have a conversation about my front door."

She looked at the TV cameras. "Do we really have to do this with them here?"

"I'm in a TV show. They're part of the package. Also, you were the one who brought them here." If she hadn't, he might have had a few more minutes with Kat. He might have been able to convince her to stay. To at least talk things out some more. He forced himself to breathe. First, he had to get through what was in front of him.

It hadn't even been an hour since they'd gotten back from the festival. How was it possible for everything to have imploded in less time than it took to make a good risotto?

"It wasn't just the front door." Emma pulled him back to the present.

"What else was it?" He could not believe they were standing here, having this conversation.

"What's your alarm code?"

"5286."

"What does that spell, Caleb?"

"Nothing. It spells nothing. It's just a number." Middle, up, down, diagonal right. He'd tapped the same pattern to unlock his phone forever.

"A number that spells Kat M."

Did it? Caleb wrenched his phone from his pocket and stared at the screen. It did.

"Do you know what people who are over

relationships do, Caleb? They talk about them. But not you. Not when it came to Kat. Every single time I asked about her, you brushed me off or changed the subject."

"Because it had been years, Em. I didn't see the point." Caleb shoved his phone back into his pocket.

"So what was the point of the box in your wardrobe?"

He stared at her. He'd forgotten about the box. When he had broken up with Kat, he'd taken everything meaningful from their relationship and put it in that box. Photos, tickets to events, letters, copies of significant emails. It was all in there. But how did Emma . . .

"Don't look at me like that. I wasn't snooping. I was looking for a blanket and it fell out. I already suspected the truth, and the box confirmed it."

"It was just a box. A box where I put a bunch of stuff in after we broke up and never looked at again." Well, almost never.

"Do I have a box, Caleb?" She asked the question softly but it packed the power of a missile.

She didn't. And they both knew it.

Emma toed the wooden floor. "Did you ever love me the way you loved her?"

"No! I loved you differently because you are two different people. But I broke up with her and I proposed to you. How does that not say everything you need to know?"

"People propose for the wrong reasons all the time."

But he hadn't. Had he?

"Anyway, that's why I came today. You looked happy at the festival, but I knew you'd sabotage yourself eventually. That you'd convince yourself that you weren't good enough for your dad to stay or for me to stay, so you'd tell yourself Kat wouldn't stay either. That's why I came today. I wanted to tell both of you the truth about why I left."

"Why didn't you tell me this four years ago?"

"Would you have believed me if I'd told you I was calling off our wedding because you weren't over your ex-girlfriend?"

No. The truth was he wouldn't have believed her for a second. Would have thought she was being ridiculous. Seeing things that weren't there.

Emma pulled a chair out from his dining table. Dropped down into it like she'd lost the energy to stand. "I knew I was right. But I wanted to be convinced I was wrong. I loved you. I would have given in, told myself I could measure up to her. But I couldn't deal with the idea of living my whole life feeling like I fell short. Knowing that one day you'd wake up and realize you had settled for me. I had to leave." She leaned forward, dark curls spilling over her shoulder. Her top teeth nibbled her bottom lip the way they always did when she was nervous.

"That would never have happened." He wasn't that guy. Once he was in he was all in. No second-guessing. No contemplating whether the grass was greener elsewhere.

Emma reached out her hand then seemed to think better of it and withdrew it. "I know you would have never left me. Not physically. But I was selfish. I wanted all of you. And when I stayed here, I realized how much of her you still carried. I knew a large part of you would never be mine. Because it had already been claimed by someone else."

CHAPTER THIRTY-THREE

Kat had been stuck in the apartment for four days. At least they'd given up trying to get her to say anything after the first two. She'd sat in front of a camera with a producer throwing everything they could at her to get her to crack and she hadn't said a word. Then a psychologist. Then Lauren from the magazine. Then Vince.

She was under contract for another ten torturous days—apparently the small print said she'd agreed to let them hold her hostage if she exited the show early. So here she was. Stuck in an apartment somewhere in Brisbane with Karissa and a cameraman babysitting her 24/7.

Her pulse skipped at a knock on the door. It would totally be a Vince thing to put Caleb on her doorstep. What would she do if it were him?

"You should get that." Karissa didn't even look up as she scrolled through her phone.

"Is it Caleb?"

"No." Karissa's voice softened and she placed her phone down. "It's not Caleb."

"Please tell me it's not my mother."

Karissa cracked a smile as she shook her head. "We're not that cruel."

Then Kat figured she could handle whoever was on the other side of the door. She released the deadbolt, pulled the door open, and peered around.

"Happy birthday!" Paige grinned at her and flung up her hands.

It was her birthday. Thirty-five. She was thirty-five today, and her cousin was here.

Kat burst into tears. She was pretty sure she'd cried more in the last four days than in the last four years.

"Shhh." Paige stepped forward and pulled Kat into her arms. "It's going to be okay."

At least she didn't say *I told you so.* Which Kat would have deserved. She snotted all over her cousin's T-shirt, her mascara streaking black marks across one shoulder.

She stepped back. "Sorry. Come in."

Paige shrugged as she closed the door behind her. "You and I both know you could weep for the next hundred days and still wouldn't come close to the number of tears I've drowned you with."

Except Paige won in the "things worth crying about stakes." Her brother. Her lifelong dream.

"I brought supplies." Out of her purse Paige pulled out a bottle of Sav, a box of Kat's favorite tea, a package of chocolate-dipped biscotti, and a block of Whittaker's chocolate, placing them all on the kitchen counter.

"He loves me." Kat hiccupped out the words to the question Paige hadn't even asked.

"The entire country knows that." Paige held up the bottle and the box. "Wine or tea?"

"Tea. Please."

"Allie's been trying to call you. Did *they* take your phone away?" Paige eyeballed Karissa over Kat's shoulder. No doubt the cameraman was filming this little reunion. Kat wasn't an idiot. Paige had only landed on her doorstep as their last-ditch attempt to get her to talk.

Fine. She'd let them win. As long as they kept the cameras out of her face. "Sort of." She'd given it to Karissa to stop herself from contacting Caleb. Or crumbling if he contacted her.

Paige flicked on the kettle as she muttered something under her breath that probably wasn't strictly appropriate for a worship megastar's future wife. Then she tore open the package of biscotti, took one, then pushed the bag toward Kat.

She took one and snapped it in two, her stomach rumbling. When was the last time she'd eaten properly? The taco at the festival? A swell of nausea hit.

Paige poured boiling water into two mugs, and the tea bags bobbed like buoys on the ocean. Kat picked up the biscotti and chocolate.

Kat sank down onto the couch, allowing the cushions to buffer her and ignoring the camera pointed in her direction. She'd stopped caring about what Australia thought of her the day she'd walked off the farm.

"Want to tell me what happened?" Paige picked up her mug, studied Kat over the rim.

"He says he always loved me. He broke up with me so I would take the job on *Alice in Wonderland*."

Paige groaned. "Oh, Caleb."

"He's not sorry. He said he would do exactly the same thing again in the same circumstances."

Paige blew her breath out as she dragged a hand through her blonde hair. "He wouldn't."

Kat shrugged. "He thinks he would. He stuck to it even though he knew I was furious with him. Even though he was trying to convince me to give him another chance."

"And you . . . turned him down?"

"How can I be with a man who thinks he's entitled to make decisions for me? He changed the course of my life, Paige. Unilaterally."

Paige took a cautious sip of her tea. "I'm not saying that's okay. I'm not defending him. But you need to be sure you can't find a way beyond it."

Kat sighed. "It doesn't matter. Even if I could, I can't give him what he needs."

"I don't understand. I may not know him. I may

406

have only seen him on screen. But I'm pretty sure the only thing that man wants is you."

Kat's heart contracted at her cousin's words. Part of her wanted to believe this crazy, messed-up thing would still find a way to end like a Nicholas Sparks movie. Preferably the ones where no one died in the end but she'd even take *The Notebook*. "The farm has been in Caleb's family for six generations."

Paige settled back, attentive but with a furrowed brow.

"He's the end of the line. The farm moving down to the next generation sits on him."

"And you don't want to have kids?" Paige's expression showed only concern, no judgement.

Kat sucked in a breath. Once she started, she'd have to explain everything. No going back. No knowing what the crew would do to her words in the editing suite or how they would be portrayed to the thousands of people watching.

"Kat?"

"Can't. I . . . I can't have kids."

Paige stayed at her end of the couch as if recognizing that if she came closer, offered any form of comfort, Kat might not be able to finish what she had to say.

"Is this why your father offered to freeze your eggs?"

Kat shook her head. "No. He doesn't know anything. No one knew except my doctors. And

407

now Caleb and . . ." She waved her hand at the camera. "Well, most of Australia sometime next week."

"What . . ."

"Endometriosis." One word. How could one word, even one with thirteen letters and six syllables, possibly cover years of agony, uncertainty, and heartbreak?

Paige's forehead wrinkled. "That's that uterine tissue thing isn't it? I don't know much about it. Do you want to tell me, or should I look it up?"

She didn't know if she could tell Paige about it. Putting the pain of the last two decades into words was unimaginable. She half-smiled, half-grimaced. "Google can tell you everything you need to know."

Paige pulled out her phone and tapped on the screen. Read and scrolled. Read and scrolled. One minute became five. Five became ten. Kat could imagine what she was reading. If anyone had ever looked at her internet history, her secrets would have been revealed in seconds.

Finally Paige lowered her phone, a sheen in her eyes. "For how long?"

"Since I was fourteen, but I was only diagnosed a couple of years ago."

"But that's . . . that's . . ." Paige did the math in her head. "Twenty *years*. How is that possible?"

"Unfortunately, it's not uncommon." Not when you had a mother who briskly informed you suffering was the price of womanhood, and a father whose go-to piece of advice was "life is pain." Along with a string of doctors who misdiagnosed her with everything from appendicitis to irritable bowel disease, or thought she was exaggerating or making up her symptoms.

Although Kat still had no idea why anyone would want to make up the humiliating and degrading symptoms that came with a reproductive system meltdown.

"Have you had surgery? A . . ." Paige lifted her phone back up and looked at her screen. "Laparoscopy?"

"Two. Last year."

"When?"

"January and September."

"But I was here in September." Paige looked panicked. "How did I miss it?"

"You thought I was on location." Kat wasn't proud of deceiving her cousin. She prided herself on being an honest person. But she had been carrying it alone for so long that she hadn't known how to let anyone in.

"I thought you were on location, but you were in hospital?" Moisture glazed Paige's eyes.

"Just a couple of days in the hospital. Then I stayed in a hotel."

"You stayed in a hotel rather than tell me what you were going through?" Paige's voice cracked, and a tear dripped down her cheek.

"I'm sorry, Paige." Kat clutched the pillow to her torso. "You had so much going on with moving to Australia and your new job and Ethan. I didn't want to add to your burdens."

And falling in love. Her cousin had been falling in love while Kat was making decisions that would change her whole life. It had been easier to compartmentalize.

"But that's what friends do. We share the burden. That's the point." Paige faced her head on. "Does Allie know?"

Kat gave a small nod. Her head felt too heavy for her neck. "She knows about the endometriosis but not how bad it got. I know it doesn't make sense, but I had to separate it all. It was the only way that I could put one foot in front of the other. You and Allie had so much stuff going on, and it felt good to be the strong one. It gave me meaning. Purpose. I didn't even know what was wrong with me until a couple of years ago. I went to so many doctors and had so many diagnoses. And those were the ones who believed me and didn't think I was a drama queen or just crazy. How could I explain it to you when I didn't know what it was?"

Paige blew out a breath. "I'm sorry. It's a lot to process. That we've been living together for over a year and I somehow missed all this. How could I have missed this?"

"It's not your fault, Paige. I've spent more than

half my life living with it. Hiding it." Admittedly having someone move in with her had upped the challenge, but it was worth it.

"What happened after you were diagnosed?"

"First, the doctors changed my medication, which helped for a while. But then the pain came back, so I had surgery. That helped for six months but my symptoms came back again. I had to take more time off work. Then it got so bad I started having to turn down contracts. That's when I had the second operation." The agony had almost been overshadowed by the euphoria. She wasn't crazy. The pain was real. Everything she'd gone through had a reason. A name. The surgeon had shown her photos and, as she'd looked at the fibrous webs and bubbles that coated her insides, vindication had coursed through her.

"And no one here knew? No one at all?"

"Dan knew a little bit. Not everything, but some." Hearing her ex-boyfriend's name was weird. She'd barely thought about him in months. "He knew having children wouldn't happen. It was a factor in our breakup."

"Wait, what? I thought you broke up with him."

"True. But I kind of jumped before I was pushed." *I love you, Kat, but I don't know if I can get past this. I'm going to need some time. Let's talk about it when I'm back.* The words had been the final nail in their coffin.

Paige looked down at her screen. "Okay, I know

411

we're bouncing all over the place here but there's still treatments, right? Fertility drugs? IVf?"

Kat shook her head. "Not for me."

"But there are, like, sixty-year-old women having twins . . . What aren't you telling me?"

Kat forced herself to look her cousin in the eye. "I had a hysterectomy."

"When?" Paige barely managed to choke out the word.

"Earlier this year."

"What? Did you tell me you were on location again when you weren't?"

Kat closed her eyes. "No. You were in the States. With the band. I didn't plan it that way. The pain got so bad I passed out on set. I ended up in hospital and said I wasn't leaving until they fixed me." Which was a lot more time and paperwork than she'd imagined. Turned out doctors were reluctant about taking out the uterus of a thirty-four-year-old woman when she hadn't had any children. While in the next breath telling her that her uterus was functionally useless.

Paige shook her head. "But I called. We talked. Texted. The entire time I was gone."

"It was fine. I had a week in the hospital then recovered at home."

"Who looked after you?" Paige's eyes widened as she processed. "No one?" Tears shone in her eyes. "You went through that all alone."

"It wasn't so bad." The physical pain, at least.

412

That was a blip compared to what she'd lived with for a large proportion of the last twenty years. The emotional pain of waking up knowing she would never be whole again, that all hope was gone. That had been what had kept her in bed for days.

"Why didn't you tell me?"

"I thought it wouldn't be as hard if I didn't tell anyone. Wouldn't be as real." *McLeods don't fail.* Yet despite doing everything right, her body had failed her in the most fundamental way. "Caleb loves kids. Loves family. He wants six. We're both only children. Even if we'd been able to have kids, they wouldn't have had cousins. He needs to marry someone with a big family. Someone who can give him all the kids he wants." *Someone like Emma.* "I'm not enough. I can't give him enough."

Paige ran her hand through her hair again, twisting it around her fingers. "Don't you think he should get to be part of that conversation?"

"Like I was part of the conversation when he decided to break up with me for my own good?"

"Touché."

"I can't do that to him. He's a good guy. He'll feel obliged to say it's okay. To try to find a way to make it work. To compromise the one thing he wants more than anything else."

"But what if that one thing isn't kids? What if it's you?"

413

"It can't be. Maybe that's what he thinks now, but eventually he'll move on. Find someone who can give him the life he deserves."

"So this is how it ends? With you doing the exact same thing to him that he did to you?"

Paige's question slapped her in the face like she'd been doused in cold water.

"Think about all the things you would've missed out on if he hadn't made that decision. Right or wrong. You wouldn't have met Allie. I wouldn't be living in Sydney. I wouldn't have met Josh." Paige quirked a smile. "Because it is all about me, after all. You wouldn't have gotten to travel the world and have your dream career. I'm not saying it hasn't cost you a lot, but it hasn't been a terrible life."

"He cost us the chance at a family, Paige. I don't know how to forgive that." And there it was. In all its brutal and ugly honesty. She was a person of faith. She believed in forgiveness. But she didn't know how to forgive Caleb for this.

Paige's fingers played with a throw pillow for a few seconds while she thought. "You can still have a family. Maybe it's not the one you'd hoped for or the one you'd imagined, but families are made in all sorts of ways."

It was true. Kat knew that. The online forums were full of stories of women like her who were navigating their new normal for families. But it wasn't enough. Whenever she looked at them, all she could see was herself at twenty-four when the prospect of one day carrying her own child was a real possibility. And Caleb had taken that away.

"Have you prayed about it?"

"We're not really talking at the moment." She slept with her Bible under her pillow. Apart from incoherent senseless prayers, that was all she'd been able to manage. As if the right answer might find its way through some form of osmosis.

"God is not indifferent to your pain."

"Really? Because it sure feels like He is." Indifferent to her pain. Indifferent to her debt. Indifferent to her humiliation. Indifferent to how she'd spent so long trying to keep her head above the water. Trying to hold it all together.

"I know it does. And I know it's not fair that our world is broken and our bodies are broken along with it. But you have power in all of this. You chose to carry this alone. You didn't have to. I would have been there. Allie would have been there. But you didn't give us that opportunity. And now you want to make that same choice again. To choose your pain over the only guy you've ever loved? To choose pain over the chance at life?"

She wasn't choosing pain. Pain had chosen her. Kat curled her arms over the part of her body that had so ruined her.

"I'm not saying it's going to be easy. It's going

to be hard. It's not the love story you imagined. But six months or a year from now, will you regret that you didn't at least try?"

Kat closed her eyes. "Once he's thought it through, once he's processed what I've told him, I don't think there's going to be anything there to try for."

CHAPTER THIRTY-FOUR

Caleb walked into the milking shed feeling like he'd been run over by a combine harvester. He'd had four hours of sleep. Maybe. Every time he closed his eyes, the slam of the door as Kat left reverberated through his dreams.

Then Emma's face appeared, as she'd told him the reason she'd left him was the same thing it had taken him a decade to figure out.

But his uncle had probably had even less sleep. The older man trudged around the perimeter of the milking shed, iodine solution in hand to clean the cows' teats.

"Morning." Caleb snapped a pair of gloves on then grabbed a handful of towels and started wiping the solution off the cows' teats to prepare them for milking.

At least in here he was safe. Safe from the prying eyes of the cameras. Safe from the probing questions of the producers and the shrink they'd brought in to check on his mental health.

The guy had pronounced him shell-shocked. Like he'd just come out of the trenches of the Somme. He wished he were shell-shocked instead of experiencing the full weight of what his fear had cost Kat. Had cost them both.

"Morning."

"How's Mum?" Now that Kat was gone, he spent most of the day either with Mum, or working on the farm at places the cameras couldn't go. But she still wouldn't let him help her when she woke at night, agitated and confused. He'd have to bring in a night nurse once his uncle moved home.

"Restless. Confused. Scared." His uncle turned his head but not before Caleb saw the way his expression crumbled like a sandcastle hit by a rogue wave. "She had a few lucid moments last night."

And he'd missed them. "What did she say?"

"She asked where you were. If you were happy. She checked, again, that I had remembered to delint the dryer."

"What did you tell her?"

"That you were doing your best to make her wish come true. I assume that's still the case."

"It's been five days. I don't know where she is. She isn't answering her phone or replying to my messages." Caleb chucked a couple of dirty towels into the laundry pile. "You didn't see her face. I don't think she can ever forgive me. And even if she did, I don't know if I can ever forgive myself."

"Funny thing about forgiveness." His uncle

418

worked quickly through the cows as they stood patiently, well used to the daily routine. "Last I checked, it's not a feeling. It's a choice. Actually, scratch that. It's not even a choice. It's a command."

Caleb grabbed another handful of clean towels, picked up his pace to match his uncle's. "I know. But even if—when—she forgives me, we can't change what's happened. Like with Emma. I've forgiven Emma, but there's no going back."

"But you love Kat."

"Yes." It was as simple and as complicated as that.

He had to tell his uncle everything. SBC were screening the day of the festival as a two-part special to string out the season. The one with his and Kat's breakup wouldn't air for another couple of days. Once that happened, everything would go crazy.

"Kat can't have kids. That's why she left. I told her I loved her and why I broke up with her. And . . . she told me that she can't have kids. That I cost us our chance to have a family. That ten years ago it would have been possible but not now. Not—" Shame choked him as surely as if there had been a hand wrapped around his throat.

His uncle listened, staying silent as he affixed suction cups onto the cows.

"Does it matter to you? Knowing we may

never have children? That I may be the end of the biological line?"

His uncle stopped and looked at him, one eyebrow quirked high. "This may be news to you, but I put that fear to bed long ago when it became apparent that Susan and I weren't going to be blessed with children. She was forty-one when we got married. There was every chance it wasn't going to happen for us. A few people even encouraged me to pursue someone younger for that very reason, especially since your mother's miscarriages were an open secret and she'd given up hope of ever having a baby. Before I asked Susan to marry me, I first had to settle in my own heart that if it was God's plan that this strand of Murphy DNA ended with me and Marion, then His plan was better than my own desires."

Caleb had never thought about that.

Jared rubbed an arm across his sparse hair. "We're not guaranteed anything more than the single second we're standing in in this life. You could get married and have thirty years together. Or it could be cut tragically short in just a few months. Making decisions on what you could have or not have is a fool's errand. You make decisions in faith with what you do have, trusting that God will be sufficient in whatever the future holds. I wouldn't have wished for a life with anyone other than Susan. Not for ten children and a guaranteed family line until Jesus returns.

I would still choose her. I would still choose the life that we had."

"Even if I can find her and tell her I was wrong and I never should have broken up with her, she may not choose me. Even if she can forgive me, she may not be able to love me."

"Welcome to free will, son. Imagine how God feels every day."

His uncle's words pierced deep down into his soul. Every day he made the wrong choices and every day he was forgiven. Loved.

"Caleb, you need to settle this in your own heart before you talk to her. And I'm not talking in a romanticized I-love-her-and-we-can-make-this-work kind of way. I'm talking in a covenant-until-death kind of way. In a way that if you never have children, biological or otherwise, a life with her and only her will be enough. You have to let go of that dream. Just like I did."

His words fell like weights into Caleb's soul. His uncle was right. If he wanted Kat to be the person he woke up with every morning and fell asleep with every night, he had to give up the dream of blond children running through the pastures. Of teaching his son how to fish and his daughter how to ride. Of small hands reaching for him and small voices calling him Dad. Of another generation of Murphys to hand this farm to.

"I—I need a moment."

"Take all the time you need." His uncle took the clean towels out of his hands and Caleb turned, stumbling, out of the shed. He made it only a few feet before his knees gave out, landing him on the cold damp ground. Caleb buried his head in his hands.

The tears rolled down his face and landed on the shoots of grass like spring rain.

In his desperation to stop Kat from walking out the door, he'd told her he didn't care if they never had children.

His words had been thoughtless and cruel.

He saw that now. She'd had years to come to terms with what her illness meant, yet the pain across her features had been fresh. And he had brushed it aside as if it was nothing. He'd spent longer deciding what kind of burger he wanted at McDonald's than he had contemplating the lifechanging news that she had told him. No wonder she'd left.

He claimed he loved her, but nothing he'd done in the last few days had been about love. It had been about what he wanted, not what she needed.

He let the enormity of the truth land on him. Kat was never going to be pregnant. She was never going to achieve her dream of four children and a family nothing like the one she'd grown up in. She'd never take a pregnancy test or lie on a bed in an obstetrician's office and watch a tiny heartbeat blip on a screen. She'd never feel new life growing inside her or know the joy of an unborn kick. She'd never get to hold a new baby minutes after birth, knowing her body had created it, nurtured it, loved it.

She'd had to sit in a doctor's office alone and be told one of the things she'd most longed for in life—something most people took for granted—was never going to happen.

His sobs echoed from the dirt as he tried to imagine what that day must have been like for her. The agony of the decision to give up on all hope of ever carrying a child to reclaim some of her life back.

Is she enough?

The words echoed through his soul. If it were her and only her for their whole lives, would that be enough? If they never had kids of any kind, would the two of them be enough? In a year? Ten? Fifty? And would he have the courage to admit it to himself if it weren't?

He closed his eyes and played back some of the last few weeks. Kat walking out of the SUV and up the front path. Kat eating her cereal at his dining room table. Kat peering over her glasses to do the crossword. Kat in the kitchen, protecting her stuffing while he bled. Kat rubbing his mum's hands, her touch careful and tender. Kat lying on the blanket and gazing at the stars. Kat's body pressed against his, her smile only for him.

His heart rate slowed, and he drew in deep breaths. He wanted a life with her, only her, like the crops wanted rain in the summer. That life would be enough. *It would be more than enough.*

Now he just had to find a way to convince the woman he loved.

Two hours later, Caleb walked up the path to his house, his steps heavier but his heart lighter.

"Caleb?" A blonde girl stood from where she was sitting on the steps to his porch. He knew exactly who she was. She was a little shorter and a bit curvier but looked enough like Kat that she had to be related.

"You must be Paige." Going by the way she'd crossed her arms and jutted out her chin, she was here to tell him exactly what she thought of his cowardice and general tomfoolery. He couldn't blame her.

Caleb strode across the cement that separated them. "Is Kat okay?"

That was all he cared about. Paige could tear as many strips off him as she liked, as long as she could tell him Kat was okay.

"What a stupid question. Of course she's not okay, you idiot."

"I deserve that."

"You don't say."

Caleb wasn't entirely sure where to go from there. He assumed Paige had something to say

424

since she'd traveled about a thousand kilometers to get here.

So he waited.

Kat's cousin studied him for a few seconds, hands on hips, chin still jutted out. The woman's fierce expression shot apprehension down his body. She and Kat clearly shared the same DNA. "Do you love my cousin? Do you love her even though she can't have babies? Do you love her enough to give this all up if she wants you to? Do you love her enough to fight for her even when she tells you not to? Do you love her enough to put it all on the line, not knowing what she might choose?"

Hope sparked to life within him. For Paige to be here she had to think there was some chance, no matter how tiny, that he and Kat could come back from this.

"Yes." His voice caught, and he gathered himself. He'd need all his wits about him to impress this firecracker of a woman. "Paige, I love your cousin with all my heart. I was hotheaded and selfish the day she left. She told me something huge, and I didn't treat it with the care it deserved. I will give her whatever time she needs. Will you please tell her that?"

She studied his face like an artist studying a masterpiece then her expression softened. "No, I can't tell her that. She needs to hear it from you."

"Do you know how I can talk to her?" He

wasn't an idiot. Even though the cameras had stopped following him around he knew the crew would never let the show finish with Kat leaving like she had. They'd probably left him alone because they were working out how to get him and Kat face-to-face.

"I can't get you to her, but I have a plan. We're going to need some help. Where are your TV people?"

Facebook Messenger

Janine: I just watched the latest episode. I'd ask if you're okay, but that would clearly be the world's most asinine question.

Kat: The show let Paige see me yesterday. That helped.

Janine: Do you want me to call you?

Kat: No—calls end up on camera. Besides, I know how crazy your schedule is. Where are you anyway?

Janine: In transit at LAX. United has just delayed my flight, so I have nothing but time. Also, I just spent the last hour and a half sitting in the United lounge with my laptop and my headphones and ugly cried so much that one man across from me became so uncomfortable he relocated himself, and another brought me a box of tissues and half a glass of vodka. I know that because I made the mistake of thinking it was water.

Kat: You know you probably shouldn't let it get out that you spent your layover doing shots and watching reality TV.

Janine: Good attempt at diversion. Now let's talk about what's really going on.

Kat: There's nothing to talk about. You just watched it. It's over.

Janine: See, here's my problem. You and Caleb are stupidly in love. Admittedly, the stupid part of that is winning right now. But lucky for you, you have one of the world's most renowned pastors on your Facebook friends list. So, just between you, me, and the free United wi-fi that may or may not have been hacked by the Russians and/or the NSA, why don't you take advantage of that?

Kat: I need some more peanut butter M&Ms.

Janine: Sold.

Kat: I'm dreading what they're going to do.

Janine: What do you mean? Who?

Kat: The producers can't let the show end with me leaving like that. Audiences need closure. Remember Rachel and Peter's hideous break up on *The Bachelorette*?

Janine: I still can't talk about that.

Kat: My point exactly. It's been over a year, and you and half of Bachelor Nation still haven't recovered. Which is how I know that sometime tomorrow, or the day after at the absolute latest, I'm going to have to face Caleb in front of a bunch of cameras. Maybe a live audience. Who knows what the producers are planning.

Janine: What are you most scared of? What the show is going to do, or that he'll try to convince you to give him another chance? Or that he won't?

Kat: I love him, but I don't know how to forgive him.

Janine: Forgiveness isn't a one-time thing. It's a choice we make over and over again. You don't have to know how to forgive him. You just have to want to try.

Kat: Even trying feels impossible. When I think of what he threw away without giving me any choice . . . presuming to make the decision for me. I'm so angry.

Janine: But how is what you're doing right now any different than what he did to you? Yes, he took a choice away from you and the consequences of that are devastating, but now you have a second chance and you're the one taking the choice away from him. Is this how you want this to end? Choosing to settle the score over the chance of rebuilding something that could be great?

Kat: I don't know how. I feel broken.

Janine: I know. But we are more than the sum of our parts. Especially our broken ones.

Kat: But my broken ones change everything.

Janine: No, they don't. And I'm sorry for

whoever it was that told you the lie that your value is somehow increased by a functioning uterus. Your value is in who you are, not your reproductive capabilities.

Kat: Even if I could forgive him, I don't know how to get beyond the idea that being with me will rob him of the family he deserves. Of him having a legacy.

Janine: There are many ways to have a legacy. Biological children are just one of them. Many people who've never had biological children have left greater legacies than those who have. I'm not trying to pretend what you've been through, and what you'd have to grapple with as a couple, isn't a big thing. But I think you're giving it a power to define your life that it doesn't deserve.

Kat: He thinks he loves me. That this doesn't change that. But I don't know if he's really grappled with what it will cost him.

Janine: Then you ask him some hard questions. You talk it through. And if he still says the same, you have the choice whether to trust him or not. But if you say you believe him, then you have to commit to trusting him. Because if you say you believe him but allow doubt to flourish in your heart, that doubt will eventually destroy your relationship from the inside out.

CHAPTER THIRTY-FIVE

*I*s *this really how you want this to end? Choosing to settle the score over the chance of rebuilding something that could be great? If you say you believe him then you have to commit to trusting him. Doubt will destroy your relationship.*

Two days later, Kat still couldn't shake Janine's words. It hurt to think of herself as a small person, the kind of person who could throw something great away just to settle a score.

Forgiving Caleb was one thing. But trusting him with her heart again when he had been so careless with it the first time? When he was still adamant he would do the same thing again? She didn't know if she was a brave enough person for that. Didn't know if her heart could bear the weight if she took the chance and it all unraveled. Again.

She didn't know if she wanted that chance. Didn't know if he were even willing to offer it.

The limo pulled into the driveway of the mansion, and Kat tried to breathe through the dress constraining her ribs and the trepidation tangling her sensibilities.

At least it wasn't a live studio audience. That would have been a million times worse.

The car rolled to a stop and her lungs seized.

She couldn't do this. She couldn't do this.

"Just breathe." Karissa offered the advice from the opposite seat. "You can do this. Just breathe."

The mic pack poked into her back, reminding her that everything that happened in a few seconds would be seen by half the women in the country. And would be on YouTube for the rest of her life.

Bright lights cut through the tinted windows of the car. Behind them, she could see movement as the crew readied themselves for her entrance.

Whatever happened, the show would soon be over. No more cameras following her every move. No more producers asking probing questions. She could leave the country until the tabloid had moved onto another celebrity breakup. Until people forgot about her and her non-existent womb.

The driver's door opened, and he got out of the car. Then her door opened, and a hand reached in.

Don't think, just do it. Grabbing the hand, she put down a stiletto-clad heel and stepped out. Every second was a second closer to the end.

She stood and discovered the man who'd

assisted her out of the car wasn't the driver but the host of the show. Mark? Matt? She hadn't seen him in weeks.

"Hi, Kat. How are you?"

She just looked at him, attempting to keep a straight face at the spray tan that had left his skin a burnt orange color.

Tucking her hand into the crook of his arm, she followed with her eyes as he gestured to the arbor, again dressed in fairy lights. They entered the tunnel but this time the cameras followed.

They walked, her heels echoing across the paving. Mark kept a firm grip on her hand as if fearing she might try and do a runner. And go where, exactly?

Just before they reached the end, Mark paused and faced her. "This is where I leave you."

"Thanks, Chris."

"What?"

"Sorry, Mark." *Stop stealing Chris Harrison's lines, dude. Then I might remember your name.*

Two cameras hovered nearby, waiting for her to move. Lifting up her skirt, she stepped forward and focused on putting one foot in front of the other. She would *not* fall into his arms this time.

She walked, focusing only on the path in front of her. If she had to look up and see him she might unravel on the spot. Collapse into a satin-spooled puddle.

Five steps, ten. Shoes came into view. Not men's ones. They were silver and sparkly.

If the producers had set up some kind of ex-girlfriend ex-fiancée showdown, she was out of here. She would walk to the road and hitch-hike home if she had to. After she'd stabbed Vince with the heel of her stiletto. That would give them good closure for TV.

Her gaze traveled up the legs to the full skirt of a cocktail-length blue dress. It wasn't Emma. The person was too tall to be Emma. What on earth was going on?

She looked up. "Paige? What are you doing here?"

Her cousin looked like a Greek goddess in a navy one-shouldered number. Someone who was almost as good as Kat had done her makeup.

She looked around. Searched for Caleb. But he wasn't there. The area was empty except for a massive screen positioned against the side of the mansion. Two directors' chairs sat in front of the screen.

"Where's Caleb? What's going on?" She spun around just in case he was about to leap out of the bushes or something.

"He'll be here. But there's something you should see first."

"What? What is it?" Of all the scenarios she had mentally prepared herself for, this was not one of them.

Paige grabbed her hands. "Do you trust me?"

Kat looked at the screen, the chairs, the mansion, the lights, the cameras, then back at her cousin. Paige had never let her down. Not ever. Paige had let Kat into her whole story. But she had let Paige down by not trusting her with her pain. The least she could do was trust her now. "Ye . . . yes." She gathered her courage. "I trust you."

"Then come sit down. It's just a few minutes, I promise."

They walked over to the chairs. One had *Kat* written on the back, and the other was blank. Kat lowered herself into the chair, unsure if her legs would hold her for much longer. Paige sat down next to her and grabbed her hand.

They were plunged into semidarkness as the big set lights snapped off and the screen lit up.

It was Caleb, sitting on the couch in his house. He looked awful. There was no other word for it. He clearly hadn't shaved for a few days. His eyes were bloodshot, and his face haggard. At least someone had managed to find him a clean and pressed set of clothes.

"I met Kat when I was twenty-four." He leaned forward on the couch, his voice rough and uneven. "She was—is—the great love of my life."

His words plastered her to her seat, and she allowed them to seep beneath her skin. This was not a man throwing out his love to try and convince her to stay. This was a man who had wrestled with the cost of her words. And still said she was the love of his life.

A tear dropped off her chin and onto her collarbone. Then another. She believed him. And she wanted another chance, whatever the risk.

"But from the moment I met her I knew I couldn't offer her enough. That my life wasn't big enough for her. She was living in Brisbane to study film and theater makeup. We had been dating for six months when she graduated and got this amazing offer to work on a film.

"I made the biggest mistake of my life because I was scared. Scared she would turn down the job for me. Scared she would wake up in three months or six and realize what I already knew. That she deserved better than me. Better than my world. Because that was what my father decided when I was six years old. I broke up with her so she would leave. And I got my wish. She left, and she's lived an amazing life for the last ten years.

"But I was wrong." He looked down, placed his hands over his face, then rubbed his eyes, resolve shining through. "I told myself I did it out of love for her, but the truth was I did it out of fear for me. Because I was afraid I might never recover if I let myself love her completely and she left me."

"I never recovered anyway. I just didn't realize it until the night I walked onto this show almost three months ago and, by the grace of God, she was there."

She was up, on her feet. She didn't want to watch some stupid movie. She needed to find him.

"Don't walk out." Paige's frantic whisper drifted toward her. "Please hear him out."

"Where is he?"

Paige pointed toward the mansion.

The clip was six minutes and thirty-two seconds long. They were two minutes and sixteen seconds in. Caleb stared at the shaking run sheet in his hand.

At four minutes Paige would slip out of her chair, if she could. At five minutes he would go and stand behind Kat's chair and, if everything they had put together still hadn't convinced her, he would put on the performance of his life. Put everything on the table.

There was movement outside. Something wasn't going to plan.

His stomach sunk into his feet. She was leaving. Before she'd even seen it all. They'd known that was a possibility but had hoped Paige being there would prevent it.

He shifted toward the door. He wouldn't let her go that easily. Not this time. If he had to run down that driveway and make his case on the side of the road he would do it.

The door flung open and he lost his breath as Kat burst through it. She stood before him, her cheeks tear streaked, the long skirt of her golden gown clutched in one hand.

"I was supposed to come to you." Yeah, not exactly the opening he'd rehearsed.

"Say it to me." The words tumbled out. "If you have something to say, say it to me. I want it from you. The real you. Not an edited version on a screen."

"I—"

She stepped forward, her dress shimmering under the lights. A second camera crew entered the room behind her.

Her gaze sought his, held his. Unwavering.

This was it. His third strike. And he was going for the home run.

"Katriona McLeod, you are the love of my life. I know I stuffed up ten years ago. I know what that has cost you can never be repaid. I'm sorry I was young and stupid and scared. I'm sorry I had the best thing in the world in front of me and I threw it away because I thought something that good couldn't possibly be for me. I thought I deserved ordinary and couldn't accept that God could bless me with someone extraordinary like you.

"I'm sorry I made you feel you weren't good enough when the truth is you are more than enough for me. Just you. If it's just you and me for fifty years that is enough. More than enough. More than I deserve."

He drew in a breath. "I'm done making choices for you. But you told me last week that you would have loved our life if I had let you choose. I know I'm ten years late, but I'm asking you to please, please let me choose you. Every day. Whatever that looks like. Wherever life takes us."

Go big or don't come home. That was what his uncle had told Caleb as he walked out the door. At least he wouldn't die not knowing.

He reached into his pocket and got down on one knee.

Kat stared at him. "What are you doing?"

"What I should have done ten years ago."

"Oh my gosh." He had no idea if it was a horrified or a stunned one, but she was still here so he was going to keep speaking until she said no or left.

"I know we have a lot to work out. I know I've caused you more pain and heartache than I can imagine. But you are the only woman I want to wake up next to every morning. The only one I want beating me at horse races and berating me for bleeding."

Kat let out what was meant to be a laugh but came out more like a sob.

"And I know you love your life, and I'm not asking you to give that up. I will travel with you and be a body double for Ryan Reynolds if he needs one. And I know this could be either way too late or way too early but I'm going to ask anyway." He held up his grandmother's ring. "Katriona Elliott McLeod, I promise I will never draw a breath when I don't love you. And after all this, I'm just crazy enough to hope that may be enough. Will you marry me?"

Kat tilted her head and was silent for so long Caleb could feel the blood pumping through his veins.

"If I say yes, do I have to wear that ring?"

"This is my grandmother's ring."

"And I'm sure she thought it was ugly as well."

"I'm down on one knee here. Did you miss the part where I asked you to marry me?"

Kat shook her head. "No, but we've had some miscommunications in the past, so I just want to be clear that when I say yes I'm saying yes to you, not that ring."

A lightness bubbled in his chest. She was still here. She was grinning down at him. And unless he was hallucinating she'd just said *when* she said yes. "Fine." He looked around. "Anyone else here have something that I can propose with. I can trade you for a 110-year-old vintage platinum and diamond ring."

"Here." One of the production assistants stepped forward while tugging on the end of her braid. "What about this?" She held out a pink hair tie.

He took it and shoved the ring back in his pocket. "Okay. Katriona Elliott McLeod, with this pink hair tie, to one day be exchanged for a ring of your choosing, will you please do me the honor of being my wife?"

Kat looked at him with a mischievous glint in her eye. "So—"

Caleb groaned. His knees were not made for this. "You know, it's really a yes or no question."

"Look. You got to give your speech. It's not my fault that you got down there before I got to say mine." She dropped to her knees beside him, her dress spreading around her like a golden wave. Taking a deep breath, she grabbed his hands and wound her fingers through his.

His quads were cramping and he was pretty sure he'd need a crane to get back up, but he wasn't moving for anything in the world.

"Caleb, I have spent so long feeling broken that I didn't know how to feel whole again. I kept telling myself God had a plan, but the truth was I didn't believe it could be that good. Like maybe in dealing the hand of life He'd given me a great career, but the trade-off was I didn't get the great love.

"Then you showed up again with this stupid show and this ridiculous plan for me to help make your mother's wish come true, and I was

440

crazy enough to think maybe I could manage it without falling back in love with you. Except that was never going to happen because I never stopped."

"Never?" He couldn't stop the grin from creeping across his face.

"Easy, Murphy, don't go getting a big head about it. I haven't said yes yet." She murmured the words against his lips.

Caleb reached up and twisted a lock of Kat's hair around his finger. "I've got all night McLeod, so you can take your time. But I'm giving you fair warning that if you get any closer, I'm going to disrupt that already too long speech of yours."

"Okay, then."

"Is that an okay to the getting married thing or an okay to the kissing thing?"

She leaned in and gave him the kind of smile that he prayed he would get to wake up to for a long, long time. "Both."

"Really?"

She nodded. "I choose you, Caleb Murphy. Always and forever."

He didn't know how it happened. It was a miracle he'd even gotten up off the floor. But the next thing he knew he was spinning Kat around, her dress flying out around them like a golden parachute, her arms around his neck and her lips on his.

"I am going to spend the rest of my life making up the last ten years to you."

Kat shook her head. "Now is enough. It's more than enough."

Paige was crying, Karissa was crying, even tough-man hipster Adam looked like he might have found an emotion.

Caleb looked around at all the cameras and lights and people for the last time then leaned into his bride-to-be. "I guess that's a wrap."

ACKNOWLEDGEMENTS

It's been almost four years since Kat McLeod appeared on the page when I was writing the first draft of the story that would one day become my debut novel, *Close to You*. From those very first words I loved her strong and sassy personality but had no plans for her to ever have her own story. As far as I knew she was perfectly content in her existing relationship! Then I started getting the first emails from readers asking when/if she would get her own story. And when she showed up in *Can't Help Falling* and again when I was writing *Then There Was You* I knew the next book had to be hers. So first my thanks has to go to all the readers who have been impatiently waiting for her story for years. It is a daunting thing to write the story of a secondary character who has taken on a life of her own over multiple books. I really hope I have done her justice.

This book has been both a joy and a challenge to write. A joy because I finally got to put my many years and embarrassing number of hours of watching the *Bachelor/ette* to good use and

I got to bring back some previous characters which feels like my own little reunion of imaginary friends! A challenge because I have never endured the heartache or physical suffering of endometriosis and my worst fear was that I would do a disservice to the many brave and courageous women who live their lives under its shadow. I owe an enormous debt of gratitude to Nicola for opening her heart, sharing her experiences and reading an early version of this book to help make Kat and her story as authentic as possible.

This story is only what it is because of the ultimate Creator. All of the best scenes are the ones where I reached my limits as a writer and had to trust Him for what came next.

No manuscript should ever complete the journey to bookdom without a team telling an author where the plot isn't working and how many thousands of words she's written that are completely unnecessary. Once again, I am grateful to Iola Goulton for her editorial expertise (she did not edit this page by the way so all punctuation and grammar errors are 100% mine!). Thank you also to Laurie Tomlinson for helping me brainstorm Kat and Caleb late one night in a hotel room in Orlando and Marisa Deshaies and Rel Mollet for their great eye for detail.

For the last nine months I've been juggling a day job with two books on deadline and the balls wouldn't have stayed in the air if it wasn't for my amazing husband, Josh. The three small people don't remember a time when mummy didn't write books (definitely a good thing) but are never shy to tell me when they have lost patience with my hours behind a screen and require me to be present with the people who really count.

Writing would be an impossibly lonely pursuit if not for the camaraderie of other writers walking alongside you every step of the way. I am so thankful that Jaime Jo Wright, Halee Matthews, Sarah Varland, Anne Love, and Laurie Tomlinson are my people.

In no specific order, thank you to all our friends and family for their tireless support and incredible friendship: Team Isaac, Team Bonnevie, Team Collins, Team Maroun, Team Beard, Team Harper, Team Benson, Team Conway, Team Holmes, Team Williams, Team Gadd-Sroufe, Team Field, Team Robilliard, Jay Athea, Steph Howe, Ally Davey, Myra Russell, and Elise Teves (and I know I've forgotten someone important—I'm sorry!).

Finally, a huge thank you to all my readers. This author thing wouldn't be nearly as fun if it wasn't for you. Thank you for trusting me with your time and everything you do to help spread the word about my books.

ABOUT THE AUTHOR

Kara Isaac is the RITA® Award-winning author of contemporary romances filled with humor and hope. When she's not chasing three adorable but spirited little people, she spends her time writing horribly bad first drafts and wishing you could get Double Stuf Oreos in New Zealand. She loves to connect with readers at www.karaisaac.com, on Facebook at Kara Isaac – Author, Twitter @KaraIsaac and on Instagram @kara.isaac.author

Books are
produced in the
United States
using U.S.-based
materials

Books are printed
using a revolutionary
new process called
THINKtech™ that
lowers energy usage
by 70% and increases
overall quality

Books are
durable and
flexible
because of
Smyth-sewing

Paper is
sourced using
environmentally
responsible
foresting methods
and the
paper is acid-free

Center Point Large Print
600 Brooks Road / PO Box 1
Thorndike, ME 04986-0001 USA

(207) 568-3717

US & Canada:
1 800 929-9108
www.centerpointlargeprint.com